AT THE STROKE O

THE 1989 IAN ST JAMES AWARDS

Judges

HAROLD CLARKE
ANDREW KEIR
JOHN MENZIES
KATE PARKIN
IAN ST JAMES
VALERIE SINGLETON
TIM WATERSTONE

AT THE STROKE
OF TWELVE

The winners of the
1989 Ian St James Award

FONTANA/COLLINS

William Collins Sons & Co. Ltd
London · Glasgow · Sydney · Auckland
Toronto · Johannesburg

All royalties from the sale of this book will be
paid to the Ian St James Trust and used for the
furtherance and expansion of the Ian St James Awards.

First published in 1989 by Fontana Paperbacks,
8 Grafton Street, London W1X 3LA
Second impression October 1989

© The Ian St James Trust 1989

Photoset in Lintron Sabon by
Rowland Phototypesetting Ltd
Bury St Edmunds, Suffolk

Printed and bound in Great Britain by
William Collins Sons & Co. Ltd, Glasgow

Introduction

They came from every town and city in England; every hamlet in Ireland, from the banks and braes of Scotland and all the valleys of Wales. Actors, bakers, doctors, clerks . . . men and women from every walk of life. Thousands of people with one thing in common – a story to tell. Funny stories, sad stories, exciting stories, stories to make you think, stories that stick in your mind . . .

This book owes so much to so many; a staggering number of people combined to make it possible. Thanks go to my many friends at Collins, especially Merric Davidson whose unflagging enthusiasm helped turn an idea into reality. Thanks to Gilly, Jane and Yvonne for co-ordinating thousands of details. Thanks to all the readers at Collins who so diligently sifted and sifted. Thanks to the judges who so generously gave of their time and who made the all-important final decisions, thanks to our adjudicator, John McEvoy, for devising such an ingenious system of marking . . . and thanks to the thousands of authors who took part in these, the first ever Ian St James Awards. Even those whose stories failed to catch the eye of the judges succeeded, because by contributing they helped establish a platform for new writers the like of which has not existed before. The quality of their writing proved the argument – that there are many writers of talent looking for that first break into print. Within the covers of this book are just twelve – twelve authors whose work will now be read by publishers, by critics, by booksellers, by literary agents and by thousands of people who enjoy the sheer pleasure of reading a good story well told.

So here they are – the twelve winners of our first ever Awards. They come highly recommended from Valerie Singleton, Harold Clarke, Andrew Keir, John Menzies, Tim Waterstone, Kate Parkin and all of my colleagues. I enjoyed every single story . . . and I'm sure you will when you read *At The Stroke of Twelve*.

IAN ST JAMES

CONTENTS

AT THE STROKE
OF TWELVE

BRONWEN'S DOWRY

Belinda Raine

Belinda Raine was born in 1959 and graduated from Bristol University with a degree in Theology and Religious Studies after which she trained as a teacher. Currently between jobs, she has spent time travelling around Britain, the Far East, Australia and New Zealand.

Belinda Raine has written a full-length fantasy novel and has begun work on a sequel.

BRONWEN'S DOWRY

The journeymen shearers called at the farms in early summer to clip the flocks of their winter wool and barter a few wares on the side. At Olber Stoson's farm the shearer had arrived with only a few tunes to trade and those from poor pipes. He was a sparely-built man, young yet weathered, with few words and fewer smiles. He was good at his craft and not a single sheep shorn was bloodied. Olber Stoson was impressed.

The price for the shearing was a small percentage of the fleeces. Pawl earned his supper with a few simple tunes. Olber Stoson was not impressed by those. He was a widower recently bereaved, soon to be remarried. He had found a new wife on the far side of the Hill, a woman somewhat younger than he, once wed but now widowed like himself, and possessing a fine piece of land. That was her only quality, it was said, but it was quality enough for Olber, for his flock grazed land that was not his and the roof over his head belonged to another – and they were required back.

Olber had but one problem – one possible snag in his plans: as a young man with a young wife he had hoped for a son who would work alongside him, support his parents in their old age. His wife had provided him with a child but it was a girl, and she never bore another. They had struggled on but the harvests were bad and the winters were worse; the lambs died and the family had nothing like

3

enough to eat, even after The Finder had visited the Hill one spring, and so when a local gentlewoman offered to take the child and raise her as her own Olber and his wife had readily agreed. That had been fourteen years ago. Then his wife had died. Alone, with nothing but sixty sheep to his name, Olber could not have hoped to find a new wife and so, to his present regret, he had gone to the fine house and demanded the return of his girl. There had been shouting and some swearing on his part, but eventually he had his way and took her off to keep house for him and help on the farm.

Then the farmer over the Hill had died out riding one day in a storm, and his plain and argumentative wife had been left a farm she could not manage and Olber had moved fast and should have moved in, but for his daughter. She was a pretty girl, even though she had lost a lot of weight since coming home and her hands were now chapped and her cheeks pinched. She would not be welcome at the farm over the Hill. The big house had made it quite clear that she was now his responsibility so he could not take her back there, and how could he marry her off? He could ill afford to part with any of his sheep and, even if he could, what sort of dowry would a few sheep be? Yet until she was gone he could not go.

'Have you a wife, Pawl?' Olber asked after Bronwen had served up a mean supper of cabbage and wheat stew.

The journeyman laughed slightly, mockingly. 'Do I look wed?'

'You would like a wife though? Or are you content to be your own man?' the farmer persisted.

Pawl looked at his hands, thin, supple with lanolin from the fleeces. 'Aye – and what man would not? But I can ill support myself, let alone another, and if there were little

4

ones . . .' the statement hung in the air and Olber knew the scene all too well.

Bronwen was brewing a nettle tea in the lean-to area where the cooking and the washing took place.

'My daughter needs a husband – and I have found no one to take her. She is a good lass . . .'

'But she has no dowry,' Pawl finished.

'And you have nothing to offer, so no other father would even let you look at his girl,' Olber countered.

And so the deal was done. When Pawl the journeyman shearer left that side of the Hill he took with him not only three fine fleeces and his sorry pipes but a pretty wife with a small satchel of threads and needles under her arm.

Bronwen did not look back, neither could she bring herself to look at the stranger walking beside her who was her husband. She was not afraid of him, for he was not a man who caused those around him to fear; rather she was shy and bewildered, and somewhat surprised at the turn her life had taken. He was no less surprised than she: he had not intended to look for a wife and in his experience of life up until this point nothing was found unless it was looked for – and even then there was no certainty. It was not that he had no wish to marry someday, rather that he had a more immediate priority, an event in the late autumn which for him marked the finishing of the old year and the start of the new. That event was the Piper's Quest.

Nightfall found them on the far side of the Hill, knocking at the solid door of a solid farmhouse. The woman who opened the door was as sturdily built as her home and she looked appraisingly at Bronwen's thin face and Pawl's bony hands and might have taken them for vagrants but that she caught sight of the shearing blades in Pawl's belt.

'About time too,' she grumbled, and directed them to the barn where they could sleep. 'I suppose you haven't eaten?'

5

she added as an afterthought, and fetched them some bread and some broth with which they celebrated their wedding feast.

Pawl woke early, as was his wont, yet Bronwen was up and gone before him. When he had worked and washed and evening was closing in he returned to the loft and Bronwen smiled her welcome.

'We're to eat in the house,' she told him.

He frowned: 'How come the invitation?'

'I too have worked today,' she said. 'I have cooked and I have mended. The woman is to marry again soon, she told me. There is a lot to do, I helped, she said eat in.'

Bronwen's dress was plain but it hung well on her, it even suited her.

Pawl knew he did not look so well in his clothes. 'I have only two shirts, the other is more worn than this . . .'

'It is mended now.'

And so it was. Mended and decorated with an intertwining pattern in green and red, gold and blue.

'The Dancing Serpents,' Pawl muttered approvingly, recognizing the design. At least that problem was solved for the Piper's Quest. Maybe old Stoson had done him a favour greater than he had guessed.

Feeling less discomforted than he would have thought possible, Pawl, with Bronwen, ate supper in the cool of the farmhouse, and when they had finished the woman asked if the journeyman could do more than shear sheep – could he perhaps mend fences?

And so they stayed. Not too many days, not too many tasks – there were others waiting on Pawl's arrival and a journey to be made, a place to be when the year ended.

They ate in daily and sometimes the woman of the house smiled and hummed along with Pawl's piping and sometimes she scowled and her eyes burnt with a hunger,

6

a desire, and she would not talk. On those evenings they left early for their straw-filled loft where they slept as secure as wintered stock.

'What does she want?' Pawl asked his wife one morning.

'Morning and evening – the promise of long life and security.'

'Meaning what?' he insisted, but she smiled and made no other reply so he shrugged and went out to secure the roof of the hen coop, as he had promised, and Bronwen opened her satchel and took out her needles and threads and some fine linen that had once been a night gown when she had lived a gentler life.

'We must be on our way soon,' Pawl said that night at supper. He was, in a way, sorry to leave. He had put on some weight in just the few days since they came here and Bronwen looked better than when he had first seen her.

'Just one more task, then I'll not keep you.' The woman was relaxed, happy even; her hunger gone, satisfied. 'A simple task – it shall not take you long.'

She spoke truly. By noon the following day he had finished the blackwood frame and Bronwen had collected their few belongings together and was ready to go. They ate a noon meal alone and when they were done the woman appeared, radiant with pleasure, and with pride.

'It looks just so,' she declared, fetching down a faded dried posy from a nail in the wall and hanging in its place the blackwood frame within which the Arc of Dawn and the River of Dusk sparkled and flowed in a barely perceivable pattern of silken threads against a milk-pale cloth. Pawl gaped and Bronwen hid a smile behind her napkin.

The woman misunderstood his expression and a guilty glimmer lit her eyes. 'I know, I know,' she soothed. 'Yet you have no home and you will get better use from the price I paid.'

'Yes,' Bronwen said quickly, 'we will.'

'Of course,' Pawl agreed, wondering what it was he was agreeing to, recalling the only other time he had seen the great symbols of home and life – a tapestry in a crowded hall, a wedding gift to the Master of Myron, where the Piper's Quest would be resolved, this year as always.

She gave them a horse instead of fleeces for the shearing and the work he had done. It was not a particularly good horse, nor a young one, but it was the first Pawl had owned and he was pleased with the bargain. They still had two of the fleeces Bronwen's father had paid, the third was spun already. Pawl felt richer than he had for many years. They even had food for a day or two. Nevertheless, he was not relaxed.

'Where did you get that embroidery?' he asked urgently as soon as they were away.

She laughed lightly, the horse pricked its ears.

'I sewed it – I made it myself. Once I lived in gentle company. I learnt . . . many things.'

'Obviously,' he muttered. 'That was what she was so anxious about.' It was a statement, not a question. She answered nevertheless, she felt she owed him that.

'She is to marry soon. She saw my design, I was working on it and she saw it. I told her it was for us but she wanted it. Eventually I agreed.' She made a little dismissive, apologetic gesture.

'What did she offer in exchange?'

Why did he feel so angry? What, he reasoned, could they have done with the embroidery if she had kept it – hung it about the horse's neck?

'I can make another,' she said contritely, though she knew it was not so, not really. The Arc of Dawn was the

8

symbol of life and of a marriage, the River of Dusk was the symbol of security and the home. These things came into the pictures once perfectly, after that they were copies only.

'Materials, threads, clothes from her past to cut and remake,' she answered his question. 'She has much, we have little, now she has something she could not have otherwise had and we have more than before. She also let me keep the spindles I borrowed; now I can spin the fleeces. I shall make you a tunic.'

Pawl, strolling beside the horse, smiled slightly despite himself. Then he raised his arm in salute to a figure in the distance, a shepherd driving a flock of sheep towards the place they had just left, and Bronwen laughed and waved too.

'That was your father!' Pawl exclaimed.

'It was,' Bronwen agreed. 'I wonder where he is going.'

Summer passed, and as the days shortened, the distance to Myron shortened too. They left in their wake a trail of shorn sheep, mended fences, cleared ditches and gentle music. Bronwen spun and sewed and was content. Pawl was growing restless. He cut himself wood for new pipes and spent long hours whittling and paring and made music that hung mist-like on the early autumn air, blending harmoniously with the melody of the woodland birds and the breezes and the streams; music that would be lost amid the high rafters of the great hall of Myron, would be muted by the tapestries that hung about its walls, would be dismissed as mere pleasant tunings from a wandering shearer and would fail, as ever, the Piper's Quest.

Bronwen listened to his playing with joy and to his misgivings with sorrow. He was committed to the Quest, each year it drew him back to Myron and each year it sent him out again to search for better tunes, to hone his skills, to long for a better set of pipes that were far beyond his reach.

On the morning when the outline of Myron crenellated the horizon Pawl sat by their campfire and traced the outline of the Dancing Serpents that adorned his wrists.

'They chase each other endlessly. No escape. So the pattern continues and the seasons follow in their rightful order. I am the winter snake,' he sighed, fingering the blue serpent, 'chasing the Piper's Quest like winter follows autumn's tail.'

Bronwen nodded, understanding. 'Chase on,' she told him. 'I shall follow you meanwhile, as spring follows winter. The cold is forgotten then.'

He smiled wistfully. 'What are you making?'

The cloth in her hands was cut small, jade green and shot through with threads of cherry red.

'A gown,' she replied, 'from an old skirt given me by that farm woman. Green for happiness, red for good health.'

'It is a child's gown,' he stated tonelessly.

'Indeed. A mother's two-fold wish for her child.' She held the tiny garment up for his inspection. 'Of course, it is not finished yet.'

Pawl looked aghast. 'We have no money, little food. I am going there,' he pointed vehemently towards their destination, 'on a fool's errand.'

She packed her handiwork away. 'I said it was a child's gown, not that we are having a child. Most of the skirt was badly worn, the good cloth was too small to do much else with.'

'I am sorry,' he muttered, after a heartbeat's silence.

'For what?' she asked mildly.

He rose to his feet and kicked the fire to ashes, saddled the horse and lifted her on to its broad back.

'Sorry that I can offer you no more than a fool's dreams.'

The Piper's Quest lasted a moonphase, marking the end of autumn when the harvests were gathered in and the animals brought off the high pastures to the valleys and farm barns and the earth lay dormant, waiting. Then the pipers of Eral gathered at Myron and made music that would seep through the frost-hardened ground and touch the seeds of new life, would bring ships safely home and would warm cold hearts and cold hearths. Eventually they would be judged and from their number one would be chosen and named The Finder. For The Finder life would never again be the same.

Even Bronwen, used as she had been to genteel living before her return to her father's house, was overwhelmed by the splendour that was Myron. Yet before long the architectural grandeur and the ostentatious wealth of the city paled beside the beauty of the gathered pipers' music. It soared to the rafters carrying its listeners' hearts, and soothed their cares and worries as it settled into alcoves and recesses. It elevated the lowly and reduced the mighty, so that all seemed in harmony. And Bronwen wept for the loveliness around her and for her husband, whose misgivings and premature sense of loss she at last understood.

Whilst he renewed old acquaintances and practised for his first recital she began to learn her way around the maze of inner corridors and outer paths, and listened as much to what was said as to what was played, and watched.

There were many like Pawl amid the contenders – skilled but ill-equipped, many others who but for their fine pipes would not have been there at all. Bronwen was not surprised by that discovery – she had learnt that life was like that.

Yet there were some present who had the good fortune to be both skilled and wealthy and it was from these that the final selection would be made, according to Pawl's somewhat gloomy predictions. Those who had been there before would have been inclined to agree with him. One such was Marika. She might have taken the title last year but for a spell of poor health which took the edge off her performance. The previous year she had taken part, but with low expectations, having just given birth to her baby daughter. This was her year, of that she was certain. She stood aloof from the crowd and practised only in private – this year everything was going her way.

Bronwen watched the women pipers with interest, and elegant Marika especially. She had thought at first that Marika, with her young daughter clinging to her skirts, like her was merely accompanying one of the contenders; some subtle quizzing had corrected that mistake: Marika was the likely Finder for the year to come, so the rumours suggested.

'Her music is her life,' said one.

'She can afford for it to be,' grumbled another.

'Always the most beautiful pipes – and new ones each year,' sighed a third.

Bronwen smiled, hopeful – an idea forming. 'She likes the best?' she suggested.

'She tolerates nothing less,' was the reply.

No one would see Marika's new pipes until the Quest reached its climax, but Bronwen had seen the set that Pawl coveted: blackwood and silver, smooth with age, bright in tone and not for sale, even if they could have afforded them. They belonged to Gloran Smithson, had been his father's and grandfather's and on the first day of the Quest they put their owner into prime position and won for him the blue sash of First Quest Leader. Pawl played well, he was not placed. Marika was elected fourth and seemed unconcerned.

'Not her best pipes,' whispered an admirer.

'Not her best playing,' scorned a detractor.

Bronwen heard the exchange but took little notice, she needed to be with her husband.

'Tell me about Marika?' she suggested when he had come out of the dark mood she had found him in and was prepared to eat and speak again.

'Marika? Well . . . she is very wealthy. She lives nearby I think, certainly her music master comes from the city, her pipes are made here. What do you want to know?'

His tone said — *Why do you want to know?*

She answered the question he had asked aloud. 'Was she rich before she wed?'

He laughed and she wished that someday he would laugh, or even smile, simply with pleasure. 'You of all people should know that without asking! Of course she was rich.' He turned away.

'As rich as she is now?'

'No!' he snarled, then rubbed his face distractedly. 'I'm tired — can we talk of something else?'

The air was cold but the sun shone brightly in a clear sky and Bronwen, well wrapped in a thick woollen shawl, sat outside in the garden, sewing. The child's gown was finished, all but the design over the heart square. The other three quarters of the breast panel held minute representations of the Bird of Joy, the Tree of Learning and the Lake of Tranquillity. Bronwen heard footsteps approaching and started to wrap her few remaining threads to pack them away.

'Surely you are not leaving the heart square!'

Bronwen glanced up with a slight smile. Marika was

standing behind her, looking over her shoulder, uncertainty in her eyes, and admiration. Bronwen ignored the gown but left it in her lap. Marika was alone, giving Bronwen a subject for conversation where she had feared she might have none.

'Where is your little girl?'

The child was always at her mother's side except during performances, and mother and daughter walked in the garden daily.

'With her aunt, she has a slight fever.'

'I am sorry,' Bronwen said sincerely, sensing the mother's concern. 'It must be worrying, she is very young I think.'

'Two years; she is not very strong,' Marika replied.

Bronwen could see she had spent a sleepless night and moved her satchel to give the other room. Marika sat down beside her while Bronwen absently fingered the cherry-red lights in the gown.

'Red for good health,' Marika said ruefully. 'Who is it for, why have you left it unfinished?'

She reached over and smoothed the fine cloth, and Bronwen, who had been waiting for that moment, turned her head away to brush an unbidden tear from her cheek. She knew what she had planned to say, planned to do. Everything had fallen into place as if it were meant to be: she had traded her marriage picture for the materials to make this gown, she knew that she could persuade Marika to trade a set of pipes for it, pipes Pawl could make real music with. Yet parting with a marriage picture was one thing – she was not searching for security; Pawl had no home, had promised her none. To give a heart gown away – that was something else again. Pawl may have reacted with horror when he thought she might be having a child, but one day she would need more than a wandering shearer's life and a yearly pilgrimage to Myron. Even with good pipes, how many years might it take him to achieve the Quest? The best pipes in the world could be no guarantee. Bronwen knew that of all the many things she wanted, what she desired most was a child of her own. She was prepared to wait, but when the time came she wanted it to have the robe she had just made: the robe of Life.

'It is for no one as yet, thus it cannot be finished.' Bronwen's heart sank as she recognized the expression that stole over Marika's face; she had seen it in the farmer's widow over the Hill when that woman had first seen the marriage token Bronwen sewed.

'Not for a child of yours, then? Do you mean to sell it?' *Yes – for the right price*, Bronwen meant to say.

'I think not, I hope to have need of it one day. May your little girl be better soon,' she said.

And she left the garden and Marika, sitting alone on a stone bench, wanting a baby's dress as dearly as she wanted the Piper's Quest.

Pawl played even better that day and won some favourable comment, though nothing else. Marika was distracted and fell from her high placing. The blacksmith's son regained the prime position and earned a purse of silver coins. The contest was into its eighth day.

Marika approached Bronwen that evening after supper. They were in the great hall and Bronwen was studying the tapestry hanging over the doorway – the wedding gift to the Master of Myron and his new wife from their overlord, the Ruler of All Eral, who would attend the final days of the Quest. Bronwen would rather have continued with her appraisal than deal with Marika's need. She turned down the offer of a bolt of sky-blue silk imported from Tesk, a second horse, a purse of silver. The child's gown was beyond price. Finally Marika bowed her head slightly, seemingly acquiescent, obviously disappointed.

'Is that your husband?' she asked, watching Pawl approach and be waylaid by a heavily-built, bearded man. 'He has much talent,' she continued casually when Bronwen indicated that he was. 'A pity he has only inferior pipes. Should you desire it I will trade you a set of mine for the gown. If your answer is still no I will not raise the matter again, but maybe you would consider it?'

Bronwen closed her eyes. She had resolved not to ask — but to refuse the offer — how, in good conscience, could she do that? Opening her eyes she saw Pawl's strained expression across the hall; he wanted to be away, alone with his frustration.

'Maybe,' she whispered. 'Let me think on it.'

'Tomorrow morning?' Marika pleaded.

Bronwen hesitated, just for a moment. 'All right. You will have an answer in the morning.'

Pawl was quiet that night; he lay down on the thin mattress provided by their host and pulled a woollen blanket Bronwen had woven over himself. He pretended to sleep; Bronwen had not mentioned Marika's offer.

As he lay quietly she unwrapped her sewing and conjured a vision of Marika's little daughter, Rosa. Not focusing her attention she let her hands select threads without reason and worked the first image that came to mind, surprised at her choice, for the child was delicate and quiet.

Beyond their window the broad crescent of the moon hung amid pale stars, muted by wispy clouds. Bronwen sat, cross-legged, beneath the casement and doubted her decision. The lightning flash filling the heart square was surely not for Rosa. Had she been untrue when she assured Pawl that they were not expecting a child? She looked at him and allowed herself a faint smile; he had relaxed and was actually sleeping.

Bronwen assumed she would meet Marika in the garden

as before and as she waited in the bower, sheltered from the driving rain, she steeled herself to say, that, despite Marika's kind offer, the answer had to be no. Time passed, the contest was about to resume and Marika had still not shown. Almost relieved, Bronwen rubbed the cold from her hands and rose, intending to go to the hall and listen to the playing. Only when her hand was on the latch did she realize that she was at Marika's door instead. The room beyond the door was rather different to the other she shared with Pawl, which was little more than a sleeping alcove with a small window. There were servants, dressed better than she, attending to their duties with quiet competence and barely suppressed concern. Bronwen guessed the cause of their unease and her resolve crumbled. Recalling the days when she too had servants to command, though admittedly far fewer than Marika, she gave directions to her room and a description of the garment to be collected. She left without seeing Marika.

Pawl had gone to the hall without waiting for Bronwen to return. He listened with admiration to Sareb Delver, the bearded man with whom he had spoken the day previously. A mood of resignation stole over him and he felt better for it. There was no reason to think this year might be different from any other and he knew from past experience that when he accepted that fact he could begin to enjoy the music for its own sake. He felt better still when he saw Bronwen walking slowly across the room towards him.

'Each day I wonder if you will still be here.' They were the first words he had spoken to her since the competition yesterday. She was glad he did not take it for granted that she would be.

Three pipers performed before she felt something being pressed into her hands; Marika, smiling, moved away. It was her turn to play next and murmurs of enquiry were already circulating as to her whereabouts.

The pipes Bronwen held were in no wood she recognized – honey-red and hard as iron, they were bound not with reed, as were Pawl's; nor with leather or bronze, as was common; nor with silver, as were the smith's son's, but with gold – or so she took it to be for she had never seen gold before, only heard tell of the precious metal found far beyond their shores.

They did not hear Marika play. Bronwen pulled Pawl away, took him outside to give him the pipes.

'What did you give for these?' The question was ungracious but his smile, for once, was genuine.

'Nothing – they are a gift freely given,' she replied with mock severity. 'Go away and learn to play them. The noon break is soon, you have little time!'

Pawl returned just as the afternoon session began. Marika had played brilliantly, Rosa was over the worst of her illness. Come the final days, according to her admirers, she would astound all with an even greater performance, from even more exquisite pipes. Bronwen had no opinion on the first matter and knew better on the second. She knew something else too – the symbol of the lightning was for little Rosa after all: two years ago, at the time of Rosa's birth, autumn in Myron had reluctantly given way to winter after days of furious storms. Bronwen felt unaccountably relieved and, as she told Marika later, if lightning was the symbol of a tempestuous character it was also the sign of genius. Marika was not unduly troubled as to what it indicated; one thing only mattered, Rosa was going to be well.

Marika took the third sash, her playing inspired by her daughter's recovery and her wish fulfilled, but among the leading contenders was Pawl, playing pipes he had never held before that morning, feeling the stir of a genuine hope in place of an unobtainable dream.

Pawl's elevation improved his mood and secured him a place in the last stage as the moon reached three-quarters full. Most of those passed over stayed at Myron to listen, nowhere else to go. As the year turned to its coldest it seemed that life was centred around the Piper's Quest.

On the night of the full moon Bronwen dreamt of a great forest of huge honey-red trees, tall and straight, rising higher than the eye could see. Trees with gold-green leaves, hard and pointed like spear heads. Trees with amber, clear as sunlight, seeping from their bark. All was gold and green, bright as morning.

The next day, while the rivers of Myron lay under a solid layer of ice, Pawl took the sash of Seventh Quest Leader.

It occurred to him that he almost wished Olber Stoson was there.

Three more times in the course of the competition Pawl regained the prime position and earned more silver than he had ever seen. If he was even more single-minded than before Bronwen did not blame him, yet she looked forward to the spring, whatever that might hold.

By the time the Ruler of All Eral arrived at Myron the moon was in decline and the tensions among the remaining contestants were almost palpable. There were twelve left in the Quest and of those six were considered likely candidates for the title of Finder. Marika seemed to harbour no regrets in having parted with her best pipes or in having given them to a man who now posed a real threat to her ambitions. Bronwen, caught up in the excitement, began to wonder what life would be like in Eral's seaport capital where The Finder would go after the Quest was achieved. By night the trees in her dreams grew broader and taller – she feared they were telling her that she really wanted to be in the forest, not at the coast. Awake, she had no firm opinion on the matter.

Pawl meanwhile tried just to live from day to day, tried not to speculate on a future still so tenuous, tried not to grasp at hopes too fragile to hold. Not that he could imagine what life would be like if he were to prove successful in the Quest. He had never met The Finders of any previous year once they had left Myron: no one spoke of what befell them once the year of their victory was over; maybe no one knew. One thing seemed certain – they would not return to the life they had left.

The final day of the competition seemed the coldest day of the year. Pawl, unable to sleep, rose long before the feeble winter sun. The water in the wash bowl was crusted over with ice but he washed as well as he could, shivering.

'Come back to bed,' Bronwen scolded. 'It's dark yet.'

'I was concerned I would disturb you.'

'You have disturbed me, now come back to bed.'

He needed no more encouragement than that and stayed there, glad of her warmth, until the low sullen gong sounded: in the dining hall the morning meal was prepared.

Pawl refused to go near the laden food-trestles, taking only a cup of hot milk. Time hung heavy. He knew he had to be patient; the twelve remaining contestants had to play before the final decision was made. He would be fifth to perform. Already his heart beat faster than normal.

Marika had drawn to play first, a position she relished, which Pawl would have loathed. She played with the same pipes she had used throughout the contest yet her recital that day surpassed all her previous performances – held her audience spellbound. Bronwen thought it sang of winds billowing in sails, of seabirds soaring effortlessly over the waves. She felt an ache when the music faded, and a pang of guilt.

Gloran, the blacksmith's son, had taken the place immediately prior to Pawl's and, unlike the three before him, gave a performance to rival Marika's. Bronwen was reminded of her early childhood, when The Finder had come to their farm and played for their harvests; the memory warmed her but, unskilled in music as she was, she would not have presumed to choose between Marika and the smith's son.

Pawl could not consider the merits of others' performances either, if for reasons other than his wife's. Gloran's final notes signalled the start of his trial; moments later he was stepping up on to the dais and moistening dry lips. Just as he could not afford to think of those who had gone before neither could he think of those who were judging. He stared into the middle distance at a memory of grassy banks and fruit-laden trees and played as if he were alone in the sheep pastures of his youth, before he had ever heard of the Piper's Quest.

Bronwen knew that it was not merely biased pride that told her Pawl's playing transcended anything she had ever heard before, for it could have quickened the buds on the trees and the seeds in the ground long before their appointed time. It sang of the great trees of her dreams, the trees from whose wood his pipes had been cut, and it sang of the spring she had yearned after, for while he played, spring slipped into the winter-bound halls of Myron.

The Ruler of All Eral smiled as the Master of Myron leant over and whispered something to him. Bronwen saw the exchange and saw also the rapt expressions about her and then Pawl had finished. For an instant there was total silence, and then cheering such as Bronwen had never heard — led by none other than Marika. Bronwen frowned, puzzled, but put the matter aside to congratulate her husband.

'That was for you,' he told her as he held her briefly.

There were still seven to play.

'Fourth place – Sareb Delver.' They had come back into the hall, the judging was complete, the moment of truth had arrived. Sareb Delver, a silver-miner from the south coast, was cheered on to the dais.

'In third place – Gloran Smithson.' A not unexpected result and well received.

'In second place . . . Pawl Shearer, and . . . The Finder . . . Marika of Myron!'

Bronwen's heart missed a beat. She glanced quickly over to Pawl but his face was unreadable. Whatever he felt he composed himself enough to take Marika's hand in a gesture of goodwill before joining Sareb and Gloran on the dais. Marika followed him to take her place amid the applause of the gathered company.

The Piper's Quest was not a competition to discover the most talented musician in all Eral; if it had been it could have been decided in a day. Rather it was exactly what it claimed to be – a Quest – undertaken by the pipers of Eral, one of whom would be successful, would be named The Finder. The greatest obstacle facing the contestants at the outset of the Quest was the fact that they had no idea what it was that they were searching for.

Pawl walked alone alongside one of Myron's twin rivers, absorbing the truth regarding the nature of the Quest, and the reality of his failure. He had left the celebrations taking only a question with him – a question put to him by Bronwen: Had he wanted to be the best piper in Eral, or had he wanted to be The Finder?

Until that day he had assumed that the two were actually one and the same. The Ruler of All Eral himself had dispelled that misunderstanding, had given him a gold ring of High Favour, had caused Bronwen to ask the question that was now troubling him. He understood, as well as one who was not chosen as Finder could, that the Quest that year had been for one in tune with the sea: with the tides and the fish shoals, the ocean winds and currents – that was Eral's need. His music was that of the forest and the field. 'Losing' in the Piper's Quest meant failing to find rather than being bettered and he had not found the songs of the ocean in his music.

When Pawl returned to the hall he found Bronwen speaking quietly with Marika, in whose arms was little Rosa, dressed in a green and cherry-red gown. As Marika turned to accept congratulations from the Mistress of Myron, Pawl presented Bronwen with two tiny white flowers.

'I discovered them by the river, struggling through the ice. Too soon – they came to their fulness too soon.'

She breathed in the delicate perfume of the blossoms. 'Yet their roots remain – they can flower again next year. It may be that the climate will be kinder then,' she suggested.

'Yes, it may be,' he agreed, 'though we shall not be here to see if it is so!'

Bronwen felt the relief flooding through her; she linked her arm through his. 'And where shall we be?' Not that it really mattered.

'North of here the Kauri grow.' He smoothed the honey-red wood of the pipes hung about his neck. 'I thought we might buy a few sheep, build a house, settle there – at least for a while. We shall still be poor, yet with time – who knows? The timber there is the best in the land, the ground beneath the trees rich in amber. The grazing is good. We have a horse, you have your spindles, maybe I can make you a spinning wheel. It will not be an easy life . . .'

23

'Can we go straight away?' she interrupted him.

'Tonight?'

'Well, in the morning then.'

They travelled all day and eventually found shelter in an abandoned cottage. Myron was behind them, out of sight.

'What are you making?' Pawl asked, coming in with his arms full of firewood. Bronwen glanced up from the small pieces of sky-blue silk on her lap.

'A gown,' she said, 'in blue for safety; sky hues for broad vision.'

'A child's gown,' he stated, in tones which clearly said *Another* child's gown!

'Yes.' She waited. He put more wood on the fire. 'Are you not supposed to remind me that we are still poor, our future still uncertain?' she asked mildly.

'Why? You know all that. Anyway, I have learnt a lot since the last time, including the folly of jumping too quickly to conclusions.'

'Last time was different,' she pointed out.

'How so?'

'That time I was merely using up old material, I was not preparing for the birth of our own child.'

And the evening rang with the pure sound of joyous laughter.

BLIND FAITH

Roland Vernon

Dedicated to Claire Heath

Roland Vernon was born in 1961 and attended school in England, but he was brought up abroad, first in Austria, then in Zambia, and finally in Greece. He was educated at Eton College and King's College, Cambridge where he was a choral scholar. After graduating with a History of Art degree, he attended the Royal College of Music where he undertook post-graduate and opera school studies. His career as a singer took him all over England and abroad, and he was under contract with Glyndebourne Festival Opera and Pavilion Opera. He now works for a compact disc recording company.

BLIND FAITH

I knew at once that something peculiar had happened to Tomasin. As soon as I caught sight of her waiting for me in front of the same old café in Bloomsbury I could see the change. She was not fixing the world with her usual, steady, uncritical gaze, but was searching the street uneasily. Her eyes darted this way and that like a nervous pet when it hears cruel children arrive home from school. It seemed that she had been stripped of her very presence, her aura was gone, and it left her looking physically shrunk. She was cringing from the world, cornered, hoping not to be noticed.

She had always been the most unwaveringly steadfast of all my friends. The very worst of traumas by anyone else's standards left her unruffled, still smiling radiantly: the very picture of self-assured goodwill. If there was anyone replete with gentle human kindness, it was Tomasin; a living example of how the best of us should be. I had a crush on her once. Even now I thought she was the embodiment of what most men hoped to find in womanhood: beautiful, intelligent, witty, strong, sensitive, caring. Fate had granted her more than her fair share of the kind of attributes that conquer hearts. Or so I had always thought, but it proved to be a misconception, and her sparse history of romantic involvement bore witness to it: the odd splash of inconsequential heart-flutters littered across years of gentle loneliness. She was still alone now, and behind that endlessly resilient confidence, I could detect her quiet awareness of the years rolling by, and the gradual evaporation of eligible partners. The conclusion one was forced to draw was that she was lacking something, though none of us could pin-point exactly what it was. It seemed like a merciless travesty of divine justice.

We had been at Cambridge together, she earnestly study-ing medicine with a determined ambition to qualify as a doctor, and me loafing around, waiting for time to drain away, without an eye to the future or a care in the world. Whereas Tomasin knew precisely what she wanted from life and where to find it, I meandered about in listless pursuit of pleasure, fat with the conviction that life had to mould itself around me. She had always been mistress of her own destiny, a concept I found hard to appreciate, assuming that everything would fall into my lap, as if by accident. She was now happily installed at the Charing Cross Hospital, while I still idled around, not through choice any more, but because nobody seemed to want me.

Something was terribly wrong. I was late as always, but instead of being greeted by her usual mock-censorious disciplinarian act, tutting and waving an admonishing finger, she ran across the street and tugged at my arm.

'Thank God you've come. I thought you'd never arrive; Christ, what's kept you?'

'I'm only five minutes late, Tom. For God's sake, you should be expecting that by now.'

'Let's get inside, I can't bear this bloody street any more.'

We hurried back across the street and into the sandwich bar. Tomasin called to the squat, hard-faced Italian woman behind the Gaggia coffee-maker that we would like two cappuccinos. When we had sat down, she unfastened her hair, fumbling agitatedly with the clip until it fell loose across her cheeks. Her face slumped into the palms of her hands with a loud smack. It would have seemed laughably melodramatic had it been anyone else sitting opposite me.

I thought I had better try the light-hearted approach: 'So what's up? Is he married? You've met the man of your dreams and he's married?'

It was immediately apparent that my flippancy had been misplaced and I bit into my lip. She did not make a sound, but began to shake, head still in her hands; short, convulsive bursts of shuddering.

'What is it, Tom?'

Still she would not answer. I thought at one point she stopped breathing altogether, but then she gasped loudly, like someone just saved from drowning. Heads began to turn.

'For heaven's sake, please say something.' I touched her hand, but she pulled away, letting out a muffled yelp. 'You're a nervous wreck.'

'I can't help it,' she screamed, suddenly lifting her head to reveal her face, flushed and puffy, eyes streaming and swollen. Everyone, it seemed, was staring at us, and the Italian mamma switched off her frothing coffee machine. 'Something horrible has happened. I don't even know if you can help me. I've never been so frightened in my life.'

My stomach turned slightly, and I could feel a slight tingling in the soles of my feet. It was a sensation I had known a few times before, usually preceding a ghastly piece of news. It was enough to make me lose awareness of my surroundings and to bring me nearer her level of distraction.

'Please tell me.'

It seemed like an eternity, during which the blood stood still in my face, and all I could do was wait until she was ready to talk. A new generation of customers came and filled the tables and chairs around us, the first having finished their hurried lunches. Our untouched cappuccinos went cold in front of us, and still I waited. At last she began to speak.

The rain had been sheeting down all weekend, an angry, resentful union of the elements that forced everyone to scamper off to their cosy little homes in search of warmth and shelter. Just sit it out, and it'll pass eventually. It was still heavy when she got on to the train on Sunday evening, but she didn't really mind. It had given her the excuse to sit indoors and ease herself into two days of blissful nostalgia. She had been to stay with Maurice and Julia, old family friends, uncle and aunt figures; the sort that make one feel safe and childlike again. She could lie in front of the fire reading a book with her chin in her hands and her feet waving around in the air. She could rest against Maurice's knees without a shred of complication jabbing at her conscience, and she could let Julia get on with the applecrumble on her own, in the safe unspoken knowledge that everyone wanted it to be so. Even the jamjars seemed to be the same ones she had eaten out of during long summer holidays years before. The same heavy floral eiderdowns enveloped her at night with as much maternal comfort as they had done in the past. The same, the same. She loved it because it was the same as ever, and they loved her because it was obvious she loved them. The weekend had gone exactly as she had wanted it, with the perfect balance of food, rest, discussion and reminiscence. Now that she was on the train, and brooding darkness was beginning to obscure the rain-swept hills and forests, she felt fine about going back to London.

Her immense calm and contentment were founded on an unwitting ability to structure her life, down to the finest detail. She possessed a rare and instinctive gift of knowing how to manage time and plan her activities with precision, so that she was never out of pace, never exhausted, and certainly never bored. This weekend had been one of her well-planned 'touchstone' breaks; a sort of refuelling, topping up the levels, getting back in touch with all the things that had gone to make her the kind of person she was; checking that they were all still there, and basking in them for a couple of days. She drew both reassurance and inspiration from the past, and would go to great lengths to keep it alive in her present. She could now return quite happily to the metropolis for another spell of perfectly ordered life.

She was flicking through her little red diary, checking the week's schedule; every planned engagement inscribed with dark blue ink in faultlessly neat handwriting. There was something satisfying in the perfectly regulated rhythm of a train's movement that had made her prefer it as a means of transport. Cars were altogether more fussy.

She was still preparing the week ahead when her compartment door opened and a man came in. He was a soldier, an officer, all pressed khaki, leather and shining metal. How much smarter uniforms look in real life, compared to films, she thought. He glanced at her and she smiled faintly back, before returning to her diary. In a moment he was seated, diagonally opposite her, brow furrowed and checking the time. She could not help noticing his carefully trained economy of movement. She had known soldiers before: terribly self-conscious about how they should look, and what their role should be in society at large, the world beyond the bashed square.

It was a long way to London, a three-hour trip, and she had come prepared. She took out of her bag the new dermatological survey she had been meaning to read for days; this would be the perfect opportunity to get to grips with it. The soldier was already engrossed in *Country*

31

Life. She prided herself on being a disciplined reader, and so began to apply herself to the text with a determination not to be distracted.

As the minutes rocked by, she discovered that the worthy medical document did not lend itself easily to concentration and she began to stare into space. The train was slowing to a halt. Another station. The soldier looked at his watch. As the train waited for its new flock of guests to board, a sharp gust of wind hit it on the side, making the whole carriage rock slightly. The rain was still pelting the window, and the world outside had disappeared into the night.

Just as they began to move again, the door of the compartment was flung open, and two more people came in, an old woman and a middle-aged man. The woman took one look at Tomasin and sat next to the soldier; judged, tried and sentenced. Do I look like a disreputable woman, she thought amusedly. The man sat next to her.

He was in a muddled state, his umbrella refusing to be packed away correctly, and a torrent of drips falling into his open, over-stuffed briefcase. In the added confusion of having to take off a raincoat, his glasses got caught on a sleeve button, and went flying across the compartment. The soldier parted his bristlingly shiny shoes, making a distinctive scratching sound on the floor, and picked the glasses up. Tomasin detected the slightest tinge of contempt in his self-satisfied smile as he handed them back to their owner, still thoroughly distraught and now blushing like a ripe fruit.

'Thank you, thank you so much. Yes, thank you,' he muttered, putting them on again and settling down; then with a great sigh of relief, 'oh dear, what a to-do. I can't see a thing without my specs.'

He looked at Tomasin for humorous support. She smiled at him with just enough geniality to ease his embarrassment and then returned to her laborious text. The four of them sat there in complete silence. Of course it was far from silent, but something about the endless inevitability of the train's background clatter provided them with a neutrality of sound that was near to silence, in that it demanded nothing of the listener except a trust in its faultless continuance. They were sitting there in blind faith. This high speed iron snake was going to take them through the terrible night storm, and bring them, after miles of wild thrashing steel against steel, into the warmth and security of a convenient London station. From where did they all find such assuredness? What formed the basis of their well-grounded trust that the system laid on for them would always work? It is like driving at top speed along the motorway, blind beyond the meagre stretch of the head-lights, yet trusting that there will not be a cliff-edge, nor a brick wall ahead. People go from day to day with a set of fundamental, taken-for-granted beliefs. The system works, and order is maintained. Tomasin lived in unquestionable faith.

The soldier kept checking his watch. The little old woman was engaged in the enthralling pursuit of needles fencing and picking around a thread of wool. Tomasin was by now on the tenth page, and her neighbour had begun to take an interest in what she was reading.

'Are you researching or something?'

'I suppose I am, sort of.'

He was a big man, acres of herring-bone tweed spreading outwards in all directions from his bulbous neck down. He had a pudgy, pig-like face, and a little turned-up nose on which were balanced the annoyingly unstable metal-rimmed glasses that had recently been returned after their flight through space. His hair was wispy, not a great deal of it left. His most startling feature was his pair of sharp little pale blue eyes. Their extraordinary colour was hard to believe. Had it been a pretty girl sitting in the compartment, or almost anyone else, Tomasin would have thought they were wearing artificially tinted contact lenses. But this clumsy lump of a man was so clearly unconcerned with his appearance, that even the idea of his resorting to beauty-enhancing cosmetics seemed absurd. He looked the type that would put on the same clothes every day without thinking, his mind taken up with other things. As long as all the elements of vaguely correct dressing were there, which they were: tweeds, woolly tie, worn-out corduroys, dirty brown shoes. A bit of an eccentric old fatty, Tomasin thought, not unkindly.

Years and years of conditioning had left their mark on her, and she never felt inclined to talk to strange men. She had an inbuilt fear of the predatory male, not because she worried about what might happen to her, but because she had no time for unnecessary or unplanned complications in her life. It disrupted the pure decision of her daily schedule. She preferred to keep her routine impenetrable. Despite this, though, she had recently reassessed her position in society, and had decided that as a doctor, if not as an adult citizen, she had a responsibility to her fellow creatures. She had become the shoulder for everyone to cry on, 'good old Tomasin' to her friends, or 'lovely Doctor Bryant' to her patients: 'you can say anything to her, she always listens and helps if she can.' It had helped her too. She felt better for the change and allowed herself a rare self-compliment: she was setting an example to the world of how you could be pleasant to everyone, even strangers, even strange men.

'What?'

'I'm sorry?' she said, taken aback by his extension of their interchange.

34

'What are you researching?'

'Oh, it's just a dermatological report that the Royal Society of Physicians brought out last month. Nothing terribly exciting.'

'Oh, right.'

They exchanged the smallest of laughs, mere forced outlets of breath through the nose. He had a pleasant, lilting northern accent, and his voice was higher in pitch than most.

'Dermatology? That's something to do with skin, isn't it?'

'That's right.'

'Are you studying it or something?' She looked up at him. 'I don't mean to pry or anything. It's just that I'm a student as well. A bit of an old one, I suppose. Is that what you're thinking?'

He giggled like a schoolboy. She smiled back at him.

'No, I'm not a student. I'm a doctor, actually.'

'A doctor, how fantastic! Great. Always feel safer with a doctor near at hand. Whereabouts do you practise?'

'I'm at a hospital, in London.'

'Well, how about that!'

He looked at the other two in the compartment, but they did not seem aware of his interest. Tomasin went back to dermatology. It won't be long before he starts again, she thought, trying to smother the grain of impatience that had sown itself already.

'Have you got a pen I could borrow?'

'I think so,' she said, and rifled through her handbag for a while, trying to find that wretched biro that was never there when she wanted it. Her fountain pen was just there, of course, but she didn't like anyone else using that. As she searched, she was aware of his intense little eyes following her every movement. He even pulled his head back at one point to get a better view into her bag. She thought it odd that in such a heavily packed briefcase he didn't even have a pen.

'Doesn't matter, I've probably got one in here,' he said.

'Here it is,' said Tomasin, finding it at last.

'Don't worry, I've got my own now. Thanks anyway. I'm studying, you see.'

She had no choice. She had to ask.

'What are you studying?'

'You guess.'

Oh my God, she thought; trapped.

'I don't know.'

'Go on, guess.'

He let out a strange, honking snigger of a laugh. The old woman opposite looked up from her knitting with an expression of distaste.

'History,' she ventured. Please, mister pig-man, please let me go now.

'Quite warm, but not spot on.'

He was really enjoying the game now. He had even moved a few inches forward in his seat, and put his hands together, rubbing them in childish anticipation.

'Give me a clue, then.'

'OK. It's to do with families in history.'

'Genealogy?'

'Very warm now.'

'I give up. Tell me.'

'No, no; please go on guessing.'

This could get seriously boring, Tomasin thought. The old woman looked at her now, as if it were her fault and she were egging him on. *Shameless hussy* was written all over her accusing expression.

'Anthropomorphic genetics?'

'I'm sorry?' he asked, his eager grin suddenly giving way

36

to troubled doubt. *Show-off, too* was the silent contribution on the face of the old woman. Damn, shouldn't 've done that, Tomasin thought.

'No, I really can't guess; please tell me.'

'All right,' he sniggered again, victory in his eyes, 'heraldry. I study heraldry.'

He turned to face her full on now, easing one massive buttock off the edge of the padded seat. She noticed a shiny, hairless shin between the top of his brown socks and the bottom of his trousers. A thin shin, a fat man.

'How interesting.'

'Yes, it is. I'm glad you think so too. I've been studying it for some years now. I'm not a member of any college or anything, but I go along to the odd club meeting and I want to publish something one day. My speciality is central Europe; from the sixteenth to the nineteenth centuries. I'll show you some of my stuff, if you're interested.'

Completely stuck now, she thought. Absolutely no way out. 'Would you like to see some? It'll only take a minute.'

The poor dear, she made herself think, it'll make his day if I show an interest. Dermatology can wait a while.

'I'd be fascinated.'

It was like letting a greyhound off the leash. He was suddenly a flurry of activity, heaving over his bag, his face reddening with the effort, flicking through piles of papers, joyously rummaging around in files and pulling off paper clips. Every so often he would toss something in her direction, either a typed sheet, or a gaudily-coloured illustration, all the while accompanying his exhibits with a muttered commentary. Tomasin's lap could hardly contain the huge array of extravagant family crests; dragons with crowns, bears with arrows, griffins with crosses, swans, stags, unicorns, bulls, lions, dogs, cats, the lot. On top of this he laid out a collection of engraved portraits, identifying them all,

37

and pairing off each one with a particular coat of arms. She listened to his potted biographies and textual addenda, showing polite interest and making all the right noises.

When it seemed that his bag was almost empty, its stretched sides caving in with relief, he pulled out one last piece of paper.

'And this is my favourite of all. That's why I've kept it to last.' One look at this guy, and some women would say that some men never grow up, she thought. 'I feel – how shall I say it? I feel – personally linked to this one. I'll tell you why in a minute. But just look at it first.'

It was another family coat of arms; a great blue shield with six leopard heads on it, and crested with the head of a horse. But it was not an ordinary horse's head. It was thin and wasted, possibly even dead, its eyes bulging out of its skull; and yet it seemed to be leering at the world, as if it knew some hideous secret and would not tell, preferring to wait so that it could watch the suffering when it was unleashed.

'Gorgeous, isn't it? Have you ever seen anything like it?' he asked.

'I wouldn't exactly describe it as gorgeous. But it's certainly different from the others. Jolly frightening, anyway.'

'You're right. You're absolutely right. That's what I thought when I first saw it. D'you know, it haunted me for days. I just could not get it out of my head. Something about that smiling horse on top. I couldn't work it out. Why did it keep coming back to me? And then, one day – you're not going to believe this – I suddenly found the answer.'

He waited to hear her anticipation.

'What happened?'

'I had a dream.'

Oh hell, Tomasin thought, it's worse than I suspected.

He really is a nut. Something in his sky-blue eyes switched off at the mention of the word 'dream'. Somewhere inside him a door had opened, and it seemed as if the agitated excitement he had shown until then had somehow been replaced by a profound, pressing sincerity that would not allow her to back away. She looked up at him and his eyes penetrated her; they seemed to be fixed on a distant spot, miles behind her head. He's a complete raving nut, and I'm in it up to my neck.

'A dream?' she asked.

'Yes, yes, a dream. About a prince who lived a hundred and fifty years ago in Germany. I couldn't remember anything else about what I'd dreamt, except all the trees.'

He paused, distracted.

'What sort of trees?'

'Oh, pine trees,' he blinked and looked at her again, 'high mountains covered in pine trees, and this German prince. That's all I remembered. But I woke up suddenly in the morning, covered in sweat and with a terrific pain in the back of my neck.'

'Too many pillows?'

'Oh no, it was far worse than anything like that. It was a real bone-splitting pain. I could hardly get up. I had to spend the morning in bed. Then when I did get up, I felt all dizzy and strange. You know, my left leg didn't know what the right was doing; that sort of thing.'

Time to get things back to earth, she thought, and scoured her memory for a possible on-the-spot diagnosis. She didn't have enough time.

'So I went to the library, the special one I go to for all my work. There's so much information on heraldry there. I took along this coat of arms because it had been bothering me for so long. After a couple of hours I managed to track it down. Very, very strange. D'you know what I found out?

The coat of arms belonged to a minor German princedom that became extinct in 1848. The last of the line lived in a castle in Bavaria, high up in the mountain forests. For some reason which it didn't say, he wasn't liked very much, because one day when he was out hunting, they caught him.'

'Who caught him?'

'The village. The mob. They dragged him to the village square and chopped his head off. And d'you know what's more? When he died he was forty-two. That's exactly how old I was when I had the dream. You see, I got the pain in my neck because he must have been reliving the beheading in my mind while I slept.'

The little eyes had gone very still. His words had got quieter and quieter, and had now stopped. There was a moment's silence, and then the soldier in the corner sneezed; an almighty roar of a sneeze that drenched the seat opposite, and doubled him up over his knees.

'Oh bless you, young man, bless you. Got a bit of a cold coming on?'

The old woman obviously liked soldiers.

'Thank you, no, I haven't,' he blew his nose heavily into a handkerchief, 'or at least I jolly well hope not.'

They had a little laugh with each other, and silence returned. It was the perfect break Tomasin needed. She could get away from him now if she wanted. She had done her bit, and just had to make her excuses and pick up her manuscript again. But the rain was streaking across the window and she paused for too long, staring at it against the darkness beyond.

'I've got a few copies of it. You can have one. Here you are.'

He handed her the horse-crested coat of arms. It was the last thing she wanted.

'No really, I couldn't.'

'I insist. Honestly, I want you to have it. Please.' She put it away in her handbag. 'So from then on I decided that dreams were very important. Do you think they are?'

'Well, that's not really my scene,' Tomasin replied, 'you'd have to ask a psychiatrist.'

'I'm not asking your professional opinion, I just want to know what you think as a person. I mean, do you believe in reincarnation, for example?'

'No, I don't.'

She decided to be firm and decisive.

'Are you sure?' he said with a wry grin. 'I think you're pretending a bit.'

She was stunned at the acuteness of his observation.

'Well, it's not an easy question, is it? I don't think – '

'Of course it's an easy question,' he interrupted, smiling at her, knowingly. 'You either believe in it or you don't.'

'Well in that case, I don't.'

'I do. I most certainly do. And I've got proof. Shall I tell you another story?'

Tomasin looked at her fellow passengers for support. The soldier had closed his eyes and seemed to be asleep. A clear wet drip was oozing out of his nostril. The old woman saw Tomasin's unease, and looked back at her knitting. *Nothing to do with me, dear. You got yourself into it, now just let's see you get out of it.* A kind of ruthless justice that ruled in the hearts of so many people. The same people who in different circumstances might have been caring and concerned. The same justice, probably, that dragged the hapless German prince to his doom at the hands of ordinary villagers. Common people stirred into action by cold-blooded obstinacy, single-minded, of vengeful purpose.

'Do you mind me talking to you like this? I don't want to bore you.'

'Of course not.' Why didn't she just tell him to leave her alone?

'So would you like to hear another story?'

'It's not long is it? I mean, I'll have to do some reading soon. We're already halfway to London.'

She wished she was there now.

'No, it's not long. I'll tell you quickly. A few years ago I had a dream that I was in an old study, surrounded by leather books. There was a beautiful view from the window, across lawns and down to a lake; then up to wooded hills. It was winter and there was a huge fire roaring in the hearth. There was a door in the corner of the room and I could hear noises coming from the room beyond. Playful noises, children having fun. I went through the door and saw this lovely child: a little girl in a frilly white dress, playing with building blocks. She looked up at me and smiled. I'll never forget that smile. I've never had children of my own, so I don't know what it would feel like. But in that dream it was so real. I knew she was my daughter. The funny thing was, that alongside the joy that that smile brought me, there was a heart-rending pain. I couldn't understand it until a month later, when I was going round a country house with a friend, a National Trust house, you know, open to the public. In Yorkshire it was. We were walking round it with the guide, when suddenly there I was, hey presto, in the same library I'd seen in the dream, the same view and all.'

He stopped. Tomasin thought he'd finished. No spooky murders in this story, thank God.

'Well, that's amazing,' she said.

'But that's not all. Not by a long chalk. I recognized it as the same library, so I looked straight for the door into the next room. But it wasn't there. I was in a right muddle. I asked the guide about it, but he'd never heard of any door having been there before. So when I got home, I wrote to the National Trust. They passed my letter on to Lord Monkton who used to own it. He was kind enough to write back to me, and you'll never guess what he said.'

Tomasin began to feel slightly sick. She had not encountered anything like this before, and didn't have a formula to follow to help ease the discomfiture.

'He said that his great-grandfather had had a door sealed off there. It used to lead to the nursery, but after a terrible accident he'd had the whole room stripped, changed and redesigned. The accident happened to a five-year-old girl, his daughter. She fell off a rocking horse and smashed her head on a brass fender. A terrible family tragedy. I ask you, if reincarnation doesn't exist, how did I know all that?'

She refused to let herself be frightened by such a story. For heaven's sake, she thought, keep a grip on yourself. Where have you just come from, who have you been staying with, who are you having lunch with tomorrow, when are you next going out to the theatre? She looked out at the houses rushing past. An Englishman's house is his castle. So many rows of castles, then. So many cosy little worlds coming into view, little centres of homeliness in the howling wind and rain. All the people, families and pets, warm and safe. There one moment and gone the next. Why didn't the sight comfort her a little? The train seemed to be getting faster and faster, like a mad roller-coaster. Calm yourself, she thought, don't get hysterical.

'So what do you think of that? The same little girl that I had seen. Killed.'

'Stuff and nonsense.' It was the old woman who spoke, packing away her knitting. 'You don't want to listen to such trash. Never heard so much balderdash in all my life. You should keep quiet, you. Instead of going round scaring young ladies like that.'

43

The train had begun to slow down. They were coming to a station. Tomasin regained control of her faculties. How absurd, she felt, to have got so worked up. She hoped she hadn't shown as much perturbation as she'd sustained.

'It's not nonsense, it's God's honest truth. It happened,' he said, fixing his little blue eyes on the old woman who had got up to leave. This was her station. She tutted, sighed and left the compartment, sliding the door behind her.

It was just the three of them now. The soldier had woken up at the old woman's outburst, and looked around confusedly. He checked his watch and picked up *Country Life* again. Tomasin asked her neighbours, as calmly as she could, if he would mind taking all the papers off her lap that had been lying there since the heraldry lecture.

'I'm so sorry, I'd forgotten all about them,' he said, forcing them back into his case in no particular order. 'You know, I don't just get dreams about things that have happened years ago,' he continued, 'things happen from day to day that I feel I've known about beforehand.'

'I get that too,' she added, trying to avert the possibility of any more scares, and put their dialogue on to a more light-hearted level, 'it's just *déjà vu*. There is a scientific explanation, you know. When the central nervous system receives a stimulus – '

'There's no scientific explanation for the sort of things that happen to me,' he cut in, turning and smiling at her again. She wondered, behind her crumbling composure, if he had got a crick in his neck by now. He finished packing away the heraldic papers. 'I meet people I've dreamt of before, I read things in newspapers I've known about before, my cat disappears and I know where to find her.'

'A very useful sort of gift, I call that,' Tomasin said, 'the right person could make a fortune out of you.'

Christ, what can you say to a lunatic like this? If only

this were the hospital. There are always people to help there, qualified people. This sort of thing shouldn't happen on a bloody train. It's not meant to happen somewhere like this.

Tomasin's tidy little world of slotted dates, a time and a place for everything, waste not want not, a bird in hand's worth two in the bush, finders keepers losers weepers, ring-a-ring of roses, little Bo-Peep: the structure she had known and built up gradually since childhood days, the quiet, logical mind that had been founded on an infancy of correct rhymes and not too much jam, the lessons learnt from smacked wrists – it all seemed thoroughly inadequate because it hadn't insured her against this. Her worthy life had been invaded by an unknown quantity; not the Bogey Man, nor the Wicked Witch, not even Dracula or Iago. This pig-man with piercing blue eyes was clearly no ordinary villain. She would have recognized conventional evil.

'It's sometimes more serious than just finding the cat, though. A little while ago, I dreamt about a young man accidentally shot by the police. The next day it was all over the papers. The same young man. I'm beginning to worry that my dreams are causing the events to happen. But on the other hand,' he added, as if about to crack an irresistible joke, 'if that's true, think what power I could have; if I could learn to control my dreams – '

The train plummeted into a tunnel at high speed. The noise was deafening. Despite the fact that the suddenness of it gave her a shock, it provided Tomasin with a welcome break during which she could think about her next move. Something about the menacing roar outside combined with the dull, slightly flickering compartment light made her feel vulnerable. Her sensibility was being bombarded by unnatural, even alien elements. She could not help but turn and look up at him. To her uncomfortable surprise, she

45

saw that his lips were still moving and his eyes were still concentratedly staring at hers. He was still talking even though it was impossible to hear a word.

'I'm sorry, you'll have to wait 'til we're out of the tunnel,' she bellowed. He nudged himself a few inches closer to her. Their knees were touching now. In a rushing instant they were out of the tunnel.

'So are you convinced?'

'About what?'

'About the importance of dreams.'

'Well, I think I am.'

She thought it best to concede.

'You'll have something to tell them back at the hospital, now, won't you? By the way, which hospital do you work in?'

Oh my God, what do I say now? She had to answer in an instant. To hesitate could prove dangerous. It was important to demonstrate that she was equal to him, on top of the situation, but she couldn't tell him where he'd be able to find her. She looked at the soldier and caught his eye for a split second. He wouldn't help.

'It's one of the ones right in the centre of town.'

She was stalling for time.

'I went to Bart's once. Cataract,' he pointed to his eye, 'they were very nice to me. I'd dreamt about that as well, by the by. It's a funny old world, isn't it?'

She'd shaken him off. It was now or never. She had to get the soldier in on the conversation to ease the pressure off her. He was a military man, after all, a man of honour. Surely they still maintained some code of gallantry in the regimental officers' mess. Maiden in distress, all that junk. He had been looking at her ever since she had glanced at him for that fleeting moment of panic. Now she looked at him hard and long, a pleading, beckoning look. He turned his head to face her full on, and smiled with one corner of his mouth. Then he uncrossed his legs and raised a questioning eyebrow. He might as well have turned green in Tomasin's eyes; his whole expression and posture had transformed into one of patient, suave lecherousness. He had turned into that repulsive lust machine, everything she hated about certain types of men.

'Excuse me, I've got to go to the loo,' she said, and left the compartment.

She hurried down the corridor, feeling sick with disgust. Once locked in the toilet, she looked at herself in the mirror. Only me, she thought, little me. It's all right, we're safe now. The train was slowing down again; last stop before London. Only half an hour to King's Cross. Why don't I get off here and get a taxi? But I have to get my bag. Now don't worry any more, just go into the compartment, grab the suitcase, say good-bye and forget about the whole thing. She felt home and dry already. Thank God for that station. Perfect timing.

Just before the train came to a complete stop, she opened the door of the toilet. The soldier was in front of her barring the way.

'Hi. Fancy meeting like this.'

'What do you mean?'

'Come on, darling, don't let's waste time. Get off here with me and we can go to my place.'

The horrible realization of his presence there in front of her, and his preposterous intentions, hit her like a slap in the face. She was momentarily stupefied, and did not know how to react.

'Coming?' he grinned, touching her under the chin.

'Let me pass, please,' she said, looking down from his face and through his torso, along the corridor.

'Changed your mind, eh? Give a man the eye, then give

47

him the slip? That's not on, you know. You're a bit of a frisky filly, aren't you?'

'Get out of my way,' she screamed as hard as she could, pushing his arm aside and running past him.

'In future, darling, don't tease what you won't please,' he called after her.

Only when she was at the sliding compartment door did she remember the gentler fear that awaited her there. There was no escape. She couldn't get off at the same stop as the soldier. She would just have to sit it out for the last half hour, alone in there with the madman.

'You're back! I thought for a moment you might have got off without your suitcase. So glad you didn't'.

She sat down opposite him this time.

To her surprise he let the minutes pass by without saying a single word. He was looking at her, nonetheless, head slightly tilted, hands together, thumbs flicking each other. She was a little unnerved at this restraint, coupled with his obviously scrutinizing stare. What could he be thinking? The rain outside seemed, if anything, to be easing slightly, but the wind still wailed its wintry melody to the quick-step accompaniment of the train's undercarriage rhythm. A full fifteen minutes went by before he spoke again. Nearly, so nearly there, Tomasin thought.

'Not far now,' he said. 'Look here, I haven't even introduced myself. My name's Colin. Colin Shepherd. I'm from Yorkshire, you know. You could probably guess that from my accent.'

He let out another string of stifled honks, like an adolescent schoolboy sniggering at his first flick through a dirty magazine.

'Whereabouts in Yorkshire?' she asked, consciously steering away from having to introduce herself.

'Halifax, or near enough. It's a funny thing you should

48

ask me that, because the other day I met someone, a young man, this was in London, who asked me the same. And I said to him, you guess where I come from, and he got it right first time. Not just Halifax, mind you, but my actual village, Brighouse. Another little unsolved mystery. I ought to write a little book of them, don't you think?'

'Yes, maybe you should,' she answered, 'it's just the sort of thing that the public always craves for; horror stories, ghouls, ghosts, voices from the past, all that sort of stuff.'

He looked at her blankly. His face lost the full-cheeked smile that it had had for the whole journey so far, and his eyebrows came together in a very slight frown.

'There's no need to get nasty, miss.'

The words were said softly, his voice at a lower pitch than before. He seemed genuinely offended.

'I'm sorry, I didn't mean to – '

'Oh yes you did,' he said, his resentfulness gaining confidence and coming to the fore. 'You've been sitting here all bloody evening, thinking I'm some mad bloody bugger giving you a hard time. Don't think I couldn't see it in your eyes. I was talking to you in good faith, sharing personal things with you, and what do you do in return?'

'I – '

'You what?' She was stunned, frozen, unable to reply. 'I'll tell you what,' he continued, 'you sit there, pretending to be all nice and sweet, little miss Doctor, and all the time wanting me to shut up, or go away or even drop dead.'

'That's not true.'

'Don't give me that. You're about as bloody transparent as a bloody piece of glass.' He was really angry now, face flushed, sitting on the edge of his seat and leaning menacingly towards her. They were rushing through suburban stations. The last lap. 'I'll tell you what's wrong with people like you, Doctor Bryant.' (When had she told him

49

her name? She was sure she hadn't told him her name. How did he know it?) 'You're so bloody self-satisfied. You think what I've been telling you is just a load of old crap; the sort of stuff to put in kiddies' books. That's what you said –'

'I didn't mean –'

'Shut up and listen to me, damn you!' He was right forward in his seat, pointing a hard, fat finger towards her face. 'It's time you started rethinking, young lady. It's time you understood that you may have got certain things wrong.'

His voice lost its hard edge, and his face eased back into its habitual leer. She found no comfort in the change. She longed with all her body and soul for that first sensation of the train decelerating. Only a matter of minutes, surely.

'Yes,' he grinned, opening wide his blue eyes, and staring right into her face, penetrating everything, fixing her inner core to the spot, 'you need to learn a thing or two, Doctor. So sure you know it all, aren't you? So safe with your little job, your little car, your little flat and your future all worked out. Why don't I tell you about my most recent dream? That might change a thing or two. Do you want to hear about my most recent dream?'

The train had at last begun to pull up.

'All right.'

'I only had it last night, but it was a real chiller.' Slower and slower. He won't have enough time, she thought. 'In fact, I think it was the most terrifying of all my dreams. Do you want to hear it? I don't care if you want to or not, you've got to hear.'

She could see the platform now, and the big white signboards: King's Cross.

'Even I was shocked by it. I only realized the full truth of it when I got on the train this evening and saw you.' His

50

face was within a couple of inches of hers. The train was grinding to a halt. 'You see, my dream last night was all about *you*.'

He gripped her wrist, but she pulled it away and slid out of the seat. Grabbing her bag, she rushed out of the compartment, and ran down the corridor without looking back. Once on the platform she pushed past the crowds and hurried into the nearest taxi.

'Where to, luv?'

'Clapham, please.'

'Where in Clapham?'

'I'll tell you in a minute; please just get driving.'

She looked behind her as the taxi moved off, but she couldn't distinguish anything or anyone in the great sea of heads.

'As soon as I got home I rang my brother. I couldn't bear the idea of staying at the flat on my own. Of course, Johnnie wasn't at home. So I had a bath. That was my first response to the whole thing: to get clean, thoroughly scrubbed. It was awful, I can't tell you how ghastly. I thought at any minute he'd be there, either in the next room or banging on the front door. I kept thinking of all those murders in Clapham recently. I could hardly blink. I got into some old homely clothes, a thick jumper knitted by Mummy. I needed the comfort. I couldn't ring Mummy and Daddy of course, or they'd panic themselves to death. All the time I was telling myself not to be stupid, and trying to think about normal things. I remembered I was having lunch with you today, and went to check the time in my diary. I was actually beginning to convince myself that it had just been a horrible nightmare. But then I saw it, and it hit me like a cold stone on the forehead.'

'You saw what?' I asked.

'In my bag. It had somehow slipped into my diary. It was the spooky coat of arms he'd given me: the skinny, smiling horse-head. I could hardly touch it. It brought it all back and into my home. It was there, in front of me, some hideous testament of his presence in my own sitting-room.'

She was about to start shaking again.

'So what did you do then?'

'I burnt it. Like some kind of ritual. I know it sounds stupid, but I had to. It helped to see it curling up and shrinking. But it burnt with a strange green flame.'

'Probably some plastic compound in the paper.'

'Probably.'

'Crisp packets have green flames as well.'

'I know.'

She hesitated.

'You can't have been frightened by that.'

'You don't understand, anything out of the ordinary scares me to death at the moment, it doesn't matter where I am.'

'Well, there's nothing out of the ordinary here. Do you feel safe here, with me?'

'Everything's out of the ordinary now. It's as if I've been blind to it all along. All the people, their faces, each hiding strange secrets, fears, joys. All the cars, different colours, dents here and there. All the sounds, sudden jabs of sound then unexpected silences. Nothing's ordinary any more. I could drop dead outside this shop. That could be ordinary. People drop dead every day. The ordinary and the unexpected are one and the same. We're living on a tight-rope and pretending that it's all normal and okay and we haven't got a care in the world. Christ, how did I get by for so long without realizing it? It honestly feels as if someone's waved a wand and opened my eyes for the first time.'

'Come on, Tom, don't get things out of proportion – '

'My name's Tomasin. I don't like being called Tom, I never have liked it.'

She was near another breakdown.

'Why haven't you said so before?'

'I'm sorry. Don't take any notice of me.'

'Look, you can't go around thinking someone's going to jump out of the crowd and bite your head off.'

'But that's what nearly happened yesterday.'

'Then by the law of averages it won't happen again.'

'Averages? Back to "ordinary life" again?'

'And why not?'

'Because I don't think there's any such thing. How could he possibly have known my name?'

'He probably saw a tag on your suitcase when you were in the loo. Is there one there?'

'It's Mummy's suitcase. Yes, I think there is a tag on it. But then it wouldn't have been my name at all.'

'He only used your surname. He still hasn't got a clue who you are. He'll be chasing the wrong girl.'

'I expect Mummy would know how to deal with him.' She was relaxing for the first time. Her face had even flickered into a smile. 'But what about those dreams he told me about?' she asked.

'For heaven's sake, you don't believe that load of weird nonsense, do you?'

'He said the last dream, the most frightening he'd ever had, was all about me.'

'So what? He was trying to scare you. Don't you see, he was just some common-or-garden pervert, most probably.'

'Like the one you might find around any street corner?'

'Exactly.'

'Well if that's your "everyday life", I'd rather be out of it.'

'Listen to me,' I said, 'you've got to pull yourself together.

53

These things happen. They don't happen very often, but when they do, they're bloody frightening. You can't let it affect you for ever. Go to the Police if it would help.'

'They wouldn't do anything. I wasn't raped or anything. They'd probably say I led him on. No, there's nothing I can do. I'm just going to have to live with it. Perhaps I should go home for a while, spend a couple of weeks with my parents, ride the horses. But then I'd probably find things had all changed there as well. I'm pathetic, aren't I?'

I hadn't managed to cheer her up very much, but she agreed to stick it out for a few days before returning to the bosom of her family. She promised to phone me whenever the fear got too intense, and I assured her I would always be there to help. I had never known her lean on anyone before, but I was glad that it should be me. The transformation was dumbfounding.

After the briefest snatch of a kiss she disappeared along the pavement, half running to the shelter of the underground station, and all the while looking around anxiously.

Tomasin hadn't slept for two days, and wouldn't be able to tonight either. So it did not matter that she was on night duty at the hospital. Casualty department: it wasn't a job that she looked forward to at the best of times. She sat in the kitchen of her flat, trying to read a book but allowing her imagination to stray. Think of all those healthy, whole people at this very moment, who before the night is out would be lying in front of her in various critical conditions. The man who'd had a heart attack at the restaurant, the boy who'd been attacked with a broken bottle, the girl who'd been knocked senseless by her own father, the mother of three who'd taken an overdose. They're all fine now, but they'll turn up tonight one by one, you could be sure of that. Accidents happen all day every day, everywhere. In fact, she thought as she stared blankly at a printed page in front of her, why call them 'accidents' at all? Why not change the word? 'Inevitables.' I inevitably crashed my car this afternoon. She died after an inevitable fall from the window. Ordinary life, so full of unplanned mishaps. For the first time in her life she felt as though the future was an unwieldy, treacherous mystery. Anything might happen to change the course of events, so it was useless even attempting to harness time. Years, minutes, calendars, clocks, all of them petty little man-made tricks to help measure time, and to fool us into believing we've got a future. What good is the day-to-day calendar for the man who gets cancer tonight and is given a month to live? What use is the expensive Swiss watch to the motorcyclist who sets out on his journey a second too soon, and just clips the bumper of the lorry? He flies across the road as helpless and fragile as the pig-man's spectacles.

She drove to the hospital in her little car, and left it in the staff car park. She could have avoided night duty if she'd really wanted to, but she preferred to be there, surrounded by people, friendly people, qualified people, and bright lights.

Everyone was the same as usual. The same smiles, hello Tomasin, good evening Doctor Bryant. No change. Familiar smells, her own white coat, the tea machine. It was good to be back.

The flood of broken people began to arrive, wheeled in by teams of hardened, eternally jolly ambulance men. I'm afraid your husband may have had a brain haemorrhage. When did you last go to the toilet? What time did she have the attack? Are you the next of kin? I don't know if we can save your son's finger. Anything like this happen to you before? Are you sure they used knives, it looks more like razor blades?

55

'There's a really critical one on the way, Doctor Bryant. Ambulance has called in. They don't know if he'll make the journey. You'd better be ready when they arrive.'

'What is it this time? Car crash?'

'No; suicide attempt. In front of a train. Nasty. Lucky to be alive at all, they said.'

She had hoped there wouldn't be any suicides tonight. She didn't want to be faced with the squirming figure of a body struggling to breathe, even though the mind had decided not to go on. She did not want the same old moral dilemma tonight. Help them back even though they've crossed the courage barrier; stepped resolutely across the line, the same as the white line along the edge of the station platform. People who cannot face another moment of ordinary life. She did not want to look into their eyes and coax them back with gentle, optimistic smiles, and words of strength. She lacked the conviction to tell them how lucky they were to be alive, and talk of bright tomorrows. Not tonight.

The ambulance had arrived, and the hefty crew were unloading their charge on to a stainless steel trolley. Tomasin could see them through the window in the swing doors. She had hardly ever seen them move so fast. This was obviously going to be a cliff-hanger. The doors crashed open: her cue, front of stage. She was in charge now. Blood was soaking through the blankets and dripping on to the floor.

'I think we might have lost him. Over to you, Doctor.'

Tomasin was running alongside the trolley, down a corridor, searching under the blanket for a wrist. Where the hell was his arm? The head was splashed, streaked and matted. She put her stethoscope to his chest, unbuttoning the tattered checked shirt. He was still wearing a tie, but it had been loosened at the knot. They had not wasted time taking his jacket off. A herring-bone tweed jacket. His head turned, a huge spherical mess of cuts, gore and splintered bone. It was when he opened a pair of sharp little pale blue eyes and stared straight into hers, that she was stung with recognition. But he was dead before she could do anything.

BLACK IS BEAUTIFUL

David Muir

David Muir was born in Buckinghamshire but now lives in Plymouth. After leaving Leeds University he joined ITN as a journalist where he worked for ten years.

In 1988 David Muir wrote a guidebook for the National Trust after which he began to write fiction. He now has two novels completed, and is hard at work on the third.

BLACK IS BEAUTIFUL

'Looking out for love, in the night so still . . .'
FLEETWOOD MAC SONG

Two lorries, shrouded in tarpaulin for secrecy, arrived, and the thirty workmen began unloading.

I went out immediately to meet their leader, a tall muscular man of my own age with a fierce sunburn. His name was Joe.

'What's the form for today?' I asked.

'It'll take about eight hours,' he advised. 'What we're going to do will scare the hell out of you. So I suggest you take your wife out for the day.'

'Will we like it when it's done?' I asked.

He grinned hugely. 'You'll learn to live with it.'

'Only eight hours . . .' I said wonderingly.

'We've had time to plan for this. I'm afraid it's going to be like living in a zoo.'

'I know that,' I snapped.

Joe stuck out his hand and said rather awkwardly: 'I admire you for what you're doing, Mr Adams.'

We shook hands.

Neither Jane nor I relished the prospect of seeing our home ripped to pieces, so we drove down to the coast for the day. We had a lousy time. Jane was nervous and irritable and took it out on me.

We'd only just parked when she said: 'I wish we could

have gone to the Cotswolds. That would've been lovely.'

'Why didn't you say when we set out?'

'You had your heart set on Swanage.'

I hadn't even mentioned Swanage.

We lolled around on the beach all day, in and out of the sea, blending anonymously with the other holidaymakers, but Jane's ill-temper continued.

The sight of the bungalow when we returned made things worse. All the doors had gone. In their place were great arches, fifteen feet wide and eight high, with electronically-controlled sliding panels. The bathroom wall had been removed so the bathroom was now part of the hall. The kitchen, living and dining-rooms had been combined into one large room. Here, the suite of furniture was pushed hard up against one wall; the table, chairs and television against the other. All other furniture was missing. The billiard room, even the bedrooms, ours and the spare, had those sliding doors.

Jane burst into silent tears and pushed me away when I tried to take her in my arms and comfort her.

I went over to the dining-room window. The back garden was unrecognizable. The lawn and flower beds had been bulldozed flat to make way for a shallow pool, a giant sand-pit and a large wooden shed.

'I suppose that's its kennel,' Jane said bitterly over my shoulder.

It had started a month before with my being called into the office of the Brigadier, an experience I'd never had before and one which scared the hell out of me.

I noticed the two pink folders on his desk: psychological profiles for Jane and me.

'We'll dispense with formalities,' he said. 'You can call me Matt.' He put his elbows on the table, hands together as if he was praying, and regarded me shrewdly for a moment. Then he said: 'We have a bit of a problem with the Thurgs.'

Perhaps I should break off here and say something about the coming of the Thurgs. Right from the start, they were so damned helpful and polite.

'Excuse me, we couldn't help noticing you've got a problem with your ozone layer. Mind if we do something about that for you?'

Next day, there's a huge block of what looks like ice in orbit round the earth. Well, you can't manage something like that in twenty-four hours, even if you're a Thurg, so they'd obviously planned it all and started the operation, only bothering to ask us when it was already under way. The block was frozen ozone, of course. Somehow they manoeuvred it over the north pole and half a dozen ships held it in suspension there for a week while it melted.

'Excuse me, we couldn't help but notice that you're cutting down trees at an alarming rate. The long term effect will be to deplete your atmosphere of oxygen and build up the percentage of carbon dioxide. Are you sure you want to do that?'

They had ships settling down all over South America the next day, unloading small trees, eight feet high. These were native to a planet they'd explored somewhere in the Orion Nebula and imported to their home world. The tree was called Xtlank – that was the nearest anyone could get to pronouncing it. Once it reaches eight feet high, the Xtlank grows at the rate of one foot a day and the wood is better than mahogany. In other respects it is just like any native species of tree, growing to the size of an oak tree.

The huge mother ship never landed. It sat up there in orbit. But we could never forget it was there.

And, of course, all the time, there was the big unanswered question: Why? Why were they being so damned helpful?

Anyway, back to the Brigadier's office . . .

'What's the problem, Matt?' I asked, taking full advantage of the offer he'd made to be informal.

'The Thurgs want to send someone down to study us, a sort of anthropologist-cum-sociologist.'

This was something new. Once contact had been made, the Thurgs had kept away from Earth. All the ambassadorial talks took place on the mother ship with unmanned drones acting as taxis.

'Just the one?'

'Just one,' he confirmed.

'And where do I come in?'

'It wants to live with a family in their home for a while. We're thinking of you and Jane.'

'A typical family?' I asked. 'Doesn't that mean kids?'

Jane and I don't have any children and we can't. To put it bluntly, I'm sterile. I've always seen this as the result of standing a little too close to a nuclear test but I've yet to persuade the military to see it that way.

'The Thurgs say any human child would be terrified of them.'

'That's an understatement,' I said, looking at Matt very hard. It wasn't just the children who were terrified. He gave me the same look back. 'Okay, with the proviso that Jane agrees, I accept. What's my role supposed to be?'

'If the Thurg wants to study us, it gives us a chance to study it. Try to find out why they're really here and what they really want. The Thurg will ask you questions. Ask yourself why it's asking specific questions and if there's one particular line it seems to be following.'

'And how do I answer its questions?'

'Quite openly and honestly. Lies and evasions might give offence, and we dare not offend them. Just in case, we'll give you a back-up. If you find out something the Thurg doesn't want us to know, and the Thurg finds out you've found out, things could turn nasty for you.'

I was introduced to Percy Rawlings: a young man with the bronzed physique of a body-builder and a conceited grin. He was to come and stay at the bungalow, posing as our gardener.

I took an immediate dislike to Percy.

It was left to me to break the news to Jane, which I did that same evening.

She was furious. Why hadn't I told her before? (I hadn't known.) Why had I agreed before asking her opinion? (I hadn't fully agreed.) It made no difference. She sulked for two whole days. Then she was hauled in for a similar interview, difficult in her case because she's a civilian.

The official letter of confirmation arrived a week later. It mentioned for the first time all the alterations that would have to be made, at the military's expense, to make my bungalow habitable for the Thurg. There was no mention of restoring my home afterwards.

Percy moved in the day after the alterations. I picked him up from headquarters and drove him home. All the way, he regaled me with his opinions on the aliens and a host of other matters, which did nothing to improve my opinion of him.

I introduced him to Jane, saying: 'Look, they've given us a gardener.'

Together, Percy and I explained his role.

'I'm supposed to act rather stupid,' said Percy, 'That way, the Thurg hopefully won't take too much notice of me.'

That shouldn't be too difficult, I thought maliciously.

Jane grinned. 'If you're going to pretend to be a gardener, Percy, you might as well be one. I'll show you what's left of our garden.' She took him by the arm as if he was a long-lost friend, and marched him outside.

Have you ever seen a Thurg close up? No, you haven't. You've only seen photographs and no photograph can do justice to a Thurg. They're midnight black all over. A photograph can only show the general shape, the detail is missing.

I remember drawing pictures of aliens as a kid. Some of my designs were quite weird, but if you looked at them carefully you could break them down into quite recognizable parts: the antennae were really snail's eyes, the arms those of a squid, the mandibles belonged to a lobster, and so on.

But alien is something different. If you're a person who believes in God and believes that God created the whole of the universe, then you look at a Thurg, suddenly your whole concept of God changes, and you're left reeling with the shock of it.

Remember those screaming newspaper headlines when the Thurgs arrived?

THE OCTOTORTS ARE HERE!

They'd done in reverse what I'd done with my childish drawings: trying to break down the alienness into recognizable parts. The name Octotort was a combination of octopus and tortoise: octopus because of the pseudopods they extend, tortoise for the basic shape of the carapace.

Start off with the idea of a shell like a king crab, only it's an almost perfect hemisphere, it's black, and it's covered with warts and nodules. There are also masses of tiny holes through which the creature breathes. All over this shell are smaller hemispheres, about thirty of them, all identical. They're like giant eyelids and you can see the cracks across the centres.

When one of these opens, you're never quite sure what's going to happen: you might see an eye, a mouth, the speech mechanism, or a rubbery pseudopod might start oozing out, shaping itself as it extends for whatever purpose the Thurg has in mind, a mass of tiny whip-like extensions or maybe a single blunt-ended extrusion, bulging out as thick as a man's thigh, which could kill you with one buffet.

I forgot to mention: the Thurg weighs a ton, literally, a ton; it's fourteen feet in diameter, and seven high.

Inside that massive carapace, the body must be like that of a giant amoeba with all the sense organs, speech box and mouth on the outside. The Thurg can move any organ internally to any of the hemispheres. Most of the time, the Thurg assigns specific organs to specific hemispheres. But you can get a shock. An aperture opens at the base of the carapace and you get a glimpse of rubbery flesh which really isn't skin but muscle fibre. Ah, you think, it's going to stick out an arm. But then the tissue writhes and a giant eye looms into view because the Thurg wants to examine something on the ground.

The eyes – there are eight of them, arranged in pairs – are the biggest shock of all. Why? Because, amidst all that black alienness, they're almost human. The whites; the pupils; irises of the purest, most beautiful, striated gold: it's all there. You gaze into a pair of eyes and you could be gazing into the eyes of a cherished friend or loved one.

The Thurg arrived on another tarpaulin-covered lorry which backed slowly up on to my driveway. There were also two carloads of officials.

IT pushed its way through the tarpaulin, slid down the ramp, and I stepped forward.

The creature stopped before me, two of the hemispheres opened, and I got my first clear sight of those terrible golden eyes, staring at me unblinkingly.

Another hemisphere lower down opened and a stumpy pseudopod extended, resolving itself into the speech apparatus. In the centre was a round, puckered hole, nothing like a human mouth. On either side was a single spoon-shaped barbel.

'Good morning, you can call me Rosie.'

I gave a formal bow. 'Good morning, Rosie, I'm Peter Adams. Pleased to meet you.' Immediately, for me the thing was feminine, and that impossible idea stayed with me for all time. In spite of what I'd been taught about the Thurgs, I instinctively held out my hand.

Rosie extruded a pseudopod. I'd expected all her movements to be sluggish or, more accurately I suppose, slug-like, but the pseudopod shot out with the speed of a striking snake. It was like an arm amputated at the wrist, terminating an inch from my still-outstretched hand. There was nothing I could do but grasp the projection and give it a gentle squeeze. It felt like hard cold rubber. I'm sure the experience was unpleasant for both of us.

While we were talking, workmen unloaded a massive black box from the flat-back.

'My things,' said Rosie vaguely.

The box was taken round the side of the bungalow to the new shed.

Jane came cautiously down the steps and I introduced them. Commonsensically, Jane didn't try to shake hands. She just nodded, rather curtly, and said: 'I am pleased to meet you, Rosie.'

A slim tentacle writhed out of one opening and disappeared momentarily into another. It reappeared, clutching a bouquet of flowers: orchid-like, but not orchids, with a smell of honeysuckle and crushed strawberries.

'For my hostess.'

Jane took them and murmured an ungracious: 'Thank you.'

After the officials had gone, we took Rosie on a guided

68

tour of the bungalow. She moved so slowly. Perhaps on her home planet with its low gravitational field she was a thing of grace and beauty, but not on Earth.

She enthused over the empty wooden shed, acted shyly for some reason over the sand-pit and commiserated over the alterations to the bungalow. 'I hope my presence hasn't put you both to too much trouble.'

'Not at all, think nothing of it,' Jane replied with a tight-lipped smile that threatened to turn into a scream. I gave her a warning frown.

Percy was introduced. I admit reluctantly his imitation of a moron was excellently done.

'I'd like to get some of my things unpacked,' said Rosie. 'Perhaps I can join you when you have your next meal, if that won't be an imposition.'

'We have our main meal at eight,' said Jane, 'but we're quite prepared to change things round to fit in with your eating habits.'

'No, don't change anything. Perhaps you'll allow me to join you for your main meal.'

'What do you eat?' asked Jane.

'Oh, I've arranged to have my meals delivered. I only eat once a day. I'll join you, but I won't eat anything myself.'

Jane's question had not been answered, I noticed.

From the dining-room window, we watched the food delivery made. Around noon, a black sphere alighted on the sand-pit and opened. Rosie waddled out of her shed across to the ship, took out a large black box, and 'man-handled' it back to the shed. The sphere closed and took off. We were no wiser.

'Slugs and snails and puppy dogs' tails,' said Jane.

'Eye of newt and wing of bat,' I replied in kind.

She shuddered.

Rosie lumbered into what was left of the dining-room at

eight. She came as near to the table as the carapace allowed, then settled firmly on the floor with enough force to leave a permanent circle in the carpet.

That evening we had a lobster salad.

Rosie wanted to know all the ingredients, where they came from, their natural history, how bread was made, everything. Jane is a biologist, so she was able to answer better than me.

'This is a cultural exchange,' Rosie explained. 'Feel free to ask any questions you wish about us. We have nothing to hide.'

Like hell, I thought.

Dinner was a dismal, stilted affair.

That night, in bed, Jane called over to me: 'Isn't it awful?'

'What's awful?'

'It!' She evidently hated Rosie.

I tried to define my own attitude: I found Rosie repulsive, but I didn't hate her. Hate is an emotional reaction and when you hate you're out of control.

'Peter, I should never have let you talk me into this.'

I wasn't aware I'd talked her into anything.

Armed with a torch, I went out of the bungalow in the middle of the night to explore the sand-pit. I poked around with a stick and unearthed a number of hard dark brown balls, slightly larger than tennis balls. Somehow it made Rosie seem less fearsome. I went back to bed.

When I got up, Rosie was there in the kitchen. She'd fixed us both breakfast: lobster salad and a stone-cold pot of coffee.

'I'll take Jane hers on a tray,' I said.

'Does Jane always have breakfast in bed?'

The truth was I didn't trust Jane's reaction to the breakfast. I muttered: 'Neither of us slept much last night.'

'My arrival has upset you.'

70

I grinned, thought of Joe, and said: 'We'll get used to it.'

Back in the bedroom, I tried to explain things to Jane. Last night we had eaten lobster salad and drunk coffee. Rosie assumed this was our staple diet. She couldn't tell if we drank the coffee hot or cold. She thought she was being helpful.

Jane took the tray from me calmly then flung it bodily across the room. 'Now I suppose we have to starve, pretending we enjoyed our lovely breakfast.'

I didn't want another argument so I returned to the kitchen. There I ate my salad and drank my coffee dutifully, watched by a pair of Rosie's unblinking golden orbs.

'Things aren't very good between you and Jane, are they?' she asked.

'They're not good,' I agreed without thinking.

'I hope my being here won't make things worse.'

'Rosie . . .' I began and then stopped. I wanted to tell her it was none of her damned business, but the Brigadier had said to answer *all* questions openly. I finished by saying: 'I have to go to work this morning.'

'Naturally.'

'You can have the run of the house.' Then I realized 'run' was a rather stupid thing to say and shook my head in self-disgust.

One of her hemispheres rattled. It sounded disarmingly like a chuckle. 'I'm familiar with your colloquialisms. Don't worry. It was a good joke, if unintentional.'

So the Thurgs had a sense of humour. Then I realized something and stared at her in alarm. She'd begun to read my body language. That was something I'd not counted on.

I reported in to the Brigadier and told him the little I knew. 'She's trying to be affable, but she's asking far too many damned personal questions for my liking,' I concluded.

The Brigadier knew Jane and I had our problems. 'Is Jane going to be okay?'

'I think I can control it. But Jane does hate her.'

'Her?'

'Rosie.'

'Peter, we're both trained psychologists. You know what you're doing, don't you? You want to make it seem less alien by giving it human characteristics – anthropomorphizing.' He was right and I admitted it. 'Can I remind you of something? Their first manned landing, we mistook them for robots and zapped the hell out of three Thurgs. They've never even raised the subject, not once. Think about that, will you?'

I told him about the noon deliveries.

'Try and find out what's in the deliveries, Peter. Any information helps. We know nothing about them. We don't even know what they eat.'

That one sent a cold shiver all the way down my backbone.

'By the way, did you have to alter the bedrooms?' I asked.

'There's no reason for the Thurg to enter them, but we don't want it to think we're hiding anything.' This made good sense. 'How's Percy making out?' he asked.

I couldn't let my irrational antagonism get in the way, so I said: 'Okay. He and Jane seem to get on fine and that takes the strain off her.'

'I thought you were at work,' said Rosie immediately I returned.

'They let me home early.' It sounded so weak, I felt compelled to say something near to the truth: 'Your being

72

here is important. They feel I should spend as much time with you as possible.'

'I'll make you some coffee and we can talk.'

I watched her make the coffee, thin tendrils lashing out all over her carapace. It must be nice to have one 'hand' for each mug, one for each of a pair of spoons, one for the coffee jar, one for the sugar barrel, one for the kettle.

'Have you and Jane been chatting?' I asked.

'She doesn't like me.'

'I'm sorry,' I said lamely.

'It's not important, Peter. It would be nice if she did, but I don't need her to like me.' She passed me my coffee, piping hot this time, and said: 'Is there anything I can do or say which will help the two of you, your relationship?'

It was such a kind thing to say, for a moment I forgot Rosie was a Thurg and replied quite openly and rather wearily: 'I can't do a damned thing myself, so nobody else can help.'

Jane and Percy came in from the garden just then. Jane was cradling a stray cat which seemed to have adopted us. Fortunately she had not overheard our conversation. She saw the coffee mug in my hand and frowned.

'Come on, Percy, I'll make us coffee. This selfish sod made himself one but didn't think about us.' She poked her tongue out at me as she passed to enter the kitchen area.

In the background I heard Rosie clicking an aperture, perhaps sympathetically.

Later, I told Jane about the sand-pit and she doubled up with laughter, the tears streaming down her cheeks. 'Elephant turds,' she cried, gasping for breath.

It was the last time she laughed for me.

Over the next two weeks, the four of us tended to pair off and only come together at meal times. Jane developed a sudden interest in gardening. I was stuck with Rosie. It reminded me of the old joke about double-dating: I don't think much of yours.

Actually, I preferred Rosie's company to Jane's. She might look abominable and I had no idea how her mind worked, but she always acted politely, sympathetically and civilized.

The sympathy was annoying at times. She seemed to want to tackle my marital problem on an intellectual basis and solve it for me. To do that she needed every scrap of information she could extract. I comforted myself by telling myself that this type of questioning was innocuous.

One day, after a particularly gruelling session, I told her exasperatedly: 'Rosie, stop worrying about it. Deep down inside, Jane and I love each other.'

'What is love?' Rosie demanded.

'If you've never experienced it, I can't explain it.'

'Can you get me some books on love?'

'I don't think there are any.' Then I thought about it more carefully, and suggested: 'Poetry. I'll get you some books on poetry. Do Thurgs write poetry?'

'We compose poetry.'

I didn't note the distinction until later.

'A lot of our poetry is about love,' I said. 'It's as close as you can get to the real thing.'

So I got the books and Rosie read them.

Thinking about love kept Rosie quiet for a couple of days. Then the questions turned to sex.

As a psychologist, the questions didn't embarrass me, and I could appreciate an anthropologist's interest.

'Are Thurgs all the same, or do you have sexes like us?' I asked.

'There are two sexes. Shall I show you the Thurgan mating?'

It was the first time she'd positively volunteered infor-

74

mation. She glided off laboriously to her hut and returned with a video player which she hooked up to my television. Then she ran the video and gave me a commentary on what was going on.

There was a green 'field' covered with some alien vegetation, craggy mountains in the background. It could have been Earth, except the sunlight was bluer.

As a biologist, Jane would have been interested in the film. But she was busy in the garden and I didn't feel like fetching her.

Two Thurgs glided towards each other and stopped with their carapaces just touching.

'Which is the male and which is the female?' I asked.

'The male is the one on the right. Males have four barbels around the voice box, females only two. There are other differences, but they're more subtle.'

So I'd been right about Rosie.

The Thurgs never spoke. It was eerie. The courtship ritual was carried out in complete silence.

'Why don't they speak?' I asked.

'What is there to say?' Rosie replied disinterestedly.

A mass of pseudopods leapt out of the shells and wrapped themselves around each other. To me it looked more like the beginning of a battle than a courtship ritual. I thought of the old joke. How do elephants make love? With difficulty.

Then the picture went into close-up. Two pseudopods extended in unison. They nudged each other gently, held contact for a moment, then withdrew a little and dropped to the ground.

On each pseudopod, the rubbery skin bulged and retracted. I was reminded of two snakes simultaneously disgorging the crushed skeletons of their digested prey.

From each, a perfectly round black sphere the size of a billiard ball emerged. The spheres lay on the ground within

75

two inches of each other, glistening in the blue sunlight.

Something nudged my shoulder and I turned in alarm. Rosie had extruded a leathery pseudopod which was now resting on my shoulder like a hand. I ignored it and looked back to the screen.

The two Thurgs gradually withdrew all their pseudopods and one by one all the hemispheres closed down. Last to close were the eyes.

'What are they doing?'

'Dying,' she replied.

'Dying?'

'When we make a sphere — I suppose you would call them eggs — part of ourselves passes into the egg. It's a form of personal immortality. We take with us from life to life our consciousness, and our sense of identity.'

My mouth gaped open. 'So you never really die?'

'In that sense, only by accident.'

I had to say it: 'Like when stupid humans panic . . .'

'They were scared. We don't bear a grudge.'

Hoping I could believe her, I looked back to the screen. The two spheres just lay there.

'Of course, this is a simulation,' said Rosie. 'The eggs aren't real, so they aren't dying. The next section is speeded up.'

The two eggs crept towards each other, touched and continued moving, pressing into each other. Gradually they merged into one egg.

'There's a one-week jump here,' said Rosie.

The egg began to bulge at opposite ends, a line appeared around the centre, and it split into two separate eggs again. Then the process was repeated to yield four eggs.

'The next part takes three years,' said Rosie.

'How long do Thurgs reckon to live?'

'About three hundred of your years.'

'And how old are you?'

'I'll be ninety in a fortnight.'

Gradually, the spheres changed into the characteristic dome-shape of the adult Thurg. Hemispheres began to blister out. The video ended with one of the hemispheres splitting open to reveal a single golden eye.

'Do you want me to get some books for you on human sexual behaviour?' I asked. 'There are plenty of those.'

She shook her head. 'I don't think sex and love are the same thing,' she said firmly. 'Books on sex won't help.'

So she was still into love.

I was reporting to Matt once or twice a week.

'Love?' he said wonderingly.

'Love. Fairly innocuous, don't you think?'

He put his head on one side and considered it for a full five minutes. Then he said: 'I think I see it.'

'You do?'

He nodded slowly. 'Pretend you're interested in human love. Completely innocuous, as you say. But slip in a few questions about other things, the things you're really interested in . . .'

'I'll keep alert for those other questions,' I said, then I added: 'Something I suspect, Matt, but I can't prove.'

'Yes?'

'I'm not sure if the Thurgs have any feelings – you know – strong emotions. Love is obviously quite alien to them.'

He either didn't recognize or didn't appreciate the joke.

Sometimes Percy took Jane out for the day. I would watch them go; Jane happy and carefree, swinging her handbag, Percy grinning like a schoolboy. I felt a tiny pain inside at the thought of something I was losing, but there was also relief. Life with Jane was becoming intolerable.

Inevitably, Rosie now took up most of my time. Jane

could have been understanding; instead she was continually moody and resentful.

I knew Jane hated Rosie, but I didn't realize how badly their relationship had deteriorated until, one day, coming home from a meeting with the Brigadier, I accidentally caught the tail-end of an enormous row in the kitchen.

First, I heard my wife's raised voice: 'It's none of your damned business!'

'Jane, can't you see he loves you?' It sounded so odd, said in that creaking metallic voice of hers.

'What's it got to do with you?'

'I can see things you can't. Love is a force of mutual attraction. If he loves you, then you must love him.'

'What does a bloody alien know about human emotions?'

'Enough to know you're a stupid self-centred bitch. Peter doesn't even realize what's going on between you and Percy.'

It was time I interrupted, I decided, before intergalactic relations were permanently damaged.

Rosie had Jane hemmed in by the sink, the enormous bulk of her carapace preventing escape, a dozen tentacles lashing the air between them. I could have sworn she was in a killing fury. Jane, cradling the stray cat, stood her ground firmly, white-faced, defiant and scared out of her wits. Percy was also there, equally pale, standing a little way off and not knowing how to intervene. Two pseudopods the size of small tree trunks, extruded menacingly in his direction, effectively kept him at bay. So much for the back-up.

'What are you two girls up to?' I asked benevolently.

A pair of golden eyes on my side clicked open.

None of them spoke.

Rosie withdrew her pseudopods and lumbered back a few inches, which gave Jane room to manoeuvre past the carapace. She ran not to me but Percy. He put a comforting arm around her shoulder and they left the room, leaving me to deal with Rosie.

'What was all that about?' I demanded.

'I was just trying to help, but I made a right mess of it, didn't I?'

'Yes, you did.' Suddenly, my heart went out to her. For all her massive intellect, she was a clumsy lumbering creature when it came to delicate emotional matters – trying to handle them with cold logic. So I added: 'It doesn't matter. You can't make things worse than they are already.' I reached out and placed my hand on the black, knobbly carapace. 'I thought for a minute you were going to kill her, Rosie.'

She seemed genuinely surprised. 'I don't think I could do that. You love her, Peter.'

I shook my head sadly. 'I don't think so. Not any more.'

She made me coffee then asked: 'Can we talk about something honestly?'

'Of course.' Some subtle change had taken place, and I could no longer regard her as an enemy.

'You're scared of all the questions I ask.'

I admitted it.

'It's just knowledge,' Rosie said, 'Some knowledge, you don't know if it's going to be useful until you have it.'

'Tell me, Rosie, what do the Thurgs really think of human beings?'

A pause, and then she said: 'We think you're rather childlike and very frightened. Of us. Even of each other. I suppose that comes naturally from being separate.'

'Separate? What does that mean?'

'Well, as you know, we have what you'd call a group mind, like ants and bees.'

The revelation was staggering. 'How does that work?' I asked.

'Suppose there are half a dozen of us all standing around in a group and one of us goes off and does something. What happens is we all simultaneously have the thought, something is going to be done and Como, or whoever, is going to do it. And then Como goes off and does it.'

'So you're telepathic.'

'A group mind and being telepathic are one and the same thing.'

'You don't need to speak to each other.'

'We don't even have a language of our own.'

'How do you know our languages? How can you speak them?'

'We've been monitoring TV signals from your satellites for years.'

My mind was still reeling, trying to work out all the implications. 'Why the hell didn't you tell us any of this?'

'Nobody asked so we assumed you knew or just weren't interested,' Rosie answered simply.

I frowned as further implications occurred to me. Things that had puzzled me made sense. 'The questions you ask – you don't record anything, do you? You don't need to. You compose poetry, but you don't write it.'

'We don't have a written language. What one knows we all know. What one experiences we all experience.'

I staggered and had to clutch at a chair for support. Suddenly I had this vision of thousands of Thurgs, maybe millions, all peering into my mind.

'What does a human being look like to a Thurg?' I asked.

'You don't look like anything we've ever encountered. The Margexalan Snurgle comes closest.'

'What's a Margexalan Snurgle?'

'It's meaningless, isn't it? You need an earth creature for comparison.'

'Yes.'

80

'All right, a blowfly maggot.'

I went rigid with shock.

She continued relentlessly: 'Strangely flabby and soft, as if you were diseased and filled with pus.' A leathery pseudopod extruded itself, the size and shape of a human arm, and gently nuzzled my own arm. I pulled away in disgust. 'That's just how you look to us, Peter. It's not how you are. Inside there's a mind, feelings and intelligence. That's the real human being. We don't worry about the outside. We like human beings.'

I was still hurt and outraged. I blurted out: 'You know what you look like to us? Something from the blackest nightmare, creatures from the darkest region of hell.'

'Well, of course we do, Peter,' she said softly.

'I'm sorry, Rosie, that was childish.'

Why did it matter to me what the Thurgs thought of humans, I wondered, why had I reacted so emotionally?

I reached out and touched the still-extended pseudopod lightly. Then I made an effort, placed my palm on it, wrapped my fingers around it. It still felt like hard rubber. What was repulsive about rubber?

The next day, I went back to see the Brigadier. I told him about the Thurg group mind and what the Thurgs thought about human beings, the whole conversation from beginning to end.

He looked horrified. 'You told her you were spying on her? You told her what humans really think of Thurgs?' He'd picked up my habit of calling Rosie 'her'.

'I honestly don't think we've anything to worry about. The group mind thing – she'd have kept quiet about that if their intentions were hostile.'

'She thought we already knew,' he pointed out.

'All they want from us is knowledge. They have a love of knowledge for the sake of knowledge.'

'What the hell can we teach them? They're thousands of years in advance of us.'

I wasn't sure.

I changed the subject to Percy Rawlings. 'He's trying to make it with my wife, if he hasn't done so already. I want him out.'

The Brigadier thought about this for a moment, head cocked to one side, then he said: 'It's not possible. If we pull out Percy, we show the Thurg what a bloody mess we humans can make of things. I'll see Percy and tell him to lay off. That's all I can do.'

I knew things had gone too far for that to work, but I said nothing.

Two days more and Rosie decided she was an expert on love.

'We Thurgs can't love each other,' she said. Was there a note of wistfulness in her voice?

'I don't understand.'

'There can only be love if there is separation. Love is to emotion what gravity is to matter: it draws separate identities together so they tend to become one. That's something you have and we don't.'

'Is that what the poetry books say?' I asked with mild amusement.

'Just as there is a force of gravitational attraction exerted on all matter, so there is love between all humans.'

I shook my head. 'We humans aren't very good at loving each other.'

'What stops the moon being drawn to the earth?' Rosie asked.

'The moon revolves around the earth and the centrifugal force counteracts the force of gravity.'

'Humans are so busy rushing round each other. When they stop, they love.'

'And how can they learn to stop?'

'Simply by trusting each other.'

'So what happens when there are two people and one trusts but the other one doesn't?'

'They get hurt.'

So here I was being lectured by an alien on something she had never experienced and never could experience, a most fundamental human experience. And yet it was so simple, it felt right. And, for that reason, I felt as suspicious as hell of it.

The same day, there was the business with Jane's stray.

Rosie was in her shed. The cat had caught a bird on the back lawn. The bird was still fluttering.

The door of the 'kennel' softly opened and Rosie appeared.

The cat looked up, startled. Either the cat had seen Rosie before and assumed her to be harmless or Rosie was too far away to appear as a threat. The cat returned its attention to the bird.

Then something extraordinary happened. One of the hemispheres opened with a clack and a snake-like pseudopod shot out. I would never have believed a pseudopod could move so far or so fast. The distance separating them must have been twenty-five metres.

Warned by some sixth sense, the cat looked up, but it was too late: the tendril raised itself, whip-like, and lashed down mercilessly. The cat gave a single scream, then there was silence. Rosie began her slow lumbering gait over towards the cat and the no-longer-fluttering bird.

I turned away in disgust, all of my loathing for the alien returning. I thought I now understood the reason for Rosie's reticence over her eating habits.

Later the disgust subsided to disappointment. Rosie was

a friend, I told myself, and there had to be trust and honesty between friends. So I tackled her about the cat.

'You weren't supposed to know,' she said; 'I buried them both in the sand-pit.'

So she hadn't eaten them. 'Why did you kill the cat?'

'It was so greedy. It gets everything it needs to eat and drink from humans, but still it has to kill a bird.'

'It's a simple creature,' I explained, 'it doesn't reason like us. A cat's behaviour is ninety-nine per cent instinct.'

'I know,' she said.

'Then why?'

'I don't know. Something is happening to me and I don't know what it is. Some change.' She was silent for a moment, then said: 'Peter, I'm frightened.'

My mind was instantly alert. First anger, now fear. Perhaps I'd been wrong about the lack of emotions. 'What is it, Rosie?'

'When I killed the cat, I had a picture in my mind. I was thinking of Jane. The cat reminded me of Jane and I was killing her.'

'Do you hate Jane?' I asked.

'No, I don't hate her. I want to punish her for hurting you. That's not hate, is it?'

'No, that's not hate.'

I sat for a while contemplating a golden eye and wondering what was really happening inside her mind. How could I advise on alien psychology? I could only do that by assuming human and Thurg minds worked the same way.

A hemisphere clicked open and five pseudopods extruded themselves. They twisted together into a plait, the ends free, and reached out towards me.

I understood. It was the closest Rosie could approximate to a human arm and hand. I took the 'hand' in mine, feeling without revulsion the leathery tendrils slipping between my

84

fingers and then exerting a gentle pressure on the back of my hand.

A hemisphere rattled: the chuckle. 'I haven't worked out yet how to simulate the elbow and the palm of the hand,' she said.

I lay awake all night thinking. By the morning, I thought I understood. If I were right, then the implications scared the hell out of me. It was time to see the Brigadier again.

'Good morning, Adams,' he said, beckoning me to a chair.

'Good morning, Brigadier.' I wondered what had happened to our informality agreement.

I gave him the whole of the business with the cat and the conversation between Rosie and me.

'I want her out of the bungalow,' I said.

'Rosie?'

'Jane, of course. And your man Rawlings. They're screwing everything up.'

'You're not doing too badly yourself, Adams,' suggested the Brigadier, giving me a bright, cold stare.

But I was right and he knew it. He picked up his phone and gave a few curt instructions. 'We'll have them out this morning,' he told me. 'Now, what are your feelings about these new developments? You say the Thurg admits itself it's no longer totally in self-control?'

I gave him my reasoning.

Start with the hypothesis that the Thurg mind is basically like the human mind. It is capable of logic and reasoning, also of feeling and emotion. Now add the fact that it's a group mind and all Thurgs are telepaths.

Rosie had admitted herself the Thurgs couldn't feel love because of the group mind. What about other emotions? Don't all emotions depend on separation? You can only fear another person, another entity. You can only hate

85

another. You can only feel jealous of another. And so on for the rest of the emotions.

What use were emotions to the Thurgs? There was no 'other' for them to get emotional about.

'So what's happened to upset the group mind?' asked the Brigadier.

'Us. We're an "other" for them to relate to emotionally.'

Then I went on to explain my fears.

Human emotions take time to mature. The young child gives way to tantrums of rage and jealousy, it is unnerved by fear, it is greedy, self-centred and demanding. Nobler emotions come only with maturity.

The Thurgs' emotional nature, dormant so long, had been re-awakened, and their emotions were likely to be as primitive as those of a young child.

'In short, they're likely to start behaving like psychopaths,' said the Brigadier shrewdly.

The parallel was precise.

'But Rosie evidently feels affection for you,' he observed.

'So can the child or the psychopath, as long as you do and say precisely what it wants.'

'You're our only contact with the Thurgs at the moment. What are you going to do, Peter?'

Suddenly we were back to Peter, and the question was what was *I* going to do. Thank you very much, Matt.

On the drive back to the bungalow, I had the radio on. My musical recipe is pop music for physical energy when there is work to be done, classics for serious contemplation. Debussy's *La Mer* was interrupted by a news bulletin.

'The Thurgan mother ship has just left its earth orbit and appears to be headed out of the solar system. No notice was given of their departure. There are believed to be no humans aboard the ship. We will bring you more news on this extraordinary development as soon as possible.'

Rosie! Her name was like a scream in my mind.

How could she have left without saying goodbye? Damn it, we were friends. She meant something to me. And I thought I had meant something to her.

There was an official car outside the bungalow with Percy sitting in the back seat together with two of Jane's suitcases. She was sitting on the wall.

'I waited,' she said, 'I couldn't just leave without seeing you first.'

I sat down beside her and told her about Rosie's state of mind and the Thurgs' departure. 'Problem solved,' I said. 'You don't have to leave any more.'

She put her hand over mine, resting on the wall. 'Peter, it's what I want,' she said hesitantly. 'We've never done anything but quarrel, have we?'

I nodded slowly. She was right, it was for the best. There was an ache of pain at the knowledge of something once very beautiful, now irretrievably lost, but no stronger feeling than that.

'Did you see Rosie before she left?' I asked. 'Was there any message?'

'I never saw her.' Then she added, in a final burst of the old spitefulness: 'Bloody Rosie! What did the two of you do together, Peter?'

I realized the implication and was too shocked to reply. I had not known her hatred went that deep. But it wasn't the last time I was to hear the question asked.

She rose stiffly, went to the car and climbed in. The car pulled away.

I entered the bungalow and she was waiting for me in the lounge. Rosie! She was still there.

'You scared the hell out of me!' I told her angrily.

She knew what I meant.

I held out my hand. The five pseudopods shot out,

intertwined, and the 'hand' grasped mine eagerly. The golden orbs watched me trustingly. Inside, I felt an ache I recognized, but could hardly believe. I loved her! Not sex, not the thing Jane had spitefully hinted at, but her mind.

'What's going on, Rosie?' I asked softly. 'Why are you still here?'

Slowly Rosie explained.

The Thurgs, despite their lack of emotional experience, had worked out what was wrong, just as I had, and they had come to the same conclusions as me. They didn't want to risk hurting us, so they had departed. Perhaps, if the emotional malaise could be resolved, they would return.

'But why have you stayed?' I asked.

'I can't do any harm,' she answered, 'One Thurg, on its own.'

The Thurgs had discovered their emotions. At the moment, they were unbalanced, and would continue to be so. There was no going back, they could only go forward. Rosie was their hope for salvation. If she could resolve her emotional difficulties, then she would solve them for them all. And to do that, she needed to remain on earth, relating to the 'other', to human beings, to me.

'Will you help us, Peter?' she concluded.

I shook my head. 'Rosie, I would do anything, give anything, to help. But, honestly, I don't know how.'

'I know how,' she said.

In that instant, I knew too. But was it possible to skip through childhood to maturity, just like that? She seemed so confident the Thurgs could do it.

'Rosie,' I said, 'I once heard you say: "love is a force of mutual attraction". Is that true?'

'Yes.'

'And all you have to do is trust?'

'Yes.'

'Rosie, I love you . . . your mind.'

'Aaah . . .'

For all their intelligence, the Thurgs have a flaw, a streak of naïvety. What did they think would happen to Rosie when the rest of them had gone?

I could see the Thurg plan.

Rosie was not yet ninety. That meant she had two hundred years before she needed to regenerate, two hundred years to solve their problem. She would remain on earth as an honoured guest. As soon as she solved the problem, they would all know, they would feel it, and then they would return for her.

I was not so naïve. Rosie wouldn't be treated as an honoured guest. She didn't have two hundred years. It was up to me to win all the time and freedom I could for her, and that would be a very short time.

How could I win time?

First thing in the morning, I was back in the Brigadier's office. He had been expecting me and he knew about Rosie.

'We'll pick her up this morning, Adams,' he said. 'I suppose on the whole things have worked out quite well. We've got more out of this than we could reasonably have hoped for, so I suppose that's a plus.'

'Do you think that's wise, sir?' I asked cautiously.

'Do I think what's wise?'

'Picking up Rosie.'

He frowned.

'If they've left her here, they've left her here for a purpose. If we bring her in, they'll know about it.'

The frown increased, and with it the uncertainty.

'Perhaps they've left her here to see how we treat her,' I suggested.

He placed his elbows on the table and put his hands together as if in prayer, his head tilted to one side, considering the problem. After five minutes, he sighed, and said: 'You want her left with you. That's what you're saying?'

I nodded. 'It's the safest thing to do.'

'You'll have to do something, Peter. The situation can't last indefinitely.'

'I'll think of something, Matt,' I said confidently.

I left the office with a feeling of triumph. I'd won us a little time. I could not guess at how much. The Brigadier had not seen the flaw in my argument, but eventually he would see it.

Human beings had killed three Thurgs and the Thurgs had not retaliated. So were they likely to retaliate over the mistreatment of a fourth? After all, we weren't going to kill Rosie. We'd just question her to death.

As things turned out, we had a week.

How did we spend our time? I've heard the sly titters and giggles. Did we try and make love to each other?

No, damn it! It was a love of two minds. That knobbly black dome with its leathery pseudopods was always repulsive to me, my soft white slug-like body was equally repulsive to her. But inside the black shell and the white maggot, there were two minds, blazing like twin suns, and they were almost identical: the thoughts, the feelings, the fears, the hopes, the aspirations – identical.

Sometimes we talked, but mostly we were silent. Sometimes she would open a hemisphere, put out the five pseudopods and we would hold 'hands'. Most times we would sit facing each other, she would open a single eye, and I would gaze into that golden orb, communing with her soul.

And all the time we fell deeper and deeper in love, not fighting it, going with the current. I could feel her mind, touching mine. And there were no boundaries. I could walk from my mind into hers as through an open door: see as the Thurgs see, feel as the Thurgs feel, think as the Thurgs think.

In her mind, I found a secret she had hidden from me out of love and even lied about.

My analysis of the Thurgs' problem had been wrong: their ability to feel emotionally was not primitive and childlike.

The Thurgs are natural telepaths and Rosie had learned to read my mind. She had picked up emotions, emotions of which I was not consciously aware. The row with Jane? Deep down, I wanted to have a blazing row with her and express all my anger and resentment. The killing of the cat? I resented that cat because Jane and Percy fed it and cosseted it. The fear of killing Jane? Yes, I was scared deep down that one day my anger would boil over and I would kill her.

My primitive emotions, a psychopathic streak in *me*.

The realization was humiliating but I forgave myself just as Rosie forgave me. She was still reading my mind and finding there the love which has the power to overcome the baser emotions.

My realization brought the release the Thurgs had been seeking. Rosie said immediately, with a sigh of relief: 'Peter, we've done it.'

The lorries arrived Monday night. I heard the engines revving and headlights seared through the curtains as the lorries backed and turned. I heard commands barked, marching feet.

Then there was silence. They were in no hurry.

'Afterwards, will they let us be together?' she asked.

'There won't be an afterwards,' I said. 'We'll never see each other again.'

A hemisphere flicked open, an eye appeared, and she wept.

Rosie actually wept. It is the one single emotional reaction the Thurgs and human beings share. Huge tears rolled down the black carapace.

'I don't think I can bear that,' she said.

'In our minds, we will always be together,' I assured her.

She was silent, the tears stopped and she stared at me solemnly with that huge eye. We just sat looking at each other for five, ten minutes, I don't know. Then another hemisphere opened slowly. The 'hand' emerged, larger than usual and knotted into a fist. By now, she had it nearly right. The 'arm' had an 'elbow' and the 'hand' a 'palm'. It advanced towards me and then the 'fingers' slowly opened. I saw the thing they held: a shining black sphere the size of a billiard ball.

'No!' I screamed, recoiling in horror, realizing immediately the implications of what she had done.

'Please,' she said, 'a gift of love.'

I took it from her 'hand'. It was rubbery in texture, but warm and soft. I cradled it gently in both my hands and gazed at her in silent awe. This 'gift of love' was her death.

The 'hand' reached out and descended to cover the egg and my own hands for a moment. Then it withdrew back inside the carapace. For a while she gazed at me solemnly with a single golden eye, then, with a rattling sigh, that last aperture closed.

At that moment, I was almost certainly insane, but there was cunning in my insanity. I leapt up immediately and sped into the billiard room. I substituted her egg for the black ball. I took the other ball into the garage, and there on the concrete floor I reduced it to an unrecognizable powder with a club hammer. Then I swept the fragments into the four corners.

They weren't going to take her egg away from me.

Apparently I was interrogated for over two months. I

92

don't remember much about that period because they used hypnosis and drugs. They thought Rosie had somehow taken over my mind and the Thurgs were still controlling it.

I told them the restoration of the ozone layer, the reforesting of the tropics, the other gifts were simply presents from a benevolent and more evolved species. They didn't want anything in return.

I tried to tell them the things that were really important. I told them about love and the Thurg group mind. I told them how the Thurgs had acquired from man the ability to love and how for them it was the most precious gift imaginable. I told them love was the most natural impulse if only we could all suspend our distrust.

I was telling them things they didn't want to hear. They just looked at each other and shook their heads.

And, of course, they were right to shake their heads. *I* couldn't do it, could I? I couldn't trust my interrogators. Otherwise I would have told them about the egg.

One thing about hypnosis and truth drugs: you can only answer direct questions. If somebody had asked me about the egg, I'd have told them willingly: it's on the billiard table. But they didn't know about the egg.

Another month and I was discharged. I was given a lump sum, a handsome pension and told to keep my mouth shut.

That's when I really cracked up. Rosie was dead. It was all I could think about, and I had nothing to do but think.

It took a month to find the solution, and then I started to heal. I've started a small business: a security firm providing personnel and advice on security. I'm looking for relationships, people or just one person I can begin to trust and who might trust me too. It hasn't happened yet, but I'm confident it will. Of course, they'll have to learn to live with my telepathic ability, which won't be easy, until they acquire the ability from me.

Most nights in fine weather I can't sleep. I take a chair out into the back garden and sit there looking up at the stars and caressing the black egg on my lap.

Then my eyes close and my mind reaches out to the stars.

I know something with absolute certainty: Rosie isn't dead.

Her identity was not transmitted to her egg but returned to the group mind. Her consciousness, all that she was and is, lives on in her people. She learned to love and through her they have all learned and experienced.

I see the shining black spheres rushing silently through the dark spaces between the stars on an endless quest to find other alien species to understand and, now, love.

Their mind is with me, here on earth, and my mind goes with them, with her, looking out for love, in the night so still.

CONDITIONAL SURRENDER

David Mallett

David Mallett joined the Royal Navy as a boy and spent nine years in the service, and joined ICI as an engineer. After teaching management in industry he has now moved to Worcestershire where he works as a management consultant.

David Mallett has become very involved in drama and has won awards as a playwright in amateur theatre. He is married with two sons.

CONDITIONAL SURRENDER

Dennis Pawley was a one-off. Whereas the rest of us are reasonably happy to go along with the comfortable security of ignorance and conformity, Dennis was a quester; seeking answers to impenetrable questions was his life. Dennis Pawley spent every second of his waking hours in an unstoppable search for knowledge and truth. Some would say his sleeping hours were similarly occupied, though there seems little chance of proving that.

Dennis was and still is a Civil Servant, holding an apparently privileged and certainly handsomely-paid position in an obscure department of a Ministry concerned with growing things and de-polluting rivers. On this latter subject, as on most, Dennis was prone to avail others of his deepest thoughts and most detailed analysis. Unconcerned that we, his friends from a rather discreet row of new houses not too far away from a commuter line to London, considered that it was not the industrialists who caused our waters to congeal, but all the dead fish which lay on their surfaces, Dennis could muster an excruciatingly sensible list of official data to disprove our arguments.

This approach to the world seldom allows its advocates the opportunity to display a humorous side to their character. In the case of Dennis Pawley, this was just as well – he didn't have one. Having been a close neighbour to him and his charmingly attractive wife Elizabeth for the last four years, I consequently often wondered how they spent their time when the curtains were drawn and the rest of us retreated to blissful hours of reading, watching television and throwing china at each other. I say the rest of us, but that isn't strictly true; the china-throwing episodes were behind me as I coped with a, hopefully temporary, state of divorced bachelorhood. This condition, though otherwise separating me from the norm of suburban home-dwellers, did at least allow even more space to ponder the Pawleys. Did they discuss themselves to sleep? Did they explore the joys of a matrimonial bed only to relax into post-coital critique of all that went before? Had Dennis covered the copy of the *Kama Sutra*, which undoubtedly lay somewhere in his house, with copious footnotes proving the cultural impossibilities embodied in most of the illustrations? Heaven and the Pawleys alone knew at that time.

The Pawleys, then, were different and were treated with a respect bordering on irony. They seldom appeared to notice this reverence and often flew in the face of it. When invited to dinner or the occasional party, they would invariably take up the invitation as if, having prior knowledge of the communal bets laid against that possibility, they were about to clean up after laying a wager of their own on its reverse.

As guests they were unusual in that Elizabeth would say almost nothing, whilst Dennis hogged any conversation going. Husbands would often try to speak to Elizabeth; sometimes because they felt sorry for her, mainly because she had the bluest of eyes and a figure that, given a particular pose, might stop the breath of a deep-sea diver. On most occasions she would smile and walk away. Sometimes she would say a delicate 'Hello', followed shortly afterwards with an even more delicious 'Goodbye', and then smile and walk away. Most of our get-togethers went on until five in the morning; if the Pawleys were present they usually wound up before ten.

Though Dennis and Elizabeth were somewhat alienated from the mainstream of street life, he sometimes joined us in the pub at the corner – always in the cocktail lounge. On these occasions, many of the resident males would uncannily scent his odour the minute he closed his door and started the quarter-mile walk down the hill. Cries of 'Oh, oh' and 'Whoops, here it comes' were commonplace at these times, as were speedy retreats into the public bar, ostensibly for a quick game of pool or darts with the locals.

Somehow, perhaps because of a marital status which made me understand loneliness, I would invariably find myself companion to Dennis for the evening. Though I was far away from the type of person Dennis was, being more of a feeling man than a thinking one, I liked him in small doses and respected his right to be the unique individual he undoubtedly was. Not that I would have been prepared to die for him, you understand; and as to whether he would have sacrificed his life for me, I both doubted it and hoped to be many miles away if anyone was thoughtless enough to ask him. Faced with such a profound humanitarian issue, Dennis was likely to crease his eyes, adjust his glasses, think in triplicate for twenty seconds or so and subsequently launch a verbal campaign of such creative inconsequence as to promote Bedlam into the ranks of our foremost universities. Unprotected ears would be pounded by an inexhaustible barrage of verbal artillery. Star-shells of 'perhaps' would light the way for bombardments of 'given a particular situation', and incendiary devices afire with 'dependent upon' would presage bayonet-sharp sorties of 'phenomenologically speaking'.

Dennis, you see, had among other pursuits studied lay psychology in all its dastardly forms. Worse, he apparently understood most of the ideas linked to that suspect discipline and was determined to deploy them at any opportunity. He once astounded a room full of dedicated alcoholics with a two-hour discourse on why, when one cheek twitched, he had a deep need to deliberately twitch the opposing one to keep his psyche in balance. On the only occasion (in my knowledge) he was able to hold an audience spellbound, he told of how the dilation of one's pupils gives a sexual come-on signal at a subconscious level; a signal which immediately causes the other party to react in similar fashion, with mutual attraction a certainty. The possibilities of this truth not being lost on the assembled host, they all retired to practise the art. Eight months on, not one of them had managed it, though interest in eye contact did tend to rise in our neighbourhood to a sometimes embarrassing degree.

Sad to say, it was this grasp of psychology that caused his downfall. Three months ago almost to the day, after returning from a trip to Cornwall, Dennis cried. This in itself was astounding enough for someone like Dennis: what is more astonishing is that he chose to knock on my door, throw himself at my feet and cry in my living-room. To be more precise, Dennis rushed through my kitchen at ten to eleven at night, threw himself on to the lounge carpet with the careless attitude of someone who didn't mind if he missed, screwed himself up into a ball and sobbed out what passes for his heart. Two coffees and one and a half hours later, when he calmed down, I asked him what was wrong. He looked up slowly, glasses askew and tears welling in eyes that, because of the oddness of the situation, I quite frankly checked for dilation on the premise that he might not be all we had always thought him to be. Far from being larger, the pupils were smaller than usual, and feeling more relaxed I sat him in an armchair. Then I did what might have been the silliest thing I have ever done; my heart races when I think of the extent of the risk.

'Tell me about it, Dennis,' I said. And he did.

I hesitate to break into this narrative at such a crucial stage in its development but, for peace of mind all round, I think it important to point out that though the story which follows belongs to Dennis, the words are mine. Just picture if you can, the burbling incoherence of that night and you will appreciate why this has to be!

The trip to Cornwall started well enough. Dennis and Elizabeth rose early; she to pack and sort out the necessary gazetteers, he to check the Jaguar for all the things Jaguars require for their efficiency.

They began their journey at ten o'clock on a gloriously sunny morning, heading for the southern route along the A272. They had travelled about forty miles, Dennis in his usual way giving a running commentary on the parlous state of modern driving, when Elizabeth took advantage of an unaccustomed lull to say, 'Dennis . . .'

Dennis stated that he was taken by surprise by this outburst and consequently ignored it until she spoke again, with more urgency this time.

'Dennis!'

'Yes, dear?' he said.

'Dennis,' she said, 'I've been reading Germaine Greer.'

'Who?' replied Dennis.

'Germaine Greer, Dennis. She's a feminist writer; or used to be, anyway.'

'I know that,' said her husband. 'Wrote *The Female Eunuch* for her doctorate.'

'Pardon?' said Elizabeth.

'Doctorate,' said Dennis. 'She's a PhD.'

'Yes?' said Elizabeth.

'Yes,' said Dennis.

'Well,' Elizabeth continued, 'I've been reading her latest and . . .'

'Yes?'

'Yes,' said Elizabeth, and paused.

'Yes, what?' asked Dennis.

'Our life together, Dennis; that is – er – our, well – our life and everything. It isn't all it should be really, is it? What do you think?'

Having said this she looked away, involuntarily clutching the side of the door as the car swerved violently to the right, causing a large articulated lorry in the process of overtaking to flash its lights and otherwise convey its driver's concern.

'What!' said Dennis, struggling to compose himself and the Jaguar.

'Nothing, really,' his wife replied quietly. 'I just thought I'd mention it.'

It took a few hours to drive down to Porthcurno; a long journey, made even longer by the total silence which accompanied it. When they arrived, cruising down the narrow road to the village, then upwards to their hotel on the cliff, the bay was its usual brilliant turquoise.

Dennis stopped the car and said, creatively, 'Look, Elizabeth, the bay is its usual brilliant turquoise.'

She glanced at him and smiled. Dennis straightened his glasses, felt somewhat relieved and asked her if she was all right now.

'Yes, thank you. I'm fine,' she said and helped him into the hotel with their luggage.

Dennis, feeling his confidence returning, determined to forget the whole episode. Minutes later, being Dennis, he had, and was deep in conversation with the lady manager.

'It's the shells, you know,' he was saying. 'That's what

gives the water its colour. Not unique, but a strange phenomenon in this country. Millions of shells crushed into tiny pieces, each piece reflecting the light through the water. Prismatic. Not sand at all. Shells.' He felt a strange desire to be considered attractive sweep over him and flashed a wide, toothy smile at the matronly figure behind the desk. 'Shells,' he said. 'That's what does it.'

'Really?' said the lady, looking a little astonished but not at all interested. 'Really. Well, I never.'

From her dialect, she had quite obviously lived in the neighbourhood for most of her life.

'Well, well,' she said again, and while Dennis signed the register she smiled knowingly over his head towards a grey-haired lady of about seventy sitting in a wicker chair by the window. Dennis, looking up, followed her gaze and saw the gentle face of this benign person looking closely at him. He grinned and walked quickly over to her, leaving Elizabeth with the luggage.

'Dennis Pawley,' he said, holding out his hand.

'Clarice Drachmer,' the lady said with a slight Germanic accent. She remained seated but stretched out to touch his hand. After a pause she added, 'And this is your wife?'

'Oh, yes,' said Dennis. 'Elizabeth, come and meet Mrs — ?'

'Miss,' said the old lady in the chair. 'Clarice Drachmer. How do you do?'

'Hello,' said Elizabeth, and a man less preoccupied than Dennis might have noticed an immediate rapport between the two women.

'Room five,' called the lady at reception. 'Room five, Mr Pawley. First on the right, up the stairs. Dinner at half past seven.' Dennis barely noticed that far from sounding Cornish, her voice now had a distinctly cockney ring to it.

'Are you staying here?' Elizabeth asked Miss Drachmer.

'For a few weeks,' said Clarice, 'I come here every year. What about you?'

'First time, isn't it Elizabeth?' said Dennis, as Elizabeth paused to reply.

'Yes,' said Elizabeth, continuing to return the broad smile of Miss Drachmer. 'Will you be joining us for dinner?' she asked.

'Never miss it,' answered Clarice.

'See you at dinner, then?' smiled Elizabeth, turning to join her husband.

'Of course,' smiled the lady, following them up the stairs with thoughtful green eyes.

Though Elizabeth said she would like a bath before dinner, Dennis insisted they walk the cliff before viewing the outdoor theatre, the existence of which had been the prime cause of their visit. He had read about it and was fascinated by the personality of the woman whose idea it was.

Whilst there, they bumped into a family of Americans and Dennis was able to give them a guided tour. Two hours later, with the Americans almost at the point of hysteria but as Bostonians unable to show it, Dennis apologized for their having to go. He grinned nonchalantly, at the woman in particular.

'Sorry,' he said. 'Dinner calls. If you'd like to pop up again at the same time tomorrow, I'll tell you the rest of it.' The Americans hurriedly explained they were going to Land's End tomorrow, thanked him politely and virtually ran to their car. 'Any time,' Dennis called after them. 'Have a nice day.' He spoke softly to a couple standing nearby. 'Americans always say that – "Have a nice day", I mean.' Then he smiled, took Elizabeth by the arm and walked the path to their hotel.

As is the way with small hotels, all the guests were to be

seated at the same table for meals. As is the way of guests in small hotels, they gathered at the bar for drinks prior to dining.

There were five in all; Dennis, Elizabeth, Clarice and a young couple, some time married, called John and Philippa Rice. John Rice was something in computers and something else in drinking. Dennis had never seen anyone who approached his talent for downing lager; a talent that expressed itself not only in speed of consumption, but in quantity. His wife quite obviously disapproved of this expertise and during the minutes before dinner she made this disapproval evident. John gave the impression that he was not unduly perturbed and carried on drinking, occasionally grinning at her and telling her 'Don't worry, darling,' or 'Come on love, don't nag.' Before long she was ignoring him completely and concentrating on Dennis, whilst Elizabeth conversed happily with Clarice.

Philippa was the kind of girl, Dennis later admitted, who exudes that subtle sensuality normally to be found only on the inner pages of tabloid newspapers. Though dressed demurely, her body language belied this modesty; especially when it came to her unnerving habit of continuously touching people she was speaking to – particularly men. As only her husband and Dennis fitted that description, and as communication with her husband was somewhat curtailed by now, she dispensed most of her pre-dinner energy fondling Dennis in the most unlikely places. Elizabeth appeared oblivious to this but Clarice, peering up from her gin and tonic through thick eyebrows, was well aware of what was going on.

By the time the gong for dinner was sounded, John had proved himself to be a bright and witty companion, able to turn most conversations his way with an ease matched only by Dennis's irritability at not being able to get a word in sideways. Elizabeth being occupied in helping Clarice from the inevitable chair, Dennis downed what was left of his drink in one and prepared to follow John into the dining room. He was astonished to feel his arm gripped firmly by Philippa, who propelled him to the table and promptly sat him between her and her husband, leaving Clarice and Elizabeth to occupy the other two seats. Elizabeth, unconcerned, sat next to John, after first helping Clarice to a seat next to Dennis.

Despite a valiant effort from Dennis, John dominated most of the conversation up to the time the pudding arrived. No matter how hard he tried, Dennis found it impossible to turn the dialogue to his advantage. His frustration was, however, somewhat mitigated by frequent caresses, above and below the table, visited on his person by Philippa.

Whether it was the second bottle of wine that did it or a growing feeling of empathy with the wife of so pompous a man, Dennis discovered both a need to protect Philippa and an overwhelming desire to put John firmly in his place. He turned to Clarice.

'I've – ah, recently acquired a deep interest in TA,' he said loudly, timing his comment perfectly to coincide with John's spooning of a large portion of treacle tart into his mouth. 'Are you aware of its existence, Miss Drachmer?'

'TA?' said Clarice, looking carefully into his eyes. She paused. 'Do you mean Transactional Analysis, by any chance, Mr Pawley?'

Dennis was taken aback: this was exactly what he had meant.

'Oh!' said Dennis, 'You know of it?'

'A little. I know of it a little,' smiled the old lady.

'What is it, Dennis?' asked Philippa, sweetly. 'Sounds awfully interesting.' Dennis removed his glasses and polished them on his tie.

'Eric Berne. *Games People Play* – he wrote it. Clinical psychologist. Used TA in his diagnosis; though it's come a long way since then.' Then he added, 'I'm quite well read on psychology, you know.'

Elizabeth was looking down at the table. Clarice glanced at her, then at Dennis.

'Are you?' she said. 'How interesting,' and she slowly sipped her drink.

'Go on then,' said John, affably chewing on his shortcrust pastry, 'go on, don't leave us in suspense.'

Dennis said, 'I'm not sure I should, really. I mean subjects like this are better left alone, perhaps. Come a bit close to home – if you know what I mean. Near the knuckle.'

Philippa nudged Dennis, put her arm through his and nestled her head on his shoulder. She giggled: 'Go on, Dennis.'

'Well, if you're sure,' he said.

'Go *on*,' crooned Philippa, and Elizabeth coughed softly.

Dennis explained Berne's theoretical model of personality and behaviour, taking twice as long as Berne would have done in emphasizing the fundamental differences between a person's Adult, Parent and Child modes and the nature of human interaction.

'I'm not sure I understand it,' said John, frowning. 'What's interaction?'

'When, for instance, two people exchange words in a conversation.'

'Yes?' probed John.

'Yes,' continued Dennis, pausing for effect. 'As, for example, when you continued your consumption of alcohol in the bar, mostly ignoring your wife but occasionally aiming patronizing remarks at her.' He looked upward; 'You were behaving as the stereotypical Parent you see, John. Philippa had little option but to respond in Childlike mode. Note,' he said turning with a smile to Philippa, 'not Child*ish*; Child*like*!'

'What are you trying to get at?' John said, frowning.

'Hmmm,' Clarice murmured. 'Perhaps you were right, Dennis. Not exactly the time, maybe.'

'Gosh!' said Philippa, moving even closer.

'It's – ah – nothing. Probably not at all important,' said Dennis airily, beginning to enjoy himself. 'Your business, really. Just an example.' He poured some more wine into his glass.

'Are you trying to say something about us?' John prickled, the lager at last beginning to take effect. 'Are you taking a dig at us, Flippa and me? – You're taking a dig at us, aren't you?'

Seeing his chance, Dennis moved in for the kill. He had read how to handle this sort of situation in a book about non-directive counselling, written by yet another clinical psychologist, and though he had never practised the techniques, he knew them backwards. 'Always ask questions; never make statements. Try to make the subject aware of any observable emotion. Allow the subject – or client as one should say – to take full responsibility for what he is thinking or feeling.'

Turning his gaze fully toward John and resting one elbow on the table, Dennis said softly, 'Would that worry you?'

'What?' said John, confused.

'Are you feeling angry?' said Dennis, sweetly.

'What?' repeated a bemused John. 'What the hell are you talking about?'

'I want to explore with you how you are coming across to me, John,' cooed Dennis. 'Reflect your feelings back to you. Why do you feel the need to express anger at this time?'

'Eh?' said John.

'Why are you getting agitated? Do you feel a need to be angry?'

John sat back in his chair and looked all around him for support. Clarice was looking closely at Dennis, as was Philippa. Elizabeth had slipped down into her seat.

'You seem worried about exploring your relationship with Philippa,' smoothed Dennis. 'Is there a reason for that? Does it concern you for some reason?'

'What's it got to do with you?' said John, finding no way out.

'Why did you say that?' probed Dennis, remembering to answer every question with a question.

'Gosh!' said Philippa, letting go of Dennis's arm and turning to watch her husband redden.

'I think I need another drink, Elizabeth.' Clarice bent her head to catch Elizabeth's eye which, along with her other one was firmly fixed on a nearby vase. 'Gin and tonic, dear. From the bar. Do you mind?'

Elizabeth rose quickly and left without a word. John appeared speechless and Dennis, remembering the importance of pauses during counselling, remained quiet, staring intently at his client.

And so it went on, for twelve minutes. Give the man his due: Dennis was pretty good at using arts he had only recently read about. In no time at all he had Philippa going at John and John blaming her for every untoward thing that had happened in their lives together. As Dennis suddenly realized, this was a technique from TA called 'Let's you and him fight!' and it was working beautifully. Clarice watched it all closely and said nothing as Dennis used his new-found skills to prove that John, in playing 'Parent', had only himself to blame if Philippa played around.

'Played around!' screamed John. 'Christ; you got it in

one there, mate; you've certainly hit the high road with that one, that's for sure.'

Dennis was surprised to see that John had worked himself into a quite violent state. He laughed, feebly. 'There, you see. Heh. Heh. Powerful stuff, isn't it? Anyone for another drink?'

'Got that one right, didn't he sweetheart?' said John to his wife, and before long they were oblivious of everyone else as insults and revelations spilled out in all directions. Dennis became immobile, trying desperately to remember a chapter covering this eventuality. Very soon, Philippa was tearfully admitting to having had an abortion prior to their meeting, John was blaming his mother for ignoring him when he was four years old and the waitress was looking slightly concerned, though much interested in all that was going on.

'That's it,' said John. 'I've had it, you bitch.'

'How dare you?' screamed Philippa, standing.

'Look,' said Dennis. 'It was only for fun, you see. No need to . . .'

'How dare you call me a bitch,' hissed Philippa. 'You bastard!'

'There really is no need to . . .' said Dennis in a strangled tone. 'What about a game of whist or something?'

'I'll give you "bastard"!' shouted John and he slapped her so hard she fell.

By the time Dennis had picked both Philippa and his own savoir faire from the ground, John had packed his bags and left the hotel; whilst Clarice, now risen, had joined a very quiet Elizabeth in the lounge.

At about this point in his story, Dennis was lying on the floor of my living room with his back against the sofa, legs clasped tightly to his chest, looking up at my face. I turned away, mouth slightly open and bottom jaw locked in a valiant attempt to hold back a smile.

'More?' I managed, offering to top up his whisky tumbler with our standard medicinal ratio of one of water to ten of scotch. He seemed interested; but as I rose to fetch it, the telephone rang.

'Aaagh!' cried Dennis and his head shot up as his body, shifting from its previous state of torpor, visibly tightened.

'You all right?' I asked; a stupid question in retrospect.

The telephone quite naturally rang again, determined to carry on until I picked it up. At every ring, Dennis appeared more agitated. His arms clamped his knees, pulling them ever closer to his chest and as if hypnotized he stared straight ahead, eyes wide beneath raised brows.

'Agh!' he cried. 'No! Off – off – !'

I paused in mid-stride as anyone would have done and asked what was the matter. He burbled something incomprehensible.

'What?' I said, and he burbled some more. The telephone rang again and his hands, now raised in a protective gesture in front of his face, had index fingers frantically pointing in its direction.

'Driiiiing!' went the telephone.

'No. No – off?' dribbled Dennis.

'Christ!' I said, and not knowing what else to do, I moved to pick up the receiver.

I tried to ignore Dennis for the short time it took to explain to an irate ex-wife why my payments were six weeks late, but it wasn't easy. The noise he made was at one point so distracting I had to put one hand over the receiver, raise my voice an octave and hiss his name in an attempt to quiet him down. 'Dennisss!' I breathed, dwelling with some sibilance on the last consonant. The noise stopped immediately. One second he was babbling like a brook, the next his arms fell to the floor, his eyes closed, his mouth fell open and the noise was gone. Then he burst into tears and lay full-length on my Axminster. Understandably concerned, I hung up on my ex-wife and spent the next few minutes trying to bring him round.

When he eventually regained his faculties, he was rational but unable to remember anything at all of what happened from the point when the telephone had broken into our conversation. Slightly baffled but definitely intrigued, I forced him to finish his tale.

Dennis, in picking Philippa up from the dining-room floor, had naturally to calm her down. He held her gently and she, in a childlike manner the potential of which she had no doubt begun to appreciate, responded by clinging to him like mad.

'Oh, Dennis,' she sobbed. 'I'm sorry. I really am. He really can be awful sometimes.'

Dennis nobly agreed. He could not recall a time in his life when anyone had behaved so badly, said so and held her tightly saying 'There, there,' and any other soothing expression he could think of. She calmed down at an astonishing rate but remained where she was, body held firmly against him and moving gently in his arms. There was a pause as he stroked her hair. She sighed, slowly raised her head and kissed him, leaning back against the table as she did so.

Some minutes later they walked into the lounge, where Clarice and Elizabeth were talking quietly together.

'How are you, my dear?' asked Clarice of Philippa. 'I believe your husband has gone.'

Philippa was not too surprised. 'Did he take the car?' was the only thing she asked.

'I believe so,' said Clarice. 'What will you do?'

'Oh!' said Philippa, looking swiftly at Dennis, 'I think I'll stay tonight. I – '

At this point she broke into a fit of sobbing and clung to the man at her side. Elizabeth stared resolutely at the carpet.

'There are trains from Penzance, Philippa,' said Dennis. 'Don't worry; I'll give you a lift to the station in the morning. There. There.'

'Oh, but – ' breathed Philippa, looking questioningly at Elizabeth until she raised her head.

Elizabeth glanced at Clarice, then smiled. 'Dennis,' she said softly, 'why don't you help Philippa pack? Settle her down? You know how good you are at helping people through times like these.'

Philippa looked back to Dennis.

'Well, yes,' he said, too quickly for his own good. 'But – well. I mean; are you certain?'

'Elizabeth, are you sure?' asked Philippa, sneaking a glance at Dennis and squeezing out a few more tears.

'Of course,' replied Elizabeth. 'Clarice and I will be fine down here; we have lots to chat about. Don't we, Clarice?'

'I think we probably do,' said Clarice, looking directly at Dennis, who should have noticed that Elizabeth was talking far more than normal but, in his excited state, didn't.

'Dennis?' said Clarice after a long pause. 'As a matter of interest; have you any knowledge of Skinner?'

'Pardon?' replied Dennis, looking puzzled.

'Oh, forgive me. It was nothing,' said Clarice.

So off went Dennis, escorting an apparently distressed

Philippa to her room, leaving Clarice and Elizabeth in the lounge. As they climbed the stairs, the hotel manager emerged from an office behind the desk.

'Everything all right, Miss Drachmer?' Dennis heard her ask as he reached the first floor.

For reasons best known to himself, Dennis refused to go into detail regarding what happened next. He merely stated that when, three hours later, he staggered shakily into his bed, Elizabeth was fast asleep.

He woke up later than he intended, to find himself alone. Dressing quickly, but not forgetting to swamp himself with aftershave, he walked along the corridor to Philippa's room, only to find it empty of both lady and luggage. Part of him breathing in the fresh air of relief but most of him still wallowing in the heady atmosphere of the previous night, he fell down the stairs to Reception and found himself face to face with a total stranger; a young woman of about twenty-two. She looked up from a ledger and gazed at him, a slightly knowing smile on her face.

'Yes, sir?' she said brightly. 'Mr Pawley is it? Can I help you?'

'Oh. Er – ' and he didn't know what to say. Then he said, 'You're new. I mean, I haven't seen you before. The other lady – the – manageress – er – manager?'

'Oh! Jean?' said the receptionist. 'She's in the office,' and she nodded towards the door. It had a window but Dennis noted that it was one of those windows where one cannot see in, but can be seen very well by anyone on the other side having the slightest motivation to look.

'Um – my wife?' asked Dennis. 'Breakfast?'

'Oh, no, sir,' the young woman said reprovingly, 'far too late for breakfast. I believe your wife has gone for a walk to the bay. It's a beautiful morning.'

Dennis tried to look nonchalant and uninterested. 'Really? And – Mrs Rice?'

'Who?' asked the receptionist, and Dennis thought he noted a mischievous smile on her lips.

He coughed; 'Mrs Rice. Mrs Philippa Rice.'

'Oh, yes,' said the young woman. 'I believe Miss Drachmer drove her to the station about an hour ago.'

'What!' said Dennis.

'Pardon?' asked the receptionist.

'Oh. Nothing,' spluttered Dennis, 'I was – that is – my wife on the cliffs, you say?'

'No, sir. The bay. Down at the bay,' she said.

'Um,' mumbled Dennis. 'Ah!' He turned; 'Um – are there any – ah – messages?'

'For you, sir?'

'Er – yes.'

'From your wife, sir?'

Dennis was beginning to dislike this female intensely.

'No – I mean, yes, of course. Messages. From – my wife. Anything?'

'Nothing, Mr Pawley,' said the receptionist.

'Right. Right; thank you.' He coughed again and walked towards the dining room which overlooked the bay.

He felt a strange mix of emotions: annoyance, disappointment, relief and, rising quickly to the surface, an incredible sense of guilt. He stared unseeing out of the window, and his hand moved to his mouth as he tried to damp down the panic. Elizabeth. His Reputation. The Service. It slowly dawned on him how lucky he was to have all of these abundant joys at his disposal.

A few trembling minutes later, his hand moved away from his face and he began to unwind. He sighed a deep sigh, feeling immensely better. Everything would be fine. Elizabeth, sanguine as ever, would behave as she always did. Philippa, on her way to patch up a marriage that already had the appearance of a coat of many colours, would never rear her seductive head again and the sun was shining on the bay. All was right and proper in his world. He spotted Elizabeth on the beach. Clarice was with her and they were talking. He turned to go.

'Oh, Mr Pawley?' said a voice and looking up he saw Jean, the hotel manager, leaning out of the office door, an envelope in her hand. A distant telephone rang and, giving the envelope to the receptionist, she vanished, closing the office door behind her.

'Sorry, Mr Pawley,' said the young woman; 'obviously a message, after all.' She took the letter and held it out to him. He felt his throat constrict and the guilt return.

'Thank you,' he said, taking the letter and almost running for the door. Leaning against the hotel wall he ripped open the envelope and, hands trembling, read what was inside.

Dearest, darling Denny, it began. 'Denny!' he croaked aloud and read on:

Thank you for the night of bliss we had together. It was so wonderful. The things we said. The things we DID. Oh Denny, you have captured me. I'm yours. I want you. I need you. Miss Drachmer has insisted that she take me to the station. I had to let you know what had happened, Denny; I couldn't refuse or she would have been suspicious. Forgive me, my dearest love. I miss you. I will phone you at the hotel as soon as I get home. I long for you. My body aches for you.

Dennis felt violently sick: *I love you, love you, love you,* said the letter; *Always and for ever, my darling. Your very own, Philippa.*

'God!' cried Dennis from within. 'Oh, my God!' and he quickly tore the paper into tiny pieces, disposing of them on the strong breeze which blew across from the bay. He stood against the hotel wall, glasses moving up and down almost imperceptibly against his nose. 'Oh, my God!' he repeated, this time aloud.

The walk down to the bay took fifteen minutes and he used them all to think it through. The guilt was back with a vengeance, as was the horror of what could happen to him if the papers found out.

'She can't phone!' he said to himself. 'She can't! What will I do? What will I say? When? Where? How? Oh, God!'

By the time he got to the bay and was walking towards Elizabeth and her companion, he had calmed down and was convinced that when Philippa arrived home, she would think better of it. 'Definitely,' he thought. 'Nothing to worry about. Mere infatuation.'

But then he said again, 'Oh, God!'

Elizabeth walked up to him and pecked him on the cheek. 'Hello, Dennis,' she said, as he looked at her warily. 'Did you sleep well? I didn't want to disturb you. You looked so peaceful.'

'Hello, Dennis,' said Clarice. 'You were sleeping in, so I took Mrs Rice to the station myself.'

'Thank you,' said Dennis, 'that was most kind of you.' He watched the old lady closely. She smiled at him, a warm, open smile.

Elizabeth took his arm, and they walked slowly along the path to the hotel as his brain grappled with the fact that their behaviour appeared normal. He was a little puzzled by this but overwhelmingly grateful. At no time in the future were Elizabeth or Clarice ever to mention Philippa again.

After their walk they sat in the lounge, at a table opposite Reception.

'Is there anything I can get you?' asked the receptionist, and they ordered toast and coffee.

Half an hour later, they were discussing the theatre on the clifftop. Dennis was thoughtful, saying very little.

Clarice said, 'Jean's the one to ask about the theatre. She's a leading light in the local amateurs. Very good, too.'

'Oh, really?' said Dennis, forgetting his worries and feeling a desperate need to tell Clarice about his unique performance as Charles in *Blithe Spirit*. He leaned back in his chair, adjusted his glasses and seemed prepared to spend some time in the telling. 'Strangely enough, I'm a thespian myself,' he said. 'When I was at College – '

'Dennisss!' Elizabeth looked up at the ceiling with an extravagant gesture and hissed his name softly. The telephone at reception rang. Dennis jumped in his seat and stared frantically at the telephone as the receptionist answered it.

'You were saying?' asked Clarice.

A terrified Dennis heard the receptionist say, 'It's for you, Mr Pawley.'

'Me?' He gulped.

'I wonder who that can be?' posed Elizabeth, and as he didn't move she continued with, 'Dennisss, you had better answer it.'

'Why did you do that?' said Dennis.

'What?' asked Elizabeth.

'Say my name like that?' he replied. 'Dennisss with a hiss?'

'Mr Pawley!' the receptionist called, offering the phone.

'Did I?' Elizabeth looked puzzled.

Dennis, realizing he would have to do something and remembering that Elizabeth knew he had left the number of the hotel with his secretary, said with a hollow laugh, 'Work. Oh dear; no peace for the wicked,' and falling over a chair on the way, he took the telephone, extending the cord as far as it would go and out of earshot of the others.

'Dennis Pawley,' he said, his heart beating faster than he could remember.

'Denny. Oh darling?' said the voice of Philippa.

'Aghh!' Dennis jumped and shot a watery smile at his wife.

'Oh, Dennis, I miss you,' said Philippa.

He whispered urgently down the mouthpiece. 'Philippa, for God's sake. You can't phone me here.'

'I can hardly hear you, darling,' crooned Philippa. 'It's a very bad line. I just want you to know that I love you and need you so. I'm at the station and – '

The line went dead.

'Philippa?' whispered Dennis. 'Philippa. Look, Philippa!'

But she was gone. He took the telephone back to the desk. His hand was shaking and he almost dropped it.

'Are you all right Mr Pawley? You look white as a sheet,' said a concerned lady of twenty-two.

He laughed nonchalantly but knew it sounded hysterical. 'Oh, yes. Fine,' he said. 'Fine, fine, fine. Work you know. Bad line. Fine. I'm fine. Yes – fine,' and he returned to the table, still ashen-faced.

Elizabeth and Clarice were laughing and talking together, totally unconcerned.

'Office?' asked Elizabeth.

'Office, yes,' said Dennis, who spent the remainder of the morning listening to the two women and jumping every time the telephone rang. None of the calls were for him.

He and Elizabeth drove into Penzance before lunch and he was very quiet, watching his behaviour carefully but finding Elizabeth as normal as ever. After an hour in the town, they drove back to the hotel.

He, Elizabeth and Clarice sat together for lunch, close to the dining-room window and in sight of the desk. The conversation drifted this way and that, with Dennis pre-occupied and the two women enjoying the opportunity to discuss things that interested them. Elizabeth told of her love of archaeology and Clarice mentioned Turkey as a place of great antiquity. The telephone had been silent for some time now and with his jumpiness beginning to dissipate, Dennis could not resist the temptation to join in.

'Ah, Turkey, I know it well; and its history.' He took a breath.

Elizabeth looked skyward. 'Dennisss,' she said and the telephone rang. He turned quickly to look at the desk.

'For you, Mr Pawley,' the receptionist called.

Clarice and Elizabeth, returning to their discussion, seemed oblivious of his stumbling retreat to the lounge.

'Pawley.' His voice was shaking.

'Denny, my darling Denny. Oh Denny, I love you,' said Philippa as Dennis dashed the receiver down with a bang.

'Wrong number,' he told the receptionist.

'She asked for you,' said the young woman.

'Ah, yes. What I meant was, wrong person. Not me, you see. Wanted someone else.'

'Oh!' she said.

'Are you all right?' Elizabeth called from the dining-room. 'Are you all right, Dennisss?'

The telephone rang again.

'For you,' the young lady at reception said.

'I'm not here!' said Dennis, absent-mindedly taking the phone.

'I love you. Oh, Denny, I need you – ' cried Philippa.

Bang went the telephone.

'I'm going for a walk,' said Dennis, and did.

It went on throughout the day. He and Elizabeth would be sitting in the lounge, on the terrace or in the dining-room when – coincidental with his recovery from understandable attacks of panic to a point where he wanted to join in a conversation – the telephone would ring and it would be for him.

Apart from the panic, the guilt, the fear and the fever that overwhelmed him, he was also aware of a deep irritation at Elizabeth's strange pronunciation of his name. The 'Dennisss' was beginning to annoy him but she insisted she was unaware of it, and he had other things to worry about.

Philippa, during one call from her home, had said she was coming back to the village after sorting things out with John, whom she had not yet seen. She was not certain when that might be, but promised not to come to the hotel. She said she would die if he didn't hold her in his arms again.

Later, thinking things over in the bedroom where, happily, calls didn't seem to occur, Dennis saw himself squeezed between two choices: if he stayed in the hotel over the next few days he would have to keep answering the telephone to a dogged Philippa; if he went out, he might bump into her with Elizabeth in tow. All in all, he wished he'd never met the woman and hoped she would go away. This, if the day were anything to go by, was most unlikely, and he eventually decided it might be better not to go out at all.

That night, having already told Elizabeth the calls were about some problem needing answers only he could provide, he added that he would have to work on it for a couple of days and did she mind if he did. Elizabeth didn't seem to mind at all, and said she would be very happy to sort out her own timetable, spending more time with Clarice whom she found an enjoyable companion. She did, though, make him promise to have meals and spend occasional times with them downstairs. With that, Elizabeth went to bed and fell asleep immediately. Dennis climbed in beside her at midnight and managed to close his eyes for ten minutes, at six.

To cut a tortuous and unsettling story slightly shorter than Dennis might have done in the past, the following three days, though not quite as terrifying as the first, were a mixture of the same. Unaccountably and worryingly, though the telephone often rang, prompting his heart to either stop dead or race out of control, Philippa's calls only occurred when Elizabeth was by his side. And Elizabeth was still calling him 'Dennisss' which, he vaguely noticed, was beginning to cause his vocal chords to constrict in mid-sentence.

With two days of the holiday to go, Philippa told him that she and John had made it up and that, though she still loved him desperately, she knew what she had to do. She would not call again but would love him for ever. Dennis, whispering in the corner, professed his disappointment and gratefully hung up on the lady for the last time. But strangely, even though he knew it was all over, whenever the telephone rang that day he could not stop himself from giving a strangled yelp, or from succumbing to the violent shaking which lasted for over a minute. Elizabeth and Clarice, to his relief, didn't seem to notice these discomforts.

That evening, more subdued than normal, he was standing at the bar with Clarice and Elizabeth when a family, recently booked into the hotel, entered and struck up a conversation which quickly turned to questions of astronomy. Dennis, feeling much better and being, of course, well-read on astronomy, saw that the husband of the family was definitely lacking a complete understanding of the subject and determined to enlighten him.

'Hmm. Yes. As I recall, the solstice – '

Looking straight at him, Elizabeth hissed, 'Dennisss!' and

Dennis, no matter how hard he tried, found it impossible to utter another word.

The seizure lasted for about ten minutes. When it passed, he discovered that he was unable to initiate a conversation. He could respond to other people but if he attempted to steer the discussion or even wax lyrical, his wife would softly whisper his name and he was dumbstruck.

That night, almost in tears, he asked Elizabeth, 'What's going on? Something's happening to me, Elizabeth. For heaven's sake, what is it? Am I losing my mind? My voice – !'

'Oh, Dennis; don't be silly,' she laughed. 'You're imagining it. You were perfectly charming tonight. Go to sleep.' She kissed him on the cheek, turned away and closed her eyes.

Unconvinced but very tired, Dennis lay back on his pillow and thought about all that had happened. He didn't understand the half of it but warning bells were beginning to ring in the back of his mind and they were no longer concerned with Philippa. He was glad they were going home in the morning.

When he awoke, Elizabeth was missing and this time she was at breakfast. Clarice was beside her.

'Good morning, Elizabeth, Clarice,' he said. 'Lovely morning.'

'Good morning, Dennis,' smiled Clarice. 'Sleep well?'

'Ah – yes, thank you. Yes. Fine, thank you,' he said and turned to his wife. 'Elizabeth. What time shall we leave?'

'I'm afraid you'll be going on your own, Dennis,' said Elizabeth directly. 'I knew you wouldn't mind so I've decided to stay for another week.'

'Pardon?' said Dennis.

'Another week,' chirped Elizabeth; 'I'm staying for another week.'

'But you can't!' her husband said, bending towards her and lowering his voice. Clarice looked out of the window discreetly. 'I mean – I have to go to work and – '

'Don't worry; I'll catch the train next Saturday,' said Elizabeth. 'There's so much to see down here and Clarice has promised to show me round. She has a car, so there's no problem. You can do without me for a week.'

'But, for God's sake, Elizabeth,' said Dennis loudly, 'this really is ridiculous. I – '

'Dennisss,' sighed his wife, and very soon he could do little else but nod in agreement.

Later, when he had packed and they were walking to the door, the telephone rang.

'Agggggh!' Dennis cried, and involuntarily his body doubled up. Clarice and Elizabeth, ignoring his predicament, carried on to the car.

Before he could straighten up, a voice called, 'Are you all right, Denny?' and it was the unmistakable voice of Philippa.

In panic, he turned to see the smiling face of Jean at the office door.

'Wha – ?' he managed.

'Goodbye, Mr Pawley,' she said, and it was still Philippa. 'Have a lovely journey.'

His mind racing and totally confused, he staggered to the Jaguar. Elizabeth opened the door and as he was about to climb in, Clarice walked up, a book in her hand.

'For you, Dennis,' she said. 'I signed it inside.' Dennis took it silently and read the cover: *Beyond Skinner. Classical conditioning and aversion therapy in the clinic – by Dr C. Drachmer.*

He turned it over, still not able to grasp what was happening. There was a picture of Clarice on the back and a short biography which included a reference to her retiring to London and owning a small hotel on the South Coast, where she spent some of her time writing.

'I think you will enjoy it,' said Clarice. 'So nice to have met you.' She walked into the hotel, leaving them together by the car. Dennis, head spinning, sat in the driver's seat. Elizabeth leaned in and kissed him.

'Goodbye, dear,' she said gently. 'Drive safely; I'll see you next week.' She paused, then continued; 'I won't phone. I'll send you a postcard instead!' Then she closed the car door and he was on his way.

Back to me and my sitting-room.

EXPOSED

Lorna Fergusson

Lorna Fergusson was born and brought up in the North East of Scotland and graduated from Aberdeen University with a first class honours degree in English Literature and English Language. She has travelled widely and had a number of jobs – including teaching Americans about Tolkien and working in a hospital for the mentally retarded. She moved to Oxford from Scotland to take up the first research post to be awarded to a woman at Merton College and is currently working in Oxford as an English teacher.

Lorna Fergusson has always written stories and poetry, but *Exposed*, her first piece of writing for a few years is also her first work to be published.

EXPOSED

Part One: The Empress

Miss Gosling picked up the pen and found herself writing 'Miss Leonie Godling requests . . .' Really, this won't do, she thought with irritation, hastily scoring out the error and starting again. At the second attempt she wrote, 'Miss Leonie Glosing . . .'

A week later she was writing her diary and after finishing, with the usual sigh of mixed satisfaction and frustration she began to read it over, as was her wont. She was her own audience: critic, reviewer and fan. To her horror, she found scarcely a line that didn't contain a strange and silly error; mostly spelling mistakes which altered the meanings of words in unexpected and disquieting ways.

It wasn't long before she became worried enough to visit her doctor, to ask him in his authority to explain to her what was going on. He was unable to do so and referred her, through the National Health Service, to a psychoanalyst.

Miss Gosling was not happy at the prospect of having her brains picked over by the tried-and-trusted method. She regarded it as a sort of mental vivisection. Privately, she was convinced, although she didn't know if it could be proved, that she had, after many years of perfect literacy, 'contracted' dyslexia. She herself used the word 'contracted', for she liked to think of dyslexia as some sort of disease; an external force barging into her nice tidy system.

As a child she had always found that words came easily to her. At school, she had won countless essay prizes. Her classmates had disliked this and placed more value on running a good race in the school sports. Spelling had *never* been a problem, and she had always had a slightly patronizing attitude towards those who found it hard. There was always a bit of the Puritan in her: no doubt if she had been a teacher in an earlier age, she'd have forced sinister pupils to write with their proper dextrous hands.

Later she moved to the city and wandered in the academic groves, entranced and more than daunted. Trees loomed over her, shut out the light. Fruit fell into her hand or was plucked with difficulty. She swayed between a feeling of having reached her home, and of being merely a visitor, a travel-writer with an antagonistic if somewhat jealous attitude towards the natives. Was she, for Heaven's sake, interpreting the rituals properly?

She did well, but – to continue the labouring metaphor – failed to become a tree herself, or a tree-surgeon. She found a minor grove, and settled down to tending the weeds there. She longed to be a sapling of promise.

Occasionally the spirit of her childhood would revisit her and the words would flow once more, as naturally as skipping and jumping waves and having dolls' tea parties in the days of her ignorance. But now, knowing too much, she would sneer at what she had written in her innocence and throw it away. The incipient sapling shrivelled and withered, but her knowledge of gardening techniques improved.

It was at this time that the spelling errors began. At first no more than a minor irritation and inconvenience, but soon a major waste of good paper. She began to phone friends rather than write to them, draw diagrams, gesticulate, anything rather than try to produce the recalcitrant little glyphs.

The psychoanalyst gave her a sage half-hour of his time one Monday, and told her this was merely the beginning. Return next week. Miss Gosling still couldn't see what good could be done. She bracketed psychoanalysis with hypnotism and had always fiercely said her mind was far too independent for her ever to 'go under'. 'They call you "subjects",' she said indignantly, 'but you're nothing but objects, really. I refuse to be an object. I refuse to be patronized.'

The psychoanalyst advised her to write as much as possible, without regard to the errors. 'Let it flow,' he said. No doubt he considered this activity therapeutic. With an ill-will she obeyed, humouring him as she would a child. Rather typically, she bought a special book, with rich pure pages and suitable severe geometric hard covers, in which to pour out what she ironically called her 'scream of consciousness'. She had always loved stationery. So white and tidy, so empty, so full of promise. She got angry when clean white notebooks became tatty and dog-eared, with untidy alterations and deletions, and half-pages scrappily torn out for shopping lists and friends' addresses. She preferred to see the pages left clean than for the wrong words to sit there, like unwanted relatives, jeering at her, saying 'We belong to you.'

The only way was not to let them get a foot in the door, not to open the door at all.

Monday next, she grimly presented the mental vivisectionist with her first 'flow'. No more than a trickle, but he was pleased. He was able to sound out depths in herself that she was unable to fathom. It was only after she had gone that he wondered if the exercise hadn't been *too* perfect. Was she contriving it? Was she mocking him? Ever afterwards, he couldn't be sure.

This is what she wrote:

> Scream of conscience stress
> I lived the word bard when I was
> A chilled loving in my home tin.

He was especially interested in the word 'bard' (she had meant 'bird', she said), with its Celtic overtones of incantation and the mystic role of the poet. 'Chilled' he delighted in, though she insisted she'd had a happy childhood, with no sense of oppression or alienation.

Week after week she returned with pieces like this, which became longer and fuller as time went on. She nodded frequently but distantly, and didn't seem to listen to his comments. She wrote one piece which began:

> The jeering condor smiles,
> The moaning teaser
> Fainting in the groove.

Her smile was indeed enigmatic as she handed it to him. He increasingly felt she was humouring him and this reminded him of his mother's soothing 'Yes, dear' when he was small, just before she forgot to take him to the zoo, or put out the light and left him in that *horrible* darkness, in which he could never find his special comfort blanket to suck. He began to dislike the glacial Miss Gosling.

At the end of the course of half-hour sessions, she presented her final opus:

> The Homeprayers knew crows
> Wear invincible
> To utter fake.

His patient, it seemed, had gone from bad to worse.

A year later the psychoanalyst, whose real name was Smith (he had been mightily offended when she wrote to him as Mr Sniff), was intrigued to find a slim volume of verse by Miss Gosling being reviewed in adulatory terms by all the major literary journals. Critics were stunned by her bold use of adventurous and unconventional language. The first volume, *Scream*, was swiftly followed by *Homeprayers Rail* and *In the Bluff*. Mr Smith watched with fascination the rise of the psycho-symbolic school of poetry. Her reputation well established, Miss Gosling appeared on TV arts programmes and wrote articles for the *TLS*. She talked winningly about the 'new freedom' movement in verse. She staunchly advocated 'letting down defences'. She was asked to edit the works of other modern poets – some of these, not being dead, felt somewhat resentful. They knew that people were buying copies of their slim verses not for their intrinsic merit but for the excellent – albeit occasionally confusing – prefaces by Miss Gosling. One particularly angry young man founded the Go Sling Your Hook Society after discovering that on the dust-jacket of his latest work, *Frankenstein was Innocent*, his photograph and biographical blurb were actually smaller than those of Miss Gosling, who had only written a two-page introduction in which she had misspelt his name three different ways. He wrote an angry letter about the orthography to *The Times*, but Miss Gosling briskly retorted that if such a practice had been good enough for Shakespeare, it ought to be good enough for him. (She actually wrote 'ham', but he hoped this was merely a typographical error.)

Meanwhile the first eager American came over to Britain to write a thesis on her work. It was entitled 'Go with the Flow: the psycho-symbolic liberation from the parameters of semantic fundamentalism, as evidenced in the post-denotative work of Leonie Gosling.'

Miss Gosling died young, almost as a duty. There was an immediate scurry for possession of the rights to her unpublished diaries and correspondence. An American university put in the largest bid, so presently British scholars had to apply for grants to go to America to study the material in the Free Flow Library, at the University of the New Consciousness, California.

Modern universities in Britain had already put her on the syllabus. Cambridge was more avant-garde in this respect than Oxford. The new school of Freedom critics were extremely prolific, if perhaps a trifle obscure. Marxism and post-structuralism were entirely *passé*.

Her small home town, Little Wittering, became a place of literary pilgrimage. Three days after her death BBC2 had transmitted a programme compiled from her own acerbic opinions, pictures of her when she was twenty, and benign and affectionate comments from benign and affectionate friends and teachers – because after all they had always known she'd be famous. Their carefully memorized accounts were formulaic and tactful, with only one or two good-humouredly bitchy remarks to remind one that the idol had had feet of endearing clay. The programme was a repeat. Perhaps its discretion was due to the fact that she had still been alive when it was made.

Channel Four had in preparation a black women's surrealist theatre group production of *Scream*, which was seen as expressing the female desire to perform autohysterectomy and fly free of the constrictions of womb-oppression. The set was to be all black, with jagged flashes of searing red. The television critics prepared themselves for a lot of primal screaming. Viewers could send for a leaflet which would explain it all to them.

The psychoanalyst read a prime obituary in *The Times*, an admirably balanced effort by one of their best critics, who claimed to have been a close friend of the subject. Cautiously he said it was perhaps too soon for any final evaluation of Miss Gosling's contribution to literature to be made. But he personally felt that once the smoke had cleared, she would ultimately be ranked highly, for she had opened up new avenues for poetry to explore and had communicated art to the intelligentsia and the man in the street alike. The article was accompanied by a rather grainy photograph of the physically deceased. She was smiling.

Mr Smith sniffed.

Part Two: The Boy

Little Wittering was a long way from Pasadena, yet it had been the goal of my pilgrimage for a number of years. Ever since I first picked up *Scream* in my local bookstore, and felt the words kind of seize me by the throat. I was still at high school then, and it seemed to me that the words expressed all the misunderstood adolescent *Angst* I was going through: I too was a 'chilled loving' in a 'home tin', and I wanted out.

I got out. Went to College, did well, and still loved Gosling's work. Bought every volume of verse as it was published and it never seemed enough. And that kind of cryptic English quality added a fascinating dimension to it. I guess I was like a lot of Americans; loving the English, respecting their culture, slightly afraid of their chilly distant politeness. They had all those unspoken *rules* and you just didn't know where you were, lumbering around like 'a fool in a tiny ship' as Miss Gosling would have said. We were all loose and hung out and they had their tweeds and their mansions and their rules. We were the gauche descendants of people who knew where they were *at*, in a big way.

What Miss Gosling had, I guess, was the ability to bridge the gap. She had all the prim prissiness of the English; photos of her made her look starched and nanny-ish and I think she was probably that way in real life. But in her poetry, there was that undercurrent, a sense of danger. By breaking the constraints of language she was breaking the rules, and it was dangerous and fun to go with her.

She certainly hit California. I wasn't the only one smitten. I remember my Uncle Jonas telling me about the sixties and how Tolkien's *The Lord of the Rings* hit the campuses, how everybody – in the midst of all that peace and love – was wearing badges saying 'Gandalf lives' and 'J. R. R. Tolkien is hobbit-forming'. And back in England there's this old Professor absolutely bemused by his success, wondering what in hell they all *saw* in it? It was the same with her, even though the era of hashish and flower power had long gone, and the era of greed and yuppies and cocaine had arrived.

I was so well into her work that I felt I wanted to devote my life to it. Maybe I had no right to: hell, I wasn't that bright. I knew that over at New Consciousness people were doing the *real* work. Although I went to College, I didn't major in Literature. I suppose that I just had one obsession and that was her. I decided I'd do something that would get me a good income and *then* I could find my own way to her. I ended up as a realtor, and pretty soon I had enough at my back to start planning the visit, what I was going to say to her and how she'd explain it all. I'd decided I wasn't going to be the usual eager Yank, full of respect and polite puppy eagerness – though God knows that's what I was –

I was going to be as cool and acid as she was in her interviews. Nobody could get close to the woman, but I was going to change all that.

All the same, it took a few years. Even with an obsession, you get side-tracked by real life. I married, got divorced, had the monthly alimony to pay, so that held me back. Luckily there wasn't a kid – then I'd *really* have been tied. Meanwhile I just kept track of her and I swear I must have known all her words by heart.

But she died. She died about three months before I was due to go to England. She'd never been to America, so I had had no chance to push my way into her attention. She'd have been such a success too – look at how well Dylan Thomas did way back, with his drunkenness and his angel-goblin looks and that big Welsh voice. I guess, though, that Miss Gosling's cracked-china voice wouldn't have carried in some great hall. Plus, she didn't seem to be into performance art.

What did she have to go and die for? She was only in her late thirties, and it was such an absurd pointless way to go.

For a while, I have to say, the heart just went out of me. I read the articles and I watched the TV – there were a lot of features imported from England and shown on PBS. Some were real weird and I don't know what she'd have thought of them. And sometimes I'd freeze-frame the picture and look at her face, flickering slightly, and those deep-set eyes, and I'd think 'Who *are* you, lady?' And I'd think that she'd have understood me, and I'd get depressed at that, but always there was the question 'Who *are* you, lady?' and that's what did it. Nobody I saw on TV or read in those articles could really tell me; they all had their axes to grind. They all showed a facet of her, or some distortion of it like one of those mirrors in a fairground, but nobody seemed to know the whole picture. So I decided I'd be the one to find out.

Maylene was angry as hell when I threw in my job: she could see her alimony trickling away, I guess. She called me all the time, with that ugly shrillness in her voice I had gotten to dislike so. She was in a panic, and I guess she was right to be: this time, for sure, I was leaving her for another woman.

Then the question arose of whether I should sell the house: it was real pretty, on a rise above the woods, and I knew as an experienced realtor I would have no trouble selling for a good price. But that was a big step, requiring consideration; it meant changing my life for good, not just the semi-break with the past I'd accomplished so far. Maylene was now established in a condo half an hour's ride away. I knew she had her lovers, and money apart, I guess we were still nearly friends. We'd spent a couple of years getting that house just right; it was the focus of all the dreams we'd had, and I'd kept it just as it was even though it was more than a year since we'd split up. It still looked as if she'd just gone out to the shopping mall.

Then one night I was re-reading *Homeprayers Rail* and I came across these lines she wrote:

> Pretty Hangland, rape with roses,
> Is there money still for me,
> Stands the kitsch clock still at twee?

It was just like when Christians shut their eyes and open the Bible, stab the page with their finger, praying to the Lord for guidance, and the verse they open their eyes to tells them what to do. And I was to go to England.

It felt like being born again, to cut away from the past. I guess she'd laugh at that kind of religious expression. But I was so eager, England was the Promised Land. When I thought of England I thought of Queen Victoria and Sherlock Holmes, and Laurence Olivier and Henry VIII chopping all those heads off and Agincourt and bowler hats. And roses and hollyhocks.

When I reached Little Wittering it was just like some film set. All those cute cottages – I just had to stop the car and it was a real effort not to get the camera out, straight off. There was a village green and a duckpond and a church with a square battlemented tower. It was as if in that poem I'd read, she knew I'd come. The stone was golden in the spring afternoon, and there were daffodils everywhere.

I checked into The Ivy Tree, the only hotel in town – only they called it a guesthouse. As it was early season, everything was still pretty quiet, but I could tell they went all out to catch tourists – particularly people like me. It seemed to me England did nothing but sell its image as this quaint old culture, pickled in the brine of the past. To be honest, even after just a couple of weeks, it was beginning to get on my nerves. To sell itself like a hooker and be so damn superior all the time, a country's got to think it's something special.

The Ivy Tree, as you'd expect, had ivy all over the front, blurring the lines of the building. It was run by a Mr and Mrs Frogmorton – quite a name – who were middle-aged and starchy. 'We pride ourselves . . .' they always said, collectively, as if they'd created England all by themselves. They prided themselves on the décor of the rooms; all chintz and frills and dark oak wood – so dark it looked as if it had been shined with boot polish. No doubt they prided themselves on the bill too. And the meals – all flabby and fat. Mrs Frogmorton wore a cardigan buttoned to the chin and coyly referred to Miss Gosling as 'our local celebrity'. Mr Frogmorton wore a brown tweed jacket and stood with his legs apart. He should have been a country squire with a gun in the crook of his elbow.

I met Harvey J. Allen in the bar, before we went into dinner, on my first night there. That afternoon, after unpacking my bags, I hadn't had time for more than a stroll around the village, to get the feel of the place. I still felt it was like a film set, only some extras from another lot had strayed into it. Sure there were quaint old inns; The Hare and Hounds, and The Cricketer's Arms, and there was the church – I went in and smelled the cold smell of old stone and lavender polish. There was a little old woman in a floral apron, she was as frail as a bird, polishing the brasses and the wood, and every sound we made echoed round the pillars in a hollow, throbbing way. I'd rather have been on my own. I sat for a while and looked at the stained glass, with medieval saints in distorted positions, and the worn straw matting and the embroidered altar-cloth, and one old faded knight lying on his tomb, staring up at heaven with his face blurred and flat. When I left, I passed through the market square, which seemed lined with tea-shops and bookshops, as if the English did nothing but read over cups of Earl Grey.

But it wasn't all like that; there were several garish-fronted 'estate-agents': with a professional interest I looked at the prices and the photos of rambling vicarages and thatched cottages. And the price of a slice of English life seemed pretty high. I couldn't believe how many agencies there were for such a small place, probably outnumbering the tea-shops.

There were people of the Frogmorton type and little old Miss Marples chatting on the corner, but there were also groups of teenagers standing around looking bored, and motorbikes roaring up and down with – it seemed – nowhere to go. Several streets had a closed and shuttered look which I couldn't understand until I realized they were weekender homes. There seemed to be few people of middle-age range; either they were young and restive, and obviously what the English call 'working class', or they were old gents in Panama hats and ladies in sensible shoes, like the whole village was some cruise-liner full of the retired.

I began to feel a bit sad and I lost the heart for the English cream tea I'd been promising myself. I felt a long way from home, and unable to understand the attitudes of this society. So when I came into the hotel, and got the 'Here is the colonial, let's educate him in the *proper* way to do things' treatment from the Frogmortons, I was fit to be tied.

They'd just asked me to dress formally for dinner, when I heard the voice of a fellow American over by the bar. I was so relieved I just went straight over, holding out my hand and saying, 'Hey, I'm Carl Bayer from Pasadena, over on a trip. Glad to meet you!'

The stranger turned with a smile, and his grip was firm and friendly as we shook hands. 'Harvey J. Allen. I'm from California too. What'll you have?'

Later, in the lounge, we both discovered we were here because of Leonie Gosling. Well, it was hardly surprising. What other reason would two Americans have for running into each other in a tiny place like this?

Harvey, it turned out, was *Doctor* Allen, of the University of the New Consciousness, and he was here to start on some post-doctoral work. He was full of enthusiasm and I was impressed by the way he could formulate his ideas. When I listened to his academic way of putting things I felt gauche and inarticulate. All my comments on her work sounded emotional; gut feelings vaguely expressed. But he never patronized me – I guess he responded to the sincerity of my feelings.

After dinner we had a few more drinks and quoted Gosling lines at each other in the easy camaraderie brought about by alcohol and by being strangers in a strange land. He put me straight on quite a few things, and I didn't argue; I figured he'd know best. I went off to bed in a haze of goodwill and respect for the guy.

It was different next morning. I came down to breakfast (swimming in grease, on a mean little plate: one rasher of bacon, one sausage, one solid fried egg, one squashed sliver of tomato), and I found Harvey had a companion, a thin intense-looking man in a dark suit.

'Carl!' shouted Harvey, half rising, and beckoning me over with his fork. 'Come on and join us.'

He introduced us while one of Mrs Frogmorton's staff leaned over me to pour some tepid tea. This meant it would be cold before my lukewarm plate of grease arrived. I thought longingly of breakfast out on the deck at our house in Pasadena. Those blueberry muffins that Maylene used to make.

'Carl, let me introduce you to Professor Charles Willoughby; he arrived too late last night to join us. He's from Cambridge University and he's *the* authority on L. G. over here,' Harvey said, heartily. 'We're lucky to have run into him. If you want to understand Gosling's work, this is the guy whose brains are most worth picking.'

Willoughby barely acknowledged my presence, probably putting me down as the puppy-dog American I was trying so hard not to be, and merely continued his conversation with Harvey, while he delicately pulled a bread roll to pieces.

'Of course, Dr Allen,' he said, 'we at Caedmon College are particularly keen to ensure that the Gosling papers stay in England, which is only right and proper. She was one of the most English of English writers, and she was that *rara avis*, an excellent *female* English poet. The most appropriate sphere for scholarship on such works remains England itself. My College is also proposing to endow a Gosling scholarship as well as the Gosling Library, in order to perpetuate her name.'

'Well, that does sound interesting, Charles, but you know that English Lit. scholars in England are a dying breed. All your Government is interested in right now is technological colleges and such, and even in *that* area things are pretty moribund. In America we have always had a proper respect for English letters – more than the English themselves, I'd say. Now, you know you have to be realistic, Charles – your colleges, even those fine old institutions of Oxford and Cambridge, they may have the clout, but they don't have the *cash*. And, Charles, it's a commercial world.

'I have to tell you, Charles, that the University of the New Consciousness has put in a major bid for those papers, bigger even than Austin put in, and we're so sure of winning that we've already started building a special Library on campus: it's going to be called the Free Flow Library, in respect to the origins of her work.'

Willoughby looked tense and disgruntled during all this; his thin lips tightened, and the bread roll was soon demolished. However, I could see that he wouldn't lose his cool completely; he preserved an icy politeness in the face of what to him must have been a body blow.

'Let us not forget, Dr Allen, the old proverb about counting chickens. Cambridge is not some superannuated house of intellectual dinosaurs: we were the first academic institution to perceive the significance of Miss Gosling's work and we feel we have a special right to be the guardians and interpreters of that work in the future.'

'Now, don't get all tight-lipped, Charles,' smiled Harvey,

'just think of all the time you can spend on the beaches when you come over on exchange to study the papers at New Consciousness.'

There was a silence. Clearly Willoughby found that no compensation.

'You mentioned interpretation,' I said hesitantly, to try to break the impasse. 'It seems to me that more than with any other writer, interpretation is everything with her work. There are so many facets, I mean, you can look at a poem and see something, look again and see something else. It's so rich, so endless. So much fun too.'

Professor Willoughby's eyebrow lifted. 'Are you writing a paper on Miss Gosling's work too?' he asked.

'Well, no, not exactly. I'm just here on my own behalf,' I answered, 'but I'm real interested in what you two have to say.'

Willoughby turned to Harvey: 'But you, Dr Allen – I understand you are writing a post-doctoral thesis on her. May I enquire as to its working title?'

Harvey beamed, eager to oblige. 'It's called "Go with the Flow: the psycho-symbolic liberation from the parameters of semantic fundamentalism, as evidenced in the post-denotative work of Leonie Gosling." '

I could have sworn I saw Willoughby wince.

'Excuse me,' I said, 'but what does all that mean?'

'Well,' said Harvey benignly, 'tell me – when you read her work, what do you get out of it?'

'I get a buzz,' I answered, 'I get a sense of adventure because I don't know where she's going to next, and I get a sense of challenge because I have to work out what she's really saying.'

'Exactly,' said Harvey. 'That's what it's all about: explaining that thrill. Criticism is all about saying *how* you got that thrill, and analysing meanings in the work that you never knew were there. It's an enrichment of the original work.'

'You make it sound creative,' I said.

'I suppose it is, in a way.'

'You see,' said Willoughby, putting the tips of his fingers together, as he rested his elbows on the table. 'Words have two values: denotative and connotative. The denotative value of a word is, more or less, its dictionary meaning, a fairly strict semantic equation between the word and its referent. The connotations of the word are those associations we have with that word, a sort of semantic halo surrounding it. To put it in simple terms, if I say 'nightmare', all sorts of pictures may appear in your mind, not just the translation of it as 'bad dream'. You may imagine all sorts of things: a skeletal horse, werewolves, falling off a cliff, suffocation, fire, rats, vampires – all sorts of things. If I say 'honey', you may associate with it childhood, sweetness, bees, Winnie-the-Pooh, and so on.

'All poets play with connotations; they use them to evoke feelings and an atmosphere – they assume you will have the same associations with certain words as they do.

'Leonie Gosling was a poet who played with semantics more than most. By subtly altering the sounds of words, she achieved a lateral dislocation of understanding, which led to a new perception of reality; a common aim of poets. Our perception of the world is tired and jaded: a poet seeks to revivify that perception by making us look at it in some new way. The metaphysical poets did it by means of astonishing conceits: comparing lovers to a pair of compasses, for instance. Miss Gosling did it by means of adaptation of common phrases: hackneyed rhymes and clichés, or familiar popular images.

'Take, for example, her lines, early in her career:

'The jeering condor smiles,
The moaning teaser,
Fainting in the groove.

'If one were to "translate" those lines back into "ordinary" English, they would become:

'The Giaconda smiles,
The Mona Lisa
Painting in the Louvre.

'This would be a very ordinary and unenlightening description: a mere statement of fact, with no "attitude" conveyed. Observe however, how by subtle alterations she preserves similarity to the original sounds while guiding our attitudes to the subject. The Mona Lisa herself is famed for her ambiguous half-smile. She is the eternal female mystery. This is conveyed in the poem by means of the words 'jeering' and 'teaser' – is she triumphing, sneering at our perplexity in some way? Is she a predatory 'condor', a literal 'culture vulture'? Or, on the other hand, is she to be seen as vulnerable and unhappy, smiling a brave smile in uncongenial circumstances, trapped, like a fly in amber, in the oppressive atmosphere of the museum: 'moaning' and 'fainting' in the conventional 'groove' all art is slotted into, so that it no longer has any natural interaction with life?'

'Hey,' said Harvey, as Willoughby at last drew breath. 'I'll have to watch my back. Can we take notes?'

'Professor Willoughby, I had no idea there was so much to it. I see now what Harvey meant: that literary criticism can truly be an enriching experience. Although, you know, sometimes it can be kind of fun *not* to know the meanings – or not too specifically, because then there's no going back. It's all cut and dried. Doesn't that sort of drain the poem, maybe?'

My voice trailed off into uncertainty. Willoughby looked professionally offended, like he was a doctor who'd just told me I had cancer and I'd said 'No I haven't.' I decided it wasn't worth making him hostile. After all, he probably knew better than I did. It was his job.

I tried looking like an eager disciple. 'Tell me, did you ever *meet* Miss Gosling?'

'On several occasions. But do not expect any personal revelations from *me*. Quite simply, the woman was an enigma. It was impossible to get close to her in any way. I've often thought,' he added pensively, 'that she herself reminded me of the Mona Lisa . . .' There was a moment's silence. 'But,' he said, more briskly, 'perhaps our visit to her house this afternoon will shed more light on her. *Not* that I am one of those critics for whom personal psychology is all. But we shall see.' Harvey and I brightened at the prospect.

In the end, we didn't all go to the house together. After lunch – steak and kidney pie, sherry trifle – Harvey and the Prof. had got into a discussion that was way above my head. I got tired of being the open-mouthed kid, and it seemed to me my ideas were getting more and more confused, the more they explained. So I said I'd see them there at three and set off to stroll through the village and on the mile or so to where her little house sat in neat detachment from all this fuss.

On the way I saw more or less the same cast of characters as yesterday. Somehow it depressed me – I seemed to have lost all that optimism I'd had when I first arrived. The house was going to be a last ditch attempt to recapture the magic.

I tried saying 'Hi' to various people on the main street, with varying degrees of response. One or two gave me an icy stare, several just looked bemused and taken aback, and a couple responded with tense smiles. Finally, just as I was on the outskirts I saw an old man out clipping his hedge. His garden was neat as pie and the hedge severely retarded in its growth, so I couldn't see the need for the clipping, but there he was, methodically trimming invisible milli-metres here and there. The sound of the shears was loud but soothing. Once again, I tried 'Hello'. There was a sideways glint of a wary eye and some sort of a grunt, and he went on clipping, sleeves rolled up and bald head gleam-ing in the sun. I decided to hold out for more interaction than this, and I knew what the British turned to in moments of conversational crisis.

'Nice weather,' I said, hopefully.

''Tain't too bad, I suppose,' he answered.

'I'm an American,' I volunteered. 'Carl Bayer. Pleased to meet you.'

He swivelled round to look at me properly.

'Ah,' he said, cryptically.

'I'm here to visit Miss Gosling's house – you know, the writer – well, of course you know. I guess you're used to lots of visitors travelling through.'

'We get all sorts, that's true. So you're another come to visit her house. Now I ask you, what's the point of that? She's dead, ain't she?'

Suddenly the floodgates were opened and the verbal cataract he unleashed overwhelmed me. He gave me no time to reply. He didn't seem to *want* a reply; he seemed to have been ruminating over all this for quite a while and he wanted it all off his chest.

'That silly old bat – I ask you, who'd she think she was? Lady Muck, *she* was. Didn't have the time of day for us once her name was in all those stuck-up papers. What'd she do to get famous? I ask you, what'd she *do*? She was

148

as daft as a brush. Just because she got her words mixed up. Good God, lad, there's twenty people in the nuthouse in Effingdean who can do that, no effort at all, and they don't get TV programmes made about them. Daft as a brush, I tell you. Couldn't say anything with any sense in it. Ought to have been locked up.

'I was sick enough of it when she was alive. God knows it was bad enough with film crews and newspapers and all that and those bloody Frogmortons making a fortune out of it all. Then the stupid woman falls downstairs – breaks her neck. I ask you, even a daft way to *die*. So I thought, well, that'll be *that*. Only it wasn't. If anything, it's worse. People parading through here, asking the way to her house the whole time, like some religious pilgrimage or something. Look at you lad – all keen to get there – don't you know, lad, that you've been took in?'

By this time the clipping shears were being held menacingly high. I'd been edging my way past him during the whole onslaught and now I raised my hand in an attempt at a cheery wave and backed away, saying something lame about how nice it had been to meet him. And I went on, feeling more jaded than ever.

Harvey and the Prof. drove up just as I arrived. The house was ordinary, I mean *really* ordinary. The sort of place that even the Little Wittering realtors might have difficulty selling. It was a square little block of dark red brick, set outside the village but right on the verge of the main highway to Effingdean, so it wasn't at all peaceful.

There was a small square garden and a small round woman at the gate to greet us. This was a Miss Dimchurch, the local librarian, who was going to show us round. Indeed, she informed us this little duty was being asked of her so frequently it had almost become a full-time occupation.

What did I expect when we got in there? I don't know, I really don't know. But this was no *literary* house: no book-lined library, no study, no chaos of papers and worn old typewriter. The place was neat as a pin and not very tasteful. Whatever individuality Miss Gosling had had must have been locked up inside her. Even Harvey looked disappointed.

There was a tidy little lounge, with a velour-covered three-piece suite and floral wallpaper. On the glass-topped coffee-table were several leaflets adjuring us to join the Gosling Society. There were few books – some were of course related to her job as a teacher – but there were also historical romances and Agatha Christies. There was a teak-effect unit against one wall, with under-shelf lighting, the shelves bearing various photographs and china ornaments, and a small television. It looked to me like the room of a woman grown old before her time, or who had been pushed so far into conventionality that nothing of her real self showed. She was playing out the role of the soon-to-be old maid.

'And now if you'll follow me,' said Miss Dimchurch in hushed, reverential tones, 'we will mount the very stairs down which Miss Gosling so precipitately descended that fateful morning. Be mindful, gentlemen, of the loose carpet on the third tread from the top. It deprived us of the full bloom of Miss Gosling's literary career – let it not nip *yours* in the bud!'

I stayed behind in the lounge for a moment, staring at a silver-framed photograph of Leonie Gosling on the wall-unit, and hearing Harvey's muffled jovial voice drift down from upstairs. A beam of sunlight, probing into the room through the net curtains, seemed to make the eyes in the photograph more deep-set than ever and the quizzical half-smile mocking and sinister.

Suddenly I remembered the first poem in *Homeprayers Rail* and I realized that all along she had been playing a game.

> The Homeprayers knew crows
> Wear invincible
> To utter fake.

More than likely, she played the game with malice. She probably shuffled Scrabble letters around or something and laughed at the pits those academics dug themselves into.

'The Emperor's new clothes were invisible to other folk.'

But nobody dared say so, except a little child.

Hadn't Professor Willoughby, his mind an instrument to prise open meaning, seen this? If he had, or if I tried to blow the whistle, it wouldn't make any difference. The whole Gosling industry would go grinding on. They'd go on pretending to see what wasn't there.

I looked the photograph in the eye. The naked truth was that there wasn't anything there but a smirk. I hated that superior smirk.

I felt a long way from home. A long way from that bookstore, where, full of hope and curiosity, I first picked up a book of her verse and thought she was speaking directly to me.

MARDY

Elizabeth Harris

Elizabeth Harris has written stories since she was a small child. She has travelled widely and draws on personal experience in her writing. The author of four unpublished full-length novels, she is hard at work on the fifth. She lives with her family in Kent.

MARDY

May is Mardy's month.

Tradition holds that May is unlucky. Bad luck will follow a May wedding. May blossom brought inside means a death within the year. The Romans believed that the spirits of the dead came back in May. And maypole dancing, Jack-in-the-green, and all those other May customs that attend the birth of new life also, of course, mark the death of the old.

Was it an unlucky month for me? Have the pain and the longing that followed the joy been May's bad luck for me?

No. For even on the worst days of yearning for her, I've known in my heart that I wouldn't have missed Mardy. Not for the world.

She got off the bus, carrying a cardboard suitcase tied round with string. I heard old Jack Gotobed call out, 'Straight down there, Miss. Big building on the right. They'll help you.' Then he shouted, 'All right, Alf!' and as the bus lurched off he leaned out of the door waving to her. I realized straight away there must be something striking about her – Jack Gotobed is the most morose man I ever met and normally speaks not a word, communicating with his passengers solely by raising or lowering his eyebrows. Usually the latter – he has an impressively thunderous scowl.

I was standing in my front garden. That's the wrong word, for it ceased to be a garden in 1940, when my elderly parents obeyed the exhortation 'Dig for Victory!' and my poor father slipped a disc in his enthusiasm. For six years the erstwhile rose-beds yielded potatoes and cabbages, and now that I was home I was doing my best to follow where my parents had led. I had an egg in my hand – one of the hens favoured the front garden over the hen-yard at the back. It was a large brown speckled egg, and I was going to have it for my tea, if I managed not to ruin it – while it wasn't quite true to say I couldn't even boil an egg, I kept forgetting to note the time they went in. The results varied from bullet-hard to the sort of pappy mess most at home in a prairie oyster. I felt I was being unfair to the hens. But I'd never learned how to cook – from the tender care of my mother I went to boarding school, then to Sandhurst, and out to India as soon as I was commissioned. And throughout the war, although we did without many things, there was always someone to bring me food.

I stood watching Mardy at the crossroads. The bus was a vague shape in the distance and the noise of its passage had died. She stood quite alone, and as I watched she straightened her back and squared her shoulders. That little gesture touched my heart. I moved over to stand at the gate, so that when at last she had gathered sufficient courage to follow Jack Gotobed's instructions, she would have to pass right by me.

She started walking. Her eyes focused on something straight in front of her, and she was frowning. Every few paces she put the suitcase down and picked it up in the other hand. I was brought up to believe that a man never lets a woman carry a weight of which he can relieve her; as she came level with the gate, years of training overcame the diffidence I've always felt with women. Especially young ones, and especially since Veronica.

I stepped out into the lane and said, 'That looks heavy. May I carry it for you?'

She jumped out of her skin. She'd been so intent on whatever it was she was thinking about that she hadn't noticed me.

'I'm sorry. I made you jump.'

'No! Oh, I mean, yes. But it's all right. My fault.'

Her face had changed from an apprehensive pallor to the blush of embarrassment. I thought probably she too was wondering how on earth my making her jump could possibly be her fault.

'Are you going into the village?'

'Er – yes. I think so. The bus conductor said there might be a room, at the pub. The Green Man. He said their son's still away, in the Navy, and that sometimes they let his room.'

She was like a child, reciting a lesson learned by heart. I picked up the suitcase, which wasn't all that heavy. It was her small stature that had made it appear so.

'That's right.' I tried to sound reassuring, and even in my own ears it came out as blustering. Whatever must she think, poor girl. 'Mrs Leavis,' I went on more quietly. 'Her husband's the landlord, but only in that it's his name painted above the pub door. She does all the work. She's not expecting you, then?'

'Oh dear! No, she isn't. Do you think it'll matter?'

I regretted my last remark. She'd brightened at my weak attempt at lightheartedness, and now I'd flung her back into her anxiety.

'No, I'm sure it won't. If you like I'll stay with you, make sure she can take you.'

Silly of me. Too pushy, to have said that. We're

trustworthy people, here in the Fens, but she wasn't to know. And here was I, a middle-aged stranger, presuming to adopt a protective role.

But I needn't have worried. She turned to me, and her smile gave an unforeseen beauty to her face. She said, 'Oh, would you? You *are* kind! My name's Mardy Russett. I've come to search for my parents.'

There was no time then to follow up her extraordinary remark, for we had reached the Green Man and Mrs Leavis herself was outside, briskly sweeping the step. Mardy's charm must have touched its fingers against her, too; on hearing that Mardy wanted a room for a week or so, she put down her broom and led her straight inside. '*I'll* take that,' she said to me, taking the suitcase, her tone implying that I was only a man and therefore not to be relied upon to do anything right. I didn't mind; marriage to Nathaniel Leavis would shake any woman's faith in the male sex.

I stood inanely on the step. Mardy, deep in conversation with Mrs Leavis, was being taken upstairs. But halfway up she turned, looking even more fragile framed by the bulk of Mrs Leavis's ascending buttocks behind her. For a moment there was the hint of that lovely smile again.

'Thank you for your help. It – ' She glanced over her shoulder, but Mrs Leavis was still panting her way upwards. 'It was so nice, to have a friendly welcome,' she hurried on. 'I hope I'll see you again. Mr . . .'

'John,' I said. 'John Langland.'

'John,' she echoed, and turned to run upstairs.

I loitered in my front garden all the next morning, despite the rain. But she must have gone out on the first bus, because I missed her. It rained without ceasing the entire morning. By midday I was soaked, and the permanent ache in my left knee had responded, as it always does to damp, with spiteful alacrity. When the sun finally put in a half-hearted appearance in the late afternoon, I was good for nothing more industrious than sitting in a deckchair on the lawn doing the *Times* crossword. I was just thinking how sweet the apple-blossom smelt, with the sunshine drying the rain, when the 4.30 p.m. bus from Cambridge pulled up at the crossroads and Mardy got off.

She looked all in. Her steps dragged, and as she approached I saw that she had been crying.

'Mardy!' I struggled to get up, and my knee gave way. She ran in through the gate and came to help me to my feet.

'Oh! Are you hurt?'

'No, no.' I felt very stupid. 'Sitting too long in one position. I was stuck on fourteen down.' I stood up, giving an involuntary wince.

She noticed. Her face winced in sympathy. 'You *are* hurt! What have you been doing?'

'Fighting a war,' I said baldly. 'Me and several million others. My driver skidded my jeep in heavy snow, in the mountains of Northern Italy.' I didn't want to elaborate. January 1945 – over a year since it happened, and still I had nightmares. Of trying to see through a worsening blizzard; of pushing on, on, desperate to keep in view the tail-lights of the vehicle in front. Of the jeep hitting a low stone wall, then cartwheeling into a ravine. I'd been lucky – concussion, neck injuries, and a smashed knee where my leg hit the dashboard. I copped a Blighty one, as they used to say in an earlier war, although until the war ended and we were all driven home up Hitler's autobahns, it got me no nearer Blighty than a Base Hospital.

My driver was killed outright.

She was watching me, her face full of concern. I managed a smile.

'What about a cup of tea?' I didn't want her to go. 'Come inside, I was just going to have one.'

'I don't . . .' she began. I walked on, along the path that led to the kichen door. She was a well-mannered girl; not wanting to offend me by simply leaving, she had no option but to follow.

'Did you go into Cambridge?' I asked. I put the kettle on, then turned to look at her. She was standing just inside the door. She didn't look at all happy.

'Yes.'

I was about to make some trite remark about the Backs or the chestnuts. But when it came to the point, I couldn't. She was trying so hard to maintain her party face, and it seemed cruel to make her go on. I put down the tea-caddy and went over to her.

'You said something yesterday about searching for your parents.' Her eyes shot to meet mine, full of pain. I pressed on before I lost my courage. 'No luck?'

'No luck,' she echoed. She tried to smile, but without success. 'There doesn't seem to be any record of my father at all.' Then her face crumpled and she started to cry.

I gave her a large cup of tea, sweet and strong, and a clean handkerchief. She sat down at my table and I perched beside her. I had no idea what to say. I had only been close to two women; my mother, who only cried when she heard *Abide With Me*, and Veronica. Crying was certainly within Veronica's repertoire; once or twice I'd watched her do it to great effect. But I doubt she shed the smallest tear over the letter she wrote to me terminating our engagement. A 'Dear John' indeed. I wonder if every other John who received one felt the extra sting of having such a suitable name? The stuff of music-hall jokes, we jilted Johns. And anyway, I wasn't even sure then that Mardy qualified as a woman. Red-eyed, runny-nosed, she looked more like a child who had fallen off its bicycle.

After a while she stopped. She sat blinking, giving the occasional hiccup. Then she looked shyly at me.

'Sorry,' she said. 'This is awful of me. I don't even know you.'

I wanted to laugh. It was acceptable, then, to break your heart in front of someone you knew? I put out my hand to touch her, but drew back.

'I don't mind.'

She reached into the pocket of her light coat and brought out an envelope. 'Look,' she said, drawing out a sheet of paper. 'My birth certificate.' She placed it down on the table. 'I'm adopted – Mum told me that when I was small. My adopted Mum, I mean. Last October I was twenty-one, and this envelope arrived from a solicitor in Cambridge.'

'May I see?'

'Of course.'

I took it from her.

'Just this? No explanatory letter?' It seemed unnecessarily melodramatic.

'Not really. The solicitor sent a brief note, but it only said that as requested in the last will and testament of the late Georgina Fearon, the enclosed papers were being sent to her daughter on her majority.' Again, she sounded as if she were repeating a lesson. 'And there was this.' She was clutching a photograph, pressing it face-down to her breast. She held it out.

I stared at the two things that made up Mardy's inheritance.

Margaret Georgina Fearon was her given name. Called, other than the first name, after her mother. Father's name was Theo Arn. I wondered irrelevantly if it could be a spelling mistake – did they make mistakes on birth certificates? – because I'd only ever seen the name Arne spelt with an 'e'. For Father's occupation it said 'student', and for name and address of informant, Georgina's name, with an address in Cambridge. I recognized it; a street where junior dons and other young professionals often had digs. No maiden name of mother was recorded.

I looked at the photograph. A head-and-shoulders study, showing a strong face with a sweep of dark hair drawn back. She wore a plain white blouse under a tailored jacket. Although attractive, an unremarkable face. Until you looked into the eyes.

Dark, heavy-lidded and thick-lashed, they were sensuous eyes, holding a challenge. And for all that their shape was like Mardy's, never in a hundred years could Mardy have imbued her eyes with that knowing, calculating look that glittered in her mother's. For this, I assumed, was Georgina.

'Why "Mardy"?' I asked. It was unworthy of the moment, but all I could think of.

She smiled, and even so soon after tears the effect was electrifying. 'I have a brother. In my adopted family. He was two when I arrived, and he couldn't manage Margaret. He called me Mardy, and it sort of stuck.'

I wasn't surprised. Margaret was too cool and sophisticated for her. Mardy was far better.

We sat in a silence so prolonged that it started to hurt. I knew I should say something, but I was torn between the awkwardness of pretending nothing had happened and wishing her a polite good-day, and the possibly greater awkwardness of inviting more of her confidences. Not to mention the gossip that would soon start were any intimacy to develop between us.

In the end she decided for me. She was, after all, younger.

Less aware, perhaps, of how cruel people can be, of the jeopardy in which we place ourselves by allowing others to become privy to our innermost feelings.

She put her hand on mine, which still held her birth certificate. I heard her draw in her breath, then she said, 'I feel so lost. I thought it'd be all right, that the excitement would keep me going. But I can't bear the thought of going back to eat my supper in the pub kitchen.'

I sympathized; Mrs Leavis as the tyrant of the Green Man was one thing, and doubtless she'd evolved her own brand of martial rule through bitter necessity. But Mrs Leavis with her elbows on the table extracting every last detail of Mardy's life story was something else again.

She was looking at me from beneath her fringe of hair. Theo Arn's hair, perhaps, for it was fair. Not dark, like Georgina's. She asked hesitantly, 'Could I – do you think I could stay here till bedtime?'

My indecision vanished, taking along with it the greater part of my awkwardness. Unto the pure all things are pure. Let them gossip in the village – at least it'd mean they were giving some other unfortunate a few days off.

'Yes,' I said, 'I shall be glad of your company. The fish van's been round today. Do you like haddock?'

That first evening with Mardy was one of the happiest I have ever spent. She was such an optimist, my Mardy, and already she was trying to put the events of the day behind her.

'It doesn't mean I have to give up, does it,' she asked, as we stood together peeling potatoes, 'just because there's no mention of my father in the parish records?'

'No,' I said emphatically. I hoped she wouldn't assume from my tone that I was brimming with helpful suggestions. I wasn't.

'Perhaps he went away, off abroad somewhere,' she mused. 'Perhaps he wasn't born in Cambridge. In England, even. It does sound a bit foreign, doesn't it? Arn.'

Something was bothering me about the name Theo Arn. I frowned, trying to pin it down.

'Yes,' I said vaguely.

She threw the last potato into the pan with a splash. 'There! We've done the messy bit, what shall we do now?'

I wiped my hands. 'We could formulate a plan of action for tomorrow for you, if you like.' I tried not to sound as reluctant as I felt.

'No,' she said surprisingly. 'I'll worry about that in the morning. Let's go outside – I'd love to have a closer look at your apple-blossom. Can we?'

'Of course.' I led the way.

She was an appreciative audience. As we walked through the arch in the rose-brick walls and our feet drowned in the soft grass, I saw the beauty of the old orchard through her eyes. For me, too, it felt like the first time.

'What are they? The trees, I mean.'

'Cox and Bramley.'

'They're ancient, aren't they? The trunks are so wrinkly.'

'I believe so.'

My parents had bought the house from the Church Commissioners, in the late twenties; it had been a vicarage until the parish had dwindled to such an extent that a vicar was no longer necessary. The Church Commissioners hadn't actually provided information about the age of the apple trees.

She was singing, running lightly down the avenues between the trees, occasionally reaching down to pick up handfuls of fallen petals. I felt a moment's keen regret that my parents were no longer alive; they'd both loved the orchard, and would have enjoyed Mardy in it.

Watching her, idly smiling in my pleasure at the picture she made, suddenly I realized what it was that bothered me about 'Theo Arn'.

Without thinking, I shouted, 'Mardy!'

'Yes, John?' She paused and turned, her face alight with happiness, and I couldn't find it in me to tell her. Like her, I'd worry about that in the morning.

I shook my head. 'Nothing. Mind you don't slip,' I said feebly.

Her smile turned to laughter. But all the same, like the obedient child she must have been, she resumed her dancing run at a slower pace.

Turning away, my mind full of warring emotions, I wondered just what it was about her that had this power to reach inside me and find my heart.

She'd said she was going to catch the early bus again, and I set my alarm so that I could get up and see her off. In fact I was awake long before it rang out. A side effect of worry, to rob us of our sleep.

I waited at the gate, and a few minutes before the bus was due I saw her emerge from the back door of the Green Man. She looked excited and happy. I walked to meet her.

'Good morning, John.'

'Hello, Mardy.'

'Come with me,' she said impulsively, tucking her arm through mine. 'Do, it's such a lovely day, and I'm sure I'm going to be lucky because . . .'

'Mardy, don't waste any more time on Theo Arn,' I said quickly. I couldn't look at her; already I knew so well how her face falling into disappointment affected me.

'What do you mean? I've got to, his name's on my birth certificate, and somebody must have heard of him!'

'No.' I made myself go on. 'Mardy, it's an anagram. I do crosswords, I recognize them. Theo Arn is an anagram of A. N. Other. Your mother . . .' I had been about to say her mother had thumbed her nose at bureaucracy, had neatly got away with a flat refusal to register the identity of her lover. But I stopped myself.

'A. N. Other,' Mardy whispered. 'My father.'

She hurried on towards the crossroads. The bus was coming round the corner, and she started to run.

'Mardy, wait!'

I set off after her. But it had been over a year since I'd been able to run, and there was no possibility of catching up with her. I stopped in the middle of the road, my weight on my good leg, watching as she boarded the bus and was driven off and wishing there was a way to damp down my increasing misgivings about Georgina Fearon.

She wasn't on the 4.30 bus that afternoon. I drank my tea alone. I went up to the crossroads soon after six, and as soon as I saw her I knew she'd had a good day. She jumped down the steps, handed down by Jack Gotobed, and I swear that as the bus drew off the old misery was actually laughing.

'Oh, John, I've had a marvellous time!' she cried, flinging her arms round me. 'There was this lovely lady in the Registrar's office, she said, why didn't I try the colleges, what with my mother's address being where it was and my father's occupation being put down as student, so I did, and guess what? The second place I went to, someone *knew* her, they really did! And it's even more extraordinary, because actually she was nothing to do with the college, she worked in the Museum, and this woman just happened to know her. Just think, I've been talking to someone who talked to my mother! Isn't it smashing? Oh, I'm so happy!'

She didn't need to tell me. She was hopping and skipping

by my side, her face shining with joy, so intent on telling me all she'd done that she didn't even break step when we got to my house but marched straight in.

Later, after we'd eaten – it was poached eggs tonight, the hens having obliged – she calmed down. Sitting over a cup of tea, her face turned reflective.

'Penny for them,' I said eventually.

She smiled, looking slightly abashed. 'You'll think me silly.'

'I doubt it.'

She stirred her tea absently. 'I was just thinking about Mother. Giving me away.' She paused, and for a moment pain flashed across her face as if she too were being made to give a child away. 'I think – I've never been *cross* with her, because Mum always told me it can't have been easy for her, having me adopted – but now I . . . well, it's as if I can understand her better now.' Her eyes had become dreamy. 'I can see her, finding out she's – you know. And being frantic, because all along there's no future for us. Then, after all that, having to part with me.' Her voice shook, 'I think she must have been very brave, doing what was best for me.' Tears ran down her cheeks, and she sniffed. 'I don't think *I* could, do you?'

No, Mardy love, I thought. I'm quite sure you couldn't. But I said briskly, 'Oh, I don't know. I should think most women would act like that, in her position.'

She looked slightly taken aback. I wondered if she resented my comment. Not that I regretted it – her determined romanticism was worrying me.

She stood up. 'I expect you're right. I think I should go now. Thank you for my supper.'

I walked with her to the village, stopping just short of the Green Man. I didn't want to part bad friends, so I said, 'What about tomorrow? Cambridge again?'

She smiled happily. 'Yes. To see the landlady, where Mother used to live. Mrs Armstead, she's called. Rosie Armstead. It should be interesting, don't you think?'

'Yes. Goodnight, Mardy. Sweet dreams.'

She turned briefly to wave, and was gone.

All next day I was uneasy. And the silly thing was, I had no definite cause for my anxiety. Someone else might have admired Georgina for her invention of Theo Arn, applauded her panache in having fooled everyone, but this hypothetical someone else hadn't looked into Georgina's jewel-hard eyes.

And he wasn't feeling in love with her sentimental, vulnerable daughter.

She got back earlier than I'd expected, soon after lunch. Her arrival took me by surprise, and in the first seconds of confusion I didn't know whether this was a good omen or a bad one. She seemed bright enough, but I noticed she was restless.

'How did it go?' I asked, pulling out a chair for her which she appeared not to notice.

'Oh, fine! It was a lovely house, in a road by a sort of meadow, with a little stream through the middle. Mrs Armstead's a keen gardener — she showed me her herbaceous borders.'

She stood with her back to me, staring out of the window.

'Did she remember your mother?'

'What? Oh, yes, she said Mother was very lively, that the house was much quieter since . . . since she'd gone.'

She didn't want to talk, for some reason. I wondered if it was because she was only now feeling sorrow that Georgina was dead. All the time Georgina had been a distant, unknown figure, it probably hadn't mattered. Now that she was materializing into a real person whom others remembered and described, perhaps Mardy was beginning to grieve for her.

I tried to steer her away from thoughts of Georgina's death.

'It's a nice compliment, isn't it, that Mrs Armstead remembered her as lively?' I said cheerfully. 'I like lively women!'

She kept her back to me. 'Yes! Mrs Armstead said there used to be lots of parties, and always people visiting, and that Mother often used to ask her in for a drink and a chat.'

'It must have been interesting for her, meeting you.'

She didn't answer. As I watched she seemed to sag. I had a feeling I knew what was coming. I stood up and went to her.

'Mardy?' I put a hand on her arm.

She lifted her head, still staring out of the window, and she moved slightly so that my hand fell away.

'Oh, I didn't tell her, actually. She – er, she was quite *frank* about Mother, and I thought it might embarrass her if I said who I was.'

My heart went out to her. But I had to ask. 'What do you mean, frank?'

She forced a laugh. 'Oh, it seems Mother had a lot of friends. You know.'

'Men friends?'

She turned on me. 'Of course! Why not? She was pretty, wasn't she, and lively, and I bet they all wanted to take her out! So what if sometimes they stayed rather late, it doesn't mean anything. Does it?'

The thought struck me that she was the wrong age for this. Younger, and she wouldn't have understood the implications. Older, and some of that innocent idealism would have had time to be eroded by the reality of life. I could think of no comforting words. I went back to the table.

But she wasn't satisfied.

'*Does* it?' she repeated. 'Or are you like Mrs Armstead, full of winks and nods and suggestive nudges?'

I was, of course. But I fell before the idea of explaining to her.

'No,' I said. 'No, Mardy, I'm not. You're right, I'm sure it doesn't mean anything.' I don't think she was convinced, but I couldn't bring myself to tell her any more lies. 'What are you going to do now?' I asked, trying to sound as if the previous matter had been finished with and I was merely going on to something else.

She looked at me for a long moment. I couldn't read her expression; she was standing in the corner by the door, and her face was in shadow.

She said very quietly, 'I think I'll go for a walk.'

She went out, closing the door behind her. I got up and hurried after her, thinking to ask her to come back for supper, but when I got outside she was running off up the lane, sprinting as fast as she could. Even if I'd called out to her, she wouldn't have heard.

She went into Cambridge once more. She hadn't told me, but Mrs Armstead had given her another contact, the name of another woman who had known Georgina. I wish she'd told me. Whatever it took, however overbearing I'd have had to be, if I'd suspected where she was going I wouldn't have let her go alone.

But I didn't know.

She was very late. The last bus had come and gone without her, and I was frantic with worry. She was so young, so unworldly. I didn't know where she'd been brought up, but I had a fair idea of by what sort of people. Good people, gentle and kindly, but without the least idea of the wickedness that is in the world.

I'd been waiting at the crossroads, thinking that she might have caught a bus to the nearest point and walked the rest of the way. I'd been there on and off for three hours, but at last I had to give in; my knee was hurting in a way it hadn't done since just after the accident. I stumbled home.

She was sitting in the kitchen.

We didn't speak: she stood up and almost fell into my arms, and before the pain in my leg made me shout out I collapsed with her into my armchair. Her whole body was trembling, and she was making awful coughing sounds in her throat. Her arms round my neck were almost choking me, and I could feel her hot tears against my cheek. I let her cry.

After a while I said gently, 'I'm sorry, so sorry, I wasn't here when you came. I was waiting for you at the crossroads.'

'W-w-were you?' Her words were uneven. 'Th-thank you. I-I thought you'd left.'

'Now why would I do that?' I tried to sound soothing. 'I wouldn't go without telling you. And anyway, I live here!'

She was too far gone to respond to my feeble attempt at humour. I should have realized. But the calm words themselves seemed to be having an effect; she was breathing more slowly and she'd stopped crying.

I stroked her hair, and it was as smooth as a young animal's coat. I laid my cheek on the top of her head, smelling the sweet scent of her. Gradually she relaxed. It was time to ask what I had to ask her.

'Mardy, what happened?'

She gave a great sigh, and it seemed wrong that such a defeated sound should come from one so young.

'I shouldn't have come,' she said. 'I should have left well alone, and gone on living with my dreams.'

'Ah.' Poor Mardy, poor love. 'Do you want to talk about it?'

She hesitated. Then she untangled herself from me and stood up, moving round the table and sitting down on a chair opposite to me. She sat as if collecting herself; as I watched the softness and trust in her face resolve into resignation, it seemed that in those few moments she put childhood and innocence behind.

'Today I saw a lady called Mrs Renwick,' she began distantly. 'Mrs Armstead gave me her name – she said she'd helped Mother, and that if I was interested in the same sort of help, I should go and see her. I had no idea what she was talking about, but I thought I'd go anyway, as this Mrs Renwick had been a friend of Mother's.'

She paused, looking down at her hands clasped tightly on the table-top.

'Mrs Renwick was a bit odd, at first. She asked me who had given me her name, and I told her. She was still reluctant to let me in, so I said I was Georgina Fearon's daughter, and that I'd come to Cambridge to find out about her. Then she did a funny thing – she apologized! She said, "My dear, I do beg your pardon." Then she said of course I must go in, and we went inside and she made a pot of tea.'

She looked up, but not at me. Her eyes were unfocused, as if she were staring inside at her memories of the day.

'She started talking about Mother. She said she'd had no hesitation in helping her the second time, because it had all gone so smoothly on the first occasion. Then she said she was so sorry, so very sorry, but these things did happen sometimes, and that she suspected Georgina hadn't taken good enough care of herself. She said, "Mrs Campbell would have given her detailed instructions, you know. She always does. But of course she can't be held responsible if people choose not to follow them." I must have looked a bit blank – I still hadn't a clue what she was talking about – because she came over and held my hand, and said we mustn't forget this was my mother we were speaking of, must we? So I explained about never having known her, about having been given away, and imagining how sad she must have been. And then – and then Mrs Renwick put her hand up to her mouth and said, "Oh, my God. What have I done?"'

She stopped again, for longer this time as if it were becoming increasingly hard to gather her courage and go on. But eventually she managed it.

'She didn't want to tell me,' she went on, her voice tight, 'she said she had no right. But I begged her, and she must have realized that by now she'd gone too far, that it would hardly be any worse for me to know the whole truth. She can't have realized how stupid and naïve I was – I don't think she appreciated that I still hadn't the least inkling.' She gave a bitter laugh. 'I was so stupid! It's obvious, isn't it? I felt such a fool when she told me. All that rot about being loved, about it being a dreadful wrench for Georgina to part with me. Well, it can't have been all that bad, because it didn't stop her getting pregnant again, twice more, only those later babies didn't even get the chance to see the light of day. She had them aborted.'

There was silence in my kitchen apart from Mardy's fast breathing. She had poured out her angry words with hardly a pause, her voice rising higher until it was almost a wail.

I sat staring at her. It didn't matter, she was no more aware of me than of the cobwebs in the corners. Her face was hard, and she didn't look like Mardy. Fleetingly, she looked like Georgina.

Then, very slowly, the mask began to crack. Her lower

lip started almost imperceptibly to tremble, and after a moment she could no longer control the downward curve of her mouth. She seemed to be holding her breath. But it was no good – grief was overcoming her faster than she could run away from it. Mourning for her mother, her dreams and her innocence, her face collapsed into anguish. In the last moment before she dropped her head on to her folded arms, Mardy came back to herself.

It was a long night. I knew I ought to return her to her room at the Green Man, but I couldn't abandon her. I thought vaguely that she could tell them in the morning she'd stayed the night in Cambridge. What the hell, it wasn't important. What mattered was that she stayed with me, that she had the small comfort of being with someone who loved her. Even though she didn't know it.

There wasn't much I could do. What can you do, for someone who had just had to say goodbye to the myth that had sustained her all her life? There was no comfort. There rarely is, in the brutal truth. We sat together in my calm old living-room, side by side on the sofa. She leaned against me, and after a while put her head down on a cushion on my lap. I think she went to sleep.

I stayed awake throughout the night.

I couldn't even hate Georgina. She'd never asked for Mardy's love; in fact she'd done the best thing, given her nature, by keeping right out of Mardy's life. She'd probably have hated it had she known that somewhere she had a daughter who entertained such fond and inaccurate thoughts about her. She'd have taken it as an insult.

Why, then, arrange for Mardy to be sent the birth certificate and the photograph? Had it been the gesture of a woman knowing she was dying and wanting somehow to be remembered? No one else would have grieved for her, for she took no husband and left no other children. Was she, I wondered, quite alone when she died? I preferred to think that one of her lovers came back to hold her hand. But perhaps by then I'd caught some of Mardy's romanticism.

In the morning she quietly slipped out of the house and went back to the Green Man. I couldn't, wouldn't believe that she would leave without saying goodbye, and she didn't. This time I had no need to haunt my front garden for fear of missing her; she came striding up the lane with her battered suitcase and turned without hesitation into my drive.

She walked up to me, putting the case down beside her. I leaned back against the warm brick wall of the house; suddenly my legs felt weak. I wanted to look at her, fix the sight of her into my head, because I knew it was the last time.

'You know I have to go, don't you?'

I nodded. 'Yes.'

'It's a dead end, this enticing trail that led me here. I've got to go back to real life, and make myself forget this dream. Haven't I?'

I wished she hadn't appealed to me like that. I wasn't sure that I could agree with her, when my whole body ached because she was leaving.

'Yes, Mardy.'

Her eyes were very bright.

'John, if I manage to forget everything else, I won't forget you. I wanted to die, yesterday. You brought me back.'

Swiftly she took a step towards me and kissed my cheek, her lips as soft as a falling petal. Then she picked up her case and ran, through the gate and away up to the crossroads. I didn't try to follow. I didn't even wait to watch her board the bus. Some things are unbearable.

I went back into the house and sat down at my table. There was her chair, where she used to sit, and all around the lonely room was the promise of a gaiety that only she could have brought.

I had no idea how I was going to cope with living without her.

May is almost here again. Lucky and unlucky month. The summer is beginning, and as always it's an optimistic time. It's five years since Mardy went, five Mays I've waited hopefully to see if she'll come back.

I planted roses, the year before last. I was sick of potatoes and cabbages, and I thought it was time we had something pretty out there again. Fragrant, too – the roses come into their own just as the last of the apple-blossom fades away. They're thriving, especially Peace. They remind me of Mardy, those ones, in that peace is what I wish for her.

I have turned my energies to writing. There are few enough jobs hereabouts, and none at all for a man with a stiff leg. I live comfortably; the house is mine, and as well as leaving me that my parents left also a fair amount of capital. It provides a small income, augmented by my Army pension. Extra, of course, for disabilities.

I write not so much to put bread in my mouth as to keep my thoughts occupied. Although, naturally, I'm gratified to have concrete, monetary proof that someone else besides me finds my articles and stories entertaining. But I find I need to have something to think about. A humorous story to tell, an informative piece about Italian wines, anything will do.

Sometimes I work in the orchard, at a little table that is light to carry, sitting under the trees that Mardy loved. I shall do so today. The blossom is glorious this year, better than I've ever seen it.

I'm glad.

For five years I've waited, and five times I've been disappointed. This year, I'm waiting with a greater optimism. The blossom, I think, is a good omen.

This January, just into the new year, I received a card. Quite plain, and unsigned. It said simply: 'I hope the blossom will be good this year.'

May, I'm quite sure, will be Mardy's month.

AN UGLY NIGHT

David Rose

David Rose has been a professional journalist for the past thirty years in Scotland and London, working for newspapers, magazines, radio and television. As an ITN reporter for eighteen years he has travelled abroad a great deal.

In 1987, David Rose took an MA in creative writing with Malcolm Bradbury at the University of East Anglia and since then he has been working on short stories and a novel. *An Ugly Night* is his first piece of fiction to be published in book form.

AN UGLY NIGHT

At the Border with the North, they made the kid get into the boot of the Mercedes among all the boxes because he hadn't got his passport.

'For fuck's sake, keep quiet or we'll all get nicked,' Tillie said, looking down at the kid's pale face. Then he closed the boot.

It was pitch-black in there and the edges of the metal cases were sharp. After a while the kid could feel the car stop and he could hear voices but he couldn't hear what they were saying. They seemed to go on for a long time. Then he couldn't hear anything.

Suddenly the lid of the boot opened. The kid put his hands over his eyes. Three big hands reached in towards his face. All the hands held guns.

'No, please, no,' he said. He took his hands away from his eyes and stuck them straight out of the boot. Three men in dark uniforms were looking down at him. Their faces were in shadow. 'Please,' he said.

'Get out the car slowly,' the man nearest his head said in a thick accent. 'Keep your hands up at all times or you're a dead man.'

The kid climbed out awkwardly. He had trouble getting over the rim of the boot without using his hands. He fell on his knees in the road. The policeman with stripes on his sleeve pointed and the other two picked the kid up below his arms and shoved him flat against the side of the car.

'Keep still now while we search you,' the Sergeant's voice said.

The big hands felt his body all over, even between his legs. They took everything out of his pockets. Then something cold and hard pressed into the back of his neck.

'We're going to take a wee walk over to the Station,' the Sergeant said. 'Don't even think of making a run for it.'

'I won't, I promise,' the kid said.

The pressure on the back of his neck steered him away from the car. He started to walk slowly towards a low, concrete building with barred windows. From the corner of his eye, he saw the crew. They were filming him, Charles' face half hidden by the camera, Tillie holding out the mike in its fat windshield. Then they started to move towards him, still filming.

The kid thought; *Mum's going to see this on the news tonight; she'll die.*

The crew moved directly in front of him. They walked backwards; he could see his reflection on the lens. Then the camera started to shake and they stopped walking and he almost bumped into them. Tillie took his arm and turned him round. John M., the reporter, was holding an empty Coke bottle up near his face. The kid felt the back of his neck where the cold circle had pressed. He looked back towards the car. The three policemen were leaning against it. One pointed at him then he took off his hat and beat his thighs. When the kid turned round, Tillie was laughing so much he'd had to sit in the road.

Charles and Tillie had been giving the kid a hard time ever since they'd arrived in Dublin two days before. It was his first trip away from London. Maybe someone had given them a rough time on their first trips.

Now they were all on their way to Derry to relieve the

crew there. After the Border, Tillie took over the driving from Charles. The kid sat in the back of the Merc with John M. There wasn't much room with the gear filling the boot. He had Tillie's box of tapes on his lap and Charles' overnight bag under his knees. Tillie asked for *Rumours* and the kid passed it forward. Tillie turned Fleetwood Mac up loud and wound the car up to eighty-five. Outside, sheets of rain were hitting the motorway from a dark grey sky. Tillie got his tin of Old Holborn out and started rolling a cigarette, steering with his knees.

The kid was scared. He wanted to talk about what it'd be like in Derry. But Charles had reclined his seat and was lying back smoking. John M. was reading newspaper cuttings and making notes. Tillie snapped the car lighter in and then held it to his roll-up. The kid pressed the rocker switch in his door so the window opened a little.

'Close it, Lassie,' Tillie said. He'd started calling the kid that after dinner the night before. He said the kid's long hair and big nose reminded him of a sheepdog. The kid's real name was Lance and he didn't like the nickname but there didn't seem to be a lot he could do about it. Tillie gave everybody names so maybe it meant they were starting to accept him.

The kid pressed the other side of the switch. 'Might things've quietened down in Derry?' he said.

'I bloody well hope not,' John M. said, putting away the cuttings into a transparent envelope. 'After we've been dragged up. Anyway, they've got to keep the temperature up to show Maggie she can't starve three of their guys to death.'

'Fucking mad Micks,' Charles said without opening his eyes. 'I hope another three've died today.'

'What happened to the other crew?' the kid said.

'I don't know exactly,' John M. said. 'Apparently they

just want out. Must've been something heavy for Andy to want to leave. News Desk said they'd lost their car, but that can't be it.'

'How could they lose their car?'

'It was stolen. Nasty men took it away from them. Luckily they had the gear out at the time . . .'

Tillie turned Fleetwood Mac down slightly. 'I bet the back was full of Nigel's empties,' he said. 'IRA probably want a reporter who's not totally Brahmsed, so they marked his card.'

'If you hadn't fucked his wife, he probably wouldn't be in such a state,' Charles said.

'If he hadn't been smashed all the time, she wouldn't have wanted it so much,' Tillie said, and he laughed. 'Anyway, that's not supposed to be general knowledge.'

'He used to be a good reporter,' John M. said. 'They shouldn't have sent him over. Considering what's been happening, he's had bloody little on . . .'

'You'd have done better with a Royal Wedding coming up?' Charles said.

'Maybe.' John M. settled back against the seat. 'We'll see tonight if you can keep the camera from shaking too much.'

The kid heard a heavy throbbing over the noise of the car and the tape. He leant across to look between the two front seats. A khaki helicopter was hovering over the motorway half a mile ahead. They rushed below it. The kid turned to look out of the back window. The chopper was still hanging there, red lights winking below its belly.

'Been thinking,' he said. 'Like it's better to ask now than mess it up when we're working.' In the front Tillie's tobacco tin clicked open. 'Can I put the lights on when there's a riot or shooting? I mean, is it OK?'

'Lassie,' Charles said. 'Do as I tell you. That's all you have to do.'

'There's only one thing you'll need to remember tonight, Lassie,' Tillie said, licking the cigarette paper.

'Yeah,' the kid said.

'Before we go out tonight,' Tillie said. He held the lighter to his cigarette. 'Before we leave the hotel, right? Go to your room, take your strides off and stick a pair of rubber pants on.'

The kid lay back and tried to make himself comfortable, but he couldn't close his eyes. His forehead felt sticky and his stomach was moving around. It was probably the heat and smoke in the car. Then he remembered that he'd had lobster the night before in Dublin. Charles had ordered it for them all but he didn't really like shellfish; he'd wanted a fillet steak.

They took the ring road round Belfast, beside the Lough, with the lights of the city starting to come on to their left. The rain was turning to drizzle as they picked up the M2. Dark clouds lay low over the hills, making it seem later in the evening. They were seventy miles from Derry, though, as the man said, if they hurried they might do it in sixty.

When they got to Derry, John M. made Tillie drive up into the Creggan for a look round before they checked into the hotel. The kid thought the big estate didn't look anything special. Earlier in the year, just after he'd got his full sparks' ticket, he'd been wiring similar houses in Mitcham. They saw a row of burnt-out cars across a side-street but they could have been there for months.

'At least it's stopped raining,' he said.

'Yeah, they'll be out to play tonight.' John M. rubbed his hands together briskly. 'Right, let's hit the hotel.'

They found the other crew round a table in the corner

of the Cocktail Bar. They all looked exhausted, even Andy.

'Hey,' John M. said. 'What the hell's that you're drinking?'

'Green Deadlies,' Ricky, the sound-recordist, said. His white sweater was unbuttoned. Several thin gold chains lay around his neck.

'You wankers,' Tillie said. 'We drive all the way up from Dublin because you're all too pissed to go out. Fuck me.'

'You're a cunt, Tillie,' Andy said. 'Except a cunt's a useful thing.' His big jaw was flecked with stubble.

'Who you calling cunt, you cunt?' Tillie said, laughing.

'Sit down and have a drink, dogsbreath,' Brian, the lighting man, said.

The kid saw the people at the bar were looking at them, but the others didn't seem to notice.

'Three Green Deadlies,' John M. said. 'Whatever they are . . .'

'Joe knows,' Ricky said.

'What are you having, Nigel?'

Nigel got to his feet without looking at any of them. 'I'm taking the crew out tonight,' he said. 'It's my patch, my story.' He gathered up a pile of papers and his drink. 'We'll leave at ten.'

'Sod that,' John M. said, watching Nigel trying to get the door open.

'Go and get the drinks, for fuck's sake,' Andy said.

The kid lifted over a chair and put it beside Brian's. He'd met Brian in the Lighting Room in London. Brian had a lot of silver hair but his face was quite young. He was staring at the kid as if he'd never seen him before.

'OK, so it's your story,' Charles said to Andy. 'I could do with an early night.'

'Fuck you, Winfield,' Andy said. 'Nigel can do what he likes. We've been pulled off the story.'

They all sat waiting for John M. to bring back the drinks, but a black-haired woman at the bar wanted his autograph. Then she asked him what Martyn Lewis was like.

When he came back with a tray, they all had to shuffle sideways to give him room to pull a chair in. He gave the kid a pint of lager. 'I thought Nigel wanted out,' he said.

'He's had a bad time,' Andy said, taking out a Marlboro. 'Yesterday and the night before and the night before that. But yesterday, when they nicked the car, they took Nigel away for over an hour.'

'Did he say what happened? Did they knock him about?'

'He didn't say.' Andy blew smoke across the table. 'But while we were waiting for him, a couple of the lads said they were pissed off we weren't getting more on about the riots. We said it was London that was dropping the stories. It wasn't Nigel's fault . . .'

'Maybe,' John M. said.

'He did say they had all the gen on his family, his London address, phone number, his kids' names and ages, his wife's phone number . . .'

'I could've given them that,' Tillie said.

'Honest Tillie, you'd fuck a barber's floor if it had hair on it,' Andy said.

'They why the hell's he suddenly talking about going out tonight?' John M. said.

'He's been drinking brandy and Benedictines since twelve.'

Ricky picked up an empty glass and clinked it against the top of another glass. 'What's that sound like?' he said.

'Nigel Buxton reading the papers in the back of the car,' Tillie said. 'First thing in the morning.'

'Right,' Ricky said. 'He's been totally out of his turret since we arrived, hasn't he, Andy?'

The cameraman shrugged his heavy shoulders and looked

away. The black-haired woman waved at him to join her.

'They shouldn't have sent him,' John M. said.

Then Tillie told them about the kid getting into the boot at the Border. After they had a couple more drinks, John M. suggested they'd better have something to eat before they went out.

'Tell you what,' Tillie said. 'Let's have an Ugly Night when we get back.'

'Jesus,' Andy said.

'What's an Ugly Night?' the kid asked.

'You'll find out, Lassie,' Tillie grinned. 'You could do pretty well, sniffing them out with that pea-shooter of yours.'

The kid hung up his good trousers and sweater in the built-in wardrobe in his room. He felt like having a shower but he couldn't be bothered. He lay on the bed. His Mum'd be expecting him to phone, but she'd worry if she knew he was in the North. She'd also know something was wrong if he rang and didn't tell her. He decided to ring the next day when everything was OK.

He went down for dinner even though he didn't feel hungry.

Tillie said there was no room for both Nigel and the kid in the Merc. The kid had to take Brian's Astra and give Nigel a lift. He felt they could've all squeezed up.

'This your first time in Derry?' Nigel said thickly.

'Yes,' the kid said. He hoped the reporter wouldn't tell him about his wife. He was having to drive as fast as he could to keep the Merc in sight. They were on a steep climb between old houses. There were no street lights. The car's headlights showed all the houses were boarded up. Most of the boards had huge slogans or flags painted on them. There were no people about.

The kid was leaning forward so as not to lose the other car. He hoped all the people had decided to stay at home. Then they could go back to the hotel and Tillie would tell jokes and maybe he'd try to tell one too. He'd like to sit beside Andy.

When they reached the top of the hill, the road levelled out. Nigel sat up. 'Welcome to the Creggan,' he said. The road bent left in a long curve, hiding the Mercedes. The kid wished Tillie would slow down.

Suddenly there were bright lights ahead. A long fire, dark figures moving around it and standing in the road ahead. The kid braked but the car arrived quickly. To the right, blocking a side-street, was a burning barricade, a couple of cars on their roofs, old furniture, boxes. The car's windscreen was filled with people, waving the car to stop, then their faces, masked and unmasked, bending to peer in.

'Drive on,' Nigel shouted. 'Don't stop.' The kid's foot moved from the brake to the accelerator and pushed it down carefully in case he hit anyone. The figures ahead divided gracefully to let them through. There were shouts and a couple of loud bangs against the side of the car.

'Faster,' Nigel screamed. 'Drive!'

The kid flinched and pressed the accelerator all the way in.

They found the Merc parked halfway down the long hill of boarded-up houses. Charles and Tillie were getting their gear out of the back. As the kid parked in front, Nigel raised his arm and took a couple of swallows. The kid locked the car.

'Get a move on, Lassie,' Tillie's voice called. 'Get your light and give us a shine.'

The kid slung the battery light over his shoulder. Charles gave him the heavy spare battery for the camera to carry, then he closed the Merc's boot. The car light went out.

Two tiny red glows showed where Tillie and Charles were. He switched on the hand-basher. They covered their eyes.

'Put it on the road, for fuck's sake,' Tillie said. 'You go ahead and show us where we're walking.'

They were stopped twice before they reached the barricade. Once by some police or Army who they never saw, but whose voices warned them not to go any further. The next time it was half a dozen men or youths who circled them like stray dogs, flashing torches in their faces and on their gear. One, called Francie, was told to go with them. On the way he tapped a cigarette off Charles. When he lit it, the kid saw he was wearing a knitted balaclava helmet like the one his Mum used to make him put on when it was freezing. He'd hated it. The man had pulled down the wool over his chin to get the fag into his mouth.

Two police Land Rovers drove up fast, as if thinking of charging the barricade. Then they stopped and the front one started to reverse but the second one hadn't got the message and was blocking the way. There were wire grilles over the windscreens and side-windows. The kid couldn't see anyone inside. Two black barrels stuck out at the side of each, moving like antennae, back and forth.

Suddenly the road was full of figures, blacker than the night, screaming and shouting, throwing rocks hard, against the steel.

The kid was shocked at their ferocity. He felt glad he was English and just there to do a job. He felt sorry for the hidden policemen who were just trying to do a job too.

A petrol bomb hit the windscreen of the first Land Rover; burning petrol covered the grille and bonnet. There were screams and cheers. The kid imagined the policemen inside, seeing the faces with their open screaming mouths, lit by the flames, trying to reach them. The first Land Rover reversed anyway, crashing into the one behind. It wheeled back in a tight arc, freeing the first one. They both sped off down the road.

In the flickering light of the barricade, the figures danced triumphantly, hands above their heads.

Charles took the camera off his shoulder and put it on the ground.

'Did youse get that?' a voice said. It might have been Francie who'd brought them up the road.

'I expect so,' Charles said, putting his cigarettes away. The crew sat on a low wall. John M. was beside the barricade talking to an older man.

'Shine your light over here, mister,' a young voice said.

In the garden, below the wall, there were twenty or thirty bottles, each with a rag stuffed in the neck. Most were milk bottles, but the kid recognized one red label: Tizer, the Appetizer. He used to buy that on the way back from school. Two young lads were loading a dozen bottles into a plastic milk crate. Then one got it on to his shoulder and went off between two houses.

'What the fuck do you think you're playing at, Lassie,' Charles said. 'Come on.'

As they crossed the road, Tillie said, 'What's the difference between an Irishman peeing in the sink and a nigger peeing in the sink?'

'I don't know,' the kid said. He was glad Tillie was telling him a joke, but he hoped no one else was close enough to hear.

'The nigger takes the dishes out first.'

There was a tall hedge on the other side of the road. 'Get ready to get behind that the next time they come,' Charles said, putting the camera down in the pathway to a house.

'They won't shoot at us,' the kid said, to show he knew they were winding him up.

A couple of wild shouts came from down the road. The kid could see a crowd shifting against the flames of the barricade. Behind the hedge, to the kid's right, there was the clink of bottles. Someone rasped a match and then swore.

The two Land Rovers came back slowly as if they were unsure. Their headlights lit four men staggering, two at each end of a telegraph pole. They dropped it on the road, blocking the Land Rovers' escape. The dark figures rushed at the vehicles, threw and then ran back to the sides of the road for more ammunition. Beside him three ran out of the garden with blazing bottles. Two hit, the front wheel and near the driver's window; one sailed over the top. The flames of the barricade and the petrol bombs seemed to the kid to freeze the attackers' movements for an instant, like strobe lighting at a disco.

There were four bangs from the Land Rovers. Two of the attackers ran back, laughing and shouting. The third tried to dive over the hedge but hit the top of it. The kid could hear him cursing and the others laughing at him. The kid couldn't see the crew. He thought he would stay where he was to show he wasn't afraid. Even he knew they were just firing plastic bullets.

The first Land Rover crunched over the barrier, then the second seemed to get stuck; its back wheels were off the ground, spinning. In front of it, dancers turned and twisted in the headlights. The two barrels sticking out of the side drew level with the kid, then they came together like a man's eyes squinting. Two petrol bombers ran out of the garden. The kid held up his unlit light above his head to show who he was. The bottles burst flaming against the Land Rover. One of the barrels looked directly at the kid then it jerked. The hedge splintered and a window broke in a house behind. The back wheels found a grip and climbed slowly over the log and away. In the street, silhouetted against the flames, the dancers were leaping and shouting.

Someone ran over the kid's legs and yelled at him. He found he was lying on the pavement. He couldn't remember deciding to get down. He got to his hands and knees. Glass fell, tinkling, from the hand-basher's reflector. A woman began screaming behind him.

Charles and Tillie and John M. walked out of the garden. 'Come on,' John M. said. 'We need the light to do an interview. There's a woman who says the glass hit her baby.'

'Lying cow,' Charles said.

'I dunno,' Tillie said. 'Free plastic surgery and they're still complaining.'

When the kid showed them the broken light, John M. said he'd better go back to the car to get a bulb. The reporter said they could interview the woman in her front room beside the broken window. She could hold the baby if it wasn't screaming too much. Then he told the kid to get a move on.

Once the hill had hidden the barricade, the road was very dark. He pointed the light at his feet and tried to switch it on. Then he remembered it was broken: that was why he was going back. It seemed a long way. He was just wondering if he could've walked past the cars, when he found he was beside the Merc. He touched it and felt his way round to the front. He held the chrome Mercedes circle and reached forward into the darkness. He felt nothing, then he took a step forward and touched the back window of the Astra.

He felt round the rim of the boot till he got the handle. He couldn't remember whether the lock was in the handle or just above or below it. He should've borrowed Tillie's lighter. Just when he was about to give up, the key slipped in. He lifted the boot and the interior light came on.

The kid rested the hand-basher on the metal case containing the telescopic stands. The bulb was broken but the reflector itself seemed OK, though the rim was bent. He found the box of spare bulbs and put one in, but it still didn't work. He wanted to close the boot and get in the car and wait till the crew came back. There wasn't much point in going back if he didn't have a light. Then he saw Brian had a spare battery light, tucked to the side of the boxes, behind the driver's seat. He pulled it out. The bright white light startled him. He put two spare bulbs in his pocket. At least he'd be able to see walking back. He put the strap over his shoulder.

He'd just pulled the boot down and was locking it when a voice said, 'We're taking your car.'

The kid turned, holding the light. Three young men, two with only their eyes showing through balaclavas, were very close. Behind him someone knocked down his arm so the light pointed at the road.

'It's not mine,' the kid said.

'Give us the keys,' the voice in front said.

He pulled the keys out of the boot and a hand took them from him. The light on the road showed two pairs of black lace-up boots, one pair of dirty tennis shoes. The driver's door opened and the tennis shoes jumped into the car. By the car's interior light he saw the man without a mask searching for the ignition. The engine started, revved and the car jerked away down the hill, the driver's door swinging.

A voice from the darkness shouted and an arm hooked the door in. After about fifty yards the lights came on and the kid watched them till they disappeared.

'Oh God,' he said. 'It's got my bag in it.' The soft black leather holdall his Mum had given him last Christmas. His

Walkman, his diary, his camera. He wondered if whoever had knocked his arm down was still behind him.

'When you see them again, can you get something out for me?' he said. 'Please.' But there didn't seem to be anyone there. After a few minutes, he started to walk back up the hill.

The crew stood in a doorway at the top of the street. To their right the barricade was burning. To their left, down the hill, a line of dark shields blocked the road. The kid could see helmets moving behind the shields. Behind the helmets were a row of lorries and Land Rovers. He pulled back into the doorway and leant against the door. A thin lad about his own height but maybe a couple of years younger crouched by the crew, staring down at the police line.

'Would you mind if we put the light on you for a few seconds?' Charles said, wiping the camera's lens carefully.

'Would that get me on the news, d'you think?' The boy was jumping from one foot to the other.

'Bloody sure it would,' Tillie said.

'Would you get me shouting about it being for Bobby, Bobby Sands?' the boy said. He pulled at his finger joints so they cracked.

'We can't guarantee that,' John M. said. 'It depends how space is, but I promise we'll say somewhere the riots are a protest at the hunger strikers' deaths . . .'

'Fuck it, you're on,' the boy said.

'Get your light on,' Charles said, lifting the camera to his shoulder. 'Keep it over me and follow exactly where I'm shooting.'

The boy picked up each of the bottles, then he selected one with a red Tizer label. He pulled a little more of the rag out of the top, then he twisted it together. Charles slid down the wall so the lens was level with the boy's face. The boy flicked a Zippo and cupped his hands. Then he stood up and peeked round the corner. John M. tapped him on the shoulder. He held out both hands opposite the camera to remind the boy where he should throw.

The boy ran back along the edge of the houses, and the crew lost sight of him.

'He won't do it,' John M. said.

'Bet you he will,' Tillie said. 'He's got the brains of a rocking horse.'

The kid hoped John M. was right and the boy had changed his mind and gone round the barricade and away into the darkness.

Then they saw him, running like an Olympic javelin thrower, his left arm straight forward, his head back, and his right arm cocked. Then his whole upper body spun, his left arm, balancing, swung behind him, while his right flew forward and upwards and the bottle rose in a long arc, flaming in the sky, and then fell, bursting, beyond the shields. Charles moved slightly out of the doorway and pulled focus on the policeman who jumped out of the line slapping at the flames which covered his head and shoulders.

Charles held the man till he fell on the ground, hidden by helmeted figures. Then he panned quickly to his right. The kid swung his reflector above the camera and the light hit the boy as he stood with his clenched fist held high. He glanced at the crew then he raised his other hand and shimmied his hips and swayed both arms as if he was holding a football scarf above his head.

'Murdering pigs,' he shouted. 'That's for Bobby Sands and Francis Hughes and Raymond . . .'

From seven feet away, the kid heard the plastic bullet break his jaw. The boy spun away from the crew holding his face and fell in the road.

The kid's arm fell.

'Keep the fucking light steady,' Charles hissed. The boy's legs were moving as if he was dreaming of running. From the other side of the road, nearer the barricade, three dark figures ran out and pulled at the body.

'Put the light out,' one shouted.

'Keep it on,' Charles said. There were no more shots from the police line.

'Jesus,' John M. said beside the kid. 'Did you get that OK?'

'No,' Charles said, lowering the camera. 'I didn't bother switching on.'

'I've never seen pictures of anyone actually getting hit with one,' John M. said. 'I'm sure that's the first ever . . .'

'Is he dead?' the kid said.

'If he ain't,' Tillie said, 'he won't be giving the police any more rabbit for a while.'

The crew walked backwards up the road, keeping close to the houses. There were only two plastic shields left at the bottom and the Land Rovers were reversing out of the line. The barricade had almost burnt out and there were only a few small boys playing behind it.

They crossed a bit of rough ground, stumbling in the dark. No one suggested the kid put his light on. Then a torch was shone in their faces.

'Was it you put the light on the boy?' someone said.

'Look,' John M. said. 'He asked us to put it on him so he could get on the news. He asked us to.'

'Would you do anything these kids asked you to?' someone else said.

'How is he?' John M. asked.

'He's on his way to the hospital now,' the first voice said. The torch was switched off and the crew walked along a street and then down the hill to the Mercedes. Somewhere along the way Nigel joined them. The kid could hear his shoes tripping and catching.

'Someone's going to have to walk,' Tillie said as he stowed the gear away. But Nigel just got into the front passenger's seat and Charles got behind the wheel and the rest of them squeezed up in the back.

'I bet they've used your wheels to take him to the hospital,' Tillie said. 'That's if they haven't gone straight to the Bjorn Borg.'

The kid thought of the boy lying on the back seat of the Astra, his legs moving as if he was dreaming of dancing or running. His head was lying on a soft black leather bag. His face went light then dark as the car rushed past street lights. Blood was flowing from his mouth.

'Honestly,' John M. said. 'I've never seen a picture of someone getting hit like that, right in front of the camera.'

'It's my story,' Nigel said slowly. 'I'm going to voice it. No one's going to drop this one.'

John M. made Charles stop the car and the two reporters got out and stood arguing in the middle of the street. In the end they tossed a coin. Nigel lost.

It was just past midnight when they got to the hotel. At Reception Nigel just walked away from them. The other crew were still in the Cocktail Bar, though the lights were off behind the bar and the grille was down.

'Go and get the night porter to take our drinks, Lassie,' Tillie said. The kid went back into Reception and found a tiny man in a crimson uniform.

When the drinks came, Tillie told the man to put them on John M.'s room.

'What the hell,' the reporter said.

'So who's for an Ugly Night?' Tillie said.

'There's not enough time,' Charles said, sniffing his Remy Martin.

'Yes, there fucking is.' Tillie laughed. 'We'll take these drinks down. Deadline a quarter to two at the bar. Twenty quid each. You in, Andy?'

The big cameraman took a bite out of the side of his glass. The kid could hear the crunching. 'Why not?' he said. Then he went on chewing the glass.

They all put their twenty pounds on to the table except John M. and the kid. The reporter said he had to ring the hospital and he wanted to start editing early in the morning in case Nigel forgot they'd tossed.

The kid got his wallet out, then he said, 'What the hell's an Ugly Night?'

'Shit,' Tillie said. 'I forgot you know fuck-all about anything, Lassie. Right, pin back your ears and listen. You go down to the Disco and try to pick up the ugliest tart you can find, chat her up, dance, do whatever you have to because at quarter to two you've got to bring her to the bar and kiss her . . .'

'Bloody hell,' the kid said. He could hear the glass cracking in Andy's mouth.

'And the winner is the bloke with the ugliest.' Tillie was counting the money. 'Give us your twenty then.'

'What do you do when you've kissed them?' the kid said. He hadn't used any of the two hundred he'd drawn in London.

'Just keep the old minces on me,' Tillie said. 'I'll show you.' He reached over and took two tens from the kid's hands. 'There we are, a hundred and twenty quid. Ready, steady, go.'

Ricky and Brian raced each other to the door. Charles said, 'It's so pointless. They're all repulsive.' He sat twirling the Remy round his glass.

Tillie folded the money and got to his feet. He stuffed the notes in the back pocket of his jeans. 'One of the three of us will win it,' he said. 'It's our lucky night, like being there when the boy was shot. We'll get an award for that, bet you any money. We're also going to win now. Charles because he hates them all or me because I need the money to support all the ugly tarts I used to be married to or Lassie here because he'll have beginner's luck.'

Two trickles of blood ran down Andy's unshaven chin. 'Bullshit,' he said. 'You won't win nothing.'

The kid watched the dancers flickering in the coloured lights. Tillie was dancing very close to a tiny, pretty girl. The kid wondered if he was being set up again. Then he saw Ricky dancing with a woman who was well over six feet tall. She looked puzzled behind her round spectacles. The kid thought she wasn't often asked to dance and certainly not by someone good-looking like Ricky, wearing white shoes and all the gear.

Ignoring the disco music, Charles steered his partner gracefully through as if she was a queen. She had a heavy square face and her mouth was surrounded by livid boils. She stared deep into Charles' eyes as they posed, still for a second, at one end of the floor, then he swept her off again.

Brian had found someone's mother, probably just as she was leaving, because she had a coat and hat on. He was unbuttoning her coat, but shouting into her ear so she didn't notice.

The kid went to the bar where Andy was leaning. He had been going to have had a pint but when Andy asked him he said he'd have a brandy. Andy made it a large one. On the way down to the disco, Tillie'd said Andy's technique was to wait until the deadline and then grab the ugliest girl in reach.

'The trouble is I fancy them all,' the kid said, smiling. Andy was taking a long time to get the cigarette packet out of his shirt pocket.

Ricky brought his girl to the bar. She was as tall as Andy or Ricky. The kid thought she must be as heavy as Andy. Ricky kept his arm round her waist.

'This is Patricia,' he said seriously. 'And this is Andy and this is Lassie.'

'Lance,' the kid said.

Ricky said something to Patricia, bringing his mouth right up to her ear, then he kissed the side of her neck. She closed her eyes behind the round spectacles.

Ricky bought two drinks. 'You two had better get a move on if you're going to find a beauty like this one,' he said. 'You gorgeous little thing.' He leant forward and kissed her big man's face. 'Yummy, yummy, yummy, I've got love in my tummy,' he sang.

The kid walked away from the bar. He found himself having a slash in the Gents on the main Reception floor. He could just go to bed, but the boys would say he'd chickened out. He could just go back and drink with Andy and grab the nearest girl. There was nearly an hour left. But she might object. It would be awful not to find anyone, to be the only one of the boys alone. He didn't mind if he didn't win. He could never ask a girl as ugly as Ricky's to dance; she'd know he was taking the piss. He'd just go out and get someone dancing.

He washed his hands and ran them through his hair, lifting it up from his forehead and trying to put the waves back in. He wasn't bad-looking, despite what Tillie said. He could get someone to dance. He'd tell her his name was Lance. He'd take her to the bar and buy a drink back for Andy but he wouldn't mock her like Ricky. Shit, he'd been looking at the wrong place, at the dancers. He should've been looking at the girls who weren't dancing, who no one had asked to dance.

Two local boys came in laughing. He stopped arranging his hair. They were both about his age.

'You're right on with her,' one said. 'Jesus, shouldn't I know?' he demanded, looking down at the urinal.

The kid passes a row of dark backs, silhouetted against the flames of candles stuck in wine bottles. If he goes inside to look at the faces, they can all look at him. As he ponders, one head turns close to him. He sees a pile of curly, blonde hair above a wide face. She smiles at him. He bends over her. She nods and rises and keeps on rising, a big girl, no, not big, the same height as him, but fat. She rises until she stands there, still smiling despite being so helplessly exposed.

She doesn't look bad to the kid who's swaying slightly as he waits for her to edge her way out, people lifting their legs and sniggering as the great bulk of her leaves its safe mooring and slips out, unstoppable once under way, towards the small tug which surely cannot, but yes, she casts an arm through his and he steers her out to the perilous dance floor.

On the way the kid takes in the fact that she's far from skinny, but his mum is fat and so's his dad. Anyway he is entranced by the kindness of her smile and he also likes the way she's holding his arm. The girl's sheer bulk could be a problem on the crowded floor except she dances lightly and gracefully. At first they dance apart, either because of the fast music or because they do not yet know each other. They don't speak either: he is satisfied to be dancing and is aware that he is not sober. She, she seems simply happy to be dancing.

Then, at first between dances, in the tiny gaps between

the records, they start to speak. Her name is Mary, Mary Hamilton. She lives just outside what she calls Londonderry. She is an international switchboard operator for British Telecom.

Soon, though they are still dancing apart, one or other is bobbing forward to speak in the other's ear, placing a steadying hand on a shoulder. Then the music slows and he stops strutting and shaking in front of her and stands, serious with possibilities, and she takes his hands and pulls him close and adjusts his slim body to her satisfaction. Soon his eyes are closed above her shoulder. Her arms are holding him; her body seems all around him. It seems to him he is safe for the first time that day.

Without opening his eyes, he tells her about coming across the Border, making a joke of it. But she doesn't laugh; in fact she stops smiling and frowns slightly.

'Why should they be so cruel to you?' she says.

'Actually I was dead scared,' he says.

While they dance, his mouth moving in the perfumed hair above her right ear, he tells her what great guys they are really, how maybe being shot at around the world has made them tough, how they don't mean any harm, it's just their way of getting through another day, how, after a few more days, they'll just accept him. He tells her how much he wants that, to be accepted as one of the boys, to be treated as an equal.

'They'll get fed up with teasing you soon,' she promises. 'People always do.' She looks sad for a moment, but he doesn't see.

'To tell the truth,' he says, 'I don't know if I can handle the job. We did a riot tonight, up at the Creggan, and I hated it. I was so scared. I really was. The others enjoyed it. They were laughing all the time. Maybe I'm too much of a coward.'

Once he's started he can't stop. He tells her about the petrol bombers and the trapped Land Rovers and the window being broken behind him, about the car being stolen and how he didn't argue but was so frightened he forgot his bag, about the hill with the fire at the top and the row of shields at the bottom, about having to put his light on the boy dancing in front of the flames, and the shot which hit him and how everyone seemed to be pleased and how he thought he was going to be sick, how he felt he had been shot himself.

And the music has stopped twice and started up again and the last two tunes are fast and they are the only couple who're hardly moving. Except when Ricky and the large woman drop in behind them and imitate them until Ricky gets fed up with not being noticed.

'Poor Lance,' she says, and it seems to him she opens up her body so he fits more deeply, more sweetly.

'But don't you see?' he insists. 'I put my light on him. I lit him up so they could shoot him . . .'

She says nothing at first, swaying gently, rocking him in her arms. 'Did he ask you not to?' she whispers. 'Did he not want to be filmed?'

'No, he wanted to be on the News. He said we should put the light on.'

'There you are then. He took the responsibility.'

It sounds as if it could be true. The kid hadn't made the boy throw petrol bombs and dance in front of the police. The kid opens his eyes again. Brian has his woman's back turned. She's still got her coat on. He winks hugely. The kid frowns and pulls away slightly.

'What's wrong?' she says.

'Nothing. You've made me feel better.'

He sinks back into her but he turns his wrist behind her neck so he can see his watch. It is nearly twenty to two.

The floor isn't so crowded. Ricky and Brian are still dancing. The kid manoevres the girl round. So is Charles. But
where's Tillie?

'They don't mean any harm,' he whispers.

'You're getting tense again,' she says, kneading his
shoulders. The kid relaxes against her again. Of course,
he'll kiss her, but while the others will be making fun of
theirs, he won't be. The other girls are much uglier than
Mary so there's no chance he'll win. He can just kiss her
and lead her back to the dance floor and sink into her again.
Someone taps his shoulder. Ricky. He points to the bar.

'Let's go and have a drink,' the kid says. The other boys
are standing out of the crush for last drinks, to the left of
the bar. Ricky's huge woman is still dancing against him
while he smiles lovingly. Charles' punkish girl is scowling
and he is kissing her hand. Brian's mother is having difficulty standing so he is hugging her.

All the men are checking their watches. The clock above
the bar says it's past five to two but bar clocks are always
fast. The kid's watch says there's less than a minute to
go.

'Why are we standing here, darling?' Mary says, because
he's not buying a drink.

'These are the other lads,' the kid says. 'We said we'd
meet here . . .'

Somebody is shouting outside. The two swing-doors to
the stairs crash open. Andy strides in. He is carrying someone. A huge black boot hangs over one of his arms. A shiny
steel frame encloses the tiny leg above the boot.

Andy makes for them, then veers off behind a pillar in
the direction of the dance floor. He reappears still spinning.
The girl's mouth is open in a scream of pleasure or panic.
Andy puts his own big red mouth over hers.

A door opens in the corner where they are all standing.

The door is marked 'Private'. The bar staff have been coming and going through it. But it is Tillie who emerges. He surveys them one by one, grinning, and then very slowly, graciously, like a conjuror, he pulls from the door a small old woman, wrapped in a patched dressing gown, her hair in curlers. Tillie stands as proudly as Nureyev. He pulls her in, across his body and passes her to his other hand. He looks at her with pride.

The old woman looks at them all shyly. 'I was asleep,' she says.

'Mrs Enwright,' Tillie says. 'This is love. This is the real thing.'

With great tenderness, he cradles her head on his left arm, touches her cheek with his right and bends his face to hers. The kid is watching, mouth open, as Tillie, mouth clearly open too, passionately kisses the old woman.

Then the kid sees that he is the only one not kissing. Mary is looking at the floor. It may be that she hasn't seen the old woman or that she is too kind to watch.

'I love you, Mary,' he says.

'Lance,' she says, smiling, and he moves back between her big arms into that soft expanse of breasts and stomach and thighs. Her lips are warm and they slip delightfully over his. He has the smell of her hair again and her fingers are stroking the back of his neck.

Then someone shouts and the kid, surprised, looks up and sees the old woman stagger and nearly fall as, laughing and shouting, Tillie suddenly withdraws her support. Andy puts the crippled girl down carefully on a chair and runs toward the swing doors. Brian and Charles and Ricky are running too, shouting and laughing, slapping each other on the back.

The kid finds they are slapping him on the back too and laughing with him and he's laughing and shouting, all the way up to Tillie's room where they fling themselves on the beds and ring room service for drinks.

And, after a while, when they ask his opinion about the winner, he stops thinking about the circle of girls standing downstairs and the flickering coloured lights playing on each of their faces in turn.

THE GETTING OF
WISDOM

Hugh Robinson

THE GETTING OF WISDOM

'How much is it, mister?'

Billy McCullough stood on tiptoes and peered anxiously over the pile of musty-smelling books and papers and magazines on the counter of Berni's Smithfield Book-shop.

He'd never seen so many books in all his life. They were everywhere and he wondered how he had never stumbled on this place before. Rows and rows of shelves packed tightly with books of every shape and size and description reached right up to the ceiling. The shelves were so tightly packed the boy was certain not even a postcard could be squeezed on to any one of them, much less another book. Two or three cardboard boxes each holding a jumble of less-valued volumes were tied up roughly with a coarse stringy twine and others were just tied up without benefit of the cardboard box. The poorest relations of all, a dozen or so battered copies of nothing in particular which appeared to have smuggled themselves into the shop when the owner wasn't looking, lay scattered forlornly about the floor. Their chances of ever being lifted to a position of honour high up on one of the shelves or even finding a place of sanctity in one of the cardboard boxes seemed hopeless. Not even valued enough to be tied together with a piece of the rough twine, they suffered the ignominy of being kicked and trodden on by every careless foot that entered the shop. The boy was one of the few who treated them with respect, and he had threaded his way carefully through them to the counter.

Billy's eyes travelled slowly around the walls of books and settled again on the little man seated behind the counter. The man made no response to his question, nor gave any indication he had even heard it. His soft little face reminded the boy of the tiny mouse his mother had asked him to kill two or three days ago when she cornered it in the scullery. Like the mouse, the man sat silent and motionless except for the impatient little eyes which scurried backward and forward across the page of his Zane Grey western. The boy hadn't the heart to kill the mouse, but he'd chased it out through a hole in the bottom of the back door. He'd forgotten all about it until now and he thought it strange the man's face should remind him of the little creature. But it did. He moved along the counter to where the pile of books wasn't quite so high and where he could see the little man without having to stand on tiptoes.

'How much is it, mister? How much is the book?'

Berni, proprietor of Berni's Smithfield Bookshop, remained motionless. His tiny eyes raced on for another line and a half, eagerly devouring the print, and then stopped suddenly. But he didn't look up. He pulled the stub of a pencil from behind his ear and very deliberately underlined the last word he'd read. It was a clever little device he'd perfected for his own convenience. Made it easier to find the place when you came back to it after seeing to a customer. It was only the second mark he'd made in the book all day.

Berni stuck the pencil back behind the same ear and got up, frowning. He didn't often get kids this age in here. If they came in to the market at all it was usually to swear at the parrot in Francie's pet shop or feed bits of soap to the monkey. But they didn't come in here. Kids didn't read books, and even if this one did, he didn't have two brass farthings to rub together to buy one. You could tell that from his thin jersey, ragged and torn and not enough material in it to keep out the chill of a cold November day like this.

The boy was conscious of the man's sceptical gaze but he didn't let it deter him. He repeated the question for the third time.

'How much is it, mister? How much is the book?'

Berni tossed the Zane Grey on to a pile of *Funny Wonder* comics in exasperation.

'What book, son? What book are you talkin' about?'

'That one,' the boy answered quickly, encouraged now he had finally captured the man's attention. He tapped the blue hardback with his forefinger and laid it down in front of Berni. 'That one, mister. *The Book of One Thousand Beautiful Things*. How much is it?'

Berni picked up the volume disinterestedly. Whatever the price, the kid couldn't afford it. He wiped the dust off the cover and squinted at the faded gold letters on the spine. *The Book of One Thousand Beautiful Things: By Arthur Mee*. He sniffed and ran the back of his hand across his mouth. He'd never heard tell of it. Must've picked it up in a job lot somewhere, probably that big house he did up the Malone two or three weeks ago. You never knew what you were going to find in them big houses. You'd be surprised. Trouble was it was hard stuff to shift.

A quick flick through the pages revealed nothing particularly exciting. Poetry. Pictures of famous paintings. Quotations from the Bible. Not the sort of stuff he'd usually carry. Too slow. *Maria Martin and the Murder at the Red Barn*, or Sexton Blake or Zane Grey. That was the stuff to give the troops. Or a good weepie. They always came back for more of that. But Arthur Mee?

'Good book that, son. Arthur Mee wrote it, y'know. Not many of his books knockin' about Belfast. Have you got any of his stuff?'

The boy shook his head. 'We've no books in our house, mister. My da' says readin' doesn't put any money in your pocket.'

Berni sniffed disdainfully. Talk like that could put him out of business in no time. He was still trying to formulate a telling response as the boy eased the book gently from his hands and slowly turned the pages. He stopped near the back of the book and traced a line of print with his finger. Then he pushed the book back towards Berni.

'How do you say that, mister? What does it mean?'

Berni's racing little eyes took off across the page, never blinking but never still for an instant. Backward and forward across the page they scurried, up and down, sometimes moving from the first line to the last and then back again to pick up the pieces in the middle. The boy watched, fascinated, and he thought again of the mouse and the way it had darted all round the scullery and had even tried to get up the wall before escaping under the back door. He was just about to burst out laughing when the racing eyes stopped suddenly and looked up at him.

'That's a poem, son. Ye Banks and Braes O' Bonny Doon. Very famous. Rabby Burns wrote it. Years ago.'

'Ye Banks and Braes O' Bonny Doon!' The boy breathed the words in an almost silent whisper, as if they were a magical incantation. His big blue eyes opened wide in wonderment as he slowly repeated the words again. 'Ye Banks and Braes O' Bonny Doon. What does that mean, mister? What's a brae? And what's Bonny Doon?'

Berni snorted and threw the book down. Poetry wasn't his strong point and he wasn't afraid to admit it. He only sold the stuff. He didn't have to understand it. But that was the trouble with poets. You never knew what they were on about and the Scotch ones were the worst of the lot. All that braw, bricht, moonlicht nicht business irritated him. You might as well try to understand Chinese as make any sense of all that nonsense.

'How do I know what it means? That was wrote a hundred years ago. In Scotland. People don't talk like that anymore. Not around here, anyway.'

The boy rescued the book from the pile on the counter and wiped the cover with his sleeve. He was disappointed the man couldn't tell him more about the poem. He thought the man would have read all the books in the shop and known everything there was to know about each of them. And especially this one. This was a good book. He knew it was.

'Well, how much is it, mister? How much is *The Book of One Thousand Beautiful Things*?"

Berni pulled the butt of a Woodbine from behind his other ear and stuck it in his mouth and then fumbled about for a match. He lit the cigarette, wheezing and coughing as he blew the cloud of hazy blue smoke into the air. You had to give the kid credit. He was a trier. Didn't have a make to his name, but he was a trier. He took another drag on the Woodbine and shook his head at the boy.

'Too dear for you, son. I'd be lookin' at a shillin' for that. Couldn't take a penny less.' He lifted a pile of old comics from the end of the counter and tossed them down in front of the boy. 'What about these? *Funny Wonder. Rainbow* and *Chips*. I'll give you six for a penny. Keep you readin' for a week. What d'ye say?'

The boy picked up a tattered copy of *Rainbow* and gazed half-heartedly at the funny little characters with the balloons of conversation issuing from their mouths. The characters were an assortment of ducks, giraffes, badgers and clowns all dressed in bright clothes of green and red and yellow and they all seemed to be having a wonderful time. The boy laid the comic down and looked at Berni.

'I like them comics, mister. But I'd rather have *The Book of One Thousand Beautiful Things*.' He paused for a moment. 'Would you take jampots for it, mister? My da' says he used to get into the pictures for a jampot.'

Berni rolled his eyes heavenward and groaned audibly. He took a last despairing suck on the Woodbine, almost swallowing it, and then flicked the butt expertly into the street. He leaned over the counter so his face was almost level with the boy's.

'Listen, son. Your da' might have got into the flicks for a jampot when he was a nipper, but he wouldn't get in now. It'll cost him four dee to get into Joe McKibben's, and Joe's is the cheapest picture-house in the town.' He straightened up and tried one last shot. 'Would your oul' fella not buy the book for you?'

It was a daft question, and he knew it, even before the words were right out of his mouth. If the kid's da' had any dough he might be able to put some decent clothes on the youngster's back.

'M' da's on relief,' the boy answered. 'He couldn't buy it.'

Berni nodded. 'Thought as much. No money comin' in, eh?' He picked up the book again and flicked through the pages, wondering if window-cleaning might be a more profitable and less demanding job than bookselling. All you needed was a bucket of water and a cloth. No shop, no books, no overheads and no worries. Just a bucket of water and a cloth. It was worth thinking about.

'Tell you what, son. Gimme tenpence and the book's yours.' He spread his arms out in an appealing gesture of generosity towards the boy. 'I can't say fairer than that, can I? At this rate I'll be out concretin' the streets with your da' for a food voucher. At tenpence I'm givin' the book away. I'm givin' it away.'

The boy's eyes widened as the prospect of owning the book suddenly became more of a reality. Tenpence was a lot of money, but it wasn't as much as a shilling. Maybe, just maybe, he could get tenpence. He didn't know where or how, but he had to try. He nodded his head up and down vigorously.

'OK, mister. I'll take it.'

Berni stared at him, his eyebrows raised and his thin mouth slightly parted in surprise.

'For tenpence?'

'Yes. Tenpence.'

Berni reached the book across the counter with one hand and held out the other for the money. 'There you are, son. That's the best tenpence-worth you'll ever buy.'

The boy stepped back from the counter. 'But I haven't got the money yet, mister. Will you keep it for me? 'Til I get the money? Will you, mister?'

Berni sighed, a long, deep and sorrowful sigh. The window-cleaning was becoming more and more attractive by the minute. Why was he wasting his time with this kid who had as much chance of getting tenpence as he had of winning the All Ireland Sweepstake? There were grown men walking the streets of Belfast who hadn't got tenpence to their name, and no chance of getting it. He tried to avoid the big blue eyes staring up at him and making him feel so uncomfortable, but he couldn't help it. He tossed the book back on the counter and made a mental note never to enter into conversation with a customer until he'd at least seen the colour of his money.

'Okay, son. I'll hold it. For a while. But don't be too long about gettin' the money. I don't reckon there's another one of them books in Smithfield. Maybe not in the whole of Belfast. Arthur Mee wrote it, y'know.'

The boy's eyes sparkled and his face launched into a great big smile.

'Aw thanks, mister. Thanks a million. I'll get it OK. I'll get the money.' He picked up the book and ran his fingers gently over the cover as if he were stroking a kitten. 'I'll get it OK. I'll get it.'

He set the book down and took a last look at it sitting among its fellows and then turned toward the centre aisle of Smithfield Market. Only then did Berni see the feet, bare and white with cold.

'Hey! Kid! Hold on.' The boy turned. 'Make that ninepence. For the book. There's a wee bit of a mark on the cover. It's damaged. Make it ninepence.'

Billy could hardly believe it. Ninepence! He was nearly sure he could get ninepence. Somewhere. He thanked Berni over and over again and then left the shop, his head already swimming with ideas how to raise the nine pennies. He stuck his hands in the pockets of his short trousers and held his head high, proudly, as if he already owned *The Book of One Thousand Beautiful Things*. He whistled, a snatch from *Phil the Fluter's Ball*, as he passed the pet shop with the white rabbits and the baldy monkey and determinedly strode on past the piles of second-hand furniture and faded paintings of wild deer in the misty Highlands of Scotland. He slowed and stopped as he drew level with an old man sharpening knives on a big grindstone at one side of the passage. He watched in fascination as the old man pushed the treadle of the contraption up and down with his foot and the stone spun round and round, and the dancing sparks leapt into the air as the Sheffield Steel was applied to the rim of the stone. The old man looked up and caught Billy's eye. He smiled. Billy smiled. Then he turned away toward Gresham Street murmuring softly, over and over again, 'Ye Banks and Braes O' Bonny Doon . . . Ye Banks and Braes O' Bonny Doon . . .'

Milligan's school in Avoca Street got out at three o'clock and Billy could hardly wait. He sat at his place in the long wooden desk, his face propped in his hands, staring blankly at the big clock above the blackboard. The brass pendulum swung to and fro in perpetual motion but the spidery black hands on the clock face refused to budge. For an eternity they seemed to have been frozen at two minutes to three and now Billy stared even more intently at them, willing them to move on and reach the appointed time when freedom came. Why was it you could never see the hands move? No matter how hard you watched you couldn't see them move, and the more you watched them the less they moved.

These two minutes were the longest two minutes of the whole day. Billy had spent the entire afternoon suffering heavy blows on the head and cruel words of insult from Mr Milligan because he didn't know his eleven-times table. But Billy didn't care. He hadn't the slightest interest in the eleven-times table or any other tables or sums of any sort. There wasn't any magic in sums. They always added up to the same thing, and if they didn't, there was something wrong. And when he did them there was usually something wrong. You either knew how to do them or you didn't. It was as simple as that. But you couldn't change them or turn them into something else, the way you could with words. You could use the same words over and over again and always get a new story or learn something new, something you hadn't known before. Like Ye Banks and Braes O' Bonny Doon. He'd never heard tell of that until yesterday, and he still didn't know what it meant. But he'd find out when he got *The Book of One Thousand Beautiful Things* and he'd find out a lot of other things as well.

He traced his finger over the initials cut deep into the rough wooden desk and wondered if the bucket would still be where he'd left it. It was a good idea hiding the bucket. It meant he didn't have to go the whole way home to pick it up, and if he got started just after school, he might get it filled before dark.

'McCullough!' The angry roar of Mr Milligan's gravel voice brought Billy back to the present and he sat up with a start as the master hurled a piece of chalk at him in a final act of frustration. The chalk bounced harmlessly off Billy's desk, hit the floor and rolled into a corner. 'You will be pleased to know, McCullough,' bellowed Mr Milligan, 'you will be pleased to know that all further attempts to instil some degree of wisdom into your thick skull have now ceased for the day.' The teacher rose from his desk and slammed the lid closed with a loud bang. 'You, and the rest of this rag-bag of the great *un*learned are now free to return to the jungle from whence you came.'

Billy was first through the school gate. It was a cold Belfast day and a stinging rain fell steadily, but he didn't care. He sprinted along Manor Street, splashing carelessly through the puddles and trying to ignore the little ginger and white mongrel which snapped playfully at his heels. The dog gave up at the junction of the Oldpark and turned back to seek new sport, but Billy kept running. He ran down Albertville Drive and didn't stop until he reached the Crumlin Road.

He leaned heavily against a lamp-post, bent almost double and pulling in great gulps of air to his aching lungs. His grey jersey and trousers were sodden with the rain and they clung heavily and uncomfortably to his sweating body, and he wondered if he should abandon his plan and just go on home. The drone of a tram buzzing its way slowly towards him on tracks of rutted silver made him look up.

The tram was nearly empty and looked warm and cosy with its lights full on even although it wasn't yet dark. It might be worth while pinching a ride on the tram. And then again, it might not. The last time he'd done that there'd been a peeler on board and he'd been lucky to get away with a clip round the ear and the promise of six months up the Crumlin if he did it again. And he couldn't afford to go to jail now. The man wouldn't keep *The Book of One Thousand Beautiful Things* for six months. He wouldn't keep it that long.

Billy wiped the rain from his face and watched the tram as it drew level with him and then rumbled on past. He could run as fast as that. Easily. He took a deep breath and sprinted after the tram. He caught it and passed it and didn't stop until he reached the piece of waste ground near Vistula Street where he'd hidden the bucket.

Thankfully, it was still there, and it was with some relief Billy pulled it out from the pile of rubbish he'd used to cover it. If someone had stolen the bucket all his plans would surely have been wrecked. But it was still here, and as he prepared to put into action the first part of his plan to raise the money to buy the book, the rain was beginning to ease. And by the time he walked down the entry and round to the door of number one Vistula Street it had ceased completely, and his sticky, steamy clothes no longer bothered him.

The old woman who answered Billy's timid knock re-minded him of a witch he'd once seen in a *Lot-O-Fun* comic. Just for a second he thought it was the witch. Her face was wrinkled in lines of pale, loose skin and like the witch, she didn't have any teeth either. A black shawl was pulled carelessly over her straggly white hair and thin shoulders.

'Any skins, missus? Potato skins? Stale bread? Any refuse at all?'

Billy stared at the woman's sunken features and studied the single white hair curling from the centre of her chin. Why did she make those awful chewing movements with her mouth when it was plain to see she hadn't anything to chew, and even if she had, she hadn't anything to chew it with? Was she trying to put a spell on him? He felt a sudden compulsion to drop the bucket and run, but he thought of *The Book of One Thousand Beautiful Things* and stood his ground.

'Any scraps at all, missus?'

The old woman stopped chewing, her mouth half open. She definitely didn't have any teeth. Her grey, watery eyes stared at Billy, almost without seeing him. Suddenly she reached out a scrawny arm and took the bucket without a word and then retreated backwards into the house. Billy thought she was never going to come back and had stolen his iron bucket to mix her magic potions in. But she did come back and she spoke to him in a thin, breathless voice.

'There y'are son. That'll help ye to get the picture money,' she cackled. The toothless smile and the pat on the head were meant to encourage but only served to make Billy all the more apprehensive. He took the bucket and looked into it, half expecting to see a collection of mutilated toads and snakes' heads. That was the sort of stuff witches usually kept about them.

But there wasn't any of that. There were only two or three pieces of potato skin lying at the bottom of the bucket, partially covered by a single decaying cabbage leaf. M'Crory paid a top rate of a penny-ha'penny for a bucket of pigswill. Suddenly *The Book of One Thousand Beautiful Things* seemed a long, long way away. Billy looked up at the woman.

'Thanks, missus. I'll call again.'

The sky darkened and the rain came again, a steady unrelenting rain, and he was cold and wet and miserable when the bucket was finally filled. Now he sat under a lamp-post in Harrison Street with the bucket of foul-smelling pigswill beside him. He didn't care about the rain which dripped from his clothes and seeped through to his bare skin, and he didn't care about the cold which nipped his fingers. He didn't care about the hard wetness of the stone kerb beneath him. He just wanted to rest, ease his aching arms and sore feet before setting out on the journey home.

Billy almost fell asleep leaning on the bucket of swill, and probably would have done, if it hadn't been for the glimpse of the old man on the bicycle which made him lift his head. The man turned waveringly into the street and pedalled the bicycle over the cobblestones towards him. He dismounted and laid the bicycle against Billy's lamp-post.

Billy had seen the old man do it a thousand times, but he watched once more, fascinated. Joe took the long wooden pole from the bicycle and reached it up to the glass globe at the top of the lamp-post. He gave a quick flick with his wrist and a gentle pull on the ring of the chain dangling from its pivoted arm, and the white mantle inside the glass ignited in a fluorescent glow. The warm light spilled on to the wet cobblestones and was thrown back by the dark puddles of water at Billy's feet. Magically, the featureless spits of rain were transformed into a shining cascade of golden needles.

Joe nodded at the bucket.

'Tryin' to get the money for a couple of fegs, son?'

Billy smiled and shook his head.

'Not fegs, Joe. A book. I'm goin' to buy a book. *The Book of One Thousand Beautiful Things*.'

'A book,' repeated Joe, securing the long pole to the bar of his bicycle. 'You're a man after my own heart. A blessed companion is a book. Aye, indeed. A blessed companion is a book.' He pulled the bicycle away from the lamp-post and wagged a finger at Billy. 'You're doin' the right thing, son. Get wisdom. Above all things, get wisdom.' Then he was gone, leaving Billy staring after him in amazement, trying to remember and make sense of the words imparted to him by the old lamplighter. But Joe's words were too deep for him. He sighed and picked up the bucket of refuse and drained the water from it, disturbing the golden pool at his feet. Then he turned and trudged wearily into the darkness and drizzling rain.

The bell above Mrs M'Gilton's wee shop in Cree Street cling-clanged sweetly as Billy pushed his way inside holding his penny-ha'penny tightly in his hand.

Billy loved the smell of Mrs M'Gilton's shop. He was never quite sure what the smell was, but he loved it just the same. At one time he'd thought the American apples were responsible. As big as a man's fist they were, crimson red and shining like a billiard ball, so shiny he imagined Mrs M'Gilton polished them every morning before opening up the shop. Then he thought the liquorice allsorts were responsible and one day he was almost sure it was the toffee-apples glued in their tray of sticky syrup that gave off the intoxicating aroma. This choice was then discarded in favour of the cigarettes, Turf, Woodbine and Craven A lined along the shelves behind Mrs M'Gilton. It could have been the tea lying loose in the wooden silver-lined chest at the end of the counter, but Billy finally decided that it wasn't any one of these at all. It was the mixture of them all, blending together, which produced the mysterious aroma. He breathed in deeply and held his breath, savouring the sweetness of it all as Mrs M'Gilton shuffled in from her back kitchen.

Mrs M'Gilton was as spick and span as her little shop and the tiny dab of French perfume, genuine French perfume, she wore behind each ear added yet another fragrance to the already heady scent of the room. She straightened a box of Mrs Cullen's Headache Powders beside the tray of toffee-apples and smiled at Billy.

'Good morning, Billy. What can I get you?'

Billy pursed his lips and feasted his eyes on the toffee-apples and the big bottle of brandy-balls at the other side of the headache powders. Then his eyes strayed to the nougat bars, pink and white and chewy. He liked nougat. The only trouble with nougat was it stuck in your teeth and made your jaws sore trying to tear a lump off. But it lasted a long time. The gob-stoppers lasted a long time too, even longer, but the flavour wasn't as good and they could break your teeth. Maybe the black liquorice pipes would be the best value of all. He knew he could have any of these and that didn't make the decision any easier. He rubbed the penny-ha'penny together between his finger and thumb and just for a moment weakened in favour of the toffee-apples. Then he thought of *The Book of One Thousand Beautiful Things*.

'Would you have an empty orange box, Mrs M'Gilton?'

Mrs M'Gilton smiled again. 'No. But I'll soon empty one.'

She disappeared under the counter and came up again with an armful of oranges, which immediately caused Billy to believe he had at last traced the source of the secret nectar in Mrs M'Gilton's wee shop. Mrs M'Gilton built the seven oranges in a pyramid between the toffee-apples and the burnished brass scales and then ducked under the counter one more time. She popped up again with a sizeable

225

box of wooden slats held together with wire and staples. She set it on the counter and wiped her hands on her dark Paisley pattern apron.

'There you are, Billy. Will that do?'

Billy nodded. 'It's bigger than I thought, Mrs M'Gilton.' He hesitated. 'Will it still be a penny-ha'penny?'

'A penny-ha'penny it is, Billy. Always the same price. Are you going to do a wee bit of work?'

Billy laid the penny-ha'penny down beside the toffee-apples. 'I'm tryin' to get the money for a book, Mrs M'Gilton.'

'Oh? What's the book?'

'*The Book of One Thousand Beautiful Things*. Arthur Mee wrote it. There's only one of them in the whole of Belfast.'

Mrs M'Gilton shook her head slowly from side to side. 'I never heard of Arthur Mee, Billy. Annie S. Swan's my favourite. She writes lovely books. But I'm sure that book of yours is good too. It's got a lovely title. You'll have to let me see it when you get it.' She dipped a hand into the jar of brandy-balls and pulled one out. She handed it to Billy. 'There you are, Billy. That'll keep you warm while you're working. And I hope you get your book.'

Billy took the brandy-ball and slipped it into his pocket and then picked up his orange box. 'Thanks very much, Mrs M'Gilton. Thanks a million.'

Mrs M'Gilton smiled, a warm smile. 'You're welcome. You're more than welcome, son.'

The bell above the door cling-clanged as Billy staggered into the street with the giant orange box. All he needed now was a hatchet.

It had taken him longer than he thought it would to chop the box into neat bundles of firewood. The problem was the wire. And the staples. Some boxes were simply nailed together with solid little blocks of wood at each corner. You could just knock them apart. But this one had been held together with wire and staples and the wire had to be removed before he could even begin the work properly. And he wanted to do it properly.

Billy knew the secret of a good bundle of sticks. It was no good just smashing the box to pieces and pulling the wire away and tying up the bits any old way. Every stick had to be a certain length, not too short, and not too long so it wouldn't fit into the grate. And they had to be more or less the correct thickness. Too thick and they wouldn't light. Too thin and they would flare up immediately and burn away like a piece of paper. If you made a bundle like that you wouldn't sell another at the same house. Neat, tidy bundles of sticks, proper size and proper thickness. That's what he needed.

And he'd done it. Patiently he'd eased the staples out from the slats with the end of a rusty screwdriver and pulled the wire away, leaving the wood free and clean and ready for the hatchet. He chopped the sticks into bundles, tied them and sold them, six bundles at a penny a bundle. Sixpence. He'd never had sixpence before, and sixpence was a lot of money, but it wasn't enough. He needed ninepence, and now it was raining again, sheeting and swirling along Royal Avenue, then twisting and turning into York Street and driving hard in his face, numbing his cheeks.

But Billy didn't mind the rain. What school-kid did? He strode jauntily along York Street with his Jackie Coogan cap perched at a ridiculous angle on his head. The cap was about two sizes too large but it didn't bother Billy. The cap was there to give him some protection from the rain. That was its sole purpose and function and it was doing a good job. His feet were cold and wet, and that was nothing new, but his head was dry and he jingled six copper pennies in his right-hand trouser pocket – the one without the hole. It would take more than a little rain to dampen his spirits today. Soon, very soon, *The Book of One Thousand Beautiful Things* would be his.

York Street was always busy on a Friday afternoon and today was no exception, despite the inclemency of the weather. Billy was glad the rain hadn't driven everyone off the streets. He needed people on the streets, and the more there were the easier it would be for him to raise the final three pennies he needed.

The crack of a horsewhip across the street made him look up. An Inglis bread-server seated high up on his cab clip-clopped his horse smartly along the wet road, heading toward Eliza Street and home. Another nag, more ancient of days and something less in the way of pedigree tossed its head and snorted great clouds of steaming breath into the air, protesting vainly against the heavy load of coal brick it was obliged to haul in and out of the little back streets.

Billy stared after the cart as it passed him, going in the opposite direction. The coal bricks were black and steaming with heat in spite of the fact they didn't have any cover from the heavy rain. He wondered if they could be as hot as they looked, and if they were, how did the man on the cart, who was as black as they were, carry them to the door of the houses where he sold them? Maybe he wore gloves. He wished he had a pair of gloves to keep his hands warm. But he hadn't. Idly, he turned and kicked an empty Woodbine packet into the river of water along the edge of the kerb. Then he looked up excitedly as he heard the sound he wanted to hear.

Stumpy Watson stood where he always stood, right on the corner of York Street and Donegal Street, bawling in

that indecipherable voice given exclusively to and inter-
preted only by fellow newsboys. Despite the fact that no
passer-by could really understand the meaning of the word
shouted intermittently by Stumpy, they did know he was
selling *Belfast Telegraphs* at that very spot.

Billy ran up to Stumpy at the street corner and watched
in admiration as his friend vocalized a particularly fine
'Teleeee-a-sixaaaa' which cracked even louder than the
bread-server's whip around the busy junction. Stumpy
prided himself that he was reckoned to have the best
'Teleeee-a-sixaaaa' in the whole of Belfast.

'Hiya B-B-Billy,' he chortled. 'W-what ye d-d-doin' down
here on a d-d-day like this? I thought you went to the
p-pictures on a F-F-Friday.'

Billy grinned up at Stumpy, a mischievous little grin.

'Not the day, Stumpy. I'm workin'. How much is your
Telegraphs?'

'P-penny-ha'penny.' advised Stumpy, who stood nearly
six foot tall and was about as broad as a brush shaft.
'D-d-d'ye want one?'

Billy shook his head as his grin grew broader. 'Not me.
How much do you pay for them, Stumpy?'

'Penny,' responded Stumpy quickly, whipping a paper
from under his arm and proffering it to a well-dressed gent
with an umbrella and trilby hat. The man gave him two
coins. He dropped the money into a pocket and then wiped
away a drop which had taken up residence at the end of
his nose. He looked down as he felt Billy tugging at his
sleeve.

'Where do you get them, Stumpy? Where do you get the
papers?'

Stumpy exchanged another paper for two coins and
turned his attention back to the youngster. 'Y-you want to
go into b-business for yourself. D-don't ye?'

229

Billy nodded eagerly, his grin growing broader by the second.

'Well,' said Stumpy, 'you'll get the p-papers round at the Hole in Li-Library Street.' He poked a long bony finger in Billy's chest. 'But listen. If you're g-goin' to flog Teles, do-don't be comin' near my pitch. It's hard enough makin' a ta-tanner without you buttin' in.'

It's doubtful if Billy heard the last piece of advice. He was already passing the *Telegraph* office and turning into Library Street. He was a little disappointed to find that the Hole wasn't really a hole, just a narrow gateway leading into the Despatch end of the newspaper building. A rough wooden bench piled high with inky newspapers barred any further progress. A couple of newsboys, not very much older than Billy, grabbed their papers from the man behind the bench and pushed past him out into the city streets.

Billy waited his turn. Then he laid his six pennies on the bench and stuck the six *Telegraphs* under his arm, just the way Stumpy did.

'I'm goin' to buy *The Book of One Thousand Beautiful Things*,' he informed the man behind the counter. 'Did you ever read it, mister?'

The man lifted a bundle of papers from the ground and heaved them on to the counter. He took a puff on his pipe and shook his head. 'Niver heerd tell of it. But I don't read much. I'm a domino man.'

Billy's eyebrows knitted together in a little frown. How could a man who didn't read much get a job selling newspapers?

'You should read it, mister. It's all about Ye Banks and Braes O' Bonny Doon and things like that. But there's only one of them in the whole of Ireland, and I'm goin' to buy it. The man in Smithfield is goin' to keep it for me. 'Til I get the money.'

He lifted the papers a bit higher under his arm and turned towards the street. Then he stopped and looked back.

'Mister?'

'What?'

'Arthur Mee wrote it, y'know.'

Selling the *Telegraphs* would be easy. That's what Billy thought, and the best place to sell them would be Corn Market. Corn Market was always full of people even on a wet day like this.

Five different streets led into the circle of space right in the centre of the city and he could have the papers sold in next to no time. It was even better than York Street where Stumpy was and he wondered why Stumpy didn't come down here. He debated in his mind whether he should tell his friend about Corn Market some time, or whether he should keep it a secret for himself.

Billy took his stance just outside Mooney's pub and held one of the *Telegraphs* across his chest so everyone could see it. That was the way Stumpy did it, and Stumpy knew all there was to know about selling newspapers.

There was only one problem. The rain. The papers were getting wet and limp and the pages were beginning to stick together. Billy gazed across the street at the warm lights of the Royal Cinema and the black and white placards of Al Jolson outside. There were plenty streaming in to see *Swanee* and it would be drier and warmer on the steps and maybe some of the people would buy his papers. That's what he would do. Move over to the picture-house.

He never saw the punch coming. He didn't even know it was a punch. He just felt the sudden pain as his lip was split open against his front teeth and the salty blood trickled into his mouth as he reeled backward. Then another blow caught him high up on the temple and sent him crashing to the ground.

Instinctively, Billy's hand went to his mouth as he tasted the blood. He stared in disbelief at the redness on his fingers and then caught a glimpse of his newspapers scattered across the street, blowing and tearing in the wind. He jumped to his feet, mad with rage as he realized what had happened, and swung a wild punch at the big newsboy who stood over him, fists held high. The punch missed by a mile and the bigger boy crashed another blow into Billy's unprotected face, sending him crashing to the ground for the second time.

He didn't give Billy time to recover. He grabbed him by the neck of his jersey and hauled him to his feet, shaking him like a wet rag.

'Listen you,' he snarled, his nose not a half-inch from Billy's. 'I don't want to hit you again. But if you come back on my pitch again I'll bust ye in two.' He pushed Billy roughly away from him. 'Now clear off, and take yer papers with ye, ye funky-lukkin' wee bastard.'

Billy spat out blood and glared at the bigger boy. He was no coward and he resented being called funky. But he was beaten. And he knew it. Even if he swung another punch he couldn't reach high enough to connect and the big boy would probably tear his papers into shreds. And he had to protect those papers, even more than he had to save his pride. Without the papers there would be no *Book of One Thousand Beautiful Things*.

He wiped the cuff of his jersey across his mouth and began to pick up the papers. They were wet, very wet, but worse than that they were torn and splattered with mud. He lifted them up in a rough bundle and shoved them under his arm.

Then he trudged wearily down Arthur Street, trying to

stem the flow of blood into his mouth and not knowing what to do next.

He couldn't even sell one paper. Not one. He cleaned and dried them as best he could, but it was all wasted effort.

An unused newspaper has a freshness and crispness and a promise to it. There may be thousands of copies of the same edition, but to its owner it is unique, unopened and untouched by any hand save his own, its hidden parts reserved for him alone. The mere expectation of the delights lying within its folds is a pleasure often deliberately delayed until it may be enjoyed at a convenient time, in comfort and ease and privacy. No one wanted a soiled paper, tainted with the mud of the streets, torn and limp and abused and uncared-for.

Billy was desperate. There were only a few people about the gas-lit streets now and anyone who had wanted an evening paper would have bought one long ago. And it wasn't only that he'd been unable to make up the other three pennies he needed. It wasn't only that. All his hard-earned money, the entire sixpence, was tied up in the six worthless newspapers stuck under his arm.

He was back where he started. With nothing. What was it his da' had said last night? He had ideas above his station? Something like that. He wasn't quite sure what it meant, but maybe it meant a kid like him would never be able to own a book like *The Book of One Thousand Beautiful Things*. Maybe that's what it meant and that's why the big lad had punched him in the mouth and kicked his papers into the gutter. Because he had ideas above his station.

He stopped outside a pub in Chichester Street and gingerly drew a finger along his bruised lip. The bleeding had stopped and so had the rain, and the bright light of the pub window cheered him up. He could hear the voices and the laughter coming from inside and he fingered his papers, wondering. It would be worth a try. Anything was worth a try. He couldn't be worse off than he was now.

The pub was comfortable and cosy and even the tiled floor felt warm to his feet. The air was thick with tobacco smoke and noisy with conversation. Over in the far corner, near a blazing fire, two old men sat staring solemnly at a draughtboard. Billy watched the men for a moment or two, interested to see the next move in the game and what the consequences of it would be. But neither man moved nor gave any indication he was likely to and Billy lost interest as his gaze started to travel round the bar.

The booths were well filled, mostly by men with bottles of Guinness and pint glasses in front of them, but there were women there too. The women were old, maybe the same age as the old woman in Vistula Street, and they sipped slowly at tiny glasses of red wine or what Billy knew to be 'half-uns'.

The group of men who stood arguing at the bar were of a slightly rougher breed, dockers probably, and the big man with the ginger curls and red-spotted neckerchief seemed to be the roughest of the lot. Billy watched as the man banged his empty glass on the counter and demanded another 'bottle by the neck' for himself and his four friends. When he'd finished speaking Billy made his move.

'*Telegraph*? Anybody want a *Telegraph*?'

No one was listening. Not to him, not to each other. Everybody was talking, but no one was listening, each voice rising higher than its fellows as it sought to make itself heard, just the way it was at home. Corks plunked as they were yanked from their bottles by the fat little barman with the black apron. Glasses chinked, 'here's to you', 'good health', and 'bottoms up' and the women laughed coarsely at some vulgar joke told by one of their number. The big man with the ginger curls demanded service at once and threatened to take his custom and that of his four companions elsewhere if his request wasn't immediately attended to. A shiny black mynah bird in a red cage just above Billy's head ordered everyone to 'finish up' because it was closing time. The bird was a good talker but wasn't quite so expert at reading clocks.

Only the draughts-players seemed aloof from it all. Billy's eyes travelled back to the two men sitting unblinking and unmoving. Suddenly, one of the men did move, lifting his right hand and holding it about an eighth of an inch above his red crowner. The man held his hand quite motionless in this position for nearly half a minute as Billy moved forward, excited to see the move and what the effect of it would be.

But there wasn't any move. Billy watched, disappointed, as the man shook his head and lowered his hand back on to the glass-topped table, bringing his other one up to stroke a worried brow. Billy moved closer.

'*Telegraph*, mister? Do you want to buy a Tele?'

The man shook his head and waved the back of his hand without even looking up. 'Go away, son. Go away. I'm in trouble. Big trouble.'

Billy nodded and turned away. Maybe he'd try the big man with the ginger hair. The man was noisy and demonstrative, but in a good-hearted way, a happy drunk. Happy drunks could sometimes be generous drunks, free with their pennies.

Billy tugged at the big man's sleeve. 'Do you want to buy a *Telegraph*, mister?'

The man stopped halfway through a bout of raucous laughter and looked down at Billy. He banged his pint on the counter and suddenly brought his face right down level with Billy so he was staring him straight in the eye.

'Do I want to buy what?' he roared.

Billy drew his head back quickly from the big man's face, not in fear, for drunk men held no terrors for him, but in order to escape the sickly, beery smell of the man's breath.

'A *Telegraph*, mister. Do you want to buy a *Telegraph*?'

The man threw back his head and began to laugh loudly, his face gradually taking on the hue of his red neckerchief, causing Billy to think the man had taken a choking fit. But just as suddenly, he stopped laughing.

'Naw!' he bellowed. 'We don't want no papers. Do we, boys?'

The boys, not one of them under fifty, shook their heads dolefully in perfect agreement with their leader.

'We don't want no papers,' repeated the man as he nipped Billy's cheek with two rough fingers. 'It's a song we want. Don't we, boys? Now, if you were able to sing a song ye might sell a paper or two in here. But if ye can't sing ye won't sell no papers.'

Billy stared hard into the man's eyes, trying to see into his mind. Would the man really buy some papers if he sang a song, or was he just using him to get a laugh?

'Well?' demanded the big man. He wasn't laughing now. His face was deadly serious. 'Well? Can ye sing?'

Billy nodded his head. 'I can sing, mister. What do you want to hear?'

The man grabbed Billy by the scruff of the neck and perched him on top of the bar. 'Anything. Sing anything ye like and we'll all buy a paper. Won't we, boys?'

The boys raised their glasses in confirmation of their leader's declaration of intent and stared expectantly at Billy. Billy set his papers beside him on the bar and nervously cleared his throat.

When Billy began to sing *I'll Take You Home Again Kathleen* he simply could not be heard above the laughter and the shouting and the clinking of bottles. Then the laughter stopped and the shouting stopped, there was no more clinking of bottles or glasses and the plunking of corks from bottles ended. Finally there wasn't a sound to be heard in the entire bar save the clear bell-like sound of an unbroken voice which hit and held every note with perfect ease and clarity.

When Billy finished singing there was a strange silence, a silence you don't often get in pubs, except when they're locked up and bolted for the night. He sat uncomfortably on the bar, feeling with embarrassment every gaze directed at him. He was about to explain he could have sung the song better if he didn't have a sore lip when the whole place erupted in a cacophony of sound: applause, whistles, cheers, demands to 'do another one' and advice that he should be 'on at the Empire'.

Relieved, Billy jumped down from the bar, beaming from ear to ear. He bowed three times as the big docker took out a dirty red handkerchief and blew his nose with great vigour, at the same time taking the opportunity to wipe away whatever it was that was escaping from his eyes. The big man stuck the hankie back in his pocket and tousled Billy's hair in a friendly gesture.

'Son, that was great,' he sniffed. 'Great. I niver heard Kathleen sung like that in all m' days. Niver. Ye hit them notes as true as amber. Ye did, son. True as amber.'

Billy basked modestly amidst the praise being showered upon him from all directions, trying at the same time to figure out what the big man meant by 'true as amber'. He declined the offer of a 'half-un' to do another song but quickly downed the tumbler of brown lemonade set up by the enthusiastic barman. Then he picked his cap up from the floor and stuck it back on his head and looked meaning-fully at the newspapers on the counter.

The big docker laughed and grabbed the papers. He held them away from him as if they were so much dead fish.

'How much are ye lukkin' for these?'

Billy looked up at the man hopefully. 'Ninepence, mister. For the whole lot.'

'Ninepence!' The man laughed derisively. 'I wuddn't give ye tuppence for them.'

Billy's heart sank and then his eyes opened wide in amazement as the big man put his hand into a pocket and pulled out a sixpenny piece and a silver thruppenny bit.

'I wouldn't give ye tuppence for them,' he laughed. 'Not if I wanted to read them. But Pat McCluskey's word is Pat McCluskey's bond. There's yer ninepence and there's yer papers as well. Ye're a brave wee singer and ye might make yer name at it, but I don't think newspaper-sellin' is the game fer you. Ye couldn't give them papers away. Ye couldn't even light the fire with them.'

Billy grinned and took the papers and took the money and thanked the man. Then he bowed one more time to his appreciative audience and promised to come back and sing for them again sometime, finally leaving the pub to another round of applause and cheers and whistles.

The rain had gone completely now and the moon hanging in the cold starry sky reminded him of the silver sixpence in his pocket. He reckoned the sixpence was just about the same size as the moon and every bit as shiny. He took it from his pocket and held it up to the sky between his finger and thumb.

The sixpence was exactly the same size as the moon and blotted it out from the sky. But the light shining from the pub window struck his silver sixpence and made it gleam, a silvery gleam, just like the moon.

Billy shoved the newspapers into a bin at the side of the pub. Then he stuck his hands into the warmth of his trouser pockets and winked up at the moon, smiling.

Tomorrow would be a great day.

Saturday morning was bright and clear, but the red mackerel sky moving slowly across the city from the direction of the shipyard gantries did nothing to take the nip out of the air. But it was early yet.

Billy stood at the corner of Smithfield Square and waited for O'Hara's bread cart to pass. The horse trotted easily, even with its full load, and the silver of its harness gleamed brightly in the cold morning sun. The amalgamated smells of horse-sweat and leather and freshly-baked bread and horse-manure hung in the air and Billy was still trying to relate each smell to its source when a whir of wings above him made him look up.

A flock of pigeons swooped low over the square on their way to the grain mills at the edge of the docks. There was always plenty of spillage at the feed mills; corn, oats, wheat and barley. No need for a pigeon to go hungry in Belfast.

Billy watched the birds arc away across the square and he wondered how they all knew to change direction at the same time and how they could do it so quickly without crashing into each other.

Pigeons were clever. Frankie M'Conkey, who was one class in front of him at school, said you could take a pigeon to Bangor in a box and let it go and it would fly right back to where it came from, even in the dark. Billy didn't believe him, but Frankie said it was true, and he didn't think Frankie told lies. Maybe there'd be something about pigeons in *The Book of One Thousand Beautiful Things*, but he didn't mind if there wasn't. There were hundreds of other things he wanted to read and look at in the book. He could hardly wait to get his hands on it.

Billy lifted a hand and shaded his eyes against the red glare of the sun and watched the pigeons disappear over Chapel Lane. Then he stepped off the footpath and made his way into the market. In a few minutes the book would be his, his very own, and he could read it from cover to cover, over and over again as many times as he liked. And he could print his name on the very first page and then everyone would know that this was Billy McCullough's book.

The old man with the grinding wheel was labouring to set up his contraption at the Gresham Street end of the market as Billy came in. Francie's pet rabbits, nearly all white with black ears and twitching pink noses, were lined up in cages along the front of his shop. The goldfish swam round and round in their tiny bowls set high up on the rabbit cages, well out of reach of tiny careless hands.

Billy stuck his tongue out at the brilliantly-coloured parrot above the doorway and laughed as it cursed him with a flurry of feathers and ruffling of wings. Then, triumphantly, he turned in to Berni's Smithfield Bookshop.

The task of threading a path through the book-strewn floor was no easier than it had been on his last visit, but he managed it without mishap. He gazed over the pile of old books and papers, which seemed even higher than they were before, but by standing on tiptoe he could just about see the little man behind the counter. There was a note of quiet pride in Billy's voice as he spoke.

'I got it, mister. I got the money. For the book.'

Berni looked up, rubbing the sleep from his eyes. He'd been at a wake the night before and the crack had been good, and the whiskey even better. But now he was feeling the worse for it and wondering if a hair of the dog that bit

240

him might not set him up for the day. Now his little racing eyes squinted in a puzzled frown.

'What book was that, son?'

Billy smiled, pleased the man was asking him to actually say the name of the book out loud.

'*The Book of One Thousand Beautiful Things*. The blue one. With Ye Banks and Braes O' Bonny Doon in it.

Berni pulled the pencil-stub from behind his ear and marked his Zane Grey. He replaced the pencil and got to his feet.

'Oh. That book. A fella was in here yesterday. A real toff. Silk scarf and everything. Offered me one and thruppence for it. Said he'd been lookin' for it for years.

The smile left Billy's face, suddenly and totally. What did the man say? Did he say he'd sold *The Book of One Thousand Beautiful Things*? His book? To somebody else?

Billy tried to speak, but the words wouldn't come out. He felt his lower lip trembling and he was afraid he was going to cry. He hadn't cried when the big lad in Corn Market had thumped him in the mouth and split it open and thrown his papers into the gutter. He hadn't cried then, but he was afraid he was going to cry now.

He stared helplessly at the man, trying to make sense of what he'd just heard. But it didn't make any sense and all he wanted to do was run, run as fast as he could from Berni's Smithfield Bookshop, run and never, ever come back again. It didn't matter now that he would never own *The Book of One Thousand Beautiful Things*. His da' was right. He had ideas above his station and the book would never be his, and no other book would ever be his because he never wanted to see another book as long as he lived. And he'd never trust anybody again.

Billy held out a shaking palm to reveal the sixpence and

the silver thruppenny bit in a final gesture of proof that he'd kept his part of the bargain.

'But I got the money, mister. I gathered refuse and broke sticks and sold papers. I got the money.'

Then his head went down and the tears brimmed over and he trudged away so the man wouldn't see. He was hurt and he was confused, and as he picked his way through the books to the door he determined that no one would ever hurt him again. He ignored Berni's pleas to come back and was almost out the door when he felt the touch at his elbow and the arm around his shoulder. He stiffened and pulled away from whatever grain of comfort the man was trying to offer. But Berni held on to his shoulder.

'Listen, son. Away over to that box underneath the counter and take a look inside.' Berni's voice was low and apologetic but still Billy didn't move. Berni squeezed his arm gently. 'Go on, son. Go over and look in the box.'

Billy wiped his sleeve across his face. Then he turned slowly and allowed himself to be led back to the counter. Berni pointed to the box.

'Go on, son. That box there. Put your hand in.'

Billy knelt down and reached into the box. His hand closed on something – a book – and when he pulled it out he knew, he just knew, without even opening it, that it was *The Book of One Thousand Beautiful Things*. But he did open it, just to be sure – and yes – they were all there, the poems, the paintings, the verses from the Bible and the wise sayings of famous men who lived long, long ago. Now the tears were gone, the sadness and sorrow of a moment ago replaced with joy and happiness and a great big smile as Billy scrambled to his feet, his big, blue eyes shining.

'You did keep it for me, mister! You did! You kept it for me,' he shouted excitedly. Then a puzzled look came across

242

his face. 'But you told me you sold it, mister. Why did you tell me you sold it?'

Berni grinned, glad he hadn't. Mind you, the offer had been tempting enough, and he almost had sold it. He'd never expected to see the kid again. But it was worth dropping the tanner just to see the youngster's face.

'I didn't say I'd sold it. I said somebody offered me one and thruppence for it. But I didn't say I'd sold it. Did you think I'd sell it, after you and me had made a deal on it?'

Billy blushed and handed Berni the coins, the sixpence and the silver thruppenny bit, glad to be rid of them so he could use both hands to skim through the book once more. This time he stopped at a picture of The Angelus. He stared at the picture intently, wondering what story lay behind these two poor people standing in a field with their heads bowed. Were they praying?

He looked up again at Berni.

'Aw, thanks, mister. Thanks a million for keepin' it for me. When I'm rich I'll buy all my books from you. I will, mister. Honest.' He paused for a moment and looked at Berni seriously. 'Maybe someday I'll write books of my own and you could sell them in your shop. That would be good, mister. Wouldn't it?'

Berni laughed. 'That would be great, son. That would be really great.' He pulled the butt from his ear and waved goodbye as Billy headed for the door. 'Oh. By the way. I found out what a brae is.'

Billy turned, eyes shining and mouth half open in expectation. 'What is it, mister? What's a brae?'

'I'm not tellin' you,' chortled Berni. 'But come back next week and I'll sell you a dictionary. Then you'll know the meanin' of every word in the English language.'

Billy took two steps forward. 'How much, mister? How much for the dictionary?'

Berni stopped fumbling for a match and smiled. 'For you? A penny. And by the way, my friends call me Berni.'

Billy waved *The Book of One Thousand Beautiful Things* above his head and grinned. 'Keep it for me, Berni. I'll be back. When I get the money. I will. Honest. And by the way, my friends call me Billy.'

Berni laughed and waved a final goodbye. The kid was a dreamer. He probably couldn't even read the book he had just bought and now he was talking about writing books of his own. The world was a hard place for dreamers. He knew. He'd been a dreamer once, just like the kid, but that was long ago and far away, before the world had moulded him to its own pattern. He didn't dream any more. But maybe the kid would have more luck than he had. He hoped so.

Berni Maguire, proprietor of Berni's Smithfield Bookshop, lit his Woodbine and settled down with the Zane Grey. But not before he'd spent a full half-hour rummaging through every single bookshelf in his little shop, searching until he found the biggest and best dictionary he had in stock.

Berni opened the flyleaf and pulled the pencil stub from behind his ear. He wasn't much of a writer, but slowly, and with great deliberation, he printed on the blank pages: TO MY FRIEND BILLY FROM HIS FRIEND BERNI.

Then, ever so carefully, he laid the book in the box underneath the counter. As his friend had said, he'd be coming back for that.

UNCLE JIM

Richard Newton

Richard Newton was born and still lives in Poole, Dorset. After a varied career as a singer in restaurants and pubs, a lorry-driver and a representative in the office furniture business, he joined Radio Victory in Portsmouth as a copywriter and commercial producer.

He has won a number of advertising awards and now works as a freelance copywriter on press, radio and television campaigns for a wide range of clients. Richard Newton is married with two young daughters.

UNCLE JIM

'You called him Uncle Jim. Was he really your uncle?'
  'No. He was my friend Jonathan's uncle.'

We had so many uncles and aunts in those days. There were the real family ones of course, then there were the friends of our parents and the next-door neighbours who all insisted on being called uncle this or aunty that. They seemed to think it granted them a special place in our affections. We didn't mind, especially if the result was a bar of chocolate or some pocket-money.

The first time I met Uncle Jim I had him marked down as a friend of the family. It was at Jonathan's house on a rainy Saturday afternoon. I'd gone round there because it's more fun being bored in someone else's house than in your own. Jonathan was in the lounge and Uncle Jim was making paper aeroplanes. Dozens of them. That's why I thought he was a family friend, not a relative. Real uncles never tried that hard.

But actually I think he just liked making paper planes. He was really good at it too. He made them with tails and wings, and ailerons that really worked.

I liked Jonathan's house. It had polished parquet floors, a fishpond and two pianos. Apparently his parents played duets, but I never heard them. Usually we played 'Chopsticks' until his father came out of his study and told us to shut up. You'd think a vicar would have more patience.

But today the pianos were landing strips. You had to stand behind the sofa and make your plane land as near to the end of the piano lid as possible. I had the modern piano by the window, Jonathan had the big old upright on the opposite wall. His had a much wider top and the surface wasn't so slippery. So he had to stand two feet further back to make it fair. Uncle Jim stood between the pianos as judge. That meant he got to throw the planes back so he had twice as many throws as us. There usually seems to be an ulterior motive where grown-ups are concerned.

The next day I asked Jonathan about Uncle Jim. He said he was actually a cousin of his mother or something like that and he lived a few streets away. I wondered why I hadn't met him before but Jonathan was a bit vague on the subject. Said he'd been out of the area for a while.

'When did you next see him?'
   'I can't remember, it was a long time ago.'
   'Well, was it a few days or a few weeks?'
   'About a fortnight I think.'

We lived in a small market town surrounded by open countryside. Jonathan and I lived a few doors from each other on the outskirts of the town. At the end of our back gardens were the playing fields of the girls' Grammar School. Beyond was open countryside with the Downs rising in the distance.

On the rare occasions that it snowed, the steep slopes of the Downs became the Cresta Run and our heavy wooden toboggans reached world-record-breaking speeds. In the summer the Downs were Roman Camps or Wild West Canyons or Cities Under Siege. In heavy August nights lightning would flicker over the ridge-tops. According to parental myth the thunder-claps were caused by the ancient

Britons throwing breeze-blocks at each other. We didn't believe that, of course. We knew it was the sound of Drake's cannons defeating the Armada.

The school summer holidays had just started and I was already at a loose end. I knew that if I hung around the house my mother would give me some jobs to do, so I went round to see if Jonathan was doing anything interesting. A motor-bike was standing in the drive. It was a BSA Bantam which had seen better days. The seat was held together with strips of black insulating tape and the mud-guards were scratched and dented.

Jonathan was in the kitchen. As I walked in I saw Uncle Jim in the larder, reaching for the biscuit tin. He said hello and offered me a biscuit. He had the knack of treating you as an equal. Not as a grown-up and not as a child. Just as . . . well, a friend I suppose.

The motor-bike was his, of course. We went outside to admire it. The three of us stood around the machine nodding wisely. Jonathan and me were desperately hoping he would take us for a ride but we wouldn't have dreamed of asking. He knew what we wanted but he waited just long enough to get us hopping from foot to foot before suggesting that we might like a trip up to the Downs. The problem of transporting three people on one bike was solved by a relay system. He would take Jonathan first, leave him there, and come back for me. The journey would only take about five minutes. We debated whether to tell anyone where we were going, but Jonathan's mother had gone to the shops and mine wasn't expecting me back until lunch-time. Anyway, Uncle Jim was a grown-up so it must be all right.

He lifted the bike off its stand and kick-started it. After four attempts it roared into life and Jonathan climbed on to the pillion seat. There were no laws about crash-helmets in those days. Uncle Jim wore a pair of goggles and a white silk scarf that streamed out behind him. He looked like Biggles.

I could still hear the bike after it had disappeared from view and after a short while I heard it coming back again. As it swung into the drive I felt a momentary panic. I had never ridden on a motor-cycle before. But it was too late to chicken out. I clambered up behind Uncle Jim and held on tight. The roar of the machine beneath me was deafening. I hadn't expected such a rush of wind against my face. Although we were only travelling about thirty miles per hour it made my eyes water. Talking was imposs-ible. When the bike leaned into the corners I instinctively leaned the other way to try to keep it upright. It must have made it very difficult to control. After a minute or two though I began to relax and go with the bike.

When I got off my legs were trembling and my ears were buzzing. But I wouldn't have missed it for the world. We sat on the grassy slope and talked about this and that. Jonathan told Uncle Jim about some of the games we played, and asked if he'd like to join in. He said he'd be honoured to any other day, but on this occasion he had one or two pressing matters to attend to and would soon have to be getting us home. He had a strange way of talking. A bit like a character in an adventure book.

On the return journey he dropped me off first, then went back for Jonathan. By this time Jonathan's mother had come back and she asked me where we had been. When I told her she didn't seem too pleased. I heard later that Uncle Jim had been hauled over the coals for not letting anyone know where we were.

'Did you tell your parents about Uncle Jim?

'Yes, of course.'

'And did they mind you seeing him?'

'Why should they?'

We didn't see Uncle Jim for about a week. The weather had turned hot and Jonathan's mother drove us down to the beach a couple of times. Then I went away with my family for a few days to visit a clutch of elderly relatives.

The morning after we got back I went round to Jonathan's to see if he wanted to go swimming. The temperature was up in the eighties and the school swimming pool was open. Some of the teachers and parents had volunteered to supervise daily sessions. The thought of walking through the school gates during the summer holiday didn't really appeal, but it was the only pool in town.

We collected towels and trunks and were about to head off to the school when a car pulled up beside us. It was Uncle Jim. His motor-bike was off the road with a puncture, so he'd borrowed his mother's old Riley. It was a lovely car – all leather and walnut with blinds you could pull down on the back window. He said he was off to the beach and would we care to join him. Of course, we told him we would and we jumped in.

I thought I'd better let my parents know where I was going so I asked him to stop outside my house while I ran in to tell my mother. She hadn't been too pleased when she'd heard about the motor-bike trip, but when I told her Uncle Jim had a car this time, she said she supposed it would be all right. She came out to the road and asked Uncle Jim if he was sure I wasn't going to be in the way. He told her it would be a pleasure to have my company and promised to have me back by two o'clock at the latest.

The nearest beach was about eight miles away at Frome Bay. We drove along the promenade and could hardly see the sand for people. It was absolutely heaving with holidaymakers. Uncle Jim said he couldn't decide if they were sardines or lemmings, but whatever they were he didn't want to be in the same zoo. We agreed of course, although secretly we thought the crowded sands looked rather exciting, and we weren't at all sure what lemmings were anyway.

Then he said he knew a little cove where hardly anyone went because it was a long walk down and when you got there it was rocky, not sandy. It was only a couple of miles away so we said OK and off we went.

We drove up a narrow lane that climbed out of the town and meandered along the line of the cliffs. It was a different world up there. We stopped at a lay-by at the top of the cliff path and there wasn't a soul in sight. Skylarks sang high above us and in the distance a dog was barking in a farmyard. A gentle breeze blew over the cliff-top, but as we trudged down the path we felt the full force of the sun. It was a long trek to the beach and by the time we got there we were very hot and sweaty.

There were narrow patches of sand between the large limestone rocks. It was quite safe to swim there on a calm day, but I knew my parents would never have let me go in. Still – Uncle Jim was old enough to know what he was doing and if he said it was all right that was good enough for us. We started to undress and put on our trunks. He already had his on under his trousers so he was in the water before us. He waded out and swam away from the shore using a smooth, powerful breaststroke. Jonathan and me weren't especially good swimmers and we were quite content to splash around by the rocks, sticking our heads under the water to see if we could see any fish. Jonathan said he saw a big striped wrasse disappear into some weed, but I didn't believe him. His mother once told me he had an over-vivid imagination. I think she was right.

We were standing side by side, bending over with our heads under water when Jonathan suddenly pitched forward and came up spluttering and yelling. I wondered what on earth had happened. I turned round in fright – and saw Uncle Jim standing just behind us, grinning. We hadn't noticed him swimming back and he'd managed to creep up, grab Jonathan's ankle and send him sprawling into the water. For a few seconds Jonathan was furious, especially when I started laughing too. Then he made a sudden dive for Uncle Jim's legs to try to trip him up. I joined in but he was too strong for us. After a few minutes of shouting and splashing we gave up and walked up the beach to where we had left our clothes. We spread out our towels and lay down in the sun to dry. It was very hot and I could feel my shoulders beginning to burn. Luckily Uncle Jim had some suntan cream. He had fair hair and pale skin, so I suppose he had to be careful in the sun too. It's funny – you don't think of grown-ups getting sun-burned. It's the sort of thing that happens to us kids. Like measles and verrucas.

Soon it was time to go, and we got changed out of our swimming gear. Jonathan and Uncle Jim just stripped off and slipped into underpants and trousers. I had always been embarrassed about taking my clothes off in front of other people. School showers were torture. I wouldn't even let my mother see me in the bath. So I went through the contortions of holding a towel round my waist as I took off my trunks. The other two had already begun to climb the path by the time I was ready, and I had to rush to catch up.

The scramble to the top of the cliffs seemed endless. Sweat was trickling into my eyes, making them sting, and my legs felt like lead. When at last we reached the car, we couldn't sit on the seats because they were burning hot from the sun. We pulled down the blinds at the back, opened all the doors and windows and spread our towels over the baking leather upholstery. When at last we got in and set off it was already twenty to two and home was a good ten miles away.

I told Uncle Jim I was worried about the time and he said I should just sit back and hold on tight. He put his foot down and we tore along the country lanes at what seemed like a hundred miles an hour. Clouds of dust billowed up and through the windows the hedges were just a blur. My father was a very sedate driver and Jonathan's never exceeded a cautious vicarly pace, so our headlong dash probably seemed faster than it really was. Still, I couldn't help thinking that Uncle Jim was the sort of driver my father always swore at.

We pulled up outside my house at about one minute past two. My parents had nearly finished their lunch and my father didn't seem too pleased when I came in. He asked me which beach we had been to. I said Frome Bay. I don't know why I lied.

'Now I want you to think very carefully before you answer this next question. Did you think there was anything . . . strange about Uncle Jim?'

'Not strange – just different.'

There really is no pleasing parents. When you're in the house they moan about you always being under their feet. When you're out of the house they moan because you're never around when they want you. If you chat to them they tell you to stop asking so many questions, for goodness sake. If you keep quiet you're being moody.

Uncle Jim wasn't like that. He was much wiser than most adults. He could tell a companionable silence from a sulk. He knew that you had to make a lot of noise when you were guarding the fort against a band of desperate savages, and he knew there was no point in buying a cone unless you got the ice-cream man to stick a chocolate flake in the top. He was more like one of us than one of them.

And yet he *was* one of them, really. He rode a motor-bike. He drove a car. He wore long trousers. He had money. He was bigger and older than us. That's what made him such fun to be with. We sometimes wondered why he spent so much time with two ten-year-old school boys. But we never asked. I suppose we were afraid he might stop.

I'm sure my parents thought he was a bit odd. I overheard them in the kitchen once. It must have been Uncle Jim they were talking about, because they were saying how surprising it was that his mother lent him her car when you see the way he rides that motor-bike. Then my mother said he was a bit of a sad case and he hadn't been the same since he lost his father – and what a dreadful way to die. No wonder they'd had to send him to Coldharbour. Still, he's better now. My father said he wasn't so sure and laughed. I think that was one of his little jokes. He could be very sarcastic at times.

Now every kid in the area knows that Coldharbour is the loony-bin over at Charport. When you go mad, men in white coats come in the middle of the night and take you away in a little yellow van. Then you are padlocked in a strait-jacket and thrown into a padded cell for years and years. Obviously my parents had got their facts wrong because Uncle Jim wasn't a lunatic. He didn't moan and groan and foam at the mouth. He didn't have mad, staring eyes. And anyway, everybody says that once they've got you in Coldharbour they never let you out.

Still, I thought I'd better check. So the next time I saw him I asked him if he'd ever worn a strait-jacket. He just laughed and said no – but he'd once had a windcheater that was a bit on the tight side. Then I asked him if he had ever been mad. He said yes, he'd been mad as hell when his motor-bike packed in. We spent the rest of the afternoon playing lunatics and wardens.

'What other games did you play?'
  'All sorts.'
  'Tell me about them.'
  'They were only kids' games, nothing important.'
  'Tell me anyway.'

One evening he drove us up to the Downs. He'd seen us playing Secret Agents in Jonathan's garden as he drove by and had stopped to watch. I was the top British agent desperately sending a last vital message from my hideaway under the laurel hedge, while Jonathan as the dastardly double double-agent was hot on my trail with his pack of ferocious Dobermans. Uncle Jim said that whilst he admired our imaginative use of the available terrain, he thought the game could be improved by a change of location to a place he knew on the top of the Downs.

Of course we leapt at the chance. Uncle Jim said he'd pick us up as soon as he'd been home to collect a couple of extra props.

It only takes five minutes to reach the edge of the Downs. In ten minutes you're up amongst the hills where sheep graze the steep slopes. In fifteen minutes you feel as though you're miles from anywhere. The ridges and dips just swallow you up. The lane we drove along soon became a track and finally petered out at the entrance to an old limestone quarry. A rusty iron gate blocked our path. Wired to the middle of the gate was a faded wooden sign. The letters had almost disappeared, but the words 'KEEP OUT – DANGER' were still visible. The gate was padlocked and topped with barbed wire.

Uncle Jim got out and walked over to the gate. He fiddled with the padlock for a couple of seconds and suddenly it was open. We asked him how he'd done it, but he said he would only divulge his name and serial number.

He drove through the gate and shut it again. Then he put the car behind an old shed so that it couldn't be seen from the track. Jonathan and I got out and looked around in amazement. Sheer walls of limestone towered over us. The evening sun didn't reach the quarry floor so although the rocks were bathed in yellow light fifty feet above our heads, we were standing in deepening gloom. The walls were pitted with narrow caves and the ground was strewn with enormous boulders.

But what was most remarkable about the place was the fact that we hadn't known it was there! We'd lived just a few miles away all our lives, yet we had never seen it. We'd never even heard of it. Uncle Jim said he'd come across it one day when he was walking the Downs with his father. It hadn't been worked for over thirty years.

You couldn't imagine a more perfect spot for Secret Agents, or Cops and Robbers, or Cowboys and Indians. Uncle Jim reckoned we only had about half an hour before the light got too bad so we'd better hurry up and get started. Jonathan and I were just about to dash off when we remembered about the extra props Uncle Jim had gone to collect. We asked him where they were and he went round to the boot of the car. As he opened it we could see a polished wooden case like a long, flat, cutlery canteen. He lifted it out and placed it on a flat-topped boulder. Slowly, he raised the lid. The inside was lined with green satin. Nestling in the shiny fabric were two black revolvers with dark wooden handles.

He said they'd belonged to his father and that they were quite safe because they weren't loaded. He handed us one each. They were very heavy and the metal felt smooth and cold.

I think it was Uncle Jim who suggested we played French Resistance Fighters in the Second World War. The Gestapo held one of our men in a cave at the far end of the quarry. They were torturing him in an unbelievably horrifying manner and he was bound to divulge the hiding place of the British Airmen unless we managed to force our way into the cave and kill him before he spilled the beans. Or spilled the haricots, as Uncle Jim said. I think it was meant to be a joke.

He volunteered to play our captured compatriot and disappeared into the cave. He began to scream as though in unbearable agony. Jonathan and I fought our way bravely up the entire length of the quarry floor. We dived behind boulders as bullets zipped and ricocheted all around us. We carefully counted the number of bullets we had fired until we each had only one left. Finally we managed to crawl to the very entrance of the cave and peered in. Uncle Jim was sitting cross-legged with his back to the wall. It was obvious to us that he could stand the pain no more and was on the point of giving the Airmen away. So we both shot him. I shot him cleanly through the head, Jonathan shot him through the heart. It was all most satisfactory.

'Did you tell anyone about the guns?'
'No.'
'Why not?'
'Because it was our secret.'
'Was there any ammunition for them?'
'I can't tell you.'
'I'm afraid you have to tell me.'

The next day was hot and oppressive. The noise of distant thunder rumbled over the Downs, and occasional big spots of rain made dark grey splodges on the pavements. After breakfast I hurried out before my mother noticed it was raining, but it had stopped by the time I reached the Gardens, where I had arranged to meet Jonathan.

The Municipal Gardens were a favourite haunt of ours. They were near the centre of town, between the brewery and the hospital. They weren't very big, but there was a bandstand, a clock tower, tennis courts, a bowling-green, a paddling pool, swings and dozens of large rhododendron bushes. It was to these bushes that we made our way, or rather to one particular bush. It was at the back of a wide flower-bed which had roses in the middle and neat rows of French marigolds at the front. Behind the bush was a tall brick wall which separated the Municipal Gardens from the grounds of the hospital. Beneath the bush was our secret den. We made sure the Park Keeper wasn't around, then stepped over the marigolds, squeezed between the roses and crept under the dense, leafy branches of the rhododendron.

It was dry under the bush and we could see almost all the Gardens without anyone being able to see us. At the brewery end we saw the Park Keeper telling a bunch of older boys to get off the swings. On the bowling-green a few old dodderers were playing a sedate game on the manicured grass. They were wearing white trousers and panamas and they kept glancing up at the heavy grey clouds, ready to abandon their game at any moment.

Jonathan first of all asked me if I had told anyone about the guns. I said of course not and he said he hadn't either. I asked him if he'd ever seen them before, and he said that Uncle Jim's father brought them back from the war and they used to be locked up in a trophy cupboard in the sitting room. He'd shown them to Jonathan when he was little, but he hadn't let him touch them. I asked him if they were really real and he said Uncle Jim's father had shot three German soldiers with one of them when he was in the desert. The other one had belonged to his close friend who had died a hero when the regiment was surrounded by an entire Panzer Division. I thought Jonathan's vivid imagination was working overtime, but you never could be sure.

Then he asked me what my parents thought of Uncle Jim. I told him what I had overheard, and he told me that his mother and father thought Uncle Jim was a bit of an oddball too. In fact, he got the impression that they weren't really very keen on us spending so much time with him, but as he was family they didn't put a stop to it. Considering he was an uncle this all seemed very strange to us. But we decided to keep quiet about any future outings. I suppose we were afraid we would be prevented from seeing him at all.

So the next time he suggested a trip to the quarry we didn't tell anyone. It was a few mornings later and he said we'd be back in plenty of time for lunch. When we reached the quarry gate he again opened the padlock in a couple of seconds and put it back in place when we were through. He hid the car behind the shed and went round to the boot. This time he didn't have the two guns. He had an air rifle. It was old, but it was very well looked-after. The wooden stock was polished to a deep shine and the barrel gleamed.

He said he'd had it ever since he was a boy, and if we liked he'd show us how to use it. Of course, we were very excited. He told us that we would have to do exactly as he said, because the lead pellets that the rifle fired could kill if they accidentally hit someone. It only took one pellet at a time and he insisted on loading it himself.

An old tin can set on a boulder fifty feet away served as a target. Uncle Jim showed us how to hold the gun and line

260

up the notch sight at the end of the barrel with the 'V' sight near the butt. He said you had to gently squeeze the trigger and hold your breath. The first time I tried it I was surprised how difficult it was to keep the barrel from swaying around. When I'd missed a few times, he suggested I rest the rifle on a rock to steady it. I did, and the next time I fired the tin can span off the boulder with a satisfying clang.

Jonathan was a much better shot than me and Uncle Jim was better than both of us. He could hit it nearly every time. After about an hour we'd run out of pellets and it was time to head back home. We told 'Knock, Knock' jokes all the way back and we were roaring with laughter as we drew up outside Jonathan's house. But we soon stopped when we noticed his mother standing at the front door. She did not look at all amused. She demanded to know where we'd been, and why we hadn't told her we were going. Uncle Jim tried to calm her down, but she just said that she was surprised at him. No one said anything about the quarry. We just said we'd been for a ride on the Downs.

I slipped off home as soon as I could, only to find that Jonathan's mother had told my mother and she was just as annoyed. As usual in these sort of circumstances I decided to say as little as possible and let the storm blow over. I thought that the real trouble would begin when my father got home. In fact, he didn't go off the deep end at all. He just said it wasn't fair to make my mother worry like that. Then he asked me exactly where I had been and what I had been doing. In the end I told him about the quarry but not about the air rifle.

'Was it the row with your parents that made you want to go on that final trip to the quarry?'

'It wasn't a row. They just told me never to go out again without letting them know where I was going.'

'But you did, didn't you?'

'No. I told them I was going to play with Jonathan – and I was.'

It was nearly the end of August, and the weather had been close and thundery for days without actually doing anything dramatic. Everyone said we needed a good storm to clear the air, but secretly nobody really wanted it to happen, because it would mean the end of the long, hot, summer. The heat made us listless and argumentative. Jonathan and I had steered clear of each other for a couple of days because there was nothing we really felt like doing, and if the truth were known, we were getting a bit fed up with each other's company.

I temporarily teamed up with the Tupper Twins in Lagland Road. They had a big tent in their garden and a sort of tennis game with the ball hung from elastic between two poles. But it was too hot to stay in the tent and they were much better than me at tennis, so I decided to mooch round to Jonathan's house in case I was missing anything.

He said he'd been having a great time with Barry Andrew's gang on Torbury Common. I wondered why he was hanging around the house in the middle of the afternoon if he was having such a wonderful time. I didn't say anything, though.

We were leaning against the garden wall talking about nothing in particular when Uncle Jim drove up. He said that by his calculations the air temperature must be at least a degree lower up on the Downs, and in the quarry it would be positively cool. He suggested we went up there to put his theory to the test. Jonathan and I looked at each other. We knew we should ask permission. We also knew that we probably wouldn't be allowed to go. But how could we tell Uncle Jim that we couldn't go with him because our parents thought he was mad? Anyway – as long as we were back for tea, who would know? Without further hesitation we piled into the back of the car.

This time when we got to the quarry gate Uncle Jim showed us the secret of opening the padlock. It was very simple really. The padlock wasn't locked at all. It had just been pushed together to look as though it was. He said he'd discovered it months ago when he'd been out walking. He thought the people who owned the quarry either hadn't noticed it was broken or they couldn't be bothered to replace it. After all, most people when they see a closed padlock assume it's locked and don't even check.

He drove the car into the shade behind the shed and we all got out. It was definitely cooler here than in the town. We felt much more energetic and started to discuss what game to play. Uncle Jim had brought the two hand-guns, the air rifle and some more pellets so the possibilities were endless. In the end Jonathan and I decided to have half an hour's target practice, then a quick session of Secret Agents.

It wasn't until we'd nearly used up the pellets that we noticed how dark it had become. A huge thunder-cloud hovered directly overhead, throwing the quarry into a deep gloom. An unnatural silence surrounded us. Not a bird sang. Not a fly buzzed. The air was still and heavy. I could feel the hairs on the back of my neck prickle.

Uncle Jim looked up anxiously at the black sky framed by the limestone cliffs. Suddenly a blinding flash of lightning crackled out of the very centre of the cloud and struck an old scrub oak that clung to the rim of the quarry. Immediately the most tremendous noise I have ever heard exploded inside the quarry. You could feel it as much as hear it. The ground shook and the cliffs seemed to vibrate. The oak tree burst into flames. Jonathan screamed. I covered my ears with my hands, and Uncle Jim grabbed hold of us both and pushed us into a narrow cave a few yards away. We cowered against the back wall and hid our heads against him. He put his arms round us and told us not to worry. But I could hear his voice trembling and feel his heart pounding.

Another flash of lightning lit up the cave and half a second later a crack of thunder shook the walls and floor. A third flash followed very quickly, and then with a rush and a roar the rain started. It was as if a river had suddenly started pouring over the top of the cliffs. Within seconds the floor of the quarry was inches deep. Luckily the ground had been sloped to provide drainage and the water poured out of the gate and down the lane, sweeping stones, mud and twigs before it.

The storm raged over our heads for what seemed like hours. At last it gradually rolled away, and the gaps between the lightning and the thunder increased with each strike. Uncle Jim got us to count the seconds to see how far away the lightning was. Every five seconds between the flash and the crash was one mile. We shouted to make ourselves heard above the din until the thunder became a distant rumble and the rain stopped as suddenly as it had begun.

We went to the entrance of the cave and peered out. The quarry floor had been scrubbed clean by the torrent of water. The hut, which had been in the path of the flood, had been turned round through ninety degrees. It now leaned against the quarry wall and its roof didn't seem to fit any more. Miraculously, Uncle Jim's car appeared to have escaped unscathed. He walked all round it and cleared away a few small boulders that had come to rest against the wheels. Without waiting to be asked Jonathan and I got in. We'd had enough of the quarry for one day.

Uncle Jim put the key in the ignition and turned it. Nothing happened. He tried again. No luck. After a few more goes he said that maybe it had got thoroughly soaked, and we'd have to leave the bonnet open for a while to give it a chance to dry out. Twenty minutes later he tried again. Still it wouldn't start.

'Do you think he really tried to start the car?'
  'Of course he did.'
  'Are you sure he wasn't just pretending?'
  'Why should he? He was worried sick about what our mothers would say if he didn't bring us back in time.'

By now we were getting very anxious. It was already nearly eight o'clock and daylight was fading. Uncle Jim dried parts of the engine with his handkerchief, but I don't think he really knew what he was doing. He kept trying to start the car and the battery got flatter and flatter, until it wouldn't turn the engine over at all. To make matters worse it started to rain again.

Uncle Jim said it was time we held a council of war. He said we had to look at the situation coolly and logically. First of all, the facts. Well, that was easy. The fact was we were stuck in a quarry, miles from anywhere, with a car that wouldn't work and parents going mad with worry because they didn't know where we were. Then Uncle Jim said we had to look at the options. They seemed to be fairly limited. We either tried to walk home through the rain and dark or we stayed put for the night and set out as soon as it was light. We all decided to stay.

No one felt the slightest bit tired and as the rain stopped again we began to play another game. This time it was Desert Rats. We were a crack corps of special commandos pinned down in the dunes by Rommel's Panzer Divisions. We had stolen the Germans' code book, and if we could only hold out until the Lancaster bomber carrying Royal

Marine parachute troops arrived, we could give the book to British Intelligence and change the course of the war.

Maybe it was because our real life predicament was similar to some of our games, or maybe it was the atmosphere of the place, or the feel of the guns in our hands — but before long we began to believe we really *were* commandos, not just pretending. The dark, deserted quarry became a steep-sided wadi. The thunder rumbling in the distance was the enemy artillery, and as darkness fell and the moon came out we expected at any moment to see Rommel's troops appear at the top of the cliffs, silhouetted against the sky.

Uncle Jim took the air rifle and went on a recce to the far end of the quarry. We could see the moonlight glinting on the barrel of the gun. It was quiet now, the thunder had grumbled away to the west. We strained our ears for the sounds of the enemy. Was that a tank engine? Were those the muffled curses of German soldiers losing their footing in the darkness? Could those lights in the sky be the plane filled with Marines?

For a while we lost sight of Uncle Jim. We could hear a scrabbling sound and the noise of stones being dislodged. Then we saw him again. He had climbed up a series of ledges on the end wall of the quarry until he was almost at the top. He was obviously going to try to see exactly where the enemy was. We stared at him in admiration. At that point the quarry face was about sixty feet tall, and he cut a dashing figure as he climbed up the last few inches and stood on the edge of the sheer cliff, his air rifle slung over his shoulder.

He crouched down and surveyed the scene. Jonathan and I listened again, and this time we believed we really could hear tanks in the lane. We crawled behind a boulder with our guns at the ready. The lights in the sky grew nearer, and there was the sound of an aeroplane engine. But was it British or German? Uncle Jim had heard it too and he stood up to get a better look. It didn't really sound like a Lancaster bomber, in fact as it got nearer it didn't sound like a World War II plane at all. Uncle Jim was taking no chances. In case it was the enemy he raised his rifle and aimed it at the approaching lights.

Suddenly a powerful searchlight beam stabbed out from beneath the machine. It caught Uncle Jim with the rifle at his shoulder. The blinding light jerked us back to reality, and we realized it was a helicopter. At the same time the gate across the lane opened and two police cars roared in and screeched to a halt. The doors were flung open but Jonathan and I hardly noticed. We were watching in horror as the searchlight showed a figure stumbling on the edge of the cliff. For a moment his arms flayed the air and the rifle flew out of his hands in a graceful arc. It landed on the quarry floor a full three seconds before Uncle Jim. It seemed like three minutes. I thought that only people in films fell in slow motion.

He didn't scream as he fell and his body hardly made a sound as it hit the ground. I felt my legs buckle, and there was a throbbing in my ears and a blackness that broke over me like a wave.

'Would you like to sit down?'
'No. I just want to go home.'
'It won't be long now. The inquest is nearly over.'

It was my father who thought of searching the old quarry after the police had discovered the empty gun cabinet at Uncle Jim's house. The police inspector knew all about the quarry. He'd been a sergeant ten years before when the body of Uncle Jim's father had been discovered there. He'd apparently commited suicide shortly after the newspaper articles had appeared accusing him of deserting his men during the North African Campaign.

I'm going to be a newspaper reporter when I get older. They enjoy make-believe as much as Jonathan and me. They made the quarry incident sound more like one of our games than an account of what really happened. There was all sorts of stuff about a desperate lunatic armed with an assortment of revolvers and high-powered rifles, kidnapping two school boys and attempting to shoot down a police helicopter.

I didn't see much of Jonathan after Uncle Jim's death. First of all we were both too upset to want to play, then my parents decided we should move to another town.

I go to a different school now, and the nightmares only happen when it thunders. I've made new friends and we have some great games. Our favourite is the one about a famous spy who gets into all sorts of scrapes around the world. The police of fifty-two countries are after him but he always manages to escape. His code name is Uncle Jim. I always play him.

ACROSS THE BORDER

Denis Sexton

Denis Sexton was born in Dublin and now lives in Kildare. He is married with four children. He worked as a teacher before becoming a schools inspector which he gave up to write full time in 1988.

Denis Sexton won an award for radio drama in 1985 and has since written full-length plays and sit-com material for radio. *Across The Border* is the first short story he has ever written.

ACROSS THE BORDER

'What time is it now?'

Pauline's mouth immediately tightened. Too late. The words had shot out of their own accord. She stared fixedly through the windscreen as if mesmerized by the line that glistened whitely down the centre of the wet road. Without looking at him she sensed Liam's reaction to her question; a slight crouch over the steering-wheel, chin pushing forward another fraction.

Outside, the gloom of the evening was cut by a flash of lightning. Pauline could feel the back of her neck press hard against the head rest. She heard Liam's breath escape in a whistle of admiration.

'One thing about Northern Ireland,' he said cheerfully, 'their weather isn't any better than ours.'

'What's the time?'

'Nearly four. We should be home before six. We've saved over an hour by cutting through the North,' said he, pleased with himself.

A hazard of the profession, she thought; sooner or later all teachers develop a tone of smug certainty. One thing for sure, the next time they drove home from Letterkenny she wouldn't be persuaded so easily to take a short cut through the North. Going round by Sligo might be longer and the road surface might not be as good but at least she'd know where she was. She looked back at the carry-cot stretched along the seat.

'How is he?' asked Liam.

'Fine.'

'Good to see that someone is enjoying the drive. He's hardly moved since we left Letterkenny.'

Pauline ignored the teasing. She noticed the tiny beads of perspiration on Ronan's upper lip and loosened the blanket.

'Could you turn down the heater,' she asked, 'it's getting muggy.' She wiped away the perspiration with a tissue. The chubby face crinkled momentarily and the pink mouth sucked at a non-existent teat. 'Wonder why he always sleeps best in the car?' she mumbled half to herself.

'Must be the bottles of Scotch at his feet.'

'Oh Liam, that was a daft idea.'

'Why?' he replied with mock innocence. 'At least he'll be able to keep a straight face when we get to the customs.'

He grinned to himself as he rehearsed in his mind the imminent question-and-answer session with the customs officer. He was sorry now he hadn't bought another bottle. Ronan wouldn't object to having a litre of Teachers under his pillow for a few miles until they crossed over the Border.

Pauline tucked in the quilt and then turned to gaze ahead. Despite the thickening blobs of rain on the glass there was still enough light outside for her to distinguish the main features of the Tyrone landscape. The countryside was much like that around Navan, rich and rolling with regular stands of mature trees. Good farming land, she surmised, and well used. Yet it all looked strange, as if it was another country, as if she was a foreigner. I'm the one who's daft, she thought. Sure, Navan is only down the road.

'Are we far from the Border?' She tried to keep her voice casual.

'About ten miles, I'd say. Ballygawley Cross should be next on the map.'

'God, I'll be glad when we cross into the Republic.'

Liam chuckled. 'Relax, Pauline. I promised you there'd be no problems. Let's see now. After Ballygawley we should be heading into Aughnacloy. Then . . .'

His voice carried on, listing the names of the towns and villages en route, those they'd passed through, those that lay ahead. When it came to maps his memory was photographic. It was only natural that Geography should be one of his subjects. Place names. Places Pauline had no memory of ever seeing but the names sprang out at her: Ballygawley, Kilgreen, Omagh, Newtownstewart, Sion Mills, Strabane, Lifford, Letterkenny. Unfamiliar places, but the names resonated in Pauline's mind. So many other names; names she had seen on clear, well-positioned sign-posts . . . Pomeroy, Enniskillen, Cookstown, Benburb. They came easily to her: Portadown, Scotstown, Clogher, Dungannon. She mouthed them silently, the list of names. She had heard them so often, on the radio, the television, in the newspapers. They echoed in her mind like a litany; a litany of horror; bombings, shootings, killings, murder, slaughter. All those familiar place names.

'Do you want it on or don't you?' Liam's question startled her.

'What?' she said, coming out of the spell.

'The radio, it's four o'clock.' His voice had an edge to it.

'Oh yes, yes.'

'You didn't fall asleep, did you?' he teased.

'You must be joking.'

Smug bastard, she thought, you never lose a chance to send me up. Before she could think of something sarcastic to say he had turned up the radio. The continuity announcer was introducing the news headlines in Irish. Pauline reached over and pushed a long-wave button.

'BBC, what's that for?' Again the mock innocent tone.

'You know bloody well I can't follow the news in Irish.'

Of course he knew, knew that her fluency in Irish was almost nil. Why should it be otherwise? She had hardly spoken a word of the language since leaving school. Not that she had anything against it, but well . . . She said no more about it; it was Liam's second subject to teach. The voice of the BBC newsreader was crisp and detached.

'In Dungannon this morning a part-time member of the UDR was shot by two men armed with revolvers.'

Dungannon! The word made Pauline shiver. The newsreader continued, voice as impersonal as ever, though dropping a half-tone in recognition of the atrocity. The same story, thought Pauline. The gunmen escape in a stolen car which is later found abandoned and a man lies in hospital in a critical condition, bullet wounds in his head. Meanwhile there is a possibility that the politicians may consider having talks about talks, about talks . . . She switched off the radio, cutting the newsreader in mid-sentence.

'What's the matter?' Liam took his eyes off the road to look at her.

'These bloody roads,' she muttered.

'What?' he asked, confused. 'I think they're marvellous; a pleasure to drive on.'

'They're so quiet,' Pauline murmured; 'you'd know you were in the North.'

'No potholes, you mean. Take it easy, Pauline. When you see the Gaelic on the signposts and hear the loose chips flying off the windscreen then you'll know you're over the Border.'

Liam smiled to himself. One of these days he was going to write that letter to the Meath County Council about the condition of the roads. It was hard enough trying to keep a home and run a car on a teacher's salary, without having to negotiate a hundred bottomless pits on every mile of road. The smile became grim. He was going to have the Council's guts for garters, one day soon.

Pauline looked back at Ronan. 'I hope he doesn't wake up before we get home,' she said.

'Haven't you a feed made up?'

'How am I supposed to heat the bottle?' she retorted.

'If he gets thirsty he can help himself to some of the whiskey in the carry-cot. That'll warm him.'

'Daft,' was all Pauline trusted herself to say. When they did get to the customs post she was going to let Liam do the talking. It might serve him right if the Customs Officer saw through his line of bullshit.

'By the way,' Liam remarked casually, 'remind me to fill up the petrol tank at Aughnacloy.'

'Do you have to?'

'I'd be mad not to. It's a pound a gallon cheaper than in the South.'

Pauline was unimpressed. 'Haven't we lost enough time?'

'What time?' he countered.

'You spent long enough in the off-licence.'

Liam laughed. 'Did you not see me nip into the chemist next door?'

'The chemist?' said Pauline.

The grin on Liam's face widened into a smirk. 'Supplies,' he said, 'supplies,' and as he spoke he sounded the car horn.

'Supplies? . . . Oh.' In spite of her irritation she laughed. 'Well done, Liam, you're not the worst.'

'I thought we'd better wean Ronan off the Scotch first before going into production again.'

No, he's not the worst, she thought. Not many other husbands would have remembered. Even now she could feel the flush coming to her face as she recalled the scene.

Old Hogan looking at her stonily as she stuttered her way to asking for a packet of Durex. 'No, Mrs Walsh, we do not stock those items in this shop,' had been Hogan's reply, spoken in the disembodied voice of a man in deep shock.

Pauline squirmed at the memory. The stupidity of it. Why hadn't she waited a few more days? She had gone to Dublin that weekend and every chemist's shop she'd gone into had been awash with condoms.

'About an hour and a half.' His voice broke in on her thoughts.

'What?'

'We'll soon be home.'

'Well, don't get any ideas,' she snapped.

Men! It had been all hours by the time they got to bed last night. Even then the post-wedding hooley was still in full flight. Her brother's wedding had turned out to be a great success. But it had been a long day. Maybe that was why she was so jumpy.

The rain outside was sheeting against the car. Liam put the wipers to full speed. A car approached them, headlights on full. The driver dimmed as it came near and the car sloshed by.

'Orange bastard,' said Liam.

'What do you mean?'

'He took his time about dimming the lights.'

Pauline stared ahead. Why waste her breath . . . There was little to see. The dark rain deepened the November gloom. Liam whistled quietly to himself as he concentrated on his driving. She admired him for that; his driving. His conversation wasn't always the kind that she liked to share but when he was behind the wheel she felt safer.

Ronan whimpered. She looked around. He was sleeping peacefully, his breathing inaudible over the rhythmical whirring of the wipers and the swish of wet tyres. She hoped he wouldn't waken. 'Where are we now?'

'Coming into Aughnacloy.' She repeated the name soundlessly. 'Last chance for petrol, booze and true blue videos.'

Aughnacloy, Aughnacloy? It had been on the news recently. Was it an ambush, gun battle or just a lone killing? She couldn't remember.

'Like to stop for a cheap pint?' said Liam.

'Piss off, would you.' He glanced at her in surprise. What had he said now? How was it women had no sense of humour? 'Liam, stop, stop the car!'

'What?'

'Jesus, Liam, what is it?'

Liam squinted through the clouded windscreen. 'I think it's probably . . .'

'For God's sake stop, slow down . . . stop the bloody car!' She wanted to grab the steering-wheel but she was frozen in her seat.

'Relax, Pauline, it's a checkpoint, an army checkpoint, nothing for you to worry about . . . just relax, okay, relax.' His words calmed her; she released her breath. Coolly he moved down through the gears and approached the barrier at a steady twenty miles per hour. A soldier stood on the centre line of the road, his arm upraised. Halt! In the crook of the other arm he nestled a submachine-gun. As Liam cruised up to the barrier he noticed other soldiers. Without turning his head he could see them along either side of the road. Some crouched along the ditch, others lay full-length in the wet grass. Their battle fatigues and dirtied faces merged with the undergrowth but Liam detected the slight head movements as he slowly cruised by them. I hope the rain freezes the balls off them, he thought as he brought the car to a halt.

'What do they want?' Pauline could feel her heart thumping. There seemed to be no air inside the car.

'Routine patrol,' said Liam. 'They'll check us out and wave us through.'

'Are you sure?'

'Pauline, they're not here to arrest us for having an extra bottle or two of Scotch. Just relax.'

She sat back in the passenger seat. Liam was right, of course. They had nothing to worry about. She rolled down the window a little to clear the mist on the glass. Pulled into the lay-by she could make out the shape of a large van or portable building of some kind. A door opened in the van and a soldier came out. For an instant the light from the interior spilled over him. He stood there in a cocoon of golden light. Pauline saw that he carried a mug in his hand. The door snapped shut.

'God, I'd love a hot drink,' she blurted.

'Yeah . . . do you want me to order you a hot whiskey?' His voice was heavy with sarcasm.

Twenty yards ahead of them was another car with three men in it. Some troops stood close by and watched as the driver spoke to the soldier at the window. Another soldier shone a torch on some papers. He shielded them from the drizzle as best he could. Pauline looked at the soldiers all around her, on the road, in the ditch, on the verge. They were like statues, impervious to the rain. Only the movement of a head indicated that they were alive.

'They look so miserable,' she said.

'Who?'

She ignored the truculence expressed in the one word. 'The soldiers, most of them are just kids.'

'Yeah, look at the artillery your kids are carrying.'

She made no reply. Liam's attitude to British troops in Northern Ireland was something he did not disguise. The last thing she wanted was an argument. She'd keep her mouth shut until they were over the Border. It couldn't be more than a few miles away.

She looked at her baby. He was still sleeping. Please God they'll get moving soon before he wakes up. She pulled the quilt closer to his sleeping face.

'What the hell is keeping them?' Liam's fingers drummed on the steering-wheel. 'Are we supposed to sit here and freeze?'

Pauline looked out again. The men in the car in front were still being questioned. Nobody made an attempt to approach their own car. What was delaying them, she wondered. Jeez! This is a right place to be stuck on a wet November evening.

She noticed that two soldiers in particular were keeping a steady eye on them. Again she was struck by how young they were. Teenagers. Maybe that's why they put dirt on their faces, she thought, to convince people that they were full-grown men, or to convince themselves. One of the two chewed gum methodically. Like a cow in a field, thought Pauline, looking at the morose figure standing there in the drizzle, large innocent eyes staring at them out of a blackened face. The soldier shifted the position of his submachine-gun. Pauline saw the water gleam on the short, squat barrel.

'Those guns terrify me.' Again the words were out before she could stop them.

Liam latched on to the slip. 'Half a chance and they'll show you what their tommy-guns are for.' Her lips tightened. But Liam was now on his way. 'Arrogant bastards. Wait until you hear the fake politeness.'

Pauline tried to keep her voice even. 'I wish you wouldn't take the whole thing so personally, Liam.'

'Huh!' The scorn was unmistakable.

279

'Every time we see a British Army uniform I can feel you getting tense,' she accused.

'Christ Almighty!' he exploded, 'You're one to talk. Every two minutes you want to know how far we are from the Border. You can't wait to be over it. You never even wanted to set foot in Northern Ireland!' He snorted at the incredulity of her criticism.

Pauline looked away. The gum-chewing soldier chewed on with the same slow rhythm. His gaze never left their car.

'It's the guns that frighten me, not the uniform,' said Pauline. 'I wouldn't know a British soldier from an Irish one.'

Liam toyed with her remark for a few seconds before squashing it. 'Let me tell you girl, there's one hell of a difference,' said he with finality.

Pauline said nothing. In his carry-cot Ronan stirred grumpily. His lips smacked together as he shifted his head on the pillow. Gently Pauline wiped the saliva that dribbled from the half-open mouth. The sucking stopped; his breathing was quiet and even.

'Liam, please don't argue with them,' she said as she put the tissue into her handbag. He didn't seem to hear her. She went on: 'Have identification ready and answer their questions and there'll be no hassle. Please.'

'Look again would you, and see if the driving licence is in the glove compartment,' he asked. She snapped her handbag shut and dropped it on the floor. She was glad to oblige him, glad to see that his anger was gone.

'Why are they taking so long with the car in front?' she enquired as she rummaged in the glove compartment. How did it get into such a mess?

'After the shooting this morning, I suppose,' said Liam in his deliberate teacher-offering-the-solution manner.

'Yes, that must be it, the shooting,' agreed Pauline. The UDR man shot on his doorstep.

'Dungannon's not too far from here.' He went on to speculate on the number of miles and on the direction in which Dungannon lay.

She didn't listen. Dungannon. The word echoed in her head. The sound seemed to draw her in, as if it wanted to reveal to her the atrocity that lay behind the name. She resisted. She didn't want to imagine a human being with part of his face blown off. She refused to picture it in her head. She attacked the glove compartment.

'Oh shit,' she hissed. 'I can't find the bloody licence.'

Liam shrugged. 'Not to worry,' he said, 'my credit card will do. In fact, a Visa card is quite appropriate.' He chuckled to himself.

At the sound of a car engine spluttering into life Pauline lifted her head. The car in front was moving off. The driver smiled and waved to the soldiers.

'Good little Prods,' said Liam, noticing the smile.

Pauline saw the soldier who had been asking the questions turn towards them. His companion noted the number plate. They spoke to one another. She grabbed at the contents of the glove compartment and dumped them in her lap. The licence must be in here someplace, she thought.

'Relax, Pauline, relax.' Liam spoke soothingly, as though he were calming a hot-headed pupil. 'Just relax.'

'I'm sorry we didn't bring our passports,' she said.

'Passports!' His mouth was open in disbelief.

'We should have brought them,' she said firmly.

'Jeez, are you gone soft in the head?' His eyes blazed with a mixture of shock and scorn.

'There's no need to raise your voice. You'll wake the baby.'

He ignored her diversionary tactic and spelled it out for her.

'We're less than sixty miles from home, on our own island, in our own country and you want us to carry passports. Maybe we should swear an oath of allegiance while we're at it.' The fists clenching the steering-wheel had turned white at the knuckles.

'I just don't want any hassle, that's all,' she pleaded quietly.

'Sure,' he said, 'no hassle.'

She flicked through the service manuals angrily. What possessed her to mention passports? A half-wit could have predicted his reaction. When was she going to learn?

She was shoving the service manuals back into the glove compartment when a shadow at the car window made her look up. Almost immediately came a sharp rapping on the glass at Liam's side. What was he up to now, she thought, why hadn't he rolled down the window?

'UDR man,' said Liam calmly.

'What?'

'The badge; UDR.'

'Liam, no trouble please, roll down the window.'

'Sure,' he replied agreeably, and just as the hand outside was raised to rap again he rolled down the glass.

'Good afternoon, sir.' Liam was right. The soldier's accent had a sharp Northern Ireland lilt. Everything else about him seemed rough and unfinished, uniform, face and his heavy moustache.

'Afternoon,' said Liam.

'Did you not hear me tapping on the glass?'

'Yes,' replied Liam.

'Or maybe you didn't notice me standing here?' The soldier's impatience was barely controlled.

Pauline glared into the glove compartment. Why did she

have to mention those bloody passports? If she'd kept her big mouth shut Liam wouldn't now be acting so thick.

'As a matter of fact, Sergeant,' said Liam sweetly, 'my wife, my child and myself are almost frozen stiff from sitting here for the past fifteen minutes.'

'Doesn't the car have a heater?'

'It does,' said Liam, 'but it's not functioning at the moment.'

Liar! thought Pauline. Then she relaxed. Maybe now that he's had his little victory he'll co-operate. He's won the point.

The sergeant paused, as if to get his voice under full control. He then proceeded with the standard questions. Who were they? Where were they coming from? What was their destination? What was the purpose of the trip? Pauline leaned across Liam and embarked on a full account of Shane's wedding and why it took place in Letterkenny and . . . The sergeant thanked her curtly. 'We're just passing through,' she added.

'That's right, Sergeant, just passing through,' said Liam pointedly.

The repetition was for her benefit; to let her know that her apologetic tone had been noted, marked and would require a further explanation.

'Could I see your driver's licence, sir?'

Liam had his answer prepared. 'I can't find it at the moment. Here's my Visa card.' He took it from his wallet and handed it to the sergeant. 'My signature's on the back,' he said, pointing, 'William Walsh.'

The sergeant studied the card dispassionately. The pause seemed to last an age. Liam whistled cheerfully under his breath. Pauline saw that other soldiers had moved into position around the car. They were watching, but when she looked at their faces their eyes slid away.

'Have you any further means of identification, sir?'

Liam opened his wallet again and produced his teachers' union card. As the sergeant inspected it Liam added, 'I'm a teacher,' in case the bedraggled soldier failed to make the connection. Pauline bent to take a tissue from her handbag. Half-hidden by the bag she saw the maroon cover.

'Something with your address on it, sir, would be helpful.' The delivery was casual, like a poker player careful not to tip his hand.

'I think I've got it,' shouted Pauline.

She opened the cover to check. It was Liam's all right. She reached across Liam to hand it to the sergeant. Liam fingered his wallet; a grin came to his face. Dourly the sergeant inspected the document. Pauline wondered what took him so long. Surely there was no need to read the fine print; the name and address was what mattered.

'It's two years out of date,' said the sergeant gruffly.

'Is it?' said Liam, eyebrows raised in surprise.

'Is this your signature, Mr Walsh?'

'Yes,' Liam replied firmly.

Again the sergeant paused before speaking. 'It doesn't correspond with that on your credit card, sir.' He was the poker player spreading his hand. Pauline wondered was it a note of triumph or could it just be the Northern accent. She could feel her heart beginning to pound. Liam gawked at the driving licence. Then he laughed.

'I signed it in Irish, Sergeant. Liam Breathnach.' He underlined the two words with his finger as if to clarify matters for a rather stupid pupil.

Pauline searched the weather-beaten face for a reaction, a face that seemed to fill the window, its dourness emphasized by the moustache that drooped unevenly past both corners of his mouth. She decided it was time for her to explain.

'Liam teaches Irish, Irish and Geography. Years ago he used to sign his name in Irish. Now he signs in English. Isn't that right, Liam?'

Liam had resumed his under-the-breath whistling. He nodded in agreement. The sergeant looked Pauline in the eye. She saw the raindrops glisten on the bushy eyebrows.

'I'm sorry madam, but I can't read Gaelic. At school I could never master foreign languages.' He continued before Liam could make a reply. 'Perhaps you could pull your car over to the side there, sir.'

'What's the problem? We've told you who we are,' retorted Liam. The poker player collected his winnings.

'Your two identities don't seem to correspond, sir. Now if you'll start up the motor and pull over beside the truck.' He moved away.

Liam swore savagely. Such a stupid waste of time! Pauline grabbed at her handbag. She wanted to tell the soldier she had more identification, letters, bankcard, children's allowance book, as much as he wanted, but his back was to them. Then he turned and waved them into the lay-by. She clung to her handbag hopefully. Liam turned the key in the ignition; the engine stalled. He pressed the accelerator hard. The motor attempted to splutter into life but the mixture was too rich. Liam cursed through his teeth as he turned the key again.

'Go easy, Liam,' Pauline said softly.

'It's not my shagging fault, is it?'

This time the engine fired; he revved it loudly to clear the carburettor. The blue smoke of the exhaust was immediately swallowed up in the drizzle. Liam released the hand-brake and the car lurched into movement. The soldiers alongside kept pace as they moved towards where the sergeant stood waiting. One of the escort then peeled off and trotted towards the large van which was now closer.

'Lousy bastard,' said Liam, his indignation growing. He clenched the steering-wheel with both hands as he glared at the arrogant figure of the sergeant who dared Liam to run him down. Liam spat noisily.

The soldier reached the van door and knocked urgently. Pauline saw him being admitted into the pool of light. They're lucky to have someplace to get out of the rain, she thought, someplace to get a hot drink.

At that moment Ronan began to cry. First a whimper, but as Pauline turned towards him, it became a full-throated wail.

'Oh blast! That's all we need.'

'Stop shouting, Liam,' hissed Pauline, 'he might settle.' But Ronan had found his voice and was crying with purpose. The wailing filled every corner of the cramped interior.

'That bloody Brit!' said Liam, spitting the words out. 'Just because I had my name in Irish.' He drove up to the sergeant's upraised hand and braked violently. The rasp of the handbrake brought a howl from Ronan.

Pauline turned her body as best she could in order to get closer to the carry-cot. She loosened the coverings and wiped away the dribbles and the tears from Ronan's face. His plump cheeks glowed brightly, the rest of his face was contorted with the effort of crying. It would be impossible to get him back to sleep, she thought. On top of everything he was probably hungry. She spoke his name soothingly in an effort to stifle the shuddering wails that permeated the enclosed space.

The sergeant spoke briskly. 'That's fine, sir.' He came to the window. 'Would you mind opening the boot, please.' Liam took the key from the ignition and offered it through the window. 'I'd prefer if you'd open it, sir,' was the sergeant's reply.

286

'I haven't got a raincoat,' protested Liam.

'You'll have to open it, sir.'

Pauline was about to lift Ronan from the cot when she sensed the deadlock. 'Liam, I can't get the baby to settle; hurry up and open the boot.' He contemplated her request; his left eyelid twitched involuntarily. 'Please, Liam, please.'

There was silence while Ronan gathered his breath. Pauline's pleading eyes tried to catch Liam's but he was staring out the windscreen. Ronan started to cry again. This time it was a full-bodied roar. As Pauline swivelled to calm him Liam pulled abruptly at the door handle. He got out, slammed the door after him and marched round to the boot. The sergeant stood beside him as he flung the boot lid open. He invited the sergeant to inspect the contents.

The two men were hidden from Pauline's view by the upraised lid. Their muffled voices came through to her but she concentrated on getting the baby out of the carry-cot and on to her lap without aggravating him further. She managed the manoeuvre and cuddled his rigid body close to her, all the time talking softly to him. She saw from the way he sucked his lips that he was hungry. Holding him with one arm she fished around at the bottom of the cot with her free hand. There was a clinking of glass and then she located his feeding-bottle. She recognized its shape by feel, same as she did at night when she left off the bedside light so as not to disturb Liam.

The howling eased into a persistent moan. As she drew the bottle from under the cot blankets Pauline knew that there was only a slim hope of satisfying him with a cold bottle. It was worth a try.

Holding the bottle to his mouth she talked to him in a mixture of encouragement and desperation. He responded eagerly to the teat. If even he takes a few mouthfuls, she hoped, it might calm him down until we get moving again.

As she pressed the bottle firmly into her baby's mouth she was aware of the voices from behind the car. An argument was clearly developing. She looked down at Ronan and launched into her usual routine of baby-talk, rhymes, jingles and high-flown praise. But the voices of the two men would not be shut out. Blunt questions, truculent answers. What was in the cases? More questions. Where had they stopped? What was in that bag, the other bag and that bag under the case, the Stewart's Pharmacy bag? She could near her husband's voice raised in anger and embarrassment as he showed the packets of condoms to the sergeant.

For God's sake, thought Pauline, won't they ever get sense? Standing out there in the rain squabbling like children. She looked in the driving mirror but the boot lid blocked her view. To her side the light from the van caught her eye as the door opened. A soldier stepped out into the rain; he pushed a fresh wad of chewing-gum into his mouth as he walked towards them. Pauline swallowed; her own throat was dry.

Suddenly Ronan wriggled in the crook of her arm. With legs kicking, body twisting and face frowning he dislodged the bottle from his mouth. He paused, took a breath and roared with all the might of his five-month-old lungs. Pauline felt an urge to ram the bottle down his throat. As she hesitated the unseen voices from behind the car came to her in snarls of mutual hostility. She looked down at the struggling child in her lap. She shook her head. What am I blaming you for, you poor little mite, she said aloud, all you want is a feed you can enjoy, but those two! Ronan stopped crying. His red-rimmed eyes looked up at her expectantly. It seemed as if his mouth was about to shape into a smile when the slamming of the boot lid made the car shudder. The tentative smile turned into a scream of terror.

'That's it,' said Pauline.

She turned and bundled the child back into the carry-cot. With the feeding bottle in her hand she ran towards the van, leaving the car door flung open behind her. Her rubber sneakers slithered on the grass but she checked her fall with her free arm. The first shout to reach her ears was from the sergeant; a clear-cut order to halt. She slowed. As she wavered, she heard her husband's voice. It ordered her to get back to the car. The command made up her mind. She rushed across the last stretch of tarmacadam to the van and pounded on the door with the heel of the bottle. It opened almost immediately. A soldier with a rifle in his hand looked down at her. Surprise showed on his face. His part-time training had not prepared him for the sight in front of him; a young woman, gasping for breath, was holding a baby's bottle towards him.

'What do you want?' he shouted, swinging the barrel of the gun towards her.

'Some hot water.' Pauline's breath came in a rush. The young soldier peered at her. Was she crazy? 'Some hot water, to warm the baby's bottle, please.'

Her voice was under control. The soldier gazed down at her from the step. He lowered the rifle; it was just a harmless lunatic arriving out of the darkness.

'Listen, ma'am,' he said slowly, 'this is an army check-point. We do not . . .'

'What is it, Mac?' a woman's voice from within interrupted his patient explanations. Before he could reply the woman came to the door. Despite her sober uniform she looked younger than Pauline.

'This lady,' said Mac, 'wants hot water.' He waited for the girl-soldier's laughter.

'Well bring her in then,' replied the girl. 'Mac,' she said as he hesitated, 'we can spare some hot water.' She turned to Pauline. The Northern accent was brisk but friendly. 'Come in out of the rain,' she said, 'come on in,' and reaching down her hand she helped Pauline to clamber on to the step. The door clanged shut behind them. Pauline stood and gathered her breath. It was warm and dry inside the van. The girl smiled at her. 'C'mon this way,' she said, 'I think it's very possible we might have some hot water on the premises.' Pauline grinned back and followed the girl-soldier towards the electric kettle.

Minutes later Pauline returned to the car. She thanked the soldier for the loan of the cape and sat into her seat. Liam handed her the whimpering child. As soon as Ronan was sucking on the warm feed Liam started up the engine. A soldier beckoned the car on to the road. The Border was three miles away.

Pauline spoke first. 'Sorry for the delay, luckily the kettle was on the boil.'

'I thought we were in a hurry,' said Liam quietly.

'We won't have to stop now. This feed should do him until we get home,' she assured him. Ronan was sucking contentedly.

'I meant in a hurry to get over the Border,' pursued Liam. She wiped the dribbling milk from Ronan's chin.

'I hope you didn't get soaked standing out in the rain.' She could smell the dampness from his clothes.

'Nope,' he said, 'I didn't get wet.'

They drove in silence. There was no other traffic on the road. Pauline knew she had to say something. Otherwise the cold silence might last until they reached Navan.

'They offered me a mug of tea.' They were the first words that came to her mind.

'What?'

'While we were waiting for the bottle to heat up.'

'You didn't drink it, did you?' He spoke with low politeness.

'Of course I drank it.' She savoured the lingering taste of the hot, sweet tea. 'I was dying for a hot drink.'

'You stupid bitch!' His eyes never left the road as he shot the words at her. 'Stupid treacherous bitch!'

'What do you mean?' said Pauline. His sudden ferocity was more frightening than the rifle pointed at her earlier.

'That Orange bastard enjoyed humiliating me. He had me out in the rain just to make a fool of me, to degrade me; then you march off and have tea with them. I hope you had a lovely tea-party!' A cyclist appeared on the road in front of them and Liam blasted him with the car horn.

Pauline clenched her lips. She looked at the feeding child in her arms. I might as well talk to the baby, she thought. If I told him that the soldiers were looking for killers, that the man gunned down this morning had died leaving a widow and two children, if I told Ronan all that and more he'd probably understand better than my husband.

The lights of the car lit up a signpost; the Border was a mile away. The Border, she thought, a line on a map doesn't make much difference . . . not when it comes to hatred and bigotry.

They drove south without talking. Liam switched on the radio. As soon as he heard the BBC voice, he pressed another button. The music was country-style, a waltz tune. Pauline was glad of it; anything was better than cold silence. She felt tears coming to her eyes. Oh no, she thought, as she held them back. She wasn't going to let him see her cry, not him, that figure hunched over the wheel, his jaw jutting over it, his mind replaying, reinventing the battle with the Orange sergeant. No tears. She would not give him that satisfaction.

Ronan wriggled in her arms; his legs stiffened. She lifted him to her shoulder and rubbed his back with her open palm. When it came, the burp was like a rifle shot, loud and sudden. For an instant the sound of it filled the car.

Why shouldn't she? Why shouldn't she cry? Not because of the slushy ballad, or for her marriage to a thick husband or for the man gunned down in Dungannon. But for Ronan. Would he grow up to be like them, chasing small victories, cursing trivial defeats? Was there anything she could do, anything that would save her son? She'd bloody-well cry if she wanted to.

Through her tears Pauline looked at him. He was again noisily sucking on the feeding-bottle, unaware of her desperation and her defiance.

ELLIE

Judy Forshaw

Judy Forshaw was brought up in a large Catholic family, the eldest of five sisters. She was educated in convent schools from the ages of four to sixteen, and later went on to Bristol University.

After leaving university in the late seventies, she first joined a touring theatre company as an actress and then moved on to become a freelance assistant film editor. It was during this time that she started writing short stories. Judy Forshaw studied script writing at the National Film and TV School and is currently working on her first commissioned feature script set in Iran in the 1950s.

ELLIE

Who did she think she was, anycase, stood there on the front step, proud as a peacock. All done up in black and red. Large red hat with black feathers hanging down over the brim so you couldn't see her eyes. Black coat. Red dress underneath. Shiny black shoes standing on the steps I'd washed down that afternoon, only half an hour earlier. Such neat little feet, couldn't've been bigger than size three, four at the most. Expensive leather with little gold buckles glinting like the brooch on her collar. A bird's claw curled round a dainty little pearl.

I must've looked a bit too long at that brooch of hers, 'cos she took a step back and covered it with her hand. She was wearing long, fancy, red gloves.

'I've come to see Mother Louis.'

'She's praying.'

'We'll wait then – it's important.'

Her hand came down from the brooch, a rare expensive thing, like the bracelet on her wrist, the string of pearls round her neck. This woman smelt of money. Not phoney, showy, made-in-a-hurry money, but real money. Money that's been about for a bit matures like a malt whiskey. It smells different. You get to recognize it.

'Darling – come on – Mummy's in a hurry.'

She had turned round and was waving one of those red-gloved hands of hers in the direction of this big black car, parked across the drive, near the statue of St Joseph.

'Mother Louis sometimes prays all day on a Sunday.'

Even if it wasn't true, I wanted this proud-peacock woman to know that Mother Louis had more important things to be dealing with than rich women in feather hats and fancy brass buckles on their shoes.

'I'm sure she won't mind sparing us a little of her time.'

A couple of the feathers on her hat blew back and I got to see her eyes. Pale green with little yellow circles round the edges of the pupils.

She was good-looking all right, which meant she probably wasn't all English. Couldn't've been, seeing as the English are the ugliest race in the world, barring the Chinese and the Irish. And it didn't look like she was mixed up with either of them. Not that I want to get into matters of race, creed and colour right here, seeing as it has no business in this story, although I do have a strong opinion on these things, stronger than a lot of people would realize. As a rule I don't like to say too much but I think a lot, enough thoughts to fill a book, fat as Mother Louis's Bible, fatter. One day maybe I'll write some of them down, mainly for the pleasure of seeing them written on the page. Maybe one day. We'll see.

That Sunday afternoon was the first time I set eyes on little Ellie, as she climbed out the back of that big black car. A Mercedes or something. She skipped, half seemed to fly, like a little elf across the gravel drive and up the steps to her mother's side, where she stood peering up at me. Same green eyes with the yellow circles round the pupils. Only Ellie was fair as her mother was dark, like the opposite sides of the same coin. And tiny. Not much bigger than the average five-year-old child. She was eight years old then.

I can't say now, exactly what was going through my mind then. Call it a sixth sense. I knew straight off that this child was different. Not especially better or worse than all the other little girls I'd seen pass through the school. Just different. And I liked that about her straight away.

'Ellie, don't stare – it's rude.'

I didn't mind being stared at. The little girl could look as long as she liked. It didn't bother me. If it was the first time she'd been this close up to a coloured person, an old black woman at that, she was entitled to take a long look. What these people don't realize is that it's seldom the children that bother me.

'Darling – say hello to the lady.' The peacock woman was prodding her with a long red finger. 'I don't know what's got into her – she's not normally this shy.'

Little Ellie didn't want to say hello. And why should she, when she was too busy staring at me, taking it all in. After she'd had her fill of looking, she crept round and hid her face in the folds of her mother's smart black coat, peering out at me from behind there with one of her big round green eyes, that didn't look to me the slightest bit shy. That little girl wasn't fooling me one bit.

As a rule I don't like to interrupt Mother Louis when she's praying. She's an old, wise woman with a lot of responsibility resting on her shoulders. What with running the school and keeping the other sisters in order, she doesn't get a lot of time on her own to be close to God.

It gets so dark and gloomy in that little chapel in the late afternoons that you need a torch to see your way around. At first I didn't see Mother Louis and it wasn't until after a bit, and my eyes got adjusted to the dim light, that I spotted her over in the corner at the back praying in front of the statue of the Virgin Mary. The Virgin Mary has always been Mother Louis' favourite. Her special confidante. And I often wonder if she isn't closer to that lady than she is to God.

When things get rough, like the time a little while back,

when it looked like they were going to have to close the convent down and there was talk of the sisters having to move to the Mother House in Rome, Mother Louis was up all night with Our Lady. And the other time when Sister Bernadette, who was old enough to know better, ran away for a long weekend with that flash Harry fellow, who pretended he knew all about sewage and nearly caused the sisters a severe bankruptcy problem with his phoney advice, she went and turned to her again. I don't suppose the Old Man minds. He must get enough people knocking on his door to be glad to have some of the responsibility lifted off his shoulders.

You would've thought though, that the sisters could've found a better likeness of the lady. That mean little mouth, close pale eyes and powder-pink face would put me off my praying if I was them. But then the sisters are supposed not to mind about those things. It's the spiritual image of her that they carry around in their hearts that counts. At least, that's how Father Benedict explained it me. And at the time it seemed to make sense. Now I only think so in Mother Louis' case. In my opinion she's one of the holiest women that walked the earth, and if they still went in for saints these days, her name would be top of the list. Pure goodness shines out of that old lady, like a light, like she's lit up on the inside with a special kind of tenderness for the world and all its creatures. And that's a rare thing.

As for most of the other sisters, a lifetime's praying doesn't seem to have got them any closer to God than the day they came in. And in my opinion, which is probably one best kept to myself here, I'd say it's taken them further away. I wonder about it sometimes. I don't know what it is with those poor sisters. But with most of them, like I say, I get the feeling that somewhere, something is nagging away at their souls, gnawing them up like a tapeworm, till they're so starved and thin inside that they don't have anything to give anyone else except the husk of their lost selves. Which sounds like a sort of a strange thing to say. But sometimes I think of them like empty pods with all the goodness taken out. And all the trying in the world to fill that emptiness with prayer only sours them worse. Because when praying's done on an empty heart it does strange things to a person inside. Maybe, I don't know, maybe in some way, they feel God cheated on them. Maybe they expected peace and happiness without having to work for it. Who knows. It's hard for a person to live with their misery. And hardest of all when it's of their own making. I suppose I should feel sorry for them. Some of them I do.

Sister Bernadette for instance, when she ran off with that flash Harry on that long weekend and came back crying. My heart went out to her. A grown woman, over forty years old, acting like a teenage girl over a man that should've had a government health warning stamped all over him. But then how was she supposed to recognize a character like that, shut up for the best years of her life in a place she was never suited to be. It was only natural she was going to want to break out, if she wasn't going to turn inwards, darken and shrivel up inside. She was fighting for her soul. Anyone could see that. I've got time for Sister Bernadette, her and Mother Louis, they're alright . . .

Back to Mother Louis. As I was saying, that afternoon, when I went into the chapel, she was over in the corner at the back, having words with her favourite person. Mother Louis as a rule is what I'd call a dainty prayer. She likes to kneel very upright, without any of herself resting on the pew, not like some of the sloppy ones I could name, sprawled all over the place like sacks of potatoes. I sneaked up close behind her. I wasn't wanting to spy or anything. And I began thinking maybe I'd got the wrong nun. Maybe it was all a mistake. You know how your mind can play those kind of tricks, when it's trying not to see what you know deep down.

Mother Louis wasn't praying like her normal self that afternoon. She was leant right forward over the pew with her head nearly touching the front. I know it doesn't sound like much. But when you've been used to seeing a woman addressing herself to God with an upright dainty dignity for the past twenty years, and then one afternoon you walk in and find her collapsed in a heap like a sack of potatoes . . . I got this uncomfortable feeling in the pit of my stomach which wasn't anything to do with what I'd had for lunch that day.

'Mary Mother of God, pray for us sinners, now and at the hour of our death . . .'

She had a rosary in her hand and her finger had stopped on this one bead. She was whispering the same bit over and over like a record that's got stuck in a groove. Ordinarily I would've waited a bit for Mother Louis to reach a natural break in her praying, but this time I didn't want to wait. I wanted to stop that whispering right away. It spooked me.

'Mother Louis.'

The whispering stopped. Mother Louis lifted her head up from the bench. She didn't turn round. 'What is it, Marsi?'

'There's a lady out in the hall that wants to see you.'

'That'll be Mrs Hollander.'

She sounded so tired, like she had the troubles of the world resting on her shoulders.

'I wouldn't let her in – only she said you were expecting her.'

She slipped the rosary into her pocket and turned to look at me. Her face was filled with a sweet peace, like a young girl in love, like a baby that's just been fed. Looking back

300

now I'll always be happy to remember that expression on Mother Louis' face that afternoon. She reached out and touched my hand, cool and dry as an autumn leaf.

'Has she come with anyone?'

'A little blonde child that's got trouble written all over her.'

'Marsi, would you mind helping me up – my strength seems to have deserted me to-day.'

It was like holding a skinny little chicken in my arms. There was almost nothing of her under that thick black cloth, nothing but skin and bones.

'What you need is a good rest.'

Mother Louis laughed. 'Rest – whatever for?'

I handed her her stick and Bible, and together we promenaded down the aisle, like a couple of old ladies taking a summer stroll down Brighton Pier.

'You don't eat and you hardly ever sleep. You spend all your time worrying about everyone else – what sort of a way is that to lead a life?'

Mother Louis liked me scolding her. It was our little game we played together, a game we'd played for over twenty years. I was the only one that could manage it with her. The sisters were scared of her. Maybe her special closeness to God made them afraid for themselves. Whatever it was, I had the edge over them as far as Mother Louis was concerned, and they hated me for it. And you can understand it. Their Reverend Mother Louis, who was holier than most saints and closer to God than the lot of them put together, she could've chosen any one of them as her friend. And instead she chose old Marsi, the black cleaning woman, a non-Catholic and a heathen unbeliever at that, who had never been baptized and never would be by the looks of things. I wouldn't've liked it. Not one bit. But then that was their problem, not mine.

Sometimes I think that old lady has a streak of the devil in her. And it's not something I haven't said to her face on a few occasions before now. She may be holy, but she's still human inside. And I've often wondered if she didn't make me into her special friend just to stick a thorn into those poor sisters' sides. I wouldn't put it past her. She's got the cunning of a snake when she wants, which more than likely accounts for her special relationship with God. Something else I've told her on more than one occasion. Anycase, back to the two of us, promenading down the aisle that afternoon.

'What sort've a way is that to lead a life?' I said.

She laughed of course, like she always does. 'That's how I've always lived,' she said.

'And don't you think it's about time you changed?'

'But I like my life.'

'You should be ashamed of yourself at your age.'

There was no reasoning with that old lady, once she'd got the bit between her teeth, which was practically all of the time. All her waking time at least. I wonder sometimes if she ever let go of it. Maybe in her prayers when she was face to face with the Old Man. They must've had some bloody battles, the pair of them. Mother Louis wasn't one to bow down easily, not even to him.

The sin of pride, that's what that old lady had, and sometimes I think she had it pretty bad, worse than I've seen in a lot of headstrong people who are always wanting their own way. And it's my guess, that it would be that proud steely part in her that was going to stop her getting to heaven straight away. But then again she's never been the sort to want things easy for herself, and most probably she would've been pretty disappointed if she'd been taken right there on a conveyor belt along with all the other good souls about. Knowing her, she'd want to fry a bit, enough to feel the heat of the flames on her back and know she'd earned her place up there.

'Stubborn as an old mule – that's what you are,' I said, just loud enough for her to hear.

'What was that?' she said, a wicked gleam coming from the corner of her eye.

'You heard,' I said.

Mother Louis chuckled, tightening her grip on my arm. 'You disapprove of me, Marsi.'

'You know what I think – Sunday's your time – for you and your praying – not for proud women in feather hats – who every time they snap their fingers are used to getting their own way.'

Mother Louis sighed. 'Her daughter's a good child.'

'Mother Louis – that little girl is nothing but trouble – she's got it written all over her – how's she ever going to fit in with the other little girls in the school?'

'Maybe you can help her, Marsi.'

'Me?'

'And why not?'

You had to hand it to her. That old lady was slyer than a pack of foxes put together . . .

'What d'you think you're staring at – never seen an old coloured woman before?'

Little Ellie was sitting at the end of the long table in the kitchen, following every move I made with those big, yellow-green eyes of hers.

Mother Louis and the lady in the feathered hat had left her here with me while they went off to the study at the back of the chapel to discuss things. And since then Little Ellie hadn't spoken a word, which must've been all of ten minutes.

Little Ellie's eyes widened with my question. She took in a sharp breath, puffing out her cheeks like a frog.

'Not one as black as you before.'

'Well, there's plenty like me – and darker – all you have to do is look around.'

I watched her out of the corner of my eye as I lifted the kettle from the hob and poured it into the pot.

'Is the jungle very far from here?' she said.

'Well, let me see,' I said. I carried the pot over and put it down on the table; 'depends which one you mean – I suppose the nearest one is about five thousand miles away – as the crow flies.'

I could see by the look in her eyes she was having difficulty.

'How do you get here?' she said.

'By bus,' I said, 'the number thirty-three.'

Ellie's eyes widened.

Maybe I should've explained that I lived a couple of miles down the road, in a house with a toilet, and a kitchen, and a bathroom and a colour TV set in the living-room. But I figured that was for her to work out in her own time when she'd gotten to know me a bit and realized I wasn't so very different from most of the other people she knew.

After mulling it over for a bit, she let it drop and changed on to something else, in the way children do. I must say though – I wasn't prepared for what came next.

'Are you a heathen unbeliever, like me?' she said.

I lifted the lid of the pot and stirred the tea. It is not something I normally do, but I wanted to be occupied to give me time to think.

'Where'd a little girl like you learn to use such long words?' I said.

'Don't you know what they mean?'

I snapped the lid back down on the pot. I felt a sharp little rush of anger stirring up in me.

'I know what people mean by them all right,' I said,

'ignorant people who should know better than to talk to a child like that.'

Little Ellie peered at me, her green-yellow eyes round as saucers. I don't suppose she'd heard a grown-up person talk that way before, but then I wasn't like all the other grown-ups she knew. She leant back in her chair and folded her arms, keeping those yellow-green eyes of hers fixed on me.

'I'm bad, you know.' She announced like it was a statement of fact, like she was telling me her name, the name she'd been born to and grown up with all her life.

'And who told you that?' I said.

'Nearly everyone – that's why they don't keep me.'

'Who don't keep you?'

'People – places like this.'

'You mean schools?'

Ellie nodded, watching me with those great round-saucer green eyes of hers, with the thin band of yellow circling them. I don't know what she was expecting from me, maybe not as much as I thought, maybe nothing, maybe the look in her eyes was curiosity, it was hard to tell.

'Tea,' I said.

She nodded. I poured her out a cup. 'Milk?' She nodded again. 'Sugar?'

'Two.'

I pushed the cup across the table. 'Watch yourself, it's hot.'

With that over we were silent again.

'How many schools have you been to, Ellie?'

A strange look came over her face, like a worried little old woman, and I wished I hadn't asked the question. But she had already begun to count on her fingers. I watched as she used up the fingers on one hand and moved on to the other. I reached across the table to stop her and touched her tiny little hand with mine.

305

Ellie looked up. 'If I go on being bad,' she said, 'will I turn out black like you?'

I squeezed her hand tight inside mine.

'Ellie,' I said, 'you're not bad.' She was staring at me. 'And besides, no amount of wickedness ever changed the colour of a person's skin – drink your tea before it gets cold.'

She picked up the cup, peering at me over the top of the rim with a look in her eye that told me she wasn't sure if I was the devil incarnate come to tempt her, or a guardian angel come to smooth all her troubles away.

So – that's how it all began with Little Ellie for me.

She didn't fit, of course. We never expected that. When I say 'we', that's me and Mother Louis I'm talking about. The other sisters, they expected different. But no amount of trying on their part 'til they were blue in the face was ever going to change that child. Little Ellie was a natural-born wild thing. A wild thing that was never going to take taming. She had too much spirit in her for that. A spirit that burnt in her so bright, it seemed sometimes as if it would burst out of her in flames and set her alight. I guess, looking back now, she was what these modern doctors would call a disturbed child. I've heard that word 'disturbed' used a lot these days – and I don't know – I don't like the sound of it. I prefer the word 'troubled'. Ellie was a little girl troubled beyond her years with things from the adult world, that most of the other little girls at the school hadn't even come across in their worst dreams.

I suppose in all the time I knew her, I never got to the bottom of what was eating away at that child. I just remember one time, it was near the beginning of her stay in the convent. I was upstairs in the vestry, washing Father Benedict's chalice down with Dettolled water, and the bell went for morning prayers. I looked up out of the window down into the courtyard, where the school congregates in the summer months, and watched the girls forming into straight lines, the tall seniors at the back, the younger ones in the front. And when everyone was there and in place, and Mother Louis had finished the morning prayer, and they had begun to sing the school hymn, a slow, turgid thing, like a funeral dirge, Sister Dolores' composition, a tiny figure streaked out across the yard fast as lightning, running like she had the wind in her feet. It was Little Ellie, over five minutes late. And I don't know if you've ever encountered a similar sensation before. It's like a bit of you has been taken out of yourself, and everything starts to run slow, like in some movies when the couple are about to kiss and they slow the film to milk the moment for all it's worth. Only in this case, it wasn't anybody kissing, just Little Ellie, running slow, out on her own across that yard, and it seemed to take her ages before she reached the other girls. And it must've been the stink of Father Benedict's Dettol, he's a very germ-conscious man, that brought me back to myself, with a sad feeling that stayed with me for the rest of the day.

Some people, they're just born to hurt, which brings me to my brother Frank.

In Frank you couldn't've found a lovelier, kinder, softer person. Pure innocence shone out of him. An untarnished innocence that hadn't dimmed any, since the day he was born. An innocence that hadn't managed to grow a second skin, that couldn't grow a second skin, because that's how Frank was, he didn't understand the necessity of such things. And I guess it was that not understanding that killed him in the end.

Poor Frank; a day, an hour almost, doesn't go by when my thoughts aren't with him.

With Ellie it wasn't the growing of a skin so much. She had a different kind of innocence, fierce as Frank's was gentle, like a wild animal that hadn't learned to live in captivity. She was always throwing herself against the bars and coming away bruised and cut. And never understanding why. Because the very next day, she'd go and do the same thing all over again.

The poor sisters, they tried their best with her. I suppose they thought if they could get Little Ellie to bend her will to God and learn a little piety, humility they called it, another word I've never liked, she'd calm down and settle in a bit.

Ellie, according to Sister Dolores, was suffering from the sin of pride. One of the worst sins in her book. Well, I don't know about that. People's pride comes in all different shapes and sizes. And Ellie's pride was a skin she wore to protect herself from the things she didn't understand. But I don't suppose Sister Dolores understood that. All she saw was a little girl who was fierce and proud and headstrong, and had to be disciplined, brought into line with all the other little girls under her care. Broken like a wild pony.

Over those first few months of that summer term, Sister Dolores tried everything with Ellie. Every trick in a nun's book designed to tame unruly children. Only in Ellie's case none of them worked.

She was put on a separate table all by herself at mealtimes to stop her incessant talking. Her bed was moved out into the corridor outside one of the sisters' rooms to stop her telling ghost stories which terrified the other children and set them off screaming at the slightest creak in the corridor at night. She was kept back to do detention in the long summer evenings while the other girls were out playing, to stop her dreaming in lesson times and decorating her exercise books with pictures of kings and queens and tall castles and big flying dogs and cats and elephants and things.

But the worst was, when Sister Dolores got Ellie to kneel down in front of the statue of St Joseph in the courtyard and confess her sins in front of the whole school.

During all of Sister Dolores' trials, Ellie never cried, not a single tear, or showed she was the least bit scared. I got the feeling she was used to this sort of thing at the other places she'd been at, and she submitted with a quiet resignation, like it was her due, part of living, and just something she had to get through. And it was that courage in Ellie that seemed to incense Sister Dolores more than anything. Whatever she did, she couldn't win. That brave little girl's spirit eluded her every time. And so she got to be called sly and cunning and deceitful by the nuns. Along with being proud and insolent and stubborn, and a whole load of other things. And it began to seem to me that that little girl had just about all the sins in the book heaped on her shoulders, which in my opinion is a lot for a child to carry, not that Ellie seemed to mind. Like I said, she accepted the blame from the adult world like it was her due, her role in life.

And so the weeks went by with Little Ellie skimming through all the trials and tribulations put in her way by Sister Dolores, staying fierce and fiery and unruly as the day she arrived.

I suppose everyone must've thought she was unbreakable, forgetting she was a child. And I might've forgotten along with the rest, if I hadn't the memory of Frank to remind me, how things all of a sudden can change and turn it all upside down. With Ellie it happened on the day of her first Holy Communion.

Leading up to that point there was a whole load of controversy stirred up by Sister Dolores. In her opinion Ellie wasn't ready, she still had the stigma of the sin of pride sticking to her and was in no condition to take the light of the Lord Jesus into her heart. Father Benedict, who was Holy Communion mad, even he thought Ellie should wait. But Mother Louis was of a different opinion. She wasn't listening to either of them. She never explained her reasons, but I knew, and Sister Dolores and Father Benedict must've known too. No one ever said as much, but as soon as Mother Louis made her opinion known, they dropped their objections fast as hot potatoes. After all, what was one little girl's spiritual unworthiness in the face of a grand old lady's dying wish.

Yes, Mother Louis was dying. For the past year we'd watched her fading away in front of our eyes, growing smaller and greyer and thinner, like the flame on a candle slowly sinking. And it wasn't going to be long now, before the light in her finally went out.

I can't remember now, exactly, the last time I spoke to her alone. It must've been about three or four days before Ellie's Holy Communion. She'd called me into her study for a chat.

It was in the late afternoon, around the end of my day's work, sometime between five and six o'clock. She was sitting at that big old desk of hers, with the curtains half drawn to cut out the sunlight. The room was dim and cool and quiet, with a patch of late summer sunshine slanting through a gap in the curtains. I don't know why, but I remember it clearly, like it happened only yesterday. We sat in silence for a long time. There wasn't any need to talk, we both knew what she was going to say. I remember watching that patch of light which slipped across the corner of the desk and dropped down in a fan shape, on to that old Persian carpet of hers, which I'd always had such difficulty making look nice. No amount of hoovering ever seemed to get it clean. I sat watching that piece of bright light, dappled like water from the branches of the sycamore tree outside her window. And although I knew what my old friend was going to say, all I could think of was how much trouble that dirty old bit of carpet had caused me. And how it was just like her to hang on to it all these years, refusing to get a new one. I suppose what I was really thinking was that now it was too late.

Mother Louis was the first to break that long silence. I looked up to see her opening the top drawer of her desk.

'I want to give you something,' she said.

I don't know why that took me by surprise. Maybe because she'd never given me anything before, which isn't as strange as it sounds, when you remember nuns as a general rule have very little that they can call their own. I suppose because I was surprised, more than anything else, I told her she didn't have to do that, which looking back now, sounds like an ungrateful thing to say. Mother Louis smiled; maybe it was my lack of grace that amused her.

'I want you to have it,' she said. 'Come here.'

She had something in her hand. I went over to her. She took hold of my hand and put it in my palm, closing my fingers around it, holding them shut. Then she let go of my hand and sat back in her chair looking at me. I opened my hand. She had given me her mother of pearl rosary. She was smiling. It was her last little joke on me.

'Mother Louis,' I said, 'if you think I'm going to start praying at my age . . .'

'I'm not expecting anything,' she said.

'Just as long as that's understood between us,' I said. I wanted to square it with her, and let her know I wasn't taking anything under false pretences.

'Of course,' she said and smiled again with a twinkle in her eye. I had to hand it to that old lady, she never gave up trying.

'Marsi,' she said, 'have you thought what you're going to do when I'm gone?'

She spoke so matter-of-factly, like she was taking a trip to the Mother House in Rome.

'Gone?' I said; for a moment I really didn't know what she was talking about.

'I had a word with a dear old friend of mine – Father McBain – it's about time he got himself a housekeeper – I gave him your name – I hope you don't mind . . .' I stared at her. 'Maybe you've made other plans . . .'

Other plans, what other plans? It's strange how the expected things are often the ones that take you most by surprise. You spend all your time waiting for them to happen, knowing it's only a matter of months, weeks, days even . . . And then when they do happen you're knocked back, and you act like it's the last thing you expected in all the world. At least, that's how it was when Frank finally killed himself. And here it was happening in the same way all over again. Only this time Mother Louis was giving me some warning.

'Mother Louis,' I said, 'you're not going anywhere.'

'I'm afraid I am, my dear – and faster than I would like – I do hope I manage to see Little Ellie take her first Holy Communion.'

I don't know what happened then. It was like somebody had pushed a switch in me that I had no control over. I started to cry, great big baby-tears came welling up in me and rolling down my cheeks. I suppose I was crying first and foremost for myself and for Frank. I don't think I was crying for her then, that grief would come later.

'Marsi, I want you to keep an eye out for Little Ellie,' she said, handing me a blue-striped handkerchief that I've still got. I never gave it back.

'That little girl spreads trouble like wildfire,' I said,

blowing my nose into Mother Louis' handkerchief. 'What good can I do her?'

Mother Louis smiled. 'I think you like her,' she said.

Like I said, that was the last time I spoke to Mother Louis, but not the last time I saw her alive. That happened on the day of Ellie's first Holy Communion. It's my guess, looking back now, that old Mother Louis held out 'til then, just long enough to see Little Ellie taken into the fold, because that same night she passed away.

Ellie was taking her communion with two other little girls. They looked pretty enough in their white frocks and white veils and little white socks. But Ellie was prettier by far. And she knew it. She had the devil in her that day. The wind in her feet. Running around, shrieking and giggling all over the place.

The two other little girls stood by, pious and prayerful as a pair of toadstools, while Ellie stole all the limelight from under their noses. They had their parents to behave for. Ellie had no one.

Like I explained before, Ellie's way to protect herself from hurting was to act wild. And the more she hurt, the wilder she acted. It's my guess, judging from her behaviour that day, she was hurting pretty bad. Her mother, the proud lady in the feathered hat I described to you, had sent a telegram that morning from somewhere in Italy, where she was acting in a film with a famous actor, saying she couldn't get away on account of bad weather conditions, which sounded like a pretty poor excuse to me.

I think, you know, I might've seen her in something, in a film with Roger Moore, where she was dangled by her little toe over a snake-pit. She had a lot of blue make-up on her eyes and not a hair out of place. But then that could've been someone else. It was a long time ago.

313

Anycase, that day Little Ellie was wild. I didn't get to see the ceremony, not being a churchgoer, which you will have probably gathered by now; it wouldn't've been right for me to be there. But I did get to see Ellie and the other little girls waiting in the hall outside the chapel for it all to begin. Ellie had calmed down a little by then, but what was strange was as soon as the organ music began to play and people started going in to get their seats, Ellie went quiet as a lamb. She closed her eyes and joined her hands and even managed to look like she was praying. Maybe she was praying. Come to think of it, at that moment I do believe she was.

Just before the organ music came to an end, Sister Dolores came out and told the little girls to come in. I saw them follow her up the aisle. Ellie was the last, with her hands joined and her head bowed in prayer. Then one of the sisters came over and closed the door, and that was all I saw.

Later, when it was all over, the organ music started up. The chapel doors opened up and the people filed out in a long line. Little Ellie was somewhere in the middle of everyone. What happened next all happened so quickly, it's difficult to separate out the stages in my mind, and tell them bit by bit. As I remember it, Ellie seemed to fly out like she had wings on her feet. All that lamblike prayerfulness in her was gone, switched out like a light, and she was back to her old self again. She dived through the crowd of nuns and parents and sped across the hall, right past me. I was standing at the bottom of the stairs, occupying myself with polishing the banisters.

That's when I saw Mother Louis. She was at the top of the stairs on her way down. She must've been in the gallery of the chapel watching it all from up there. It's funny how you remember things. I looked up and saw her hand on the banister. And then Ellie's little feet on the foot of the stairs, and the sound of her laughter. And Mother Louis coming down towards her smiling. And Ellie taking the stairs in leaps, two at a time. It was like she was flying towards her. Mother Louis' hand came away from the banister, and Ellie was getting nearer and nearer, laughing all the time. Mother Louis was still smiling when she started to fall in a black heap like a sack. I remember the sound, a soft thudding that didn't seem real. And little Ellie's eyes open wide, staring. And the sweep of her veil to the back of her head as she turned and ran away. I looked round. No one else had seen her on the stairs but me.

That night Mother Louis died in her sleep. By all accounts quiet as a whisper, having made her peace with God. Happy. Her heart stopped beating and she slipped away to the place where she'd always wanted to be.

And I'll say this now, knowing that old lady like I did, I'll defy anyone to say it was that fall which finished her. Mother Louis had made up her mind she was going that night and the only thing that kept her hanging on so long, was the old lady's stubborn determination to see Ellie right with God. Only as it turned out, she lived just long enough to see the start of something go all wrong.

Well – the very next day at the morning assembly after the Lord's prayer, Sister Dolores climbed up on to the platform. She stood there for a long time with her head bowed and her hands clasped in prayer. Everyone was silent, waiting for her to say something. She looked up, just at the point where it seemed like she was losing their attention, and stared over their heads straight at me. I was standing in the corner of the courtyard, a bit away from the assembly, washing down St Augustine's statue with soapy water and a little Vim, which helps to get the worst of the pigeons' doings off of him. I don't suppose she liked seeing me getting on with my work while she was up there making an impression on everyone. Well, it wasn't working on me. I bent down and wetted my cloth, getting ready to start on the saint's head, when she began to speak in this loud and sombre sounding voice, like she had it all rehearsed.

'Girls – I have a very sad announcement to make . . .'

That's when my heart stood still. Mother Louis was dead.

And in my mind, my thoughts flew to Frank and that Sunday afternoon when there was a knock on the door. As soon as I opened it and saw that little bald plain-clothed person standing there with his briefcase tucked under his arm, it was like I'd been waiting for that moment all my life. And I was calm and cold as steel inside, watching as he unzipped his case and brought out the black and white shiny photographs with little white specks on them. Photographs of Frank in the road, with his arms spread out and his head twisted round like he was pinned to a cross. Frank, with every bone broken in his body, smashed to pieces with the leap he'd taken from the balcony of his thirteenth-floor flat. The plain-clothed person had it written down on his form as an accident. He said he must've tripped on something which sent him over the edge. Well, if that's what he wanted to have down on his piece of paper I wasn't going to put him right. After all, what was the point? He didn't know Frank. None of them knew Frank. He was just a name and a number of a body on a slab as far as they were concerned. Frank's reasons were private. And they were best kept that way.

I didn't hear the rest of Sister Dolores' speech. And by the time I came round, she had everyone kneeling on the ground with their heads bowed and hands joined in silent prayer. Only one little girl was standing up at the front. And as I could only see the back of her head, it took me a while to realize the little girl was Ellie. One moment she was standing there stock-still as a lamp-post and the next moment she was down on the ground. I walked up the side of the courtyard to see what was going on. A group of girls had collected around the place where she fell, and from where I was standing, I thought I saw little Ellie lying on the ground, with her arms spread out and her head twisted back. It was only a brief glimpse, quick as the blink of an eyelid, before one of the sisters came over and cut off my view with a sweep of her long black skirt.

Later that morning I heard little Ellie had been taken to the infirmary to rest. Over that week I didn't see her around, not that I thought much about it, I had troubles of my own to be worrying about.

When the call came to go to see Sister Dolores, I was prepared, ready and waiting, I'd been expecting it all week. Sister Dolores had become Mother Dolores now, and had moved into my old friend's study.

When I went in, she was stood by the window, watching something through a pair of binoculars. She told me to take a seat, without turning round, and went on watching whatever it was occupying her attention, making me wait 'til she was good and ready to say her piece. Not that I minded. I knew what was coming, and besides, it gave me the opportunity to notice the changes she'd made to Mother Louis' room. The gold curtains were gone, and so was the bit of old carpet, and all of the pictures of Our Lady that used to be hanging on the walls. She'd got Venetian blinds put in, and a rug with the pattern of what looked like a bulldog woven into it, and a calendar with a photograph of three little bulldog puppies on the wall beside the desk. The only other pictures she had were one of St Augustine sitting on a cloud looking glum, and another of an old bulldog balanced on a tightrope on one hindleg. Well, I suppose I learnt something new about Sister Dolores that morning. I never knew she liked bulldogs that much, better than the Virgin Mary by the looks of things.

Sister Dolores was a strange one. Over six feet tall, with great big hands and feet, and a square jaw like a man's with grey whiskers on the chin that she'd never troubled to cut back like some of the other nuns. There was always something about her that put me in mind of John Wayne, out of one of those cowboy films. The way she stood sometimes, with one leg up on a chair and an elbow resting on her knee, like cowboys do when they're having it out with the sheriff, or dallying with dancing girls in smoky saloon-bars. And if it hadn't been for her voice, which was soft and sweet as a young girl's, I think I would've had a difficult time believing that there wasn't a man hidden inside that big black habit of hers.

Anycase, to get back to that morning. Sister Dolores, who had recently become Mother Dolores, which was a change of name I was never going to get used to thinking of her as, put the binoculars in her pocket and came round and leant herself against the front of the desk, with her arms folded and one foot crossed over the other, like a policeman at the start of an interrogation.

'Marsi,' she said, 'I think you know what I'm going to say . . .'

Well of course I did. As I said, I'd been waiting for it to come all week. But I wasn't going to play ball.

'No,' I said.

'I think you do,' she said, as she took a little nail file from her pocket.

Now if there's one thing I hate it's that sound, it sends shivers all up and down my spine. I'm uncomfortable as a cat dropped in a puddle of water, and I have an intuition Sister Dolores knew that. When you have that sort of antipathy towards another person, like the two of us had, it's a chemistry that binds you both in a strange sort of intimacy, like you can see into the other person's soul. And I suppose that's the thing that makes you hate them, 'cos you don't like what you see, at least I didn't with Sister Dolores, and I guessed she felt the same way about me.

'The time has come,' she said, 'for a parting of the ways.' She looked up, putting the nail file back in her pocket. 'Your position here was never intended to be permanent.' I'd only been in the job for over twenty years. 'And I'm sure you realize that I for one have never shared Mother Louis' opinion of your suitability for the post – and I think you'll know what I'm referring to when I say that you'd be happier and far better off working in a non-religious establishment, where impressionable young Catholic minds weren't at risk.'

'I've always kept my beliefs to myself,' I said.

'That's hardly the point,' she said.

'No, it isn't, is it,' I said, managing to meet her in the eye for the first time since I'd come into the room.

The point was, she and most of the other sisters, apart from Sister Bernadette, who was too preoccupied with matters of the flesh to mind, hated me for my special friendship with Mother Louis. I'd got close where none of them could even get a toe in the door. And her preferring me for myself over the rest of them cut deep. And seeing as the point, at this time, was understood between me and Sister Dolores, I didn't see much sense in pressing on, and I let her get on tying up the loose ends of my dismissal. At the end of it all, in which I was graciously granted one month's notice before I had to quit, she asked me if I had anything I wanted to say.

I asked her if I could go and visit Ellie in the infirmary. She said Ellie wasn't in any fit condition to be seeing anyone.

And when I suggested that if Ellie was unhappy, maybe I could help her, that's when a nasty look came into her eye. A sixth sense must've told her it was something discussed between Mother Louis and me.

I saw my mistake straightaway but by then it was too late and Sister Dolores was expressly forbidding me to do something I could otherwise have done without blinking an eyelid, if I hadn't been fool enough to bring it up with her that afternoon.

I suppose these things work two ways. If I'd never asked Sister Dolores' permission to visit Ellie in the infirmary I never would've been forbidden. And if I hadn't been forbidden, I don't think I would've got along there so fast, that same day around lunchtime, which as it turns out it was lucky I did, despite the amount of trouble it caused later.

Twelve thirty is the time the sisters go to their midday prayers, which meant there'd only be old Mrs White in the dispensary up at the end. And seeing as her drinking problem prevented her from noticing much of what was going on around her, I figured I'd be safe to sneak in and get to see little Ellie for myself.

The infirmary around that time of year is usually pretty empty. When I went in there was nobody around, apart from old Mrs White snoozing in a patch of sunshine behind the glass of the dispensary, and a little girl asleep in her bed at the far end. I couldn't see Ellie anywhere, and I began to wonder if they'd taken her away somewhere, when I remembered the isolation room at the back near the bathroom. I went along there. The door was locked. The key for it was kept in the dispensary. Old Mrs White was well away, snoozing with her jaw dropped down and making those little grunting sounds. The smell of whiskey was powerful. It stank like a distillery in there. I reached up and took the key for the isolation room off a rack above her head. She grunted and belched a fresh wave of whiskey fumes, and as my hand came down across her face, holding the key, one of her eyes snapped open and stared straight at me, with an expression in it that was mean and fierce as an old jungle cat. For a moment I thought she had me, then the lid dropped down and the soft grunting snores started up again, sending sharp little twitches down her body, like a fat old dog asleep in front of the fire after mealtime.

I left old Mrs White to her mean whiskey dreams and went to find little Ellie. The curtain behind the bed, which was drawn across the window, billowed out like a full sail, with a pale light shining through. It took a while for my eyes to adjust to the dimness before I saw the dark shape of a child in a long nightdress silhouetted against the pale cream-coloured light. At first I didn't understand. Ellie wasn't in the bed or under it. I felt like I was seeing a ghost. And when I realized, I ran across that room like lightning and pushed back the curtain. Ellie was standing on the window-ledge staring down. I didn't stop to think. I grabbed hold of her by the waist and pushed her back into the room, sitting her down on the bed. I was shaking all over, trembling like a leaf.

She stared up at me, with those round-saucer green eyes of hers, calm as you like.

'I'm bad,' she said.

I sat down on the bed beside her and put my arms around her and held her to me very tight. We stayed like that for a long time. I was thinking of Frank. Frank on the window-ledge, thirteen floors up. Frank lying on the ground with his arms spread out and his head twisted back.

She lay in my arms, limp as a little fish, not moving a muscle. My heart ached, and all I could think about was

Frank, over and over, the same thing again and again, on the window-ledge, on the ground, and nothing in between.

After a bit I let go of her. She was looking beyond me, past my shoulder at something in the corner of the room. I turned round to look. There was nothing there. But she kept on staring.

'Ellie – what is it?'

She pointed to the corner of the room. 'Make him go away.'

I forced her head round so that she was looking at me. 'Make who go away?'

She whispered. 'The black man with wings.'

Well, there was no black man with wings that I could see in the room. But I wasn't going to tell her that. To that frightened little girl he was standing there plain as day.

'Who is he, Ellie?' I said.

'You know,' she whispered.

'No – I don't – tell me.'

Keeping her eyes fixed on that spot in the corner of the room, she leant forward and whispered into my ear.

'Mother Louis' friend.'

'What does he want?' I whispered back in her ear.

She was staring over my shoulder into the corner of the room. Her face crumpled up. She started to cry.

'Tell him to go away.'

Well it may sound strange to you, but I knew what I had to do. I got up off that bed, went over to the corner of the room. I raised my hands, jumped up in the air as far as I could and bellowed at the top of my voice. It felt good. I turned round to Ellie.

'Has he gone?' I said.

She pointed to another corner of the room by the basin. 'He's up there,' she said.

I went over to the basin and repeated the same performance all over again.

'What about now?' I said.

She pointed to the window-ledge. I went over to the window and pulled the curtains back. Now I know this is going to sound even stranger, and you're not going to believe it, but I saw my brother standing on that window-ledge clear as day, clear as I'm speaking to you now. And I can assure you I've never been one for imagining things. It was Frank standing there in his old checked shirt I gave him one Christmas and old trousers, and no shoes. Standing there smiling at me.

I turned round and looked at her. She could see him too. I walked over to the bed and picked her up in my arms and carried her over to the window.

'Ellie,' I said, 'I want you to meet my brother Frank.'

She was looking straight at him, seeing what I saw. Her face cleared, like a dark sky after rain. She held out her hand and their fingers touched. She was smiling. And he was smiling. And I was crying like a great big baby, for the first time since he'd been gone.

'Don't cry,' she said. 'Mother Louis sends her love, and says thank you for looking after me, and when she grows wings she'll come and see you for a chat and tea.'

Well, I never did see Mother Louis again, or Frank for that matter. By the time I turned to look around, he was gone.

'Where is he?' I said to Ellie.

She pointed up into the sky. A big white cloud was passing across the sun.

'Home,' she said, 'over there.'

LANDSCAPE, GIRL, LION

Clive Lancaster

Clive Lancaster grew up on the South Coast in the years after the war. After failing the eleven-plus, he left school early. He did National Service in the RAF, and went on to work in London for a small paperback publisher and in 1966 moved to Labrador, Canada, where he worked as a school master in a remote fishing village for three years. He received a state scholarship and moved back to Sussex University where he read social anthropology – followed by two years at Oxford.

Landscape, Girl, Lion is set in Africa where Clive Lancaster spent a year. He is married with two children and has resumed writing after a gap of many years.

LANDSCAPE, GIRL, LION

Suki was born in a faraway country, a high windy country under an African sky where on a clear night the stars were so many and seemed so close you thought you could cast a net and haul them in by their thousands like little silver fish.

You could find Suki's country in the atlas, somewhere west of Somalia, north of Kenya, east of the stupefying plains of the Sudan, but even the best maps would tell you very little. It would seem to be a largely blank space of indeterminate size, occupied by a couple of roads, two or three rivers, perhaps half a dozen small towns. Nothing could be further from the truth. In reality it was a big country in which there were enough names to astonish a team of lexicographers. People say we live on a shrinking planet, a global village they say, but if you dropped out of the sky to stand on a high place in Suki's country you would soon see how vast is spaceship Earth. Your aching legs could measure it out pace by pace, and your lungs and your sweating skin, and your eyes dazzled in the dry, dusty plains, your mouth dry and no water-hole in sight. And what had been an empty space on the map would become filled with names. Every hill, every clump of low, thorny trees, every rock, would have its name, as would all the streams, the old wells dug deep in the red rock, the strangely shaped termite mound on the ridge, the great plain beneath the escarpment where baboons lived, the place where there had long ago been a river, the place where your grandfather was killed by a wild boar, or where the very first people saw God, or where it had once rained three times in one year or where it had never in the memory of men rained at all.

All the animals had names, all the plants, all the insects, everything that roared or ran or flew or muttered or howled or grunted or burrowed silently in the earth. So many names and not a dictionary in sight. Adam had been this way, too, and walked every inch of it; apt deviser of names, archivist of the planet and all its creatures. Even Suki knew many names, thousands of them, and she was only a girl and young at that. When the old men started on the names of things and their stories there was no end to it.

Most names were so ancient that no one could say where they had come from; others were newer and some were so new that they had not yet, so to speak, settled down properly and so were suitable subjects for discussion and interpretation. Since the war with the Somalis, for instance, many people now called the praying mantis, elegant creatures ranging from the big green ones to tiny creations like jewels from a nightmare, by a name that meant Somali ghosts. Then there was the great bush-covered outcrop of rock by the water-hole. A few years ago a foreigner had come that way, a red-faced man who spoke of a book; from a certain point of view, so he said, the rock looked like the head of a lion, and so a new name came into existence. Even for those who still preferred the old name, the new one had its uses, since it reminded people of the red-faced foreigner and of his book. No one had been much impressed by him and indeed few had listened to him talking about his god who, it seemed, had allowed himself to be tied up and beaten and slaughtered like an ox. Even so, strangers of any sort were rare in Suki's world and gave people something to talk about at night when the cows came back and were milked, each wife with her own cows and every cow with its own name, like so many dogs.

That's how it was every evening in Suki's world. Early in the morning, before the sun rose, the boys, the unmarried men, even some men who were married but who were poor and had no cattle of their own, drove the cows away from the village, out into the rolling plains beyond the thorn fence. All day they wandered while the patient beasts grazed at the sparse grass. Where they went depended on the time of the year, on the condition of the grazing, on the location of the water-holes, even on the whereabouts and disposition of other people, people who were sometimes enemies, who spoke a different language and who therefore knew different names. At dusk they returned to Suki's village, the cows already lowing as they came nearer, the men following with their long spears resting across their shoulders, the dappled bull always in the lead.

Then all the men in the village stood outside the thorn fence and watched the animals, noting their condition, commenting on their pedigrees and their fertility. They were like bankers keeping a watchful eye on an important investment. Inside the thorn fence the women and children waited. As the cows ambled in the women called their names and the cows answered.

Between the time the cattle left at dawn and returned at night there were many things to do. There was wood to be cut and gathered from the forest and water to be brought from the wells that had been dug many years ago in the rocky foothills of the great escarpment. There was sour milk to be made and butter, and there were the endless minor repairs to the hut where Suki lived with her mother. Suki's mother was her husband's second wife and his favourite, so he often stayed the night, although at other times, of course, it was necessary to visit his other two wives. When all the work of the household was done Suki visited her friends and they plaited each other's hair, a business of great elaboration that took up many pleasant hours.

Up to this time, if anyone had asked Suki was she happy she would probably have shrugged her shoulders, perhaps laughed at such a curious question. But then she became thirteen years old and things changed. First, things in her body changed, and then things in the world. How it seemed to Suki, when later in life she thought about it, was that she had been a girl and then she was a woman. Among her people the women made a great business of the menarche; the first showing of the blood was a thing to be celebrated, a ceremony of solidarity among the women in which they welcomed the girl who had become a woman. Everything had changed and yet Suki felt as if nothing had changed; something secret had happened inside her and however hard she thought about it she could never quite pin it down.

From now on, once a month, she would have to remain hidden in the back of her mother's hut so as not to be seen by any male creature. Following these changes in her body there came changes of another sort. One day Suki's mother spoke to her as they were cleaning milk pots with hot ashes. She told Suki that her father had gone to a distant village to talk to a man he knew. For a while Suki's mother was silent, staring down intently at her work with the pots. Suki kept her tongue still for a long time and then gave in.

'What man is this?' she said.

Still looking down at her work, Suki's mother said, 'A man who wishes to marry you.'

This was the most ordinary thing in the world. Nothing could be more commonplace than that her father, now she was a woman, would seek to negotiate her marriage. He would look for a man of wealth, a man with many cattle, a person of influence with important kin, a man of vigorous middle-age already proven to be virile; a man, it now occurred to her, very much like himself.

All this was only to be expected, it was something that everyone knew, something the young girls approaching womanhood often gossiped about. Just the same, now it had happened at last, she felt pole-axed like a dumb beast. The hut suddenly seemed strangely silent and things seemed muffled and distant; she could feel the blood pulsing in her eardrums. If she felt anything else at all it was a great dismay. She knew she did not want to marry this old man her father was talking to. In such moments thoughts come in waves, seldom one at a time; another thought was that she did not want to marry anyone, the thought of it made her feel she wanted to turn her head from side to side and shut her eyes against the world. Yet another thought was what was the use of being one kind of thing only to have to change into another and always have your fate in other people's hands?

Why Suki should find the normal fate of girls so repugnant was something of a mystery; in due course, when the business became a village scandal, all the usual people were consulted. Some said an evil eye had been put on her, others that she was perhaps a little mad, others that she preferred a younger secret lover, still others that she was simply a wicked and obstinate child.

Not having thought about marriage before she was astonished at the force of this distaste; her mother, who knew her better, was less surprised which is why she had averted her gaze. The mother comforted herself with the thought that by and by the girl would come round to the idea. After all, what other fate than marriage was there for women? This was a society in which there were girls, married women and widows; there was no such creature as a spinster. Even so, Suki's mother could not forget the look on her daughter's face.

Sitting alone in the dim light of the hut the woman tried to recall how things had been when she was a young girl; rhythmically shaking the sour-milk pot up and down she let her mind drift back to that distant time. But although she could remember many things, see faces clearly and even hear the words, she could not recall herself, could not penetrate a kind of cloud in her mind in which her young self moved invisibly.

As was the custom among Suki's people, her father said nothing to his daughter about his plans for her marriage. Such a course would never have entered his mind and would, in any case, have been regarded as deeply shocking, a profound breach of etiquette. As his negotiation proceeded slowly he informed Suki's mother and she, in turn, informed her daughter.

The dry season moved slowly through one hot, dry day after another until one afternoon a big wind got up and blew dust and tumbleweed everywhere, making both people and animals irritable all day long until darkness came, sudden and without twilight, and the wind dropped as suddenly as it began. Those who studied such things, the sky, the wind, the behaviour of beasts and birds, went round the village with the good news. First the wind, they reminded people, then the clouds, then the long rains. Herdsmen took to looking at the sky from time to time, the cattle became noisier and more quarrelsome, the hyenas became bolder at night and boys dug pits and baited them so that in the morning they could spear those ugly brutes who stole things from men. All the signs were clear; soon the rains would come, the new grass would spring up and the milk would flow. There would be feasts, ceremonies, much visiting among kinsfolk and there would be the season for marriages.

The nearer this time came the unhappier Suki grew. She was certain now that she did not want to marry this man, a man she had never seen and who already had two wives. But she did not know how to disobey her father and neither could she think of anyone to whom she could turn for help. By day she went silently about her work, no longer playing or gossiping with the other unmarried girls, and at night she lay on her low couch of dressed hides and stared up into the darkness until she drifted into a shallow and troubled sleep with many bad dreams.

No one takes the despair of the young seriously, reasoning that it always passes in time and not seeing how this might make it worse, but even so Suki's mother could not bear to see her daughter so miserable and confused. One morning she said: 'Go and talk to the old woman who lives alone.'

Suki could hardly believe her ears. 'The old woman is crazy,' she said to her mother. 'She has the evil eye and everyone knows she is a witch.'

Suki's mother paused as she pounded the maize grains and wiped sweat from her eyes. With her small, elegant head and the great silver earrings she could have been a queen in old Egypt; in her youth she had been judged a great beauty.

'Ah yes,' she said thoughtfully, 'everyone knows ... I still say talk to her.'

The old woman lived alone at the north end of the village. Her hut was close to the great thorn fence and just to one side of the entrance through which the cattle passed every morning and every night. As was only proper for such a strange old woman her hut was set at a distance from all the others as though this physical space spoke for the social distance between this solitary and the rest of the village. Living in a distant village in the east of the country she had a son, a middle-aged man who had never visited his mother since her husband died, many years ago. This in itself was a disgrace that gave rise to all manner of speculation.

Among Suki's people no one lived alone; the great, branching networks of kinship, stretching out across time and space, were such that solitude was thought of as both a vice and an absurdity. Even those old men, widowers who had no hut of their own, who wandered the countryside from one camp to another, leading prayer, presiding at ceremonies, discussing law and custom, never spent a night on their own. No wonder then that stories and rumours gathered around this strange old woman. Once a big, handsome woman she was now a tall, stooping figure with a sardonic eye and a low, harsh voice, still vigorous in spite of her great age.

Ever since Suki was a tiny child she had known about the old woman who seemed never to have changed but although she had seen her hundreds of times she knew nothing about her, not even how she managed to live. Having neither kin nor cattle, how could she stay alive, what did she eat? Quite suddenly, as a consequence of her mother's apparently casual suggestion, this eccentric stranger emerged from the generality of village life into sharp focus. Suki took to loitering near the old woman's hut, pretending to be on some errand, making a business of collecting dried cattle dung for the fire, and trying to watch the old woman without being herself watched. She soon saw that things were not as she had thought and that the old woman was not as solitary as she had unthinkingly supposed. Quietly, furtively one could say, various women of the village appeared from time to time, hovered at the entrance of the hut then slipped inside. Each woman carried a gift, a dish of maize, a pot of milk, a length of cloth, a bundle of tobacco, even once some stewed goat meat in a covered dish. Suki saw these things, a few episodes observed among so many missed, and began to see how it might be possible for this old woman to survive. Curiously enough this observation pleased her; in simply watching the old woman Suki had rediscovered the pure pleasure of paying attention and learning things.

Some of the women stayed only a few minutes, others remained in the hut for a long time. Once a woman stayed inside for what seemed hours, to emerge weeping silently, standing in the sudden fierce light like a shipwrecked mariner, tears flooding down her cheeks, before stumbling blindly away. A small boy hunting with a toy spear for the lizards drowsing in the thorn fence stood in the dusty soil and gazed at this strange and incomprehensible scene.

All afternoon Suki stood in the shade of an acacia tree and watched these strange comings and goings until the sun began to dip towards the rim of hills and it was time to go back to her mother's hut and help with the evening meal.

For three days things went on like this. Every night Suki's mother asked her if she had spoken to the old lady yet and each time Suki had to say, increasingly sullenly, that she had not.

On the fourth day it was very hot although the sky was dull and leaden. Soon the clouds would begin to mass over the escarpment, heavy with moisture gathered from a distant sea. On the night before Suki had heard her father talking to her mother about the man who wanted to marry her. The voices were indistinct but she knew what they were talking about. Her father sounded angry more than once.

In the heat of the afternoon she leaned against the tree trunk, watching the termites running up and down, always bumping into each other, strange creatures that taken one by one seemed stupid and yet, in the mass, were not. Perhaps she dozed off for a few seconds; at any rate there she was at one moment alone, half asleep in the heavy air, and then from nowhere there was someone else. The old woman, grinning at her, a nose like a spear blade, wrinkles, bloodshot eyes, teeth missing; all these without any diminution of vitality. This was not one of those old ladies who went round begging bowls of milk and muttering blessings or curses to which no one paid attention.

'Suki spies on me,' the old woman said. 'Why does she spy on me?' The woman's voice was deep and hoarse, her eyes were glittering. For a moment Suki thought that perhaps it would be wiser to run away. 'The daughter of Dida the son of Boru has no tongue?'

'How do you know my name?'

The old woman grinned and showed her tobacco-stained teeth.

'I know everything,' she said slyly.

'Everything?'

'Everything.'

'Then what do I want, do you know that, old woman?'

The old woman laughed and clapped her hands. 'Take care of your tongue, girl,' she said. 'Come inside out of the sun and we will talk.'

'What is your name?' Suki said.

'Name? Oh, my name. Let me see, yesterday I was Elbow, tomorrow I shall be Sore Foot, so today I am Eye.'

None of these words was a name among Suki's people. The two women stood for a moment by the entrance to the hut; the old one reached out and very gently stroked the young one's shoulder and upper arm, her long, thin fingers dry and cool on the girl's glossy skin. As she stroked she made curious little grunting noises and nodded her head. Then Suki pushed past her and went into the hut.

Here she found a cool, dim space, much smaller than inside her mother's hut but tidy enough, even comfortable, although there was a strange smell. Suki bowed her head for a moment and concentrated on this odour; it was not the smell of cattle hides or of the packed earth floor or the dried woven branches of the roof or even of the tobacco bundles hanging up to dry. It was a different smell, in part sweet and in part sharp, bitter even, that she thought she knew but could not for the moment give a name.

There were two low, carved stools set either side of the hearth with its heap of white ash still glowing between the three hearth-stones. The old woman blew on the ash and threw a handful of dried leaves on the glowing mound and at once the strange sweet and bitter smell grew strong as a thick plume of white smoke rose, thinned and vanished in the roof. As for the old woman, she leaned forward with her face turned down into the rising smoke and took in a single, long, shuddering breath.

Somewhere outside a hornbill screeched its monotonous challenge; dappled light filtered down through the roof; Suki could hardly tell how long she had been in this dim, silent place, whether minutes or hours. An ant, one of the big black ones, rushed about on her bare foot and from somewhere in the back of the hut, beyond the partitioned sleeping area, there came a strange, dry, rustling sound, something between a hiss and a rapid clicking, that swelled up angrily and then subsided into silence.

At last the old woman spoke. 'Why does Suki come to trouble this poor old woman?' Her tone was now perfunctory, almost bored.

'Why must girls always marry?' Suki said.

337

The old woman who called herself Eye replied in a rapid mumble: 'How else would they live?' She poked irritably at the ashes with a pointed stick.

'Why must they marry?' Suki said again. She would have liked to ask a more interesting question but could not for the moment think of one.

Eye spoke in a low voice without looking up. 'Because they have no cattle.'

'Must all the world have cattle? Is there no other way to live?'

The old woman looked straight at the girl now. 'You ask questions to which you already know the answers. I have no cattle, will you live like me? The red-faced man with the book had no cattle and far away in the city there are untold thousands with no cattle. Perhaps you can find one of the red-faced men or live in the city where you can serve beer and sleep with strangers for money or be a farmer's wife and scratch all day in the earth.'

Suki knew that Eye was mocking her but even so these were not things that anyone else had ever said to her. 'Why have women no cattle?' she said.

'What! You don't know even that! Things must have changed since I was a girl if you don't know that. Listen: in the beginning the people had no cattle. They lived in a flat country far to the south and they were all farmers. God lived nearby in those days, he came and walked among the people, sometimes he was in the sky, but very close, just here, so – ' she lifted one hand to a level just above her head. 'A woman quarrelled with her husband because he took a second wife and neglected her. She was working in the fields with a hoe and she was angry. God came very close and asked the woman why she was angry and she raised her hoe and struck God. Then God went away, far away up in the sky, and the people gave up farming because

338

God cursed them and nothing would grow. The elders prayed and God gave them cattle and they came to this place. The elders said that a woman had ruined the farming and driven God away and if another woman ruined the cattle we would all die. So that is why women have no cattle.'

Suki thought about this for a while and then admitted: 'It is a good story.'

'It is a very good story,' Eye said and grinned. 'One of the best.'

Suki felt she had been in the old woman's hut for a very long time. Once more there was the strange rustling sound in the back of the hut and then a snake, one of the big cobras, came gliding across the earth floor, turning its head from side to side and tasting the air with its flickering tongue. Right in front of the girl it lapped milk from a dish as daintily as may be imagined. For a moment the snake raised its flat head and stared at Suki from its tiny black eyes, then it glided between her bare feet, a snake longer than a man, and passed outside into the sun and then on into the great thorn hedge where it vanished in a moment.

Eye seemed not to have noticed the cobra. 'It is more than a question of cattle,' she said. 'Life is not only a question of milk and maize and meat. We must have a name, we must speak and hear, it is necessary to be known. If you will not marry then how can you live among people and if you cannot live among people how will you live at all? One thing leads to another in this life, girl, and things cannot be easily untangled from each other.'

'I don't want to marry,' Suki said.

'Your father will make you marry.'

'But I don't want to.'

'You will have nowhere to live.' Eye held up a warning

finger. 'That's twice,' she said mockingly, 'the third time is for truth.'

'I will not marry,' the girl said angrily.

'Then if you can't live with people,' the old woman said maliciously, 'you must go and live with the beasts. Find a cave in the hills and live with baboons and hyenas, perhaps even lions. Would you like that, Suki daughter of Dida son of Boru, to live with the wild beasts?'

Suki said: 'You are mad. They say you are mad and so you are.'

'They say, they say,' Eye sneered. 'What do they not say? You call me names and yet you have not brought me a gift, not even a drink of milk or a little tobacco to chew. Strange times when girls of good family have such fine manners.'

After a while Suki said: 'I will bring you a gift. What would you like?'

'You will think of something. And I too, have something to give. Take this and think very carefully. If you cannot use it then you must return it to me.'

She went to the back of the hut and came back with a bag of strange design, quite like a satchel if Suki had ever seen such a thing. It had a long strap to pass over the shoulder and a wooden peg to fasten the flap through a loop of leather. It looked very old and as she took it from Eye Suki could feel the weight of it and hear a clinking sound like stones knocking together.

'There is no point in looking in it now,' the old woman said. 'Do not let anyone see it, not even your mother, keep it secret. Remember, if you cannot live with people then you must live with the beasts. Or you can go to the city, which is even worse, since at least among the beasts you will remain yourself whereas in the city you would soon start to disappear.'

Suki stood up. 'What you say is impossible,' she said,

but the old woman made no reply. Then Suki was outside in the hot sunshine, blinking in the sudden light, hardly able to say whether she was awake or dreaming.

The old woman called from within the hut: 'Impossible you say. All the same, it has been done.'

Later that night, when her mother was asleep, Suki took the bag out from under her bed and felt about in it, trying to guess what it contained. Very early in the morning before anyone was awake she emptied the bag on the floor. There was an old dagger with a horn handle, the blade thinned by age and use but still sharp; there were three hearth-stones showing scorchmarks from the fire; there was a leather water-bottle with a wooden stopper carved like a snake's head; there was a milk bowl fashioned from a gourd; there was an iron and flintstone for making fire. All these things were commonplace enough except for the iron and flintstone. The making of fire was something that belonged to men; in all her life Suki had only ever once seen a fire being lit. It had not looked a very difficult affair at the time. In any case, what man would show a girl how to make fire?

After she had helped her mother in the house Suki went for a long walk, far beyond the thorn hedge and up into the foothills of the escarpment. Again the sky was grey and the air was dull, hot, oppressive. On her way from the village she saw the usual group of older men sitting in the shade of the big acacia tree. Two men were arguing about the rights to a distant watering hole, each rising to his feet to make his case, then squatting again to listen to the reply. The other men listened, grunted occasionally at a fine point or a striking image, cleaned their teeth with little sticks, looked bored and yawned, passed around chewing tobacco. From a distance Suki saw a stranger among them, a thin, hook-nosed man, sitting straight-backed and cross-legged next to her father. Suki's father said something to the stranger who turned and stared at the girl. She stepped back into the shade of a thorn bush and the man turned away.

Later she found a secluded place, a little clearing among high rocks, where she tried her hand at the fire-stones. She had wrapped them in a piece of cloth; all the other things were in the old leather bag hidden under her bed. She could see almost at once that there was more to this business than she had thought. After an hour she had produced nothing more than a couple of feeble sparks and made her hands sore. This was one of those things that looked easy but was not. Suki sat in the shade of an old termite hill and blew on her sore fingers. On a distant hillside she saw a troop of baboons, darting here and there and shouting at each other. In this oppressive heat birds of all kinds sat sullenly in trees or on rocks, opening and closing their beaks and spreading their wings to catch the smallest breeze.

She turned the fire iron over and over and studied the marks scratched on one side: three short wavy lines beneath the sign of a new moon. After a little while the solution of this elementary problem became obvious. The sign on the iron was the maker's mark and who else but the smiths worked in iron? She went down the hill and set off across the plain towards the market town. It was now shortly before midday and if she walked well she could get to the town, find a smith, and still be home before dark. It was a long walk but she was strong and she knew the way. There was a water-hole under the hill at Golbu and she knew that in the market town there would be smiths, squatting in the dust, selling the products of their craft alongside other workers in wood and in leather. Although the smiths spoke the same language as Suki's people theirs was a dangerous craft, forbidden to Suki's people just as the smiths were forbidden to own cattle. In that respect, Suki thought, they are like women. No doubt there was a story about that, too, which she would learn in time.

The town was a rambling settlement of mud houses with corrugated iron roofs set out in a pattern of squares on a dusty plain at the foot of wooded hills. Here were all manner of strange people, traders mostly, but also officials, army men and government people, women who ran beer-houses and other places where it was said you could sit inside and eat food for money, men who traded in cattle for the distant city, people from far away places who spoke strange languages, even European tourists who sometimes arrived on the bus from Kenya and stood in the dusty square gaping around them. Small mangy dogs ran aimlessly about, panting with their tongues hanging out, and an old leper woman begged outside the place where strangers could rent a partitioned-off space for the night. In the centre of the square there stalked a madman, mumbling, cursing or praying, no one knew which. Suki knew of him, he was a young man of her own village. He had gone away to be educated in the great city and there had lost his wits.

Just for once she did not stop to look at all these strange things but hurried to the market-place. It was getting late in the day and she feared that the market would be empty and all the smiths gone to their cluster of huts at the foot of the mountains or else taken their earnings to the beer-houses where no woman could go. She saw a town woman hoping to sell the last of her eggs, two men arguing about the price of a spavined camel that no one would ever buy or sell again, two government men in suits supervising a load of maize and there, sitting in the shade of a thorn tree, a solitary smith packing the tools of his craft into a leather sack.

He was a very small man, tiny even, with a deerskin apron and a cloth draped over a spare bony frame; he had more wrinkles on his face than Suki had ever seen on a human countenance. On the other hand he had all his teeth and his small, deep-set eyes flashed lively enough. Suki loomed over this strange little man, feeling large and clumsy in contrast to such neat and merry composure. Casting around in her mind for a suitable opening she found none and simply showed the man the iron and the flintstone. Then she squatted on the dry, sandy ground while the little man turned the iron over and over and made thoughtful clicking noises.

'This is very old,' the smith said. 'From the time of my grandfather, perhaps even older. No one has used this sign since the time of the great war when foreigners came here.'

The first thing everyone tells you, Suki said to herself, is how old things are; we are a great people for long ago. She took the iron and the flintstone from the little man and held them out in the palms of her hands.

'Show me how to make fire,' she said. The little man raised his eyebrows and rocked back and forth on his heels in silent laughter. 'Show me and I will give you a goat.'

The smith clapped his hands in pleasure. Ah, a goat, how tender, how succulent, how aromatic with herbs and chillies! As for this crazy girl, if she wanted to learn secrets then let her learn, it was nothing to him. Even so there were necessary precautions; if any of Suki's people saw him with the girl there would be trouble and he wanted no trouble with those tall men and their long spears. This troubling thought lent an edge of malice to his instructions in the little clearing on the edge of the town, away from the road; he was brusque with the girl and jeered at her clumsiness. 'Have you two left hands?' he asked, grinning. Still, she learned quickly enough how to hold the stones, how to strike them, what sorts of dried grass were best, what kinds of wood, even about the kind of bark that would burn when wet, and how to keep the ashes hot in a little clay pot with a grass stopper. Over and over again the little man made the girl go through it until he was satisfied.

'You may be the first woman to know this,' the smith said. 'Be a good girl and do not tell people. At any rate, leave my name out of it.' It was easy to see how excited she was, like a drunk, hardly able to contain her delight at this new and rare skill. 'Well, don't forget my goat. A young one, female, if it's all the same to you.'

Long after Suki had gone out of sight the smith squatted on his heels in the dust and thought about this strange girl who had wanted to learn how to make fire. Over the years the women of her people had asked him many things, when their men weren't looking, but none of them had ever asked how to make fire. But then these were strange times. Only a month ago a foreigner, one of the red-faced men, had spoken to the smith in his own language, badly it was true, but badly was extraordinary enough.

The smith knew his kind were despised by Suki's people but still, he thought, they fear us a little, too, and come to us for the many things they do not understand, knowing that we are the first people who owned all this land long ago before they came with their cattle and their spears.

Suki arrived at her village just before evening milking. She supposed that everyone would see at once that she was different, as though what was in her head must show in her body, but no one even noticed that she had been gone.

That night she hardly slept and in the morning she rose early, made her preparations and was gone from the village before the sun had risen above the distant rim of the great escarpment.

Later that same day, before Suki's mother had thought much about her daughter's absence from morning milking, the clouds massed in the sky and this time did not move on even though there was a strong wind for nearly an hour. Then the wind dropped and the sky became dark. Everywhere people stood staring up into the sky, saying nothing, waiting. Quite suddenly the air was filled with water as great drops of rain, at first a few and then a torrent, crashed to the earth and bounced as high as a man's knee. Within minutes everything and everyone was soaked; children ran in the sudden rivulets laughing; out in the bush the grazing cattle raised their heads as the rain steamed on their hot bodies.

Such a downpour could not last long and in less than an hour it settled to a steady drizzle and then stopped altogether. But in that time water poured down from the hills near the town in a sudden flood and washed away the sandy path that led to the market-place. Instead of the red sand there was now a deep ditch filled with thick, reddish water that ran in a jagged line right through the middle of the town. In places its sides were as high as a man. Children ran up and down along its crumbling banks following the misadventures of a goat which suddenly found the world opened up beneath it and now spun helplessly in the flooded ditch where it found no foothold. Eventually it found a shallower place and clambered up to dry land where it wandered about, shaking itself like a dog and bleating loudly.

Men came out from one of the beer-houses and laid long planks over the flooded ditch. They sat at a trestle-table with rain running down their faces and drank beer and laughed. The youth who had lost his wits jumped up and down in a big puddle until one of the men gave him beer. Then he became silly and tried to walk along the wooden railing that ran around the beer-house verandah. He soon fell off there and lay unhurt on his back in the wet, sandy earth until he fell asleep, snoring loudly.

In Suki's village her mother went from hut to hut looking for her daughter. No one had seen the girl although there was no shortage of advice and opinions. She would be with so and so, would she not, or she would have gone to such and such a place, had she not mentioned it only yesterday or perhaps last week? No one was alarmed; theirs was a world of visibilities, people did not vanish or come to mysterious ends, but only went off for a while to reappear shortly.

Suki's father was displeased but calm. Like a great spider's web his network of kinship would surely vibrate soon enough and send him a message. Besides, everyone knew that girls sometimes behaved badly before marriage and he was well aware that this daughter was a girl with a strong mind. Suki had merely gone astray for a while like a temperamental heifer wandering off before the bull led her back. Such bovine metaphors came naturally to Suki's father. It was not that he couldn't tell the difference between people and cattle but rather that so much of his life had led him to dwell on the similarities.

Suki's mother was more uneasy. She didn't yet suppose that her daughter had come to any harm but among other things taken from her hut was a bag of sun-dried beef strips and a quantity of coarsely ground maize flour. Mixed with a little water and left to ferment on a flat stone in the sun and then baked this would make a chewy, unleavened bread. Going through things more carefully Suki's mother soon found that other things were also gone; an iron dish, made long ago by a smith from metal scavenged from a wrecked lorry, a little clay pot, a bed cover of supple, dressed cowhide from Suki's couch. Later still she found that an old spear, kept up in the hut rafters, was also missing.

Among her people Suki's mother was known to be a

woman of substance. She would not miss these few things but the question remained; where had they and Suki gone? She asked the old woman, of course, but might just as well have saved her breath. It was impossible to say what amused such a strange person but undoubtedly she was amused.

'Fine times,' she said to Suki's mother, 'when women of good family lose their daughters.'

Time passed and no news came. After a while it became clear that Suki's father had decided she must be dead; either dead or hitched a lift to the faraway city with a lorry driver. This was more or less the same thing as being dead as far as he was concerned. Quite naturally this extraordinary disappearance was a great scandal and gave rise to much gossip among the women of the village, some of whom, it has to be admitted, were not altogether sad to observe that family misfortunes occurred even to such a woman as Suki's mother. To be the favourite wife of the wealthiest stock-owner for miles around, to have been a great beauty and to possess wit were all very well, but to have only one child and that a female was in itself a misfortune and now the wretched girl had vanished only weeks before her wedding. But then, as the gossips soon recalled, she had always been a difficult child, sullen, unco-operative, too fond of her own company. It was clear to everyone that other people's misfortunes often had a moral foundation.

As days became weeks the gossip died away and in a little while Suki's name was hardly mentioned any more. Her mother never told her husband about the things taken from her hut; about some things she knew it was better to say nothing and that theft, it seemed, was among them.

The long rains continued, not the daylong steady rain of misty, northern countries, but sudden thunderous rain-storms that ceased almost as soon as they began, giving way once more to a blue sky and a sun whose power was so great that for an hour or so after each downpour the whole land steamed to the height of a man's thighs like some vast hot bath.

Under this double blessing of rain and sun the land flourished wonderfully. Stock ponds filled and became loud with the chorus of frogs, streams reappeared that people had forgotten about, the grass sprang up, green and juicy, and a multitude of edible plants suddenly appeared, all manner of bulbs, stems, leaves and berries which the women and girls gathered for a salad.

Dida's third wife, a very young woman, bore her first child, a sturdy boy who was inevitably named Rain. Irritated by a sudden intrusion of the feminine in her hut and disliking the routines of infancy, he spent even more time with his second wife. In this way he both pleased himself and silently admonished the gossips. Sometimes, as he watched her passing around coffee or sour milk to a gathering of his friends and clients, Dida was greatly moved by her grace, her elegance, her charm. He bought her many ornaments and lengths of gaudy cloth and never spoke of the vanished girl.

The would-be husband, mollified by gifts of cattle and many expressions of goodwill, returned to his own part of the country where in due course he took someone else's daughter for his third wife.

Sometimes Suki's mother would stand at the entrance of the great thorn fence and look out across the country, shielding her eyes against the sun's glare, although whether she expected to see her daughter is impossible to say.

One day, well into the dry season that followed the long rains, the same boy who had been hunting lizards and had watched the weeping wife stumble out of the old woman's hut, was playing with a scorpion he had dug out, tormenting

349

the fearsome little beast with a twig, laughing to see its rushes, the claws high and the arched tail with its curved sting. How angry the scorpion was to be dragged out into this hostile sunlight and how it would claw him and sting him if it could.

It was late in the afternoon and very hot. The village of grass-roofed huts within the thorn fence was silent, people were dozing or sitting in the shade, listening to the buzzing of the bush crickets whose stridulations came in sudden bursts that as suddenly ceased, leaving the hot, windless afternoon even more profoundly silent.

The boy playing with the angry scorpion became bored and flicked the creature away with the end of his twig. Unhurt, it righted itself in a moment and scuttled away into the shadow of the thorn fence. Far away on the hill that rose towards the south and west the boy could see a human figure, tiny at this distance, walking towards the village. Twice he saw the sun flash on bright metal but it was a long time before the figure came close enough to be clearly seen. Even so, something about this distant person caught the boy's interest. In a little while he saw a tall, dirty female, clothes ragged, hair matted and tangled, feet grey with dust. Over one shoulder she carried a strange leather bag and on the other a long spear.

The boy could hardly believe his eyes and ran through the village, from one hut to another, shouting at the top of his voice. In moments the entrance of the thorn fence was jammed with women and children, all staring at this strange sight, a woman from nowhere and carrying a spear, as if she were a man. Of course it was Suki, it must be, who else could it be, and yet was it not possible that some trick was being played here? It was well known that there were spirits in the bush who could take on the forms of human beings or domestic animals so perfectly that no one could tell the real from the simulacrum. There was no harm in these spirits although it was alarming when they abruptly vanished, leaving nothing behind, it was said, but a faint tinkling sound that soon faded into silence.

Eventually Suki's mother pushed her way through the crowd. The dusty, dishevelled girl grinned at her mother and the woman wrung her hands, laughed and cried, and turned her face to the sky as she alternately mumbled and called prayers to God who had preserved her only child.

Suki grounded her spear and the two women embraced. As they walked through the crowd of curious onlookers towards the woman's hut the questions had already begun. When a young woman walks out of her village one morning, without a word to anyone, vanishes for more than two months, then it is certain when she suddenly reappears that many questions will be asked.

Suki did the best she could. Of facts there were many although even with those she had to take care since many of them were discreditable or worse. Even such trivial things as having eaten fish and birds' eggs would have caused a scandal. These were things regarded by Suki's people as unclean, the sort of disgusting things eaten by the despised smiths and other low types of humanity. Facing so many questions and with her head still full of silence and great distances, Suki experienced for the first time in her life the difficulty of narrating a unique experience.

She tried her best until she could bear it no longer. 'Go away, mother,' she said. 'Leave me in peace.' She spoke quietly enough but her mother stopped talking and left the hut. Later she brought a dish of sour milk. Suki was lying on her back on her couch staring up at the domed roof of woven sticks and grass. Suki's mother put the dish down and withdrew in silence.

Suki sighed as she realized how long it would take her to get used to everything again. So many people, such a racket of voices! At any rate, she had already decided, there would be no more interrogation. She had been gone for a few weeks, she had lived alone in the bush, things had happened to her, she had survived, and had now returned to live with people again. Let that be enough for them. In any case, she thought coldly, they will soon find something else to gossip about. She feared too, that if she talked too much it would all fade away. Already these familiar sights and sounds and smells were reasserting their easy dominance. The wild had its power, but what was that compared to the power of the domestic, the tame, with its vast weight of custom, of routine, above all of habit. She was like an explorer of wild places who comes home to find people drinking tea.

She ate the sour milk and then lay back on her couch and soon fell into a light, dreamless sleep. When she awoke it was evening and already dark; she could hear all around her the cows milling about at the evening milking, feel their hooves juddering on the hard soil, smell their bodies. Later her mother came into the hut and, soon afterwards, her father. Lying on her low couch behind the woven partition Suki heard them moving about and saw their shadows suddenly thrown against the walls as the fire momentarily flared. Her father spoke from beyond the partition. He spoke in a formal manner, as though she were another man, a style belonging to ceremonies or the greeting of important visitors.

'Are you strong, daughter?'
'I am strong. And you, are you strong?'
'I am strong. Will you stay?'
'I shall stay, father.'
The man grunted in the manner of one who, if not exactly

satisfied by what he has heard, is content with it for the time being.

In the days that followed he sometimes looked at his daughter in a speculative, almost dreamy, way. Although he was a laconic and even austere man, he too had his share of curiosity and she could see how much he would like to know about what happened to her alone in the bush, how she had lived, what thoughts had come into her mind in that wild solitude.

Lying on her couch in the warm darkness, listening to the many sounds and voices of the village, she could see clearly how difficult it would be to say all the things that had happened to her, even to her father who of all people was perhaps the one who really did want to know. How could she tell anyone of the emptiness, the solitude, the silence, the appalling tedium that turned first to intense irritability and then to a lethargy so profound that she lay on her back in the cave for three days and nights until hunger drove her stumbling out, weak and dizzy.

That was the day she found the eggs. One was addled and the stink made her retch. Another she broke so that most of it ran down her chin; with the remaining three she did better. Raw eggs, she learned, were not so bad after all.

Other things of which she could never speak were the terrible noises her thoughts made when there was no one to talk to, and the hallucinations, the voices she heard in the cave as plainly as she heard them now. The voices only lasted a little while before fading; always both domestic and admonitory they said things like: 'Clean this pot again, girl,' or 'Why is there no clean water?' It was strange, she now thought, how these voices always manifested themselves as such commonplace utterances, and how poignant an effect they had.

Then there was the cave. The cave was dry and cool

with a sandy floor. In its entrance she set out the three hearth-stones and made her first fire. To make your own fire – how could you tell anyone a thing like that!

Higher up the hill from her cave there were baboons; down the bottom there was a spring in a rocky outcrop. As the rain fell each day during the rainy season a small pond grew among the rocks and there she found fish; ugly, sluggish creatures that could dig into the dried mud and live out the dry season. She ate these, too, speared them on a pointed stick and roasted them over her little fire.

At the back of the cave there were leopard droppings but they were very old; Suki sniffed them and crumbled them to dust between her fingers. In any case, everyone knew that leopards were shy creatures that kept clear of people.

Sometimes she ate nothing all day. She supposed she was always hungry but after a time it hurt less. Twice she found a bees' nest in a high tree. Among the dried, rustling remnants there were a few sticky comb pieces with a little honey still attached.

Once a wild pig came bursting out of the bushes and stood glaring at her, legs asplay, head down, before crashing back the way it came. In the mornings and evenings birds sat in the trees and called, shrieked, muttered or clanked monotonously. Suki had not realized there were so many different birds and so many different voices.

The rainy season passed and the temporary pond vanished. In a little while the spring began to fail; full on one morning, almost empty on another.

At night she liked to sit in the cave with the little fire crackling and spitting. Moths and beetles blundered into the unexpected light and crashed into the glowing cinders. The stars were scattered like jewels on a black cloth and sometimes she could hear, further down the hill, the hyenas as they whooped at each other for hours on end.

The hallucinations passed and there were no more voices. Now only the failing spring remained; the berries were all gone, no more edible leaves or roots to be found. The dried meat and the maize that she had stolen were long gone. On the thirtieth day she found a young wild pig hiding in a thicket with a broken leg. She pushed the spear up under the animal's ribs and felt the polished shaft vibrate as the little pig thrashed about for a time before it died. Leaning down hard on the spear she shouted at the animal but could not drown out its squeals of mortal agony.

The pig lasted four days. She buried the guts under a tree far from the cave. Long before dawn the hyenas had already dug them up again.

One day she took her spear and her wallet and walked west all morning until she came to the slopes overlooking the market town. Here foreigners from the north had been settled by the government after the great famine. They grew maize, potatoes, onions and millet and kept a few scrawny chickens to sell to the houses where strangers could eat for money. At the edge of a maize field far from the farmer's shack, Suki waited in hiding until the boy sent to scare off birds would walk to the shack for his lunch of coarse maize bread and barley beer. For two hours she waited and still the boy never moved far but just sat under a makeshift canopy or occasionally walked around shaking his bird-scarer's rattle before returning to the welcome shade.

Suki sat patiently on the dry, powdery soil and listened to the tall plants rustling drily in the wind. All this land had once belonged to her people until the soldiers came and dumped truckloads of farmers from the starving north, a far-off country, even further than the city. At last she stood up and strode through the maize until she came out in a clearing about twenty feet from the bird-scaring boy. He looked at this strange figure and then ran, never stopping until he came to the farmer's shack where, panting for breath and sweating freely, he babbled of a wild woman from the bush with a great spear.

The farmer's wife scolded the boy and hit him with a stick. No sensible person believed in wild women from the bush. For three more days Suki did well, taking bags of maize and even a chicken once. On the fifth day, as Suki strode through the maize path a man suddenly stepped from behind a distant tree and shot at her, one round from an old Lee-Enfield left over from the great war long before either Suki or the bird-scaring boy were born.

The bullet went wild and Suki heard it hissing through the maize. She loaded her satchel once more with the smooth, heavy cobs with their silky ears and tassels and went back to her cave.

All these were things she might have told her father. Then there were the animals, among which were the wild pigs and the hyenas, the ostriches, grave and ridiculous creatures, the zebras, brilliant beasts looking as though they had been newly delivered from some celestial paintshop; there were troops of baboons, noisy and quarrelsome, and the tiny colobus monkeys in their priestly colours. There were birds of many kinds, bush rats, snakes, beetles, ants, ticks, creatures she knew well and many others she had never even heard of.

Last of all there was the lion. The lion came one morning to drink from the spring below her cave. She could see at once that, like the solitude, the dreams, the hallucinations and the immense silent nights, the lion was not something she could tell people about. He was big, full-maned, a little mangy to tell the truth and with a limp in one of his front legs. He had strange yellow eyes with tiny black pupils shaped like diamonds. Among Suki's people it was said that if you looked too long in a lion's yellow eyes you would begin to feel remote and disinterested; everything would go quiet and fear would fade from your mind.

Five mornings the lion came and each time Suki went a little closer until on the fifth morning she stood just across the spring from the great beast as he lapped daintily at the spring water. She was almost close enough to reach out and touch him. Years later she sometimes thought that perhaps she had touched him, although at other times she thought not. Over the years she touched him many times in her dreams, and these dreams blurred confusingly with her memories. Sometimes the lion lifted its heavy head and stared at her, yawning to show the great fangs and the moist, red interior of its mouth. Perhaps she had been in the bush long enough not to smell like other humans; whatever it was the lion neither threatened nor retreated. It drank its fill, shook its mane, slouched off down the hill to the dense cover at the edge of the plain.

Twice at dusk she heard him growling in the cover beyond the spring. On the sixth day there was no lion, nor on the seventh.

On the eighth day Suki climbed higher up the hill to an outcrop of rocks near the rim of the escarpment. It was early, still cool, there were beads of dew glittering on grass, on stems, on leaves, spurshoots, calyx and petal, on all the secret green places of plants, the kingdom of small birds, lizards and insects. She sat on the rock and looked out across the great plain of Golbu that stretched south and west further than the eye could see, an immense, tree-dotted landscape as level as if it had been sliced off with a knife. At the furthest extremity of vision she saw the low blue haze of invisible mountains.

Suki sat there for a long time gazing out across the plain and then returned to her cave, gathered her things together, and set off back home to her village. She had lost weight, she looked a good deal the worse for wear and she had smelled sweeter but, taken all in all, she was in fine condition, never felt better, as she stepped out on the long walk.

In the course of time Suki did marry after all, a little late in life by the standards of her people it is true. She married a man who had been educated in the city and who had not lost his wits but had returned to his native country and resumed his old life. He became a man of two worlds, a man with many cattle and a voice in the councils of the people, as well as three trucks and a share in a bar run by his brothers in the distant city. Suki had three sons and a daughter and became a famous woman, as her mother had before her. Many women and girls came to her hut with their troubles; it was well known that she was a woman who knew more than other people.

Once, just before she married, she met the old woman coming from the water-hole with her water-gourd balanced on her head.

'They say you will marry, after all,' the old woman said.

'Of course,' Suki said mockingly, 'what else would a woman do but marry?'

The old woman laughed. 'So, Suki daughter of Dida son of Boru, now you have lived with beasts, why should you have trouble living with people?'

Then without waiting for an answer the old woman turned and strode away, laughing sardonically, her back as straight as a spear shaft, never spilling so much as a single drop of water.